Paul Nagle was born in Dublin in 1959 and brought up in a large close-knit family of nine boys and two girls. After dabbling in a number of entrepreneurial businesses in the eighties and early nineties, he settled in Johannesburg in 1995 and began a career in computer software. At the time South Africa was taking a giant leap towards democracy, leaving behind its apartheid past, and the initial idea for *Ironic* was born. However, with burgeoning business commitments, work on the novel was put on hold until 2004 when researching and writing started in earnest.

Paul now divides his time between his homes in London and the Algarve. He is married with three children.

IRONIC

Paul Nagle

Book Guild Publishing
Sussex, England

First published in Great Britain in 2008 by
The Book Guild Ltd
Pavilion View
19 New Road
Brighton, BN1 1UF

Typeset in Baskerville by
Ellipsis Books Limited, Glasgow

Printed in Great Britain by
CPI Mackays

A catalogue record for this book is available from
The British Library.

ISBN 978 1 84624 256 4

For Anna

In memory of my mother
Breda
your light guides me

1

Lex Goldman appeared as composed as always, but beneath the serene surface his blood was so chilled it took all his self-control not to shiver visibly.

He stared hard at the muted city scenes passing the darkened windows of the limousine, trying to calm and order his thoughts, still wondering how he'd got himself into such a grave predicament. Standing accused of the brutal murder of a young NYPD detective, he could be facing the death penalty for a crime he hadn't committed.

He'd been in peril before and in many life-threatening situations, but he'd never had so much time to consider the precariousness of his position. Sudden danger was never a torture, only the slow, fearful anticipation of it. Immediate dangers had always allowed him to use his powers of self-reliance, but now his fate lay in the hands of other, anonymous people.

As always in life, there was an element of misfortune in his current situation. In 1995 New York Governor Pataki had reinstated the death penalty, making his the thirty-eighth state in the union to put miscreants to death. So much in life depended on being in the right or wrong place at the right or wrong time.

If he had been born at a different time in a different country to different people . . . if he had made different choices . . .

Fate had been kind to Lex more often than not. Without its help he would never have experienced the wealth and power that had passed through his fingers down the years, but now it was exacting a terrible price for those favours.

No one on the planet would be able to avoid seeing the image of Lex Goldman entering the gladiatorial pit of the New York courtroom on that sharp, bright spring morning. The world's media had been staking out positions on neighbouring rooftops and at windows overlooking the door for days, all fearful of losing them to competitors. Local landlords and office managers could ask any price if they had a few square yards with visual access to the best angles.

Few of the deals done for these little pieces of real estate were ever committed to writing; so many of the more trusting members of the media had turned up at reserved addresses on the day, only to find higher bidders had moved in and they had to hunt for a new vantage point, handing over inflated wads of money to someone unable to believe their luck and anxious to cash in before the opportunity passed.

At street level, competition for elbow space was even more ferocious and frequently descended to physical violence as cameramen and reporters jostled to get to the front. Barriers supposed to herd them back onto the pavement proved inadequate hours before Lex actually appeared, and the police department had sent reinforcements to ensure that traffic could continue to flow. Drivers who slowed down to rubberneck were moved along with only curt civility. The authorities knew this could easily turn from a media circus into a full-scale riot. They didn't want pictures of the police becoming heavy handed in the world's greatest city to be spread across the television screens and front pages.

Cameras had been primed and alert since the first sign of light made it through the surrounding buildings. Anyone who came in or out of the court entrance was snapped and filmed a thousand times in the course of a few seconds, the resulting pictures beamed back through satellites for producers and editors to try to work out if they were someone of importance. No one wanted to print a picture of an office cleaner and claim it was one of Lex's army of top attorneys.

When Lex finally made his appearance he didn't disappoint the waiting horde. As he stepped out from the black limousine a roar went up from all around. It wasn't an indication of approval or disapproval; simply the sound of the world's media shouting in vain attempts to make their voices heard above one another. There was no possibility that the tall, perfectly groomed focus of their attention was going to do anything more than smile at them politely, but they were paid to try and elicit some sort of response from him. Hundreds of voices shouted his name to make him turn in their direction for the nanosecond they needed to get a memorable image.

More police appeared from the convoy of cars surrounding the limousine, and a dozen or more neatly suited attorneys, their arms filled with files and boxes of information and records, which would be combed through and quoted as every detail of Lex Goldman's life was laid bare for the world to enjoy, examine and judge.

The man himself looked every inch the star of the show. Always handsome, the weight he'd lost in the previous decade had accentuated the gauntness of his strong face. His silver hair had been recently trimmed and contrasted with the mahogany tan of a man who'd spent most of his life bathed in sunshine. To accommodate his slimmer appearance he'd had a new made-to-measure wardrobe created, and the early morning breeze made the light cashmere overcoat fly behind him as he walked, revealing the immaculate lines of the navy pin-striped suit and deep red Hermes tie. Ralph Lauren couldn't have asked for a more perfect model of the good life.

As far as the media were concerned, however, Lex's physical glamour was only the icing on the cake. The reason this court-room was the hottest news ticket around was because it was a symbolic trial of the world's elite. This was far more than a simple murder trial. There was no disputing that Lex had been one of the richest men in the world of commerce, and part of the contro-versy now raging was over his claims that the entire fortune had gone. The thousands of eyes watching him striding into the court-room saw a man of apparently limitless self-confidence. At the same time as being thrilled by such a spectacle, they felt a frisson of excitement at the thought of so much hubris being brought to its knees, the twin mysteries of wealth and power exposed in the merciless spotlight of the justice system.

The myths that surrounded the rise and fall of Lex Goldman had allowed every conspiracy theorist on earth to feel vindicated. Anyone who'd ever claimed that power corrupts and that great personal wealth can only be accrued at speed if the recipient resorts to crime could now point a finger at the evidence, even though the trial hadn't even started. The media had been full of colourful speculation for weeks, once his resurrection had been revealed.

However much lip-service the authorities in every country paid to the evil of drug trafficking, the general public still remained fascinated by those who knew their way around such a rich and dangerous world.

Lex had the added attraction of seeming not to belong exclusively to any one country or continent. Although born and raised in Africa, his parents had emigrated from the Baltics and most of his adult life had been spent in America, Europe or travelling. He was the ultimate global man, which added to the sense of mystery that shrouded him. Few had lived a life quite like his and the huge crowd of onlookers could only imagine how his mind worked or what the details of his daily life might really be. In every man's heart there was a small corner that longed to be more like Lex, and another that was hungry to learn more about him. Every woman wondered what it would be like to be a part of his life. Half the world wanted to see him put to death while the other half longed to see him leap free of his small-minded tormentors with a single bound, like comic book heroes had always done.

It was a few seconds before the crowd noticed the woman standing beside Lex. At first glance she looked young, her greying blonde hair sparkling in the sunlight, but as a thousand lenses focused in on her they showed a face of ageing beauty. Sophie Goldman, a name they'd all read about in their files but a face they hadn't been able to catch on camera for more than a decade, had emerged from hiding to support her husband. Did that mean they'd been together all through those years when she had never been seen, or was this a cynical move by Goldman's attorneys to make him seem like a regular upstanding family man? A new wave of questions rose from the throats of the crowd but Sophie appeared not to hear, her face as tranquil and composed as a hostess graciously welcoming guests to her dinner table.

Lex paused in the doorway and turned slowly, as if taking in the beauty of the spring morning. His wife slipped her arm through his, allowing the audience one last look at them before they disappeared from sight.

The judge had agreed to allow cameras inside the courtroom, partly because his wife had insisted. She had explained repeatedly, and with increasing exasperation, that he'd reached an age where he had to think seriously about his pension, and a famous retired judge would attract more lucrative directorships and speaking engagements than an equally distinguished one who had not managed to turn himself into a household name.

The presence of those cameras meant Lex would not be able to let his guard down for even a moment. It was crucial the world never saw him looking shifty or tired. They must see no nervous tics or signs of weakness. However long this case stretched on, he had to maintain the appearance of a wronged hero; his life depended on it. He glanced at Sophie as she took her seat, as impressed by her as he had been the first time he set eyes on her many years earlier, before she had led him to the darker sides of her life. Looking at her now, serene and immaculate, it was hard to imagine some of the places they'd been to together and some of the sights they'd seen.

Across the court he saw the lead attorney for the Justice Department settling behind his desk, surrounded by another phalanx of file-bearing clerks and assistants. Lex had heard a little about the man from his defence attorney. He knew his name was Kal Woodson and that he was in his mid-thirties, about twenty years younger than himself. In legal circles he was considered to be one of the brightest attorneys in the state of New York and had proved himself to be more interested in justice than in making money. Examining him now, Lex was surprised by how young his rival looked; maybe that was his reward for leading a virtuous life. His hair was still jet black and his olive skin unlined. Lex Goldman knew better than to underestimate anyone who had the potential to do him damage, and this man had the ability to take away his freedom for ever, and possibly even his life.

Back in the media newsrooms the background material was piling up as high as in the courtroom. Journalists specialising in subject matter as diverse as business, crime, international relations and society gossip were being forced to collaborate by their editors and producers to make sense of the web of information and misinformation that rose to the surface whenever the name 'Lex Goldman' was fed into the Internet search engines or into the ears of any known source. It was almost impossible to disentangle the facts from the lies, myths and propaganda. They could already see that as the story emerged day by day in the courtroom they would be able to sell thousands of extra copies of their newspapers, or substantially raise their viewing figures; as long as they could stay ahead of the competition. That meant always being the first to reveal the most shocking facts and fictions, the moment the attorneys on each side unveiled them.

'God, I can hear her from here,' Lex complained.

It was 1962, he was nineteen years old and his mother's voice was drilling through the night air above all the other guests, making him want to run a mile.

Lex and his best friend Zak had found a quiet corner on one of the terraces overlooking the illuminated swimming pool and the view beyond, which had become a twinkling canopy of lights in the blackness.

'You shouldn't be so disrespectful towards your mother,' Zak reprimanded. 'Your parents do a lot for you.'

Lex raised an eyebrow at his friend, a gesture too subtle to come across in the gloom. He didn't say any more, knowing Zak was right. His mother's heart was in the right place, if only her voice wasn't so loud and her opinions so bizarre.

Out of sight of the other guests, the two boys had lit up the cigars they'd taken from one of the many boxes dotted around the house for guests to dip into, and were trying to enjoy the smoke without coughing as they lounged in the cushioned chairs and sipped their drinks, unable to avoid overhearing the conversation going on behind them.

'I can't tell you how many times I have explained it all to the stupid girl,' Eva Goldman was saying to an audience the boys couldn't see. 'But she understands nothing. I might as well be talking to the wall.'

'She's talking about Beauty,' Lex explained, 'the new kitchen girl. She thinks the girl looks at her the way she does because she's stupid – she's not stupid.'

'What is she then?' Zak sniggered but Lex didn't rise to the bait.

'She's angry,' he said. 'And she hates my mother.'

'She probably hates all of you,' Zak suggested. 'I would if I had to clean up after you.'

Lex nodded thoughtfully, listening to the crackling of the cigar and enjoying the aroma for a few seconds longer before taking another puff. He couldn't quite explain why his mother's way of dealing with the black house staff made him as uneasy as it did, when most of his friends' mothers were far worse, but it still made him cringe every time he heard it.

'So, what are you two doing, skulking in the corner there?'

Sol Goldman probably meant his enquiry to be jocular, bu the final traces of his Lithuanian accent, overlaid with the South African vowels he'd assimilated in the twenty or so years he'd lived in Johannesburg, made it sound more like an accusation. He had never been good at social small talk, preferring the black and white rules of business negotiations. Both the boys sprang to their feet, unable to hide the glowing cigars in time.

'Ah, sit down, relax,' he waved them back to their chairs. 'Enjoy yourselves, why don't you? This is a party. There is a time to work and a time to play.'

The boys sat back down again on the edges of their chairs as Sol leant on the balustrade, took a deep contented lungful of air and surveyed the party going on around them. The pool lights illuminated the purple blossom of the gently swaying jacaranda trees and the night breeze was perfumed with an intoxicating blend of scents. Carefully placed lights throughout the manicured landscape picked out the rarest and most fragrant of the plants and shrubs, leading the observer's eye into the far distance.

'And what a party this is,' he went on.

'It's good,' Zak agreed, aware his friend had been struck dumb by his father's arrival. Sol carried with him a charisma that crushed lesser spirits, even when he didn't intend it to. Lex had a similar air about him, but lacked the gravitas of age and experience.

'Have you any idea how much of this country's wealth is walking around this house tonight?' Sol asked.

'No, sir,' Zak admitted, aware of Lex's embarrassment at his father's question. 'I have no idea.'

'A hell of a lot, my boy, a hell of a lot, and most of it around the necks of our wives!'

Zak knew this was intended as a joke because Sol let out a short bark of a laugh. He did his best to join in, while Lex stared the whole of life as a giant chessboard, and e, particularly when it led to victory. Placing ticular board had been a masterful move and like enjoying it to the full.

'Have you seen Lex's mother tonight?' Sol went on, oblivious to his son's embarrassed body language.

'No, sir,' Zak said, 'I haven't had a chance to talk to her yet.'

'With the jewels she's wearing tonight I could have bought a fleet of Rolls Royces,' Sol said. 'That's all I'm going to say. Are your parents here tonight?'

'Yes, sir, they're in the house somewhere.'

'Your father will be doing some deals here tonight. Rare paintings, that's his business isn't it?'

'That's right, sir, yes.'

'Seen what's hanging on the walls in there?'

'No, I'm not too good on history of art . . .'

'There's Rembrandts and Van Goghs and all those impressionists everyone goes on about. It's like a shop window for him, and all these people have mansions they need to fill. I've been meaning to talk to your father about investing in some more art myself. Eva's been going on about it.'

'I'm sure he'd be delighted,' Zak said, knowing his father had believed for some time that the pile of money Sol Goldman was amassing would soon rival some of the oldest fortunes in the country.

'That family should be investing more money in art,' he'd been saying, 'but that wife of his wouldn't know a good painting from a hole in the ground.'

'When we came here to escape the Nazis it was touch and go whether they would let us in,' Sol said and it was all Lex could do not to let out an audible groan. 'We had nothing, Eva and I, except a few names and addresses of people who might be able to help. And now I'm talking to you about buying another Rembrandt. That's the wonder of this country of opportunity. It's all out there for the taking.'

'Just as long as you have those names and addresses,' Lex said, almost inaudibly.

'Come back to the party,' Sol gestured to them both, pretending not to have heard his son's sarcasm. 'Two young guys like you should be circulating amongst the girls. All the best families in the country are here tonight, you could marry any one of them and never have to work again!'

He let out another short, sharp laugh as he steered them back into the mansion and towards Eva and the group of women she was talking to. The boys knew the parents of the eligible girls were eyeing them up in just the same way. Everyone wanted their children to make a good marriage to a good family, preferably one they already knew and had business links with. No one wanted their children to marry out of the faith and complicate things.

Zak couldn't help but notice Eva's jewels now that Sol had pointed them out, and every other woman seemed to be wearing similar splendid pieces, the diamonds sparkling and glittering as they caught the light, nobody wanting to be outshone. A waiter, perspiring uncomfortably in a formal footman's outfit, came past with a tray and both boys changed their glasses for fresh ones.

'Look who I found hiding on the terrace,' Sol boomed to the group, making heads turn all over the room.

'You boys should be talking with the girls,' Eva screeched and both Lex and Zak felt their faces reddening. Sol nodded benevolently and the other women chirped their agreement. One of the reasons for the gathering this evening was for their offspring to spend time with potential partners from other suitable Jewish families. Time and money had been lavished on the girls' appearances, dresses flown in from Europe, hair and make-up applied by professionals. Many of the mothers had lent their daughters just the right amount of jewels to show off their slender young necks to best advantage. A good safe marriage would make all the investment worthwhile, bringing a many thousandfold return.

'We'd better circulate, then,' Lex said, backing away from his parents and steering Zak through to another room filled with more people. 'If we stand still for too long we'll find ourselves engaged already!' he grumbled.

'Do you want to go somewhere else?' Zak asked as they surveyed the expensively dressed crowd. 'Somewhere a bit different to this?'

'Anywhere,' Lex said, 'as long as you can promise me there's no chance anyone who knows my parents will turn up.'

'Oh, I can definitely guarantee you that,' Zak laughed. 'But I'll have to blindfold you because the location's a secret.'

Lex thought his friend was joking about the blindfold until they were actually in the car and Zak was passing him the white silk scarf he'd been wearing with his evening suit.

'You're joking, aren't you?'

'No,' Zak grinned. 'If you want to come you have to put it on. You can't know where we're going. It's for your own protection as much as anything.'

Lex opened his mouth to argue but thought better of it. He had an idea he knew the sort of party Zak was planning to take him to, and if that was the case he definitely wanted to go.

'Okay,' he agreed, tying the scarf around his eyes. 'Let's go!'

Zak chatted all the way and Lex tried in vain to work out from the noises outside the car where they might be going. After driving for about half an hour Zak pulled up and cut the engine. Lex was struck by the silence; they'd obviously driven away from the city centre.

'Keep it on,' Zak warned as he put his hand up to remove the scarf and Lex sensed a serious note in his voice. He heard him winding down the car window.

'Hi,' he said to someone on the outside. Lex felt stupid and was tempted to pull the scarf off before anyone else saw him, but Zak put a hand on top of his to stop him. 'Rudi said to come round. This is a friend of mine. He's been blindfolded all the way.'

'Rudi said?' a man's voice replied. It sounded like a black voice to Lex.

'He said there was a party and just to ask for him.'

'What's your name?'

'Zak.'

'Wait there.'

Lex heard footsteps walking away from the car. 'Who the hell is Rudi?'

'An artist friend of my father's. Just keep quiet and do what I tell you.'

The footsteps came back.

'Okay, Rudi says to come on in. Keep his eyes covered till he gets inside.'

Lex allowed Zak to steer him out of the car and along a path. They bumped into a few things as they went. Lex guessed there were no lights. A door opened and they were surrounded by the noise of voices, all talking at once. Lex coughed, his lungs surprised by the wall of cigarette smoke after the fresh night air. Zak pulled the scarf off his head, looping it back round his own neck.

Lex blinked and looked around him, waiting for his eyes to accustom to the low lights. For a boy who'd never been outside white South African society it was a shocking scene. There were groups of people sitting together and talking, some of them black, some of them white and some of them coloured. They didn't seem to recognise any differences. There were people holding hands with others of different colours, one couple were even locked in an embrace in a dark corner. The initial shock turned to a thrill when he realised he'd entered a forbidden land, a mixed-race party. If the police turned up now they'd all be arrested and most of them – those who couldn't buy their way out of trouble – would end up in prison. But no one in the room seemed to be concerned. It was as if they didn't realise they were doing anything wrong. The thought that excited Lex the most was just how shocked his mother would be if she were to see where he was. She wouldn't even dream that such a scene was possible.

Now he was inside the house, having passed whatever security there had been outside, Lex felt completely accepted; no one was looking at him suspiciously and everyone was smiling. He found a drink in a chipped mug pressed into his hand and, when he sipped it, discovered it to be beer. When he pulled out a cigarette a black man standing close by flared a match for him.

'Thanks,' Lex said, holding out his hand, 'my name's . . .'

'No names, friend,' the man said with a grin. 'If no one knows who's here no one can tell any stories.'

He beckoned Lex over to a group of people sitting on an old mattress; the lighting was so dim he had trouble working out how many people were mingled there. There was an argument going on. Everyone was talking about someone called Nelson who'd just been arrested. Lex didn't want to show his ignorance so he sipped his beer and listened. Whoever this Nelson was he seemed to be both a friend and a hero to everyone in the room.

'They wouldn't dare kill him,' one voice was saying.

'They won't dare to keep him alive,' another said.

'There are plenty of ways to make someone wish they were dead,' said another.

'They'll never let him out now.'

'He's been arrested before . . .'

'This will be different!'

As he grew accustomed to the gloom and the different voices he realised that one of the most ardent speakers was the girl sitting next to him. He could see she was coloured, probably Indian, and she smelled of perfumes and spices he'd never encountered before. Just being close to her was a heady, delicious experience. She was so wrapped up in her conversation she hadn't even turned to acknowledge his arrival, and all he could make out was her profile. Her thick hair was pulled back untidily to reveal delicate features. When she did eventually turn and smile with a flash of perfect white teeth and coal black eyes, it felt as if the breath had been knocked out of his chest.

'Hi,' he said, wishing he could think of something else to say.

'Hi.' She didn't move her gaze from him and there was a slightly puzzled look in her eyes, as if she was trying to work out what had just passed between them in those few seconds.

'Is Nelson a friend of yours?' he asked, cringing at the sound of his own ignorance.

'Nelson is a friend to everyone,' she said. 'Men like him are the only hope for this country.'

She shifted her position as if relieving the cramp in her legs, bringing her face close to his.

'You are really handsome,' she said. 'How come I've never seen you before?'

Lex was lost for words. He'd never met a girl like this before.

It wasn't just the fact that she was coloured, her whole behaviour was unlike anything he'd ever come across. His mother would be horrified by such forward behaviour, which made it all the more tempting.

'So are you,' he said, 'beautiful I mean.'

'Thank you,' she laughed at his discomfort and squeezed his hand. 'Have you ever kissed a coloured woman before?'

'No,' he said, feeling giddy as she brushed her lips across his.

'Are you a student?' she asked.

'No,' he said, wanting to kiss her again but aware she'd been teasing him and now wanted to talk. 'I'm starting work. What about you?'

'Studying law. What kind of work?'

'Mining,' he said, hoping it sounded like a noble profession.

'I bet you don't go below ground too often.'

He blushed but she couldn't see in the gloom. 'No. It's more the business side of it.'

'Raping the land of its riches?'

'I guess . . .' he laughed. 'Maybe I should think of something else to do.'

'Maybe you should. There are more important things to do here than collecting sparkly rocks.'

As they talked they touched all the time, her fingers brushing the back of his hand, his shoulder pressing against hers, his thigh feeling the warmth of hers.

'You certainly came dressed for a party,' she said, tugging at his dinner jacket.

'Oh, yes,' he looked down at his clothes, all memories of the party he'd just come from driven from his head.

He undid his bow tie, letting it fall loosely round his neck and undid the top stud of his shirt. The girl undid another one, staring into his eyes. It was as if there was no one else in the room around them.

'Hey, mate, I wondered where you'd got to,' Zak thumped down on the mattress beside them. 'Hi,' he said to the girl in a manner that suggested they knew each other.

'Is this guy a friend of yours?' she asked Zak.

'Yes, he likes to think so,' Zak joked.

'How come you never introduced us before?'

'He moves in a different world. I've only just managed to subvert him.'

They chatted for a few more minutes and then Zak took Lex away to meet someone else.

'My God, she's fantastic!' Lex whispered once they were out of her earshot.

'Who, Reshmine?'

'I thought we weren't supposed to know names.'

'No, you're right, sorry. I've known her all my life. Her dad works for my dad. Do you fancy her then?'

Lex opened his mouth but no words came out.

'I'll take that as a yes. Looked like she liked you too. Don't worry, you can find her again later. Be careful though, she's a real little firebrand. She could get a nice boy like you into a lot of trouble.'

'Who's this Nelson chap they all talk about?'

'Do you *ever* read a newspaper? Nelson Mandela runs the ANC; he's been arrested and it looks likely they'll throw away the key this time.'

'My God, I had no idea you knew people like this.'

'It's not something you shout about, if you want to stay healthy.'

For the next couple of hours Zak introduced him to a series of nameless people, but he couldn't stop himself from glancing back across the room at the girl he now knew was called Reshmine. Often he would find her eyes on him as well and it was as if a magnet was drawing them together. Eventually she got up from the mattress and came over to him, her fingers closing lightly around his.

'Come with me,' she said.

He glanced nervously at Zak, who gave him an encouraging wink. They went out into a courtyard at the back of the house, where more people were sitting and talking. She led him on through a door on the other side, and into a simple bedroom, which looked as if it belonged to one of the servants of the house. Without saying a word she drew him down onto the bed and undid the rest of the studs on his shirt, kissing his neck and running her fingers over his chest and stomach as she went. Her scent mingled with the alcohol and made his head spin as they lay down together on the rough blanket.

When Lex woke up in his own bed the next morning he felt disorientated for a few seconds and unable to explain the strange feeling of joy deep inside him. As he remembered what had happened, the same feeling rose and swept over him like a wave across a beach, leaving a residue of fear as it withdrew. He'd had sexual relations with a coloured woman and that was a punishable offence under the laws of apartheid. What was even worse was that it had been the most wonderful moment of his life and he knew he wouldn't be able to resist going in search of Reshmine, which meant he would be putting both her and himself in more danger.

'Where did you disappear to?' his mother asked when he managed to get downstairs for some breakfast, finding his parents reading the papers. 'I hope you didn't do anything that is going to cause us any embarrassment!'

She raised her eyebrows questioningly and he knew she was imagining him slipping away with one of the little Jewish heiresses she was lining up as a potential daughter-in-law. Sol lowered his paper to witness his son's response.

'Zak took me to some friends of his,' Lex said. 'Don't worry, mother, no one you would know! Your reputation sails on intact!'

'Don't be smart with me!' Eva snapped. 'You don't know the damage you could do . . .'

'Be careful of Zak and his friends,' Sol interrupted, eager to take charge of the conversation before it ran out of control into emotionally uncharted territories. 'That boy keeps some bad company.'

'They seemed very nice to me,' Lex pouted, aware he mustn't allow his adolescent indignation to lead him into a childish indiscretion.

His mother let out a contemptuous little hiss and went back to eating, signalling him to do the same. His father sank back into his newspaper, leaving Lex free to nurse his hangover and try to remember how he got home after the party.

Later that day he drove over to Zak's house, to find his friend asleep in the sun on an inflatable mattress, floating in the swimming pool. Stripping off quietly, Lex lowered himself into the warm water and disappeared below the surface, rising up underneath the mattress and tipping his friend off.

'You bastard!' Zak spluttered as he came back up and set off in pursuit, catching Lex by the legs as he tried to pull himself out of the pool and dragging him back for a revenge ducking.

'How did I get home last night?' Lex asked as they lay on the hot coping-stones a few minutes later in the sort of contented, peaceful state of companionship that can only be achieved when you've known someone all your life.

'I carried you and you're a bloody dead-weight,' Zak laughed. 'You were completely out of your head.'

'I want to see her again, Zak,' he said after a few moments silence. 'I really do.'

'Don't be stupid, mate.' Zak sat up, suddenly serious. 'You had a great night. Leave it at that.'

'I can't.'

'You have to. You could be endangering everything. You have a lot to lose. Your dad's money won't be able to protect you in a situation like this, you know.'

Lex suppressed the urge to punch him, knowing that he needed Zak on his side. 'I don't have a choice. I have to see her again. Can you arrange it?'

'No way, man!' Zak sounded truly horrified at the prospect. 'Listen, you don't know what it's like for people who get on the wrong side of the law like this. You live in an ivory tower. I've met some of the people who've come back alive from police custody and they're broken men. Believe me, this is not possible.'

'So why did you take me to the party?'

'Going to a party is not the same as starting a serious relationship with one of them!'

'What do you mean, "one of them"?'

'You know what I mean. Don't try to make me into the villain here!'

'I'm asking you to do this for me as a friend,' Lex insisted, as calmly as he could manage.

'As a friend, I'm telling you to leave it!' Zak replied. 'Another year or two and your parents will have arranged for you to make a sensible marriage and you'll be a pillar of society. Something like this could rise up and haunt you for the rest of your life. As it is you could put last night down to a youthful indiscretion –

boys will be boys after all. You get involved with her seriously and you could mess up your whole life. I care too much about you to be part of that.'

The argument continued for over an hour but in the end Lex wore Zak down. It hadn't occurred to him that he would not be able to do so, since he'd always been able to get whatever he wanted out of other people, even as a small child. He liked Zak because he was almost his equal in strength of character, but ultimately Lex had never met anyone he couldn't persuade in an argument, apart from his father.

'Okay, all right.' Zak was irritated to lose the argument, but could think of no other way to shut his friend up. 'Leave it to me.'

Lex didn't leave it to him; he pestered him every moment of every day until Zak gave him a time and a place to turn up.

'Okay, already,' Zak said. 'Come to my dad's house this evening. He's got a meeting with Reshmine's father and she's going to be coming along. For fuck's sake don't let anyone else see what's going on between you or we'll all end up behind bars.'

'I'll never forget this,' Lex said, hugging him. 'You are a true friend.'

'I still think it's a bloody stupid thing to do,' Zak protested, but Lex had already gone. He wanted to compose a letter in the hope that he would be able to pass it to Reshmine that evening.

Set at an altitude of five-and-a-half thousand feet, Jo'burg's air was always thin and breathless, but that evening, as he made his way to Zak's house, Lex was afraid he wasn't going to be able to pull enough oxygen into his lungs to survive. Every nerve in his body was tense. He'd never felt anything like it before. The fumes from the traffic and buildings hung suspended like a cloud.

Zak's father was unwrapping a consignment of paintings that had just been delivered from Europe. Reshmine's father, who was cataloguing them and dealing with the paperwork, had been pleasantly surprised when his daughter showed an interest in coming to watch him work. There was a close bond between them and he worried all the time that his headstrong girl would get herself into trouble with the authorities. Any sign that she was showing an interest in something less inflammatory than politics, like art, was a relief. At the same time he was proud she was willing to stand up against injustice whenever she saw it and did everything he could to help her with her education so she could become a civil rights lawyer, despite the dangers.

The current of electricity that passed between Lex and Reshmine as he came into the room gave both of them a jolt, and even the older men looked up from their work, as if puzzled by the change in the atmosphere. The lovers made sure they kept their eyes averted and talked to one another only as polite strangers might do when first introduced. Zak, unable to bear the tension, made an excuse and left, telling his father that Lex wanted to stay to see the paintings.

The two older men were so absorbed in their work as the crates were prised open and the old masters carefully lifted out, that they paid little attention to anything else. They didn't notice when a letter dropped from Lex's hand into a bag Reshmine had left on the floor.

The next day Lex put his plan into action, not knowing whether Reshmine would be there. He left work and got into his car as usual. He drove to the spot he'd chosen and parked, getting out without locking the doors. Without looking around he walked across the street and into the tobacconist to buy a packet of cigarettes. When he came back out his heart was crashing in his ears. He crossed to the car and climbed into the driving seat, forcing himself not even to glance at the back seat. He drew out into the traffic.

'Are you there?' he asked, his eyes on the road ahead.

'Yes,' came a muffled voice from beneath the blanket.

'Stay down and I'll tell you when it's clear.'

He drove for half an hour out of the city, passing by some of the shanty towns that haunted the Vaal triangle. Even from the high road it was possible to see how squalid the living conditions were for the inmates, with family shacks constructed from no more than scraps of wood, tin cladding and old boxes thrown together. Hardly able to contain his impatience, he frequently pulled out to pass 'bakkies' and bigger trucks packed tightly with black labourers on their way to and from the mines in the area. He tried to keep his eyes averted but something always drew him to glance at their faces, all wearing the same desperate, vacant expression. They starkly reminded him of the stories his father had told him about the Nazis in Europe loading Jews onto trucks and railways carriages as if they were nothing more than goods to be moved from one place to another. Eventually he pulled up in front of a small anonymous white house.

'When I say go,' he said, 'get out and walk straight down the side of the white house I've parked in front of. There's a kitchen door, which will be unlocked. Let yourself in. The woman who lives there is called Beauty.'

He looked all around. There was no one in sight.

'Go.'

Reshmine sat up and their eyes met for only a fraction of a second before she was gone. He watched her disappear down the side of the house. He waited a few seconds before climbing out of the car himself, casually locking the doors and strolling in through the front door as if he owned the house.

'Beauty!' he called as he came in.

'I'm in here, Master Lex!'

He walked through to the kitchen to find Reshmine sitting at the table with Beauty, a rotund, smiling black woman in her sixties. He gave Beauty a hug and then threw his arms around Reshmine.

'I was so frightened you wouldn't come,' he said.

'You should have had more faith,' she teased.

'I'm going to visit my sister now,' Beauty announced, standing up and pulling on her hat. 'Don't you two go answering the door to anyone.'

'Thanks, Beauty,' Lex said as she waddled out of the back door.

'You're very welcome, Master Lex,' she smiled conspiratorially. 'I'll be back later tonight.'

Once the door closed behind her the young lovers fell into one another's arms again, both too hungry to be able to wait another second. A bang on the back door made them jump apart.

'I don't hear no one locking this door!' Beauty shouted.

'Okay,' Lex laughed and turned the key before going through to do the same with the front door.

'She's lovely,' Reshmine said as they embraced again. 'How did you meet her?'

'She was my nurse when I was tiny. Beauty isn't her real name but my mother likes to keep things simple so she gives all the servants the same names.'

Reshmine pulled a face.

'I know,' he grinned. 'But in their defence my father did buy her this house when she retired.'

Unable to wait a second longer he took her by the hand and led her into Beauty's neat bedroom. They made love on the sweet smelling bed beneath a crucifix and a picture of a smiling Jesus, all flowing blond hair and bright blue eyes. Beauty had placed a small bunch of flowers in a vase on the bedside table.

The routine was set and every evening Lex would leave work and park in the same place. Some days Reshmine wouldn't be able to make it and he would drive to Zak's house instead, where he would then spend the rest of the evening talking about Reshmine and fretting that this one missed liaison might be an indication her ardour was cooling. So obsessed was he by his passion he hardly heard the warnings his friend kept giving him. Most nights Reshmine was able to make the meetings and Beauty would dutifully go to visit her sister. As long as no one saw Reshmine getting in or out of the back of the car Lex believed there was little danger of discovery, since it was perfectly feasible he would be visiting the woman who had brought him up. The constant fear of discovery, however, added another layer of intensity to the romance.

In the hours they lay together after making love, they would talk endlessly about what they were going to have to do to be together for the rest of their lives. Both knew the only option open to them if they wanted to conduct their affair in public was to move to another country. They pretended to themselves, and to one another, that this would be easy to achieve, although both of them, in moments of despair when they weren't together, knew that in truth it was going to be almost impossible. They had been brought up to believe their destinies were entwined with the country of their birth, his with the Goldman financial empire and hers with the anti-apartheid movement. To cut themselves away from such roots was going to take every ounce of courage they could muster.

* * *

One night, as they lay together on Beauty's bed there was an explosion of noise outside: screaming tyres and brakes, shouting, gunshots and running feet. For a moment Lex thought it was the sound of thunder, one of the regular electrical storms that hit the city. On the drive over there had been spectacular daggers of lightning slashing through the night sky.

'There's going to be torrential rain tonight,' he'd said to his hidden companion.

The moment he realised it wasn't the sound of the storm, Lex pushed Reshmine to the floor and rolled over to fall beside her. They crawled quickly out into the front hall, keeping themselves below the level of the windows, even though they were all curtained. Pausing in a corner for a second, they tried to work out what was happening and in which direction they would be attacked from first, their eyes wide as they watched both the front and back doors.

The noise became closer and louder, angry voices and screaming, but the house remained untouched. There was a crashing noise, like the sound of an approaching herd of elephants, signalling the arrival of the rains he'd predicted on the way over. Cautiously, Lex knelt up and lifted the corner of a curtain. Outside it was dark, but the headlights of two police cars had created an arena of light in the street where four policemen were beating a young black boy with batons. The rain slashed through the beams of light as the boy kicked and squirmed in the puddles that had suddenly appeared on the ground, trying to escape the blows. Realising the futility of the struggle, he curled into a foetus-like shape, his bleeding head tucked into his arms, and still the blows crashed down. He became still and they started to kick him instead, making his unresisting body roll back and forth, coating him in a mixture of blood and mud. When they finally tired of their sport the policemen ran back to their cars as if suddenly anxious to get out of the rain, the last one drawing his pistol from its holster and firing a single shot into the back of their victim's head. The cars drove away, sending up sheets of spray. When the sound of the engines died away there was only the roar of the rain on the surrounding tin roofs.

Reshmine stood up and ran to the door, fumbling clumsily with the lock.

'Wait!' Lex grabbed her from behind, pinning her arms to her sides.

'Let me go,' she shouted, 'we have to help him.'

'There's nothing you can do for him, you'll only endanger yourself. There will be others, just wait a second.'

She struggled for a moment and he could feel her heart thumping against his as he held her. Then they heard voices and she relaxed. They went back to the window and watched as figures emerged timidly from the shadows, lifted the sodden, broken body and carried it into the house opposite. Then, above the sound of the rain, they heard the wailing of a woman's heart breaking.

Reshmine turned and buried her face into Lex's bare shoulder, too shocked and angry even to cry as he held her tight.

When Sol's secretary rang to announce Zak was in the outer office and wanted to talk, he felt a premonition run through him and he took a second to compose himself before telling her to send the boy in. He never liked taking meetings when he hadn't been thoroughly briefed beforehand. Sol always liked to have the upper hand, so he could plan what moves he would make in advance. If Zak was bringing bad news about Lex – and he could think of no other reason why the boy would arrive unannounced – he wanted to prepare himself for the blow.

Zak, already nervous and unsure whether he was doing the right thing, had been further unnerved by the grandeur of the Goldman head office. Sol had commissioned the building specifically to have that effect on visitors. He wanted them to know the moment they stepped through the doors that they were in the presence of enormous wealth and power. Just eight years before, his office had been a wooden shed above one of the mines.

Zak's palm was clammy as the older man shook it firmly and directed him to a leather chair on the other side of the desk without saying a word.

'What can I do for you, Zak?' he asked, when they were both seated.

'I'm not sure I'm doing the right thing, Mr Goldman,' Zak said, swallowing uncomfortably.

Sol steepled his fingers in front of his mouth and waited to hear what was coming next. At least it didn't sound as if he was going to be told Lex was dead or injured in any way.

'Lex is the best friend I've ever had,' he stumbled on under Sol's piercing stare, 'and I know I'm betraying him by coming to you, but he's putting himself in danger and he won't listen to me.'

'In what way is he putting himself in danger?' Sol asked, comfortable now that this was going to be a problem he would be able to find a solution for. His opinion of Zak had plummeted the moment he realised the boy was about to betray his son's confidence, but he still wanted the information Zak was about to impart. Sol had been in business long enough to know that information was power. Without it you were always at a disadvantage.

'He's fallen in love with a coloured girl.'

'Are they having an affair?' Sol's voice gave away none of the emotions that were suddenly swirling around inside him; none of the fear or the anger.

'Yes.' Zak was relieved by the calmness with which the older man was taking the news.

'Does anyone else know?'

'I don't think so, apart from Lex's old nurse Beauty who lets them use her house. I don't know if the girl has confided in anyone. I doubt she has.'

'Do you know her?'

'A little. If we were in any other country in the world I'd say they were perfect for one another. She's beautiful, intelligent and highly motivated to fight against apartheid and other injustices.'

'Oh my God, she's a political activist?' For a second Sol's guard dropped and he looked worried.

'She's training to be a lawyer. She wants to work in human rights.'

'Can you give me the name and address of her father?'

Zak hesitated for a second but Sol's eyes didn't waver from his face. He pulled a piece of paper from his pocket and passed it over with a shaking hand.

'He doesn't have to know who has told me this,' Sol said.

'I wouldn't be able to lie to him,' Zak said, and Sol thought he could see tears welling up in the boy's eyes.

'Say nothing at the moment, let me deal with it,' Sol said before standing up and extending his hand to indicate the interview was over.

'You've done the right thing.'

The moment Zak was out of the office Sol looked at the piece of paper again and picked up the phone to his secretary.

'Get them to bring a car to the front door, but no driver. I want to drive myself.'

That evening Sol asked Lex to stay in for dinner with him and Eva. Lex knew his father well enough to be able to tell from the tone of his voice that it was an order, not an invitation. Throughout the meal his mother fussed over the food and insulted the staff just as she always did, and although Lex made some attempts at conversation, his father did not respond. At the end of the meal Sol invited Lex into the library and the two of them sat down together beneath the ceiling fans. Lex assumed his father wanted to talk business.

'You've been born in fortunate times, Lex,' Sol said.

'In what way, Father?'

'You know a little of what happened to your mother and me before you were born, and to most of the members of our family.' Lex had been told a thousand times by both of them about how they'd been the only members of the family to escape the Nazi death camps in the early nineteen forties.

'No one else in the family was able to get permission to come to South Africa,' Sol said, 'and when your mother heard that her sister wasn't going to be able to come with us she didn't want to leave. In many ways she was closer to her sister than she was to me, or even you.' Sol fell silent for a moment, nodding slightly in agreement with his own pronouncement.

'I had to insist. If we had stayed in Lithuania we would have been taken to the camps too and we would have been killed. We had to make a sacrifice. I don't think your mother has ever forgiven me for that. If I hadn't insisted, we would both be dead and you would never have been born.'

Lex opened his mouth to respond but was unable to find any words, so he waited for his father to continue.

'It wasn't just the Nazis. Before them it was the Russian tsarists who tried to crush our people. Can you imagine how it feels to be put in a position where you have no power to save yourself, other than running away and leaving your loved ones behind to their fate? Can you imagine how it feels to have to walk away from your home with nothing but a suitcase, knowing you're going to have to throw yourself at the mercy of strangers?'

Lex nodded, remaining silent, knowing he had to allow his father's monologue to run its course; knowing also that Sol had earned the right to say whatever he wanted.

'Everything I've done since then has been aimed at ensuring that never happens to us or you or your children ever again. If we'd had money and influence in Lithuania we could have saved more of the family, maybe all of them. The wealth we have found here has put us amongst the most powerful people in the country. We must never do anything to endanger that position again. You never want to find that you have to run away with nothing more than a suitcase, Lex. Do you understand what I'm saying?'

'Yes, Father,' Lex said, although he still wasn't sure why he was being given this lecture.

'As long as we remain on the right side of the law there is nothing they can do to hurt us.'

'The right side of the law?' Lex wondered if his father was referring to the ways in which they traded their gold around the international markets.

'Different countries have different laws, and when you choose to live in a society you must abide by its rules, whether you agree with them or not. If you break them you risk everything. Instead of being one of the powerful ones you become a criminal, a part of the underclass. That cannot happen to us, we have too much to lose. Your mother could not go through that again.'

In a blinding flash, Lex realised what his father was referring to. He said nothing, in case he was wrong.

'You have to give the girl up,' Sol said. 'If you don't you are not only endangering yourself and her, but also her family and your family, your unborn children and grandchildren. You will be throwing away everything and you will be running for the rest of your life.'

'Some laws are wrong,' Lex said, his voice cracking.

'Then work to change them if you must,' Sol said, 'but never break them!'

Lex fell silent, torn between anger at his father's interference and sadness at the realisation he was right. But he couldn't possibly give her up; it would be easier to cut out his own heart. He had never before been confronted with a problem that appeared to have no happy solution. It felt as if he was being torn in half. He tried to make sense of it all.

'Who told you about her?' he asked after what seemed like an eternity.

'It doesn't matter,' Sol said. 'If even one other person knew then you put yourself and the girl in danger. You must sever all connections with her immediately.'

'I can't do that,' Lex said, standing up to leave the room. 'If you met her you would understand.'

'I do understand, Lex,' Sol replied sadly, 'but understanding how hard it will be does not change anything. You have to do it. I am insisting.'

'There is nothing further for us to talk about on this subject,' Lex said, feeling physically sick from the amount of adrenaline it took to defy his father in this way. He turned and walked out of the room.

* * *

Zak heard Lex's car long before it reached the house. He'd been listening out for it. He was studying on the porch and put down his books as the engine cut out and Lex's footsteps approached.

'My father's found out,' Lex said, not even taking the trouble to lower his voice.

'I'm so sorry, Lex,' Zak said, standing up to face his friend.

'Sorry? Why are you sorry?' Lex didn't understand. 'Was it you who told him?'

'I had no choice. You wouldn't listen to me. I was scared for both of you. You're both my friends.'

Lex threw a punch before either of them expected and caught Zak squarely on the chin, sending him spinning back across the porch.

'A friend would never betray someone like that!' He spat out the words, turned and walked back to the car.

He'd been intending to stay the night at Zak's, not wanting to go home, but now he found himself betrayed twice over. He drove to a nearby hotel where Goldman Enterprises had an account and booked into a room. He lay on the bed, staring at the ceiling, trying to calm the dozens of thoughts that were racing in different directions. There was no question that he could give up Reshmine, so he had to lay plans for them both to leave the country. He would be sorry to leave Goldman Enterprises where he had so much ambition for how he would develop it once he took over from his father, but he could always start another company. He was sure he would never find another Reshmine. He lay for hours, eventually falling into a fitful sleep, where his plans and fears mingled with his dreams.

The following day he drove the car to the usual place at the usual time, parked and went into the tobacconist. When he got back to the car he didn't even have to look behind him to know there was no one on the back seat. He told himself not to panic, there had been other days when she hadn't managed to get away for their liaisons. He would just have to wait until the same time tomorrow.

Back at the hotel, the hours crawled by. He couldn't concentrate on anything except his own desperate need to see her, hold her in his arms and tell her of his plans for their future together.

The following day the car seat remained empty again and he wasn't sure how he would endure another twenty-four hours without seeing her. He thought about going to her house, but knew that would be madness. Although he'd found out the address from Zak weeks earlier, just because he was hungry for every scrap of information about Reshmine that he could possibly glean, he'd never been to the area and knew he would be conspicuous there. There had been one or two occasions when she'd missed two days in a row, but never more than two. If she wasn't there the next day he would go in search of her. If the first twenty-four hours had been bad, the second was like a water torture. By the time he was able to get into the car and set out for the same location he was having trouble holding on to his sanity. His anger at Zak and his father, coupled with his fear that he might be losing Reshmine at the same time as losing his footing in his father's company, left him feeling like he was hanging in mid air, a sort of mental limbo.

The back seat was empty when he got back into the car and he felt as if his world had finally ended. Unable to judge any longer if it was a wise or a rash thing to do, he drove to Reshmine's house. Faces appeared at the neighbouring windows at the sight of a young white man driving into the area in a new Mercedes, but it meant nothing to him. He didn't care if the whole world knew about his love for Reshmine. He didn't care if the police came and beat him to a pulp, as long as he could see her again.

Her father answered the door and his face was grave. His eyes still flickered up and down the street, alert for danger, before letting the agitated boy into the house. Lex could hear a woman crying in the kitchen and only just managed to stop himself from barging rudely past to find her and comfort her.

'May I see Reshmine?' he asked.

'She's gone,' her father said.

Angry at being lied to, Lex pushed past and burst into the kitchen. A woman, who he guessed to be Reshmine's mother, was sitting at the table, sobbing.

'She's gone?' Lex asked, turning back to the man.

He nodded.

'What do you mean?'

'They killed her.'

'Who?'

'What does it matter, who? A gang of them beat her to death.'

'Because of me?' Lex asked.

The man nodded and the woman covered her face and wailed louder.

'We have to do something,' Lex protested. 'We have to report it to the authorities.'

The man laughed but there was no humour in the sound. 'You, a privileged European Jew expect the authorities to care about people like us?'

Lex opened his mouth to protest but no words came out.

'Please, you must leave now or they'll come to the house,' her father said.

'Yes.' Lex allowed himself to be walked to the door, unable to take in what he'd heard.

'I'm so sorry,' he said as the older man closed the door behind him.

2

The sirens were superfluous; everyone had heard the crash of the rocks falling already. The noise had been deafening for the miners underground and had continued for minutes, echoes of one fall mingling with the impact of the next. Lex and the other managers felt the vibration beneath the floorboards of the manager's hut before they heard the roar emitting from the mouth of the mine. Everything shook and rattled around them as they ran out into the night to see what was happening.

Workers who were able to escape were struggling to the surface through the choking clouds of dust. The only ones who wouldn't make it to the surface in the next few minutes would be the ones trapped or crushed by the rocks.

'Kill the sirens!' Lex shouted, wanting to bring down the levels of noise and panic as quickly as possible. The sooner he could restore order the quicker he could assess the damage and get them back to work in the seams that were still accessible. He was acutely aware of how much money they were losing every minute the workforce was out. He knew exactly how much money the mine made at any hour of the day or night and he knew how to push it to its maximum.

The sirens faded obediently, but the shouting and screaming didn't lessen. Lex waded into the crowd, bellowing orders, but the chaos was impenetrable. Pulling out the pistol he always kept beneath his shirt, he fired it into the air three times. A shocked silence fell on the crowd around him, although those still stumbling out of the mine entrance continued coughing and calling out to one another.

'More lights!' Lex ordered and lanterns flickered into life amongst the crowd, casting eerie shadows and illuminating the dust and blood-caked masks of the survivors.

As the dust settled, he started to piece the story together from those who were able to talk coherently.

'It's shaft two,' he shouted to his assistants who were looking as confused and panicked as the workers.

Lex snatched a lantern from a nearby hand, pressed a handkerchief over his mouth and nose and pushed his way against the tide of stumbling bodies to the opening. To begin with it was hard to make out anything in the gloom, but his eyes gradually accustomed themselves and a couple of the braver managers found hard hats and came in behind him with more lights. He could see shaft two had entirely vanished. Away from the chaos of the crowd outside the silence below ground was sudden and uncomfortable.

'How many men would be in there?' he asked the shell-shocked manager beside him.

'Fifty, maybe more,' he replied.

'None of the other shafts are affected?'

'Doesn't look like it.'

'Then let's start getting them back to work, we've lost enough time over this already.'

Lex was aware of the minutes ticking away while the mine lay idle, money was evaporating before his eyes and it made him angry. It had been such a smooth shift and now things had been wrenched from his control.

The managers exchanged shocked looks.

'We could use this shift to try to get to any survivors,' one of them suggested.

'There won't be many of those,' Lex replied curtly. 'We'll get professionals in tomorrow to assess the situation. That seam was nearly spent anyway. I doubt it'll be viable to open it up again now.'

None of the others said anything. They all averted their eyes. No one on the management team ever argued with Lex, any more than they argued with Sol. The last man who'd questioned the way the workforce was treated had not only been fired, he'd ended up beaten to a pulp in a dark alley late at night. No one would actually be brave enough to suggest out loud that the two events were connected, but in everyone's minds the link between defying the Goldman family and meeting a sticky end had been established.

Lex was well aware of the way people thought about him, but he didn't care. From the day he heard about Reshmine's death, his heart had hardened and he realised the only way to survive was to be more ruthless than everyone else.

As he emerged back into the crowd, with his managers behind him, the workforce fell quiet. They respected him for walking bareheaded into a collapsing mine and they all looked to him for the leadership needed to co-ordinate the rescue operation.

'Okay,' he shouted. 'Everything is sound in there. Nothing's going to happen in the other shafts, so get back to work. We've got a lot of catching up to do now.'

A murmur of disquiet rumbled around the back of the mob.

One man near the front, emboldened by the voices he could hear behind him, stepped forward.

'We need to get them out,' he said.

Lex pulled his gun out again and pressed it against the man's temple so that others could see. There was a hiss of shock and everyone pulled back. Lex recognised this man, he was a troublemaker, trying to stir up unrest amongst the labour force. If he had to shoot him it would at least serve as a lesson to anyone else thinking of challenging the way things were done.

'Are you running this fucking mine or am I?' Lex snarled.

'You are.' The man was obviously afraid, but was brave enough to keep talking. 'But some of them may still be alive.'

'If you're wanting to give up your job, go ahead,' Lex said. 'If you want to keep it, get back to work, now!'

For a few seconds he couldn't be sure which way the mood of the crowd was going to go. All eyes were on him and the man at the end of his gun. If they'd decided to rush him there wouldn't have been anything he could have done. He would have been able to shoot a few of them but he doubted if his managers would have the guts to follow his lead; he would have been overrun within seconds and he doubted they would show him any mercy.

'Okay, boss,' the man said, lifting his hands in a small, resentful gesture of surrender.

The tension had been broken and the men moved slowly back towards the entrance. One or two of them shot angry looks at Lex, which he ignored, but most kept their eyes on the ground.

At the next board meeting several of the directors wanted to talk about the accident, which annoyed Lex.

'No good crying over spilt milk,' he told them, smiling in a way he hoped would look benign. 'There are always going to be setbacks, we just have to move on and open new seams to replace spent ones, business as usual.'

'There were a lot of lives lost that night,' one of them said. 'You could have done more to save them.'

'Mining is a dangerous business,' Lex said, the grin still fixed on his face. 'That's why the rewards are so good.'

'There is a lot of disquiet in the workforce,' the director persevered. 'They're starting to organise themselves. An incident like this gives the ring leaders a platform to denounce us from.'

'I know who the troublemakers are,' Lex assured him. 'I'm dealing with them. Can we talk about Levy's now?'

'He's right,' Sol agreed. 'There's nothing to be gained by going over the accident again. Let's talk about Levy's. They need help if they aren't going to go under.'

'The company is basically sound,' Lex remarked, pleased to have steered the meeting in the direction he intended. 'I think we should make an offer.'

'An offer?' Sol looked puzzled. 'An offer to help? They just need a cash injection to update their machinery, that's all.'

'If we owned them we could inject the cash and reap the rewards,' Lex pointed out.

'They've been family friends for twenty years,' Sol reminded him. 'They've come to us for help, told us things in confidence. We can't betray that.'

'Betrayal has nothing to do with it,' Lex sighed as if his father exasperated him. 'This is business. If we make them an offer they can take the money and invest it in another business. They've become too small a player for today's mining business. We could rescue them this year and they would be back in trouble in two years' time. Put them out of their misery for God's sake, and salvage something good from the wreckage.'

'You're suggesting we take advantage of someone when they're down on their luck, someone who's been a good friend?' Sol asked. 'How would you be able to face them again?'

Lex smiled contentedly. 'I would rather ask for forgiveness afterwards than permission before – that way you move forward. Our job is to take every opportunity to make Goldman's more profitable. Buying Levy's at a rock bottom price would be a good deal for us.'

A chair scraped noisily on the polished wood flooring as one of the directors stood up.

'If you decide to go ahead with this,' he said, 'I'll be resigning.'

'Anyone else want to resign?' Lex asked, looking round the room, one eyebrow arched. The man had played into his hands, he'd been thinking for months it was time to get some new blood into the boardroom; there were too many of Sol's old cronies there, men who'd lost their hunger for making money and spent too much time worrying about the rights or wrongs of their decisions rather than the business sense.

'Wait a minute,' Sol said and Lex noticed for the first time how tired his father looked. Eva had told him about the cancer diagnosis, but this was the first time he'd seen a physical sign of the illness. 'Can we just calm down about this and think it through sensibly?'

'If we don't do it someone else will,' Lex said. 'We have an opportunity to get this company at a fraction of its true value. Wait another couple of days and we'll have lost the chance. Anyone who doesn't believe we should do it doesn't have the best interests of Goldman's at heart.'

He stared straight at the man who was still standing beside his chair, calling his bluff. Sol fumbled in his jacket pocket for the painkillers the doctor had given him, and no one else spoke. The rebellious director eventually shrugged, knowing he was beaten, and sat back down again.

'Good,' Lex said. 'Let's work out an offer.'

Lex always knew that if his father was drinking whisky when he arrived at their house for dinner, there was likely to be trouble. It always brought out the worst in Sol, released all the fear, resentment and bitterness that he usually managed to suppress. Eva might not have been able to connect her husband's bad moods to his choice of drink, but she recognised other signs and made sure she didn't aggravate him any more than she had to. She knew Lex would be bound to do that.

She hated it when her husband and son argued, particularly now the doctor had told her Sol's days were numbered. In many ways she could see they were too alike to be able to get on easily; neither of them could ever admit there might be a valid alternative viewpoint to their own. The older Sol became the less he was able to keep control of his tongue, and the older Lex grew the more ruthless he seemed to become. She had watched as Lex's views grew more like his father's as he took greater control of the company, and she was sad to see his heart hardening. She said nothing because she assumed it was the natural way of things; in order to survive in a hostile world men had to make difficult decisions and sometimes people got hurt. She appreciated there was often no alternative. She preferred not to think about it, to distract herself with other less painful thoughts.

'Sometimes you have to be cruel to be kind,' she would say when anyone challenged her on the morality of her husband and son's thriving company. Or possibly, 'You can't make an omelette without breaking some eggs,' which was a phrase she'd heard both of them use to justify the high death rates amongst their workforce.

'You make enemies of people who've been your friends and pretty soon you end up on your own if you keep pushing them too hard,' Sol said as he and Lex came through from the veranda and sat down to supper. 'All those people on the board have been with me for a long time. There's such a thing as loyalty.'

'They're all getting old. If the company is going to thrive in the future it needs new people.'

'People you can bully, you mean.'

Even when it was just herself and Sol, Eva always insisted they dine formally, making her husband change into a dinner suit and spending at least an hour on her own make-up and hair before descending the main staircase. If Lex was joining them she went to even more trouble, fussing around the staff all day to ensure everything would be perfect by the time they came to the table.

'A company needs strong leadership,' Lex reminded his father. He didn't have to add that Sol was weakening by the day – they both knew that.

'You bring outsiders into the company and you never know who you're dealing with,' Sol said, changing his tack.

'Who are all these outsiders, Dad?'

'You know perfectly well who,' Sol scoffed. 'There's us and then there's the rest of the world.'

'Us Litvaks you mean?'

'Do you have to use that word?' Eva tutted, 'it's so vulgar.'

'Yes, Litvaks,' Sol spat back at him before turning on his wife. 'We are what we are. If we're vulgar then that's what we are!'

Eva tutted again, shrugged and concentrated her efforts on ticking off the butler over an imagined smear on one of the gleaming crystal glasses set out before her.

'You can't go on distrusting the whole world for ever,' Lex insisted. 'Successful business is about co-operation and teamwork. If we never work with anyone we aren't related to there's a limit to how big we can grow.'

'We're not doing so badly,' Sol grumbled. 'Do you think we're doing badly? Eva, the boy thinks we're not doing well enough, when everything is being handed to him on a plate!'

Eva kept issuing orders at the butler as if she hadn't heard her husband, and Lex took a deep breath, determined to keep his voice low.

'Of course we're not doing badly,' he said, 'in this country. But if we want to take this company truly international we have to work with foreigners. We have to hire experts in different markets and different skills; we have to put some trust in other people.'

'This country has been good to us:' Sol added a mouthful of wine to the mixture already coursing through his veins. 'If it wasn't for South Africa you wouldn't even exist.'

'I know.' Lex was holding onto his patience with all his strength: 'I'm not being ungrateful to this country, but not everyone in the outside world thinks this is the greatest political system. As long as Goldman Enterprises is linked to apartheid there's going to be a resistance to doing business with us. Other people don't want to be seen to be tarred with the same brush.'

'You think we have something to be ashamed of?' The glint in Sol's eyes showed he was ready to take the gloves off, he just needed an excuse. 'You think I shouldn't be proud of what I've achieved?'

'You should be proud,' Lex said, 'just as I'm proud of you and everything you've built.'

Unable to find fault for a moment, Sol started eating, waving the butler away irritably as the man tried to help him to vegetables, and Lex was able to continue.

'We need to diversify into diamonds, to hedge ourselves against fluctuations in the gold markets. And we need to move away from being just a mining company. The big profits are being made by the commodity traders and they don't even have to get their hands dirty. We should be a dominant force in the dealing rooms. We need to be seen as an international name, not a South African one. People mustn't feel guilty about doing business with us.'

'Why should anyone feel guilty about making a profit,' Sol asked, his mouth now full of food, 'as long as they've earned the money honestly?'

'They don't feel guilty about that,' Lex said, 'but they're being made to feel guilty about the exploitation of the blacks who we pay next to nothing to dig the stuff out of the ground.'

'We pay the rate for the job,' Sol snapped back.

'Come on, Dad,' Lex tried to keep his tone reasonable. 'We both know the blacks were forced to work in the mines when the British started taxing them and disallowing them from owning property. The men are separated from their families and they have no rights at all. You know all this. We wouldn't be able to produce the profits we do if we didn't exploit those facts. But it's not going to last for ever. Sooner or later they're going to call our bluff, we're going to have to start paying higher wages and our profits are going to be hit. We need to diversify and consolidate before that happens.'

Sol looked uncomfortable for a moment. When a man knew he was going to be meeting his maker in the near future he didn't want to have too much on his conscience. 'There are worse employers than us,' he said eventually.

'I know there are, Dad, but someone reading an article in some left-wing paper in Europe doesn't know that. They don't see any difference between us and every other rich white South African racist oppressor.'

'Listen to this,' Sol shouted at Eva, making both her and the butler jump. 'Our son is calling me an oppressor! Me, who lost everything in Europe!' He pointed a short, thick finger at Lex. 'I'll tell you about oppression. Oppression is what happened to our people in Lithuania. Ninety-four per cent of us were murdered in those camps – ninety-four percent! There's nothing left over there, all our culture is here in this great country. They wiped us out in our own country, but we have survived here. Here we're free, there we were oppressed. Am I sending anyone to the gas chambers? Am I raping their women and experimenting on their children? Am I doing any of these things?'

'No, Father, of course you're doing none of these things, but over forty thousand black labourers have died in the gold mines here over the last seventy years. It's easy for people to turn that into bad press.'

'Whites too. A white man's skull is crushed as easily as a black man's'.

'Sol,' Eva looked up, 'we're eating.'

The butler showed no sign of having heard a word of the conversation. None of them even glanced in his direction.

'I'm just explaining what we need to do to improve the image of the company abroad so that we can expand,' Lex sighed. He hated the way Sol made him go through this ritual of explaining himself. He didn't have to do it. He was going to take the company wherever he wanted anyway; it was only out of respect to his father that he even bothered to discuss his plans. He'd already talked to every investment banker in the country, explaining to them how Sol was getting old and that he was no more than a figurehead; that the real power now lay with him.

'Image?' Sol let out a hiss of disgust. 'Propaganda, you mean.'

'Whatever you like to call it, if you want this company to become a force internationally you are going to have to move with the times.'

'We're doing okay,' Sol said, obviously keen to change the subject.

'We're doing more than okay, and you know it,' Lex continued. 'But that's mainly because the South African economy is booming. Everyone down here is doing well. But when the bad times come we need to have diversified and we need to have alternative profit-streams. Attitudes towards apartheid are hardening all over the world.'

'So you make scapegoats of our friends?'

'I haven't made scapegoats of anyone,' Lex sighed. He'd hoped they'd laid this argument to rest.

'You sack people who had been loyal to me for years without even telling me.'

'They retired,' Lex said for the hundredth time. 'And they all have more than enough money to last them, I doubt their children or grandchildren will have to work with the money they took from the company.'

'And you cheat the Levys out of a fair price for their company, a company they've built up over three generations!'

'It was a fair price for a company with no cash and out-of-date equipment. We have to keep driving this business forward or the company will die with . . .'

'Go on,' Sol snarled, 'say it. The company will die with me!'

'The company was stagnant and your cronies were not earning their keep,' Lex snapped. 'The Levys are not sharp enough to survive without being propped up – better they take what they can get and open a bakery!'

'Enough!' Sol slammed his fork down on his plate and stood up, sending his wine glass flying across the table. 'I've heard enough. I'm going to bed.'

Eva tried half-heartedly to dissuade her husband from leaving the table, keeping one eye on the butler's frantic efforts to mop up the wine before it damaged the surface of the priceless table.

'You shouldn't upset him so,' she scolded Lex once the dining-room door had banged behind Sol's departing back. 'Now, tell me how you're getting on with Helen.'

Lex never spoke of Reshmine to anyone. His mother had no idea that such a person had ever existed and he certainly wasn't going to bring the subject up with Sol. His friendship with Zak had ended the day he discovered his treachery, and none of the girls that Eva had matched him up with in the intervening years could have been trusted with the information that the love of his life had been a coloured Indian woman.

'This is a lovely girl,' Eva would say every time she told him she'd arranged for him to meet someone new.

The routine was always the same: Eva would arrange one of her impossibly formal dinner parties, at which everyone would be in couples apart from Lex and whoever the young lady of Eva's choice might be. Usually the girl's parents were also invited and no one was under any illusions as to why they were all there. No one would have dreamed of turning down one of Eva's invitations, not when Goldman Enterprises was doing so well. Sol was now amongst the richest men in the country and everyone knew that Lex was considered to be an even more brilliant and ruthless businessman than his father.

What right-thinking parents, from the right Litvak background, would think twice about their daughter marrying into such an assured future?

Lex had to admit his mother had a good eye for pretty girls. He ended up having relationships with most of them, although he never had any intention of marrying any of them. Helen had come the closest so far to having a similar effect on him to Reshmine, but it still wasn't the same. Eva sensed there was something more than usual going on between her son and Helen, but she could never have guessed it was the girl's mind that interested her son more than her looks. Helen was generally considered to be one of the most beautiful girls in South African society. During her short modelling career she'd appeared on virtually all the front covers of the national women's magazines, but she'd given it all up to pursue her political interests. Lex suspected it was her beauty that had helped her to stay out of trouble when she voiced the sort of opinions that led to many others being arrested and imprisoned. He suspected it was only a matter of time before she overstepped the mark and the authorities decided it was time to teach her a lesson. She knew that too, which was why he admired her courage so much.

'You could never marry me,' she teased him one evening, as they lay in bed together after making love.

'Why's that?'

'I'd hamper your rise to the top.'

'And how would you do that?'

'I would be your conscience, making you think each time before you did some mega-deal that would make you even richer and thousands of blacks even poorer.'

'I don't get rich at their expense,' he laughed, 'I get rich at the expense of my competitors, other whites.'

'Bullshit.'

'You think?'

'If that's the case why don't you give all your workers a living wage and allow them to live with their families?'

'I don't make government policy.'

'You don't have to do everything you're told, do you?'

'If I started to rock the boat it wouldn't be long before I ended up in prison or worse. If the government didn't have me assassinated, the business community would.'

She fell silent for a moment, her head on his chest so he couldn't see her expression. It worried her that she adored him so much when she could find no evidence that the man had any heart. She'd never once heard him say anything empathetic about the thousands of blacks who slaved for Goldman Enterprises, often dying in the process. But she couldn't stop herself from coming back for more.

'Someone has to rock the boat,' she said eventually, 'otherwise it'll sail on for ever.'

'People in other countries are doing a pretty good job. You should leave it to them. No one's going to come knocking on their doors in the middle of the night.'

'Sanctions are never going to work.' She tweaked his chest hair, making him jump.

'Ouch! I don't see why not.'

'Because too many people are breaking them.'

'Seriously,' he said, stroking her hair, knowing perfectly well she was right. 'You should be careful what you say; people have disappeared for saying less than you.'

'Don't worry, your mother would soon find you a replacement,' she teased.

'That's not funny. You won't help anyone by getting yourself murdered. Go slowly and you could end up changing things forever; go too fast and they'll kill you.'

They both fell silent and thoughtful again. Lex found it exciting and disquieting to be with Helen. It was exciting because she was so full of idealism and hope, but it was disquieting because he knew she was right. He knew he should feel bad about the thousands of blacks who worked for Goldman in conditions no different to slavery, but he didn't. From the moment he heard of Reshmine's death he'd realised the absolute truth: life was cheap. The only way to make your own life worth anything was to become richer and more powerful than everyone else. So that was what he planned to do. He said nothing, knowing that if she thought there was any chance she could win him over to the cause, Helen would never leave him alone.

He knew he really should be telling her that he would never be able to love her the way she needed, because his heart would always belong to Reshmine. He hadn't lied to her or given her any false hopes, but he was pretty sure she would move on if she knew the true state of his feelings and he didn't want her to do that, not yet. She helped him to forget how lonely he was most of the time. There were moments when he wondered if he was being unrealistic. Would he ever meet anyone who would drive the constant thoughts of Reshmine from his head? He liked the idea of having children, and not just because his mother was constantly reminding him she wanted to be made a grandmother before it was too late. But creating a life with anyone but Reshmine seemed like an act of treachery. How would he ever be able to look his child in the eyes, knowing he wasn't completely in love with its mother, knowing that in the place where his emotions had once been there was now nothing but a chilling emptiness?

* * *

'Listen,' Sol said one evening, suddenly too tired to go on arguing with his son. 'Soon it's going to be your company. You must do what you think is best.'

'Don't talk like that,' Eva scolded her husband. 'You're as strong as a thousand oxen.'

'Don't be a fool, woman. I'm an old man. I'm going to die. What do you care? You'll still have your bridge and your damn tea parties.'

'Dad!' Lex saw the tears start in his mother's eyes before she was able to look away.

'The doctors said you could go on for years,' Eva said.

'The doctors said they didn't have any idea how long I had,' Sol corrected her. 'They admit they can't diagnose whatever it is that's eating into me. Listen,' he turned his attention back to his son. 'Do what you want. Go travel while I'm still around to run things here.'

'Thank you,' Lex said with a respectful nod. He was glad he hadn't had to tell his father he'd already booked flights to New York and London and had a list of appointments with many of the most powerful bankers and traders in the world. He now had the whole of the board on his side. Although none of them would ever have been brave enough to stand up to Sol on his own, each of them had caved in when confronted with Lex's determination. Now it would look to Sol as if his son had waited for his permission, while everyone else in the company knew that Lex was more ruthless than his father had ever been. It was the best of all possible outcomes and Lex knew he'd played the game skilfully.

It was easy to see that Sol's strength was waning as the cancer increased its hold on his system. The flesh was disappearing from his face and his neck no longer filled the collars of his shirts. The weaker his body grew, the more fiercely the fire in his eyes burned, as if with a renewed fury. Lex wished he could think of a way to win the old man's blessing before it was too late. If he could produce a real result with his expansion outside South Africa before Sol died he would be able to believe he had finally won his father's respect, at the same time as preparing the ground for a real programme of modernisation within the company.

The money was continuing to pour into the coffers, despite Sol's reluctance to move forward, but there was a limit to what could be achieved with the company in its current form. Lex knew that with the capital mountain they were sitting on he could turn Goldman's into one of the world's most powerful trading and minerals corporations, but was less sure that his father would live long enough to see it happen. The thought made him even more determined to drive through the changes he knew were necessary with all speed possible, regardless of what had to be done.

Although many who met Lex found him arrogant and overbearing, he was always realistic about his own shortcomings. He knew that working in a family company all his adult life had not given him a rounded business apprenticeship. He understood how to make money and how to grind costs down to the lowest possible figure, which meant he was rich, but he knew he needed a great deal more international business experience before he would be in a position to compete on the global playing field. Lex realised he had a lot to learn if Goldman's was going to become a world-player, and he wasn't going to achieve that by staying in Johannesburg counting the money.

America was a revelation to him, making him wish he'd travelled outside South Africa more in his twenties. There had always been so much to occupy his mind at the company. If he'd managed to keep a relationship with a woman going for more than a few months, she might have been able to persuade him to take her to see a bit of the world. Travelling on his own had seemed pointless, until now.

Now he was a man on a mission. Spending weeks in meetings with some of the most successful businessmen alive made him realise more acutely than ever just how limited his horizons had been, but also just what a strong position Goldman's was in. Many of the much larger companies he met with were not sitting on cash mountains the size of Goldman's. They were all tied to borrowing and surviving on their cashflows. Every time there was a dip in business, their situation became precarious. He could see that his hunches had been right: Goldman was in the perfect position to spread its wings and become one of the major players.

In the initial few weeks he hardly slept, wanting to soak up every piece of information, both in meetings and in the social settings where people he wanted to do business with mixed and talked with their guard down. For the first time he realised the potential of the technology that some of the big computer companies were researching and testing. He could see that within a few years it would change the world and the way business was being done. He also realised that while everyone's eyes were on the Japanese and their phenomenal business growth, the oil dollars pouring into the Gulf were creating some of the wealthiest people on the planet, people who could be useful customers and partners for a firm that dealt in money, investment and precious metals, people who would have no qualms about dealing with South Africa or parent companies based there.

On his first return home he was shocked to see how Sol's health had deteriorated in his absence. He could see from the dreamy look in his eyes that his father had lost interest in the future and knew he would never share his enthusiasm for taking the company global.

'We need to build the company into a globally recognisable brand name,' he explained one evening, determined to get his point across.

'Do whatever you must do,' Sol said with an impatient wave of his hand, as if slapping away an annoying fly.

'It will probably mean a new company name and a lot of investment.'

'It'll be your company soon,' Sol shrugged, 'just don't piss it all away too quickly.'

That, Lex decided, was the closest he was going to get to receiving his father's blessing.

News that Goldman Enterprises was looking for an international agency to create a brand image for them from scratch spread through the advertising and financial public relations worlds like a virus. All the big players wanted to get themselves in on the ground floor. Within hours of Lex making the initial enquiries from his suite at the Waldorf, the calls started to arrive from all over America and Europe. All the big groups were willing to fly creative teams over to New York to present to him, each one assuring him of just how excited they would be at the prospect of working on such an internationally prestigious project. Lex spent a month being wined, dined and flown from continent to continent as the most creative brains in the industry attempted to convince him that they were the ones to turn his vision into a reality.

To begin with he would ring his father to report back on progress, but it was obvious Sol wasn't interested. All he would do was grumble at the expenses he could see Lex running up, and then sigh wearily as if there was nothing he could do to stop his son from ruining the company. Lex swallowed his disappointment; he just hoped his father would live long enough to see some of the results he knew he could achieve.

When the last of the pitches had been made and the agency group had been selected, the money began to pour out. Lex leased prestigious offices in the financial districts of New York, Tokyo and London, and architects and designers were hired to oversee everything from the letter headings to the facades of the buildings. After months of research it was decided to rename the business 'Goldfields Corporation'. The corporate material would feature sun-drenched fields of corn, stretching as far as the eye could see, being harvested and spun into gold and into the most exquisite diamond jewellery to be hung on the most beautiful models. Dewdrops on flowers were filmed being transformed into ravishing diamonds. Aged craftsmen were shown working on minutely detailed pieces in places like Venice and London. No film was shot around the mines of South Africa or the noisy, crowded trading rooms of the financial districts. No black faces appeared anywhere in the branding. It was as if the precious metals had appeared fully formed on the workmen's benches. No one saw the dirt and squalor of the shanty towns that the miners lived in, or the ugly, prison-like vaults filled with gold bars.

'Goldfields means wealth and luxury,' the creative mantra went, 'just like Rolls-Royce, Coutts, Rothschild or Asprey. It's a company that people aspire to work for or do business with.'

The rest of the world didn't need to know that Goldfields was supplying gold and diamonds to industry and to governments as well as to the makers of cheap, shoddy jewellery. It was in everyone's interest to keep that quiet, to maintain the purity of the image.

It was about safe investment in the two most glamorous commodities the earth could produce.

Every serious investment banker in the world wanted to reach Lex and persuade him to borrow money to finance his expansion. Lex quietly let each one think he was doing business with a rival, but all the time he and Sol were bankrolling the entire operation from their cash mountain.

'Whatever you do don't borrow money,' Sol had snapped at him when Lex had suggested that perhaps they should let the banks take some of the strain. 'It's bad enough that you're squandering all this money in the first place, without you paying interest on it.'

From other sources Lex heard that Sol was actually congratulating himself on making a sound investment in his son and the growth of his own business.

'If the banks think they'll get a good return on their money,' he told one of his oldest friends, 'then it should be a good bet.'

Lex was pleased to hear this, but wished his father could have told him to his face that he had faith in him.

Most of the time Lex was so busy he didn't have a moment to think how lonely he was. There were always people around him, decisions to be made, planes to be caught. But every so often he would find himself in a hotel room in a foreign city on a Saturday with the prospect of a whole evening stretching ahead of him and no one to call. It was on one of those nights in London, staying at Claridge's Hotel, that he reached for the telephone and called an escort agency. This was the first time he had ever admitted to himself that what he really craved was company, someone to be with and talk to about things other than business, someone to enjoy a few hours with.

The voice at the other end of the line assured him it would be no problem to find someone at short notice and, two hours later, they rang up from reception to say that Miss Bizzykhan was waiting for him. When he came out of the lift to meet her he was startled to see that Miss Bizzykhan was coloured. Although she didn't look pure Indian, almost everything about her reminded him of Reshmine, from the dazzling white smile she unleashed on him the moment he introduced himself to the tiny fingers that gripped his so firmly as they shook hands. He caught a hint of her scent as she raised her flawless olive cheek for him to brush against his and was transported back nearly twenty years.

'Would you like a drink?' he enquired, as shyly as a young boy on a first date.

'That would be lovely.'

He led her through into the hotel bar, grateful to her for covering his awkwardness with the easy chat of a professional. She asked him what business he was in, but was quite happy to change the subject when she realised he didn't want to talk about it. They stayed on neutral subjects, discussing where they would go for dinner and what else they might do to pass the evening, and all the time he kept thinking that even if they spent the night together she would still be gone the next morning and the loneliness would return. But she wasn't Reshmine, however much she might look like her, and there was no point kidding himself that she could be the answer to his problems. He drained his glass and ordered a refill, determined to enjoy himself.

They ate at the hotel and then moved to the Ritz casino. Despite being able to see how wealthy her date was, Miss Bizzykhan made no attempt to pretend she had any feelings for him beyond the professional, which made him like her even more. A number of Middle Eastern contacts came over to shake his hand at the casino and complimented him on the beauty of his companion. By the end of the evening he'd lost nearly a hundred thousand pounds, but he'd had a good evening. Miss Bizzykhan agreed to stay the night with him and the next morning he rewarded her generously for her services.

Once she'd gone he stood for a while at the window of his suite in his dressing-gown, staring down at the street. He liked London and felt no wish to return to South Africa. He knew the emptiness in his heart would never be filled as long as he was in the same country where Reshmine had died. His reverie was interrupted by the phone call he'd been dreading for so long: Sol had passed away peacefully in his sleep, finally losing his battle with cancer.

His mother kept whimpering, but Lex suspected it was more to do with self-pity than with the fact that they'd just buried her husband.

'But I'll be living here all alone,' she moaned, 'with you God knows how many thousands of miles away.'

'You won't be alone, Mother,' he replied. 'You have more friends than any woman I've ever met, and the staff are here. Your life will hardly change.'

'How can you say that? Your father was my life. Without him I have nothing. How will I fill my days until I can join him?'

'You will play bridge, go to parties and buy hugely expensive paintings just like always. There will be a succession of old men hoping to marry you. I'm not moving back to South Africa at the moment, so stop the manipulating.'

Eva pouted for a few moments while Lex made some calls, then decided to try a different tack and ordered one of the staff to help her get to her bedroom to rest. Lex was too distracted by then to notice the performance she was putting on, and by the time she came back downstairs a few hours later, he was already on his way to the airport, heading back to London. With Sol gone there was nothing to stop him doing whatever he wanted. Now one of the richest and most powerful businessmen in the world, he was determined to have a lot of fun working out how to enjoy it.

3

The 'For Sale' signs never even went up; they didn't have to on a house worth as much as Hampstead Hall. There weren't many people in the world rich enough to afford such a property, and only a few of them would be likely to be looking in north London at any one time, so the list of potential buyers could be reached with some discreet networking on the part of the estate agents.

'Have you any idea who it is?' Joanna Feinstein asked. 'You were so close to Barbara, did she not tell you who she was selling to?'

'She had no idea,' Ellen Rothberg replied. She had been having an afternoon nap, in preparation for an evening dinner party when Joanna rang. 'Apparently it was bought by some trust in Switzerland or somewhere.'

'Maybe it's a banker,' Joanna suggested. 'They're the only people who could afford a place like that.'

'It could be a pop star, or an actor,' Ellen suggested. 'They sometimes like to guard their privacy.'

'Oh, God,' Joanna sighed, 'I hope not. If those sort of people start moving in, the area wouldn't last long.'

'Don't be such a snob, Joey,' Ellen chuckled. 'You could do

worse than have a film star, they can sometimes put up the property values.'

'It wouldn't be one of the royal family, would it?' Joanna had thought of something that to her would have been even worse than a pop star.

Ellen laughed outright. 'I don't think so, dear. They usually prefer to move out to the suburbs if they can't be in Kensington.'

'Or the country,' Joanna agreed.

'Quite. Why are you so desperate to find out, anyway? You're bound to know soon enough.'

'I'm just trying to be a good neighbour,' Joanna protested. 'I was thinking of sending round a welcome hamper or something, making a gesture.'

'You are just desperate to get in ahead of the crowd,' Ellen teased. 'Are you going to be at the Epsteins tonight?'

'We are, of course.'

'We'll talk more then.'

Joanna and Ellen were not the only ones consumed with curiosity. No one in London had any idea that it was Lex who had bought Hampstead Hall, one of the oldest and largest mansions in Hampstead. He hadn't even been to see it, leaving that to his agents, who had no idea they were working for him, having received their instructions from a Swiss banker who had feigned deafness whenever he was asked who might actually be planning to live in the house they were purchasing. There were one or two alert journalists, particularly on the business pages of the papers, who were also keeping their ears to the ground in the hope of being the first to find out. Anyone who was moving into a house of that size was bound to be a player in the business world, and if they were choosing to move to London from abroad, it was bound to be significant.

'It's someone from South Africa,' Ellen told Joanna in a return call a couple of weeks later.

'What is?'

'The buyer of Hampstead Hall.'

'Oh my God,' Joanna was aghast. 'South African? That's appalling. If it's someone from the government we won't be able to accept any invitations.'

'I know, I know.'

'Is there any chance you're wrong?'

'I don't think so,' Ellen said. 'Ralph's cousin works at Credit Suisse. He was lunching with someone in Geneva who works for the bank overseeing the purchase – his wife's brother-in-law I think; the man who advised Betty what to do after Jacob died.'

'I remember him, he dined with us a few times.'

'So, a reliable source then.'

'Could be,' Joanna thought for a moment. 'I'll ask Phillip when he gets home this evening. He knows most of the South African families.'

Phillip Feinstein was a surgeon of international reputation. He had frequently been flown out to South Africa at the request of women wanting to take a few years off their faces, or a few inches added to their bust measurement. Marrying Joanna had made him financially secure enough to set himself up in a practice, which was now one of the most lucrative in Harley Street.

'Coming from where in South Africa?' he wanted to know when she told him the news as they dressed to go out.

'She didn't know. Does it make a difference? Are there that many families?'

'Not that many. I'll ask around.'

Phillip had learnt long ago that his wife's social antenna was good for business. The parties she threw were always full of people who other people never managed to get through their doors, and most of them led to business one way or another. The next day he phoned a few people in South Africa who he knew liked to gossip, and some names were suggested. One name in particular kept cropping up.

'Goldman?' Ellen couldn't hide her surprise when she heard. 'Sol Goldman? I thought he was dead.'

'He is. It's the son.'

'Little Lex?'

'He's not that little, Ellen, he's thirty-six years old.'

'Is he married?'

'No,' Joanna wasn't able to keep the glee from her voice, 'he's not married.'

'Where are the Goldmans originally from?'

'Somewhere in the Baltic, I think.'

'That's right, I remember that now. Ralph's father used to do business with Sol's uncle. How come the boy's not married? Is he queer?'

'Apparently not. He's dated virtually every girl in Cape Town and Johannesburg.'

'We'll have to see if we can do better for him up here. Does he control the whole company now if Sol's dead?'

'Phillip says he thinks so.'

'My God, Joey, he is such a catch!'

'I know, I know.'

Unable to find the time to do it himself, Lex had hired an interior decorator to prepare Hampstead Hall for him, a fellow South African who had moved to England many years before, had just finished decorating the American ambassador's residence, and a few years later would go on to revamp Kensington Palace for

Prince Charles' young bride. It was costing Lex nearly as much to renovate and furnish the house as it had to buy, but he wasn't bothered. London property was always a good investment and he needed a base. He was very happy to leave everything to a professional, and when he arrived he found that everything had been done exactly as he'd hoped. It was like walking into an English country house that had been in the same family for generations. Amongst the post, neatly laid out for him on the inlaid hall table by the butler, was a dinner invitation from Joanna Feinstein. Lex knew enough about the leading Jewish families of Europe to know that Joanna was one of the best-connected women in London. As well as being married to one of the most celebrated plastic surgeons in the world, her father and uncles ran one of the largest and most successful chains of retail stores in Britain.

One of the reasons he'd decided to buy himself a house in town was that he wanted to become part of the community. He could have hired a permanent suite at one of the hotels and saved himself a lot of trouble, but he'd had enough of spending his evenings in casinos with paid company on his arm. He wanted to belong again, to have neighbours and friends, as he remembered from his youth. He made accepting the invitation one of his first tasks of the evening.

Over the following days his hours were so full of business meetings and decisions that he didn't think of the invitation again until a couple of hours before he was due to arrive. As a result, he was late, an irritation that Joanna was prepared to overlook the moment she saw how handsome her new neighbour was in a dinner suit. Although the main drawing-room didn't exactly fall silent as he walked in, there were certainly a great many heads turning in his direction as Joanna moved him through the throng, looping her arm firmly through his.

The Feinstein dinner parties were always popular, not just because many of the richest people in London tended to come to them, but because Joanna was careful to intersperse the usual crowd, all of whom knew one another and enjoyed distraction, with people from completely different fields. If a well-known American star was appearing in the West End, it was likely Joanna would coax him or her up for dinner, likewise an artist who had a major show on, provided the show was receiving plenty of coverage in the media. Now and then she would even invite sports people, if she was reasonably confident they would be entertaining. She was also not above inviting beautiful young women, since there were always a smattering of male guests who would be there without partners, and she needed to balance her seating plans.

'I've put you next to me,' Joanna told Lex as she steered him towards the dining-room, aware that her chef was beginning to fret in the kitchen, 'because I have so much I want to ask you about South Africa. And on your other side I have put a charming young thing called Sophie.' She lowered her husky voice as if about to impart a terrible secret. 'She's a bit of a "*cause célèbre*" at the moment, very daring. Be careful she doesn't seduce you.'

The palatial dining-room had been decorated to look like a formal eighteenth-century dinner party; even the waiters had been dressed up as footmen in powdered wigs and satin britches. Lit by huge candelabras filled with flickering candles, the table glittered with glass and silver, the centre filled with enough flowers to stock a large herbaceous border.

'This is beautiful,' Lex told his hostess.

'It's nice to give people something different,' Joanna murmured, 'don't you think?' She led him to the end of the table and showed him where he would be sitting. 'Excuse me just a moment while I herd the others in.'

Lex stood dutifully behind his chair, watching the other guests coming through, smiling and nodding to those who caught his eye.

'Hello.' A girl was standing by his left shoulder. 'Who are you?'

She didn't wait for him to answer, leaning across him to pick up his place card and read it, brushing so close to him he caught a waft of her perfume.

'Lex Goldman,' she read. 'You sound like some sort of superhero. Are you a superhero, Lex Goldman?'

She giggled at her own joke. He opened his mouth to say something but, to his surprise, nothing occurred to him. All he could think was she was the most extraordinary looking creature he had ever seen. Her thick blonde hair shone in the candlelight, framing a strong, tanned face at the top of the longest, slimmest neck he had ever seen. Her huge eyes were staring at him through thick lashes, as if waiting for him to say something.

'You smell really good.'

He heard the words coming out of his mouth, although he was sure he hadn't told them to. He could see the look of surprise in her eyes and tried to think of something else to say to cover his awkwardness. He hadn't felt this uncomfortable since he was fourteen.

'What perfume are you wearing?'

'I have no idea,' she laughed, touching him lightly on the arm. 'I'm Sophie, nice to meet you. Are you South African?'

He took her hand in his and knew he would never forget how it felt, small and light but strong.

'Yes, from Johannesburg.'

'Oh yes. A wonderful country, terrible people.'

'Yes,' he said, wishing something witty would come into his head. 'I rather agree. That's why I'm here, I suppose.'

'I hope you're fighting for the cause,' Sophie said, sitting down as a footman adjusted her chair beneath her, and indicating that he should do the same.

'The cause?'

'The abolition of apartheid, of course. They have to let Mandela out of prison, don't you think?'

'Yes, I suppose so. It's complicated.'

'Not as complicated as your people like to pretend. We've stolen the African's country. We should give it back to them and then ask nicely if they mind if we stay as their guests. Not so complicated.'

'Many of the white families have been there several generations, it would be like trying to throw anyone with French blood out of England.'

'That's a ridiculous analogy.' Sophie stared at him hard. 'The French blood has been mingled into the Anglo Saxon, they have been assimilated. It is the complete opposite to apartheid, where such mingling is against the law.'

'So, what do you do?' Lex asked, keen to change the subject.

'I haven't completely decided what to do,' she said. 'What do you think I should do?'

Lex laughed, feeling his confidence returning as he grew a little more used to her. 'Joanna has warned me to be careful in case you seduce me,' he said, pleased to see the remark catch her unawares. 'So perhaps you should become a famous courtesan.'

Now it was Sophie's turn to search for a suitable reply. She'd been thinking how attractive he was and wondering if he was married; she didn't like having the initiative removed so unexpectedly. Before she could think of a response Joanna returned to her place and the business of the meal was under way.

'Tell me more about the lady on my left,' Lex said later that evening as he and Joanna sat with coffee cups in the drawing-room. Many of the other guests, including Sophie, had already gone. Most of those who were left were the people who attended all of Joanna's parties, the ones she would refer to as her 'nucleus', either related or linked through their family businesses.

'Ah, Sophie Rae,' Joanna smiled understandingly. 'Stunning, isn't she? The Raes are one of the big brewing dynasties. Her great grandfather founded the company in Ireland. I don't think they have much to do with the day-to-day running of it now, they're more into their horses. Sophie's an Olympic standard showjumper, you know.'

'No, she didn't mention that.' Lex had to admit the girl was able to surprise him, even when she wasn't there.

'Her father's one of the top breeders in England, I believe. I'm afraid I don't know too much about horses. She likes to live dangerously.'

'Riding you mean?'

'Oh no,' Joanna laughed, 'she has a taste for dangerous men. She's always getting herself into the gossip columns, linked to some gangster or other. I'm glad she's not my daughter.'

As he lay in bed later that night, unable to sleep, Lex realised that Sophie Rae had managed to disturb him in a way no one else had in more than fifteen years. It was an uncomfortable feeling, and exciting at the same time.

The next morning he found himself awake earlier than he'd intended. He had a great many other things he should have been thinking about, but he found it impossible to concentrate. Sophie had written her telephone number on the cuff of his evening shirt as she was leaving the party. It was a gesture that had reminded him just how big the age gap was between them. Wasn't that the sort of thing teenagers did? Now he was glad she'd done it; it showed she was interested in hearing from him and it meant he had a number to call without the embarrassment of having to ring his hostess and ask for it.

'Good morning,' he said when Sophie answered. He could tell he'd woken her. 'It's Lex Goldman. What are you doing next weekend?'

'I don't know, I'm not much good at planning.'

'Let's go somewhere and get to know one another better.'

'Where do you suggest?'

'A friend of mine has a yacht; he keeps telling me I should make use of it while he's away. It's in the South of France at the moment, maybe we should use that.'

'Okay.' She was beginning to sound more awake, although she didn't seem as impressed by the offer as he'd hoped.

'I'll charter a plane,' he said, hoping that would impress her. 'We'll pick the boat up at Cannes and go down to Saint-Tropez, if you like.'

'Okay,' Sophie said, as if they'd just made a date to meet in the local pub.

'Okay,' Lex echoed, feeling deflated and unsure how to proceed. 'I'll talk to you later, then.'

If she lacked enthusiasm on the phone, Sophie more than made up for it when they arrived at Cannes and boarded the *m.v. Jacaranda Bleu*, a ninety-six foot long motor yacht so gleaming white in the sunshine it hurt their eyes as they drew up to it in the tender. Her enthusiasm wasn't for the luxury of the cabins or the superb cuisine it was for the opportunities the boat offered for her to indulge in physical activity.

Within an hour of arriving, while Lex was still settling himself into his luxurious cabin, Sophie had persuaded the crew to launch the speedboat so she could water-ski. Lex had trouble persuading her to come back on board an hour later, so that the captain could sail them round to Saint-Tropez while it was still light enough to enjoy the views of the spectacular coastline. As the mighty engines gunned into life they settled down on the lower front deck, soaking up the rays of the late afternoon sun. The occasional splash of surf rose up as they bounced along, while a fresh sea breeze cooled their skins and made their hair fly. A steward served them with a bottle of chilled Cristal champagne, and after filling their glasses, they raised them in a toast to each other with the majestic background capturing the magic of the moment.

As soon as dusk fell, they moored in Saint-Tropez, the captain skilfully nestling into the front dock amongst the other fabulous yachts. A number of passers-by stopped to take in the new arrival and to wonder if this latest addition to the glittering collection on view contained any famous faces. Sophie was impatient to go ashore and explore the wonderful shops and cafes of the famous old town, and after pausing for only a few hours sleep she was up with the sun, grabbing a quick breakfast of orange juice and croissants at one of the waterfront cafes before heading back into the side streets to shop, dragging Lex in her wake.

It had been many years since Lex had taken a holiday, and he couldn't remember when he had ever allowed someone else to dictate what he did with the hours of his day. The strangest thing, however, was that he found he didn't resent any of it. In fact he loved it. Clubs he would never normally have gone near suddenly took on a magical quality when Sophie was dancing and laughing in them, boutiques he would normally not even have noticed suddenly seemed to be filled with the most fascinating items, every one of which he wanted to buy for her. The fact that she wouldn't let him pay for anything puzzled him. If she didn't want him for his money, what did she want?

The answer soon became apparent. He had gallantly arranged for them to have separate cabins, not wanting her to think he believed she would automatically sleep with him simply because he had flown her to the South of France. On the first night, exhausted from the trip and the dancing, they had slept apart, but on the second night she came to his cabin without him asking. She slid between the sheets without a word, naked and warm and loving, and he could tell she was as magnetically attracted to him as he was to her. Their bodies fused together as if it was always meant to be, and he realised just how much he'd missed all the years since he last made love to Reshmine. All the women his mother had set him up with had meant nothing compared to the way he felt when he held Sophie in his arms, drinking in the scent of her skin and hair, feeling her body pressed against his. For the first time since he heard of her death, he felt guilty about betraying the memory of Reshmine, because he was now experiencing the same overwhelming passion he had felt with her. He couldn't imagine how he would ever bear to be apart from Sophie again.

Each time they made love they would fall asleep in one another's arms and he would be woken a few hours later by her gentle caresses as her appetite returned for more. He expected to be exhausted by the morning, but in fact her energy seemed to empower him.

Halfway through Sunday she said she wanted to go water-skiing again. He left her in the capable hands of the on-board instructor and made his way down the gangplank. Ignoring the curious stares of passers-by, he wandered into town to try to gather his thoughts.

The little winding roads of what had once been a simple fishing village, until Brigitte Bardot and her friends made it one of the most fashionable spots on earth, led him out through the old port until he found himself standing beside a graveyard, gazing out past the gravestones towards the azure sea, wondering which of the tiny figures trailing streams of white behind them might be Sophie. Soothed by the peace and warmth of the place, he sat down on one of the stones and read the inscriptions around him. Some dated from the last war, and many of them told the stories of young boys felled in the fight against the Nazis and occupation.

His mind drifted back to the many stories his father had told him of those years, and of how many millions had suffered and died in defence of something they believed in. Gazing out across the sea, studded with yachts and small craft, he imagined what life must have been like for Sol and Eva, and all the kids who were lying in this graveyard. He wished he'd been less dismissive of his father whenever Sol started to tell stories of how his generation had suffered. Still suffused in a glow of happiness from Sophie's embraces, he realised more than ever just how profoundly grateful he was to his father and to everyone else who had made his privileged life possible. He smiled to himself, remembering his father once saying to him, 'Remember, Lex, the graveyard is full of indispensable people.'

Just thinking of Sol and his homespun wisdom made Lex's eyes smart, and he rubbed them quickly before a tear could form. For the first time in many years he wondered if his headlong pursuit of money and power had been the best way to use his youth. He liked to think of himself as indispensable to the company, just as Sol had done before the cancer began to weaken him, but he was no more so than any of the men lying at rest around him. Was now the time, as Sophie kept telling him whenever the conversation strayed onto the subject of apartheid, for him to start giving back something to the world?

'So why aren't you fighting apartheid?' she'd asked as they sat together on the plane down, snacking on smoked salmon and caviar.

'How do you know I'm not?'

'Just a hunch. You're someone who prefers to be on the side dishing out the beatings.'

'My people are Lithuanian Jews,' he replied. 'Most of them took so many beatings from the tsars and then the Nazis, they didn't live to tell the tale.'

'I'm not talking about your people,' she said, 'so don't try the emotional blackmail on me. I'm talking about you. Just because someone picked on your uncles you think it's right to pick on a whole lot of other people?'

He knew she was right. It was time he created some sort of fitting legacy for his father and all those like him.

A few nights after their return to London, the phone woke Lex in the middle of the night. There was a lot of background noise, as if the caller was at a party or in a pub somewhere. He could hear music and shouting.

'Hello?' He was irritated at being woken by what he thought was almost certainly a wrong number.

'Is that you?'

'Yes, Sophie,' he said, his anger at the disturbance immediately melting away at the sound of her voice.

'You doing anything this weekend?' she asked. 'Do you want to go riding?'

'Sure, that would be great.'

Two days later he drove down to Sussex and managed to find the gates Sophie had described to him: great towering things, topped with rampant stone lions and almost obliterated with ivy. There was no indication where the drive inside would lead as it wound its way through paddocks of horses, past a lake and woods. The fencing began to look better cared for and more recently painted, and then the house appeared through the trees, standing at the end of an avenue of ancient oak trees, huge and beautiful and tranquil.

As he drew the Range Rover to a halt on the gravel outside the house, a pack of labradors, spaniels and terriers appeared from round the corner of the house to investigate him, some barking, some sniffing at his legs and wagging their tails in welcome. A yellow Porsche with a personalised number plate bearing the initials 'SR' suggested Sophie was around somewhere, but there was no sign of anyone.

He couldn't find a doorbell at the front door, which was standing open, and no one responded to his calls. He decided to walk round the side of the house the dogs had appeared from. The tranquillity of the place was already seeping into his soul, reducing his usually brisk pace to a stroll. As he came through a gate in an ancient wall he found himself in a garden, with immaculately tended lawns stretching away to freshly trimmed hedges, which divided them from the fields beyond where yet more horses grazed in the sunshine. An arch at the back of the house seemed to lead to some stables where he thought he could hear voices. He walked across the deeply worn flagstones, coming out into a stable yard.

'Sophie?' he called.

'Can I help you?' a man's voice replied.

Lex swivelled to face the speaker, a slim man whose erect bearing gave the impression he was taller and younger than he probably was.

'I was looking for Sophie Rae.'

'She's in the sand school I think, round the corner.'

'Thank you.'

Lex followed the direction the man pointed him in. The sight of Sophie, putting a huge, shining black horse through its dressage paces knocked the breath out of his body, as she had intended. Sophie knew exactly how good she looked when her long legs were encased in riding boots and jodhpurs, and she had a tailored jacket to show off her tiny waist.

Lex said nothing, simply standing and watching as the horse moved gracefully beneath her, alarmed by the strength of the chemical reaction this woman created in him. She sensed he was there but didn't acknowledge it for several minutes. When she did she gave a curt wave.

'Want to go for a hack?' she asked, without bothering with a greeting.

'That would be great.'

She led the way back into the stable yard and tied the horse up.

'Let's find you some boots. Size nine or ten?'

'Something like that.'

She led him into a tack room and gestured towards the hats while she picked the boots. 'Find yourself something there that fits.'

The man he'd seen when he arrived came in with a bridle and saddle to put away.

'This is my father,' Sophie said. 'Daddy, this is Lex. He's from South Africa.'

'South Africa? Really? Jolly good.' Tom Rae smiled politely and went on about his business. Lex had a feeling he was a man who liked to be left alone.

Ten minutes later, mounted on a heavy bay mare who seemed to resent being mounted by a stranger, he was riding out beside Sophie.

'Can you keep up?' she asked.

'I'll try my best.'

Sophie immediately broke into a canter. Lex smiled grimly and kicked hard, sending his horse in fast pursuit. Sophie swerved into a field and he followed, invigorated by the feel of the wind on his face and aware that he didn't yet know this horse well enough to predict what it would do next.

Sophie headed straight for a hedge and it was obvious she was going to jump it. He was going to have to trust her judgement since he had no idea what was on the other side. By the time he reached the jump she was only a few yards ahead. He paced himself well and gave the horse one last kick to spur it on. As it skidded to a halt he found himself flying, landing on the other side with an explosion of escaping air. Sophie was standing, calmly waiting.

'You all right?' she asked, not looking particularly concerned.

He raised his hand in acknowledgement, unable to find enough breath to force any words out. She dismounted smartly and sat beside him with her horse's reins still in her hands.

'Shouldn't we go after her?' he gestured over the hedge.

'She'll be back in the stables by now.' Sophie pulled a packet of cigarettes from her pocket and lit one, offering him a puff. He declined, still unsure if he would ever breathe easily again. 'Perhaps we should find you an easier horse for starters.'

'Maybe,' he said, quite certain she had deliberately set him up with a mount that she knew would give him trouble first time out. 'This is a beautiful place.' He gestured at the views stretching away in every direction without a building in sight.

'Hmm,' she shrugged. 'It's okay. I always preferred the house in Ireland. I like the Irish.'

'You don't like the English?'

'The English are bullies.'

'Like white South Africans?'

'Exactly, you're all little empire builders. The Irish have a better grasp on what life should be about, at least they do when they're allowed to. Do you want to stay for dinner?'

'If I'm invited.'

'It won't be anything as grand as your friends in Hampstead, or your chef in the South of France.'

'They're not my friends. I thought they were yours.'

'No, I'm just there to decorate the room and make the rich old bachelors think they're meeting eligible young women.'

'So why do you go?'

'To meet people like you.' She stubbed out her cigarette, having taken only a few puffs. 'Think you can limp back now?'

'I can probably make it,' he smiled, pulling himself to his feet.

That evening at the dinner table she was still picking fights with him.

'Sophie, dear, do leave the poor man alone so he can eat,' her mother said eventually. 'Tell her, Tom.'

'Absolutely.' Sophie's father appeared to wake up from whatever trance he'd been in. 'Give the man a rest.'

There were other relatives and family friends around the table and Lex had been introduced to all of them. He'd forgotten their names already and couldn't bring himself to tear his eyes away from Sophie long enough to engage any of them in conversation.

'Okay,' she raised her exquisitely arched eyebrows at him. 'I'll lay off diddums. Wouldn't want to get myself a reputation as a bully, would I?'

After dinner she suggested they went outside for some fresh air, while the relatives retired to watch television and play bridge. Lex put his arm around her shoulder as they walked through the moonlit gardens, breathing in the night time scents of the lavishly planted flower-beds. She slid her hand around his waist and pulled his hips against hers as they walked, bringing back memories of their nights on the yacht. She led him to an elegant Palladian folly overlooking the lake he'd passed on his way up the drive. Inside she found an oil lamp and lit it with her cigarette lighter, then turned to kiss him. The touch of her lips made him feel dizzy.

'Stay here with me tonight,' she whispered in his ear and there was no question that he would be able to do anything else.

Lex never noticed the ten-year age gap when he was with Sophie, but whenever they mixed with her friends he was suddenly aware that he was from another generation. During the week she lived in a family-owned flat behind Sloane Square, and usually socialised with other people from the same area, whom she knew from the various schools she'd attended. They would go out as a group to restaurants and bars in the Kings Road. Most of the girls seemed to be in public relations while most of the boys were estate agents. All of them had money to burn.

'What exactly do you do?' he asked Sophie one evening as they lay in bed after making love.

'Do?' she asked. 'What do you mean?'

'Well, your friends all seem to have jobs . . .'

'Most of the girls are just filling in time until the boys are earning enough to marry them,' she said.

'Still haven't answered the question.'

'I'm a writer.'

'Really?' How could he have known her for several weeks and only just discovered this? 'Writing what?'

'I'm writing a book.'

'On what?'

'The Irish troubles.'

Lex was surprised, never having seen her writing anything, although he had noticed there were books on the subject lying around the flat. She talked a lot about Ireland, remembering a romantic childhood before she was packed off to boarding school in England.

'I'd like you to meet some friends of mine tonight,' she said one morning as they were having breakfast in her flat.

'I'm not sure . . .' Lex began, his heart sinking a little at the thought of another evening in a Kings Road trattoria with a bunch of spoiled kids.

'These people are different,' she interrupted him. 'They're from my childhood. You'll like them.'

'Okay.' He was surprised by the sudden seriousness of her tone. 'Sure.'

During the day she rang him with the name of a pub where they could meet in the evening.

'Where's Kilburn?' he asked when she told him the address.

'Just across from Hampstead,' she said, 'not far.'

He checked it on the map before he left the house. She was right, it wasn't far. But it was a very different area to the immaculately kept village streets of Hampstead. The Kilburn High

Road had a rundown, uncared for air about it, with bags of rubbish stacked up outside budget and charity shops, and drunks outside the pubs. A lot of windows were boarded up. He wondered if it was going to be safe to leave the car. The pub she'd directed him to was dirty and covered in graffiti. The frosted glass windows obscured the view from the outside. Once through the unwelcoming doors, inside it was dark, and the burble of talk quietened as Lex came in. All eyes turned to size up the stranger. He looked around for Sophie but couldn't see any girls at all. The only woman was the one behind the bar who was eyeing him with the same blank-faced hostility as the customers. He suddenly wished he hadn't bothered to shave and shower before coming out, and had chosen some clothes that weren't quite so expensive and quite so well pressed.

There was no way he could turn round and walk out now, so he walked the gauntlet of stares to the bar and ordered a beer. The woman served him without speaking.

'Is this your only bar?' he asked. 'Only I'm meant to be meeting someone.'

'Who would that be?' she asked in a strong Irish accent without looking up from the beer she was pouring.

'A girl called Sophie,' he said, realising his words sounded incongruous in a pub full of men, all of whom seemed to be listening in.

'This is the only bar,' she confirmed, banging the glass down in front of him and holding out her hand for his money.

'Thanks.'

He decided to say no more, just sat at the bar sipping his drink and staring straight ahead. The wall behind the drinks dispensers was mirrored and he was able to make out fractured images of what was happening behind him, aware he was now being studiously ignored by all the men in there. He wondered how these people fitted into Sophie's romantic memories of Ireland and the Irish.

Several men came and went through the doors as he drank his pint. He didn't intend to order another. If Sophie hadn't turned up by the time he finished this one he was going home.

'You made it.' He jumped to hear her voice so close.

'Where did you come from?'

'I was out the back. They only just told me you were here, sorry. There's some good Irish whiskey out the back, come through.'

She didn't wait for his reply, just walked away, expecting him to follow. Even dressed in torn jeans and a shapeless anorak, her hair pulled back savagely into a pony-tail, she moved like a model. He glanced around, expecting every man's eyes to be on her, but it was if they were both invisible. The whole pub was continuing about its usual rowdy business without reference to them.

The room she led him to was so thick with cigarette smoke he wasn't able to stop himself from coughing. Everyone looked up as he came in this time and Sophie reeled off a number of names. As each was introduced they extended their hands for him to shake. There were a couple of women and half a dozen men, most of them sitting around a kitchen table, some on a thread-bare sofa pushed against the wall.

'This is Mudge,' she said when she got to the last man in the room. 'He and I played as children. He's my oldest friend.'

'Just one of the servants, Lex,' Mudge O'Connor laughed as he shook Lex's hand. Lex was surprised by the strength of the young man's grip. 'There to keep the young mistress amused.'

'Oh, shut up, Mudge,' she laughed and leant against him. He put his arm around her shoulders in what looked to Lex like a genuinely brotherly show of affection. 'He likes to put himself down. It's all bullshit.'

Room was made for Lex at the table and a glass of whiskey appeared in front of him. Everyone talked like old friends, as if they'd known him forever. No one asked him any questions about what he did for a living or about his intentions regarding Sophie. It was as if they already knew everything they needed to know about him. He couldn't work out why the gathering felt so strange when everyone was making such an effort to be charming. They kept filling his glass, thumping him approvingly on the back at everything he said, and by the time he staggered from the pub he was far too drunk to drive.

'I can't leave the car here all night,' he protested when Sophie insisted on taking his keys away from him.

'Don't worry,' she said. 'We'll get a cab. I'll get one of the guys to bring the car back to you in the morning. It'll be fine here, they'll keep an eye on it.'

For some reason he knew she was right; these people would look after his car. It must, he told himself, be because they think so much of Sophie.

The following morning he was woken by a persistent ringing on the doorbell. When he opened his eyes he realised Sophie was not in the bed beside him. He spotted a note on the bedside table.

'Hope you slept well. Talk to you later.'

His head was pumping and his mouth was so dry he could barely raise enough saliva to speak when there was a light tap on the bedroom door.

'Urrrgh,' was all that came out.

'A gentleman by the name of Mudge is downstairs,' the butler informed him, in a tone that suggested he didn't approve of this particular visitor.

'Mudge?'

'An Irish person, sir.'

'Here?' Lex tried to shake himself awake as some vague memories of the previous evening floated to the surface. 'Okay, take him into the kitchen and make us some coffee. I'll be down in a minute.'

Having tried to revive himself in the bathroom he arrived in the kitchen to discover Mudge settling in to coffee and croissants at the table as the staff worked silently around him.

'You look bright eyed,' Lex commented.

'You look feckin' terrible,' Mudge responded cheerfully. 'Coffee?'

Lex took the proffered mug of black coffee from his visitor and sipped at it cautiously.

'This is a fine old house you have here, Lex,' Mudge said. 'Want to give me a guided tour?'

'Really?' Lex was surprised to find Mudge had an interest in domestic architecture.

'Come on,' Mudge stood up. 'We can take our coffee with us.'

As they wandered from room to room it was soon obvious that Mudge was more interested in finding out about Lex and his business activities than he was in admiring the furniture or the drapes.

'You ask a lot of questions,' Lex complained as his head continued to throb.

'I'm a student of life, Lex,' Mudge replied. 'Interested in how the whole thing works, how it all comes together, you know? And, of course, I want to be sure Miss Sophie will be taken care of.'

Lex raised an eyebrow and Mudge grinned.

'She's very special to a lot of people,' he said. 'We wouldn't want her mixing with the wrong crowd.'

Lex didn't have the energy to respond, leading him through a small study where there were some comfortable armchairs he could sink into while he waited for the caffeine to revive him.

By the time Mudge left, Lex had no more idea what their conversation had been in aid of. The boy was charming enough, and Lex was quite happy to give him some time since he was obviously important to Sophie. He was less amused when he received a phone call later that afternoon.

'Lex,' the Irish voice growled. 'It's Mudge.'

'Yes, Mudge,' he said, not bothering to hide the hint of exasperation at being disturbed again. 'What can I do for you?'

'Would you mind coming to meet some people this evening?'

'People?'

'People who would be very interested in doing some business with you.'

'I don't think . . .'

'Sophie would like it if you came,' Mudge interrupted his protest.

'Is Sophie going to be there?' Lex wasn't comfortable with the idea of asking another man about Sophie's whereabouts. There was so much about Sophie that was unsettling, so much that was fascinating.

'I'm sure that can be arranged.'

Mudge gave him an address in Kilburn and suggested a time, before hanging up. Lex was left feeling irritated but curious. It would have been a difficult invitation to turn down.

The address he was given wasn't far from the pub. He recognised some of the faces that were waiting for him in the kitchen. There was an air of seriousness about them. Someone called up to Sophie who came downstairs with two other men. It looked as if they'd been having a separate meeting. Sophie kissed him on the cheek and squeezed his shoulder as if thanking him for coming. He said nothing, unable to work out what was going on.

'We want to put a few ideas to you, Lex,' Mudge said. It seemed he was the spokesman although Lex suspected one or two of the older men were senior to him. 'But we need to be sure that nothing said here will ever go outside these walls. Even if you decide what we're discussing is not for you. Sophie has vouched for you.'

Lex looked to Sophie for guidance, but she gave him none.

'Not sure I follow you,' he said.

'Let me lay my cards on the table then, Lex,' Mudge said, all hint of friendliness gone from his voice. 'If you don't want to give us an assurance that you will never speak to anyone about what we are about to discuss, then you can turn and leave now. If you give your word and then break it we will hunt you down and kill you.'

He glanced at Sophie but was unable to catch her eye. A small voice of reason in the back of his head was telling him to turn and walk out now, but then he would be walking out on Sophie, which was not an option, and he would never know what it was they were going to propose, which was more than his curiosity could stand.

'Okay,' he said after a few silent seconds, 'I give you my word never to discuss anything I have heard in this room with anyone else.'

'Good.' Mudge visibly relaxed and there was a lifting of the atmosphere. 'We would like to make you a business proposition. We have a number of activities which generate a great deal of cash. It is cash that we can't spend for a variety of reasons, until it has been cleaned. We need the help of someone with a business that does enough international deals to be able to handle the movement of our cash without drawing any attention.'

'A business like mine?'

'Exactly.'

'And what would be the benefit to my business?'

'Cash flow, use of the funds for investment when we don't need them, and a commission.'

'What sort of sums are we talking about?'

'It depends,' Mudge shrugged, 'several million a year, sometimes more.'

'What are these activities that generate so much?'

'That's more than you need to know.'

Lex nodded his understanding.

'You would be helping the people of Ireland achieve their freedom,' Sophie interrupted, unable to suppress her excitement a moment longer. 'You would be doing something that matters. Wouldn't your father have been proud of you, fighting back against the oppressors?'

Lex couldn't stop himself from smiling; he realised Sophie was manipulating him, but he didn't care. What he wanted most at that moment was to please her. If he could make some money at the same time he would be even happier.

'I would certainly be happy to discuss the possibilities of doing business,' he said. 'Although I don't at any stage want to know where the money is coming from.'

'You don't need to know anything, but remember, once you are in, you are with us for life.'

Two years after their first meeting, Lex and Sophie were married. The reception for five hundred guests was held at her parents' house. On her side it was nearly all family and friends; on his it was mostly business contacts. Eva flew over from South Africa with two of her oldest friends, and wept copiously throughout. She was saddened that he had married outside the faith, but the grandeur of the Raes' house more than compensated.

'Your father would be so proud,' she kept saying, before dissolving once more into tears.

Sophie looked more beautiful than he could ever have imagined a woman could look. As he watched her coming down the aisle on her father's arm, he realised that for the first time he was able to think of Reshmine without a stab of pain or guilt. She had finally taken her rightful place in his memory. He had succeeded in moving on.

Some of the guests on Sophie's side had travelled from Ireland. Most of them were people who'd worked on the Rae estates all their lives, and part of the reason they came was to help with the preparations and the security. Anyone watching the way Lex interacted with the Irishmen would never have suspected that his relationship with them was anything other than commonplace. No one would have guessed that by the time of the wedding he and the men he had met in Kilburn had constructed an elaborate network of bank accounts that were allowing money to flow freely via Libya and Switzerland, giving the Irishmen the ability to buy large amounts of arms and explosives, and allowing Lex even greater financial power.

Lex was pleased that Sophie had so many friends. He knew from his own experience, and the experience of many of his most successful male friends, that one of the difficulties with balancing a career and a home life was making sure that spouses did not grow resentful of the amount of time that had to be dedicated to work matters. Sophie never seemed to complain when he had to be away on trips or was delayed at meetings. In fact it was often he who was complaining because she wasn't there when he got home and didn't always remember to tell him where she could be contacted. He never felt the remotest hint of suspicion that she might be being unfaithful to him, which made it easier for him to put aside his occasional irritation at not having her company when he would have liked it. She was, as far as he could tell, the perfect wife for him.

The thought that he was working for a worthy cause by helping to keep the funds moving around the world, gave him some pleasure, although he never really had a great deal of time to think about where the money might end up or what actual use it would be put to.

When the bombs went off in London's Oxford Street he was as shocked as anyone else watching the television coverage of the carnage. He was sitting in his office in Hampstead, with the television on when newsflashes started to light up the screen. Initial pictures showed the mangled remains of a car, little more than a tangle of blacked metal, and dreadful stains on the walls of the surrounding shops. As soon as the television producers realised the stains were from the blood of shoppers innocently going about their business just a few minutes earlier, they instructed their cameramen to keep their cameras pointing downwards. Some sights were just too horrible to contemplate.

Lex wished he knew where Sophie was, although he had no reason to think she would be in the area of the explosion. Shocked witnesses were being interviewed, none of them quite sure what had happened, all choking on their words and some weeping uncontrollably. They talked of severed heads and limbs and survivors begging for help as they bled on the pavements. The police were still not speculating how many fatalities there had been.

A knock at the door of his office made him jump.

'Yes?' he barked, hoping this might be someone to say Sophie had called the house to say she was okay.

'The Irish gentleman is in the kitchen, sir,' the butler informed him, 'asking for a meal. He said it would be all right with you.'

'What do you mean, what Irish gentleman?' Lex tried to grasp what the man was talking about, his attention still focussed on the television screen.

'He has been to the house before, sir, which was why I didn't throw him straight back on the street. He let himself in.'

'Okay, ask him to come up and bring whatever food he wants.' Lex now knew who the mysterious man was. He resented the way Mudge felt he could just walk in and out of the house uninvited and, had he not known how fond Sophie was of the man, he would have told him so. He was aware, however, that his wife and this man had a very special bond from their childhood and he didn't want to do anything to cause a rift.

As he waited for Mudge to be brought up he continued to watch the news coverage. The Provisional IRA had claimed responsibility and it was without doubt the worst atrocity of their campaign so far. It seemed there had been two bombs. Ashen-faced witnesses were beginning to tell reporters of what had happened when the first one went off in the department store. Shoppers had rushed out into the street just as the second bomb exploded in an illegally parked white car. The police were being cagey; it looked as if there had been a warning call but it hadn't arrived in time for them to evacuate the store.

'You've heard the news then.' Mudge nodded towards the television as he walked into the room.

'Yes.' Lex was about to add the word 'terrible', which would have been anyone's knee-jerk reaction to such a scene, but stopped himself just in time. The sight of Mudge standing across the room, dressed almost totally in black, as the television presenter's frantic voice continued to spill the facts of the bombing as they were so far known, made him start.

'Sophie's not here,' Lex said after a moment, 'if you've come to see her.'

'Indeed she isn't,' Mudge agreed, sitting down on the other side of the desk and falling silent as the butler placed a plate full of sandwiches in front of him and withdrew. 'She's done well today,' Mudge continued once the door had clicked firmly shut behind the butler.

'I'm not sure where she is,' Lex went on, as if deliberately ignoring the innuendo in the other man's voice. 'She may have popped down to see her parents in the country.'

'Yes of course.' Mudge's expression had a smugness that Lex had never seen before. 'Sure, most blokes think they've the prettiest wife at home!'

Suddenly Lex saw everything with a ferocious clarity.

4

'Fucking bastards!' George Docker shouted as the message crackled through his radio, making everyone around him jump. Nerves were stretched anyway as they all waited for a different sort of explosion. None of them could afford to give any indication of the panic they felt. 'They've blown up Oxford Street.'

'The Home Office is on the line,' one of his constables shouted from the open door of the car he'd just jumped out of.

'Is this the work of the IRA?' one of the reporters called out, his face lit eerily by the flashing blue light.

'Get back behind the fucking cordon,' Docker spat at the reporter. How did these people manage to get here so fast, he wondered?

'Are they starting to win the war do you think, Inspector?' another reporter taunted him. They knew they had him in a corner and they intended to make the most of it. The public liked to see a scapegoat, especially one as senior and ill-tempered as Docker.

Docker's unit was swarming over the Kings Road, clearing people away from the area surrounding the Chelsea Barracks, headquarters of the Royal Green Jackets Regiment, trying to ascertain the exact location of the bomb the informant had told them about. The bomb disposal crew was gearing up to approach a battered white car, illegally parked, when the message came through about the explosions in Oxford Street.

'Oxford Street?' one of Docker's men queried. 'But there was no fucking warning.'

'There are no fucking military targets up there,' another added.

'Are we still going in?' the major from the bomb disposal squad asked.

'Of course we have to go in,' Docker snapped. 'This one came with the right code word. They must be hitting several targets at once.'

The warning call had come through from the Salvation Army, using 'Starlite' with an 'E'. Very few people knew that code word. There was no question that someone in the know in the Provisional IRA had wanted Docker's unit to come to this location. Never before had they sent him on a wild goose chase. If they said there was a bomb here, then he was sure there was. The bomb squad and all the logistical resources were ready; even if it was a false alarm they had to search until they were sure that the area was safe, but now they were needed several miles away across London as well.

'Now the bastards are really starting to play dirty,' Docker muttered.

He ran to the car where the call from the Home Office was waiting, past the growing crowd of shouting reporters and flashing cameras, ignoring them all.

'What's happening, Docker?' the voice from Whitehall wanted to know. 'It looks like the Provos are running rings around you. The Home Secretary is concerned.'

'We're all fucking concerned!' Docker retorted. 'I'll get back to you.'

He gave the car radio back to the constable and indicated for him to get back behind the wheel. 'Get me to Oxford Street.' He spoke into his own radio again as he climbed into the back. 'I'm on my way!' he yelled.

The driver's foot hit the floor and the press pack broke through the cordon to run alongside, shouting questions and grabbing a few last pictures before the car picked up speed, the wailing of its siren forcing everyone else off the road, onto the pavements of Sloane Square. Hurtling onto the wrong side of the road, its speed rose to ninety as it ploughed north, ignoring all the red lights and give way signs.

The emergency services were converging from all directions – ambulances, fire engines and other police cars – as the daylight faded and the streetlights flickered on, casting shadows over the ugly scene. Frightened pedestrians were still running from the area, fearful that there might be a third bomb. The first police to arrive were attempting to stem the panic and move the crowds back so they could assess the damage. A helicopter circled overhead. Docker saw that more media were already arriving and he knew he was going to be roasted alive.

Lex could hear the clanking of the plumbing as Sophie ran herself a bath next door. The whole house needed a complete overhaul, but he doubted it would get it as long as Sophie's parents were still alive. Despite its fading grandeur, it was still one of the most comfortable homes in Ireland and no one in the Rae family wanted to change a thing about it. They loved the worn Persian rugs, the noisy water pipes and basic electrical appliances. Lying in County Kildare, the next county to Dublin and home of the Curragh Racecourse at the heart of the horse-loving world, it was one of the most beautiful settings in the country. It was the views from every window that brought a feeling of peace to anyone who stayed there.

Although he had initially been taken aback by the shabbiness of the place, Lex could now understand why his in-laws were content to keep it the way it was, becoming fonder of it himself with every visit. It was late morning and there were still some embers glowing in the bedroom fireplace from the previous evening. The night before he and Sophie had made love, having spread the antique eiderdown out on the mats in front of the fire. The more volatile and dangerous their relationship became, the hungrier they both seemed to become for one another physically. Their mutual desire was so intense that sex between them was now so violent it seemed more like fighting than lovemaking. But this morning some of the frost that was beginning to fringe their relationship had returned.

Things had started to go wrong after the Oxford Street bombings. Sophie had sworn to him that she knew nothing about them.

'I would never want to be involved with any attacks on anything other than military targets,' she assured him. 'They told me they planned to bomb Chelsea Barracks. I had no idea I was just a decoy.'

Lex had felt a shiver of fear, mingled with excitement, at the thought that his wife was capable of being a bomber.

'How come you never told me?' he asked.

'Told you what?' It sounded like she was playing for time.

'How deeply involved you were becoming. I mean, planting bombs, Soph, for God's sake!'

She shrugged and narrowed her eyes, half defensive, half aggressive. 'This information is dangerous. You don't go talking about it.'

'I'm your husband. How many other secrets are you keeping from me?'

'None,' she said, sounding indignant but looking, he thought, furtive. Her eyes flashed angrily. 'I don't ask you for every detail of your money laundering deals.'

'It's not the same,' he protested.

'Of course it's the same. It takes money to buy explosives, and you're facilitating that.'

'Tell me if there are any other secrets,' he said, anxious to move the conversation away from his activities.

'There are no other secrets.' She stared him straight in the eye, challenging him to disbelieve her.

He wanted to believe her, but Mudge had introduced an element of doubt into their relationship with his enigmatic comments. It wasn't that Lex trusted Mudge, he didn't, but he could no longer tell if Sophie was telling the truth or not. She and Mudge went back a long way together and there were bonds between them that he knew nothing about.

'Was he christened Mudge?' Lex had asked Sophie one night when they were lying in bed together, after making love.

'No,' she laughed. 'He used to be Patrick. Mudge is just a nickname.'

'What does it mean?'

'It started out as Smudge and then just sort of got shortened.' She didn't seem to want to elaborate.

'Smudge? I'm guessing it wasn't because he forgot to use blotting paper at school.'

'No.'

'So, what was it?' It annoyed him when she held back on him, as if she and Mudge had shared memories that Lex had to be excluded from.

'It was back in 1978, he had to deal with a British army informer inside the ranks and he used a baseball bat to "smudge" his features,' she said, speaking quickly as if that would make it sound less unpleasant.

'Lovely,' Lex made a wry face. 'Remind me not to upset him unnecessarily.'

'You won't,' she laughed. 'He thinks a lot of you. He says you're doing a lot for the cause.'

Knowing that she was now safely in the bath, Lex finished dressing quietly and pulled the briefcase out from under the bed. He'd been shocked to discover the house had no safe on his first visit.

'Safe?' Sophie had looked puzzled when he asked. 'We don't need a safe here. We don't even lock the doors at night.'

He hadn't told Sophie where he was going that morning. It had become a bad habit with both of them, not communicating. As he passed through the kitchen on his way to the back door the cook was already working on Sunday lunch, and several estate workers were sitting around the table with the newspapers. Lex greeted each by name and received a respectful, if not warm, response. Sophie had warned him it would be at least ten years before they started to look on him as anything other than an outsider.

There was a Landrover parked in the rear courtyard with the keys in the ignition, so he climbed in and started the engine. He'd tried getting to the O'Connors' house in a normal car before and practically lost the exhaust pipe on one of the bumps.

'Why doesn't your father do some maintenance on this estate?' he'd asked Sophie irritably as he viewed the chips in the paintwork from flying stones.

'He's not bothered about things like that,' she smiled. 'Only when it comes to the stables.'

Lex had noticed how there was no expense spared for the horses, with heated stables and security cameras on every corner.

'Don't the O'Connors complain?'

'Mudge prefers it if the house is a little inaccessible.'

The Landrover took the bumps in its stride, and twenty minutes later Lex was sitting in Ma O'Connor's kitchen, being fed freshly baked soda bread and hot coffee. She was a powerful matriarch of a woman, with arms like tree trunks and white hair tied up in a bun. Her husband's picture hung above the stove where she spent most of her days, the glass often shrouded in steam. Lex had been told that it would be unwise to mention the man's name when Mudge was around.

'Mudge was still a teenager when the British army killed his father,' Sophie had told him. 'They opened fire on him at a road-block, without giving any warning; they executed him. That was the day Mudge vowed to take bitter revenge in any way he could. He was very, very close to his father.'

Lex could still remember how he felt when he heard that Reshmine had been killed. He remembered the feeling of hatred that had gripped his insides, making him want to scream out in the night whenever he imagined her face. He had sublimated his hatred into ambition, distracting himself with work, but he could understand how easy it would have been to channel that hatred into violence.

'So, how long have the O'Connors lived in this house?' he asked, as he waited for Mudge to arrive.

'Three or four hundred years, I believe,' Ma replied. 'They were here before the Rae family. I dare say they'll be here after they've gone as well.'

'Sure we'll all be burned by the flames of time,' Mudge said as he came in, catching the tail-end of the conversation, giving his mother a playful slap on the backside, which she appeared not to notice. Lex wished he could be sure he understood what Mudge meant when he uttered these cryptic comments. They made him feel uneasy, like an outsider to a secret society.

'How are yer?' Mudge asked, extending a hand to Lex. 'How are things at the big house?'

Lex chose to ignore the question and gestured at the briefcase standing by his feet without saying anything.

'We'll be back in a moment, Ma,' Mudge said, lifting the case and nodding for Lex to follow him.

They pushed through a curtain dividing the kitchen from a sitting-room, which was so full of junk it would have been impossible to sit down.

'Is everything you promised here?' Mudge asked.

'And some,' Lex said. 'The deal went better than expected, you made a handsome profit.'

'And I bet you did too,' Mudge grinned and Lex ignored him again.

'I just hope you're gonna spend it wisely,' Lex said, attempting some levity of his own.

Mudge looked up and for a moment Lex thought he'd overstepped the mark and was going to get a warning. 'Come on,' Mudge said. 'I'm gonna show yer something to gladden yer heart.'

Still clutching the briefcase, he opened a door to what looked like a store cupboard, moved a few boxes around and lifted a trap door, revealing a wooden staircase down to a basement. He flicked on a light and indicated for Lex to go down. Mudge followed, pulling the trapdoor shut after him. Lex was expecting the normal musty smell of a basement, but instead was met by the clean taste of artificially cooled air. There were arches leading in three directions, so he waited for Mudge to join him and lead the way, flicking lights as he went. The tiny cottage that the O'Connors had lived in for so many years was no more than the tip of an iceberg. Beneath the ground rested a labyrinth of buried rooms, each one filled with arms. There were rifles and rocket launchers, packets of Semtex and handguns, and boxes of ammunition piled up to the ceiling.

'My God,' Lex said as he looked around him, trying to gauge just how much money must be invested in this cache. 'I had no idea.'

'Nor do the British,' Mudge grinned, 'I hope.'

It wasn't just the air conditioning that sent a shiver down Lex's spine. This, he realised, had all been bought with money laundered by people like him. It wasn't that he hadn't realised he was becoming involved in criminal activity, it was just that he hadn't understood the sheer scale of Mudge's operation. If the authorities ever came across this lot and traced his connection they would be throwing away the prison key. The British Government might pretend that it had no use for torture, but if they thought he could lead them to a cache like this they would be willing to take some risks. Once they had him behind bars they would ensure that he never came out again and he had no illusions that he would receive any help from Mudge and his colleagues. He was an outsider, expendable, no one would be campaigning for his release or signing petitions.

'This will have to be the last of the deals,' Lex said.

'What's that you're saying?' Mudge asked, without looking up from the wads of money he was counting from the briefcase.

'It's becoming too risky. The amounts are becoming too big. People in my company are starting to ask questions.' Lex felt a physical pain of regret at the thought of the future profits he might be losing by bowing out now.

'Then think up some answers for them,' Mudge said quietly. 'And find new ways of hiding the deals. You can't stop now.'

'I'm not asking your permission,' Lex said, 'I'm telling you I've done all I can for you.'

Had he seen Mudge's lunge coming towards him he might have done something to protect himself. As it was it came as a nasty surprise and the first thing he knew about it he was up against the wall with Mudge's forearm pressing painfully into his throat and the full weight of the Irishman's body pinning him helplessly to the cold stone. Lex was struggling for breath, his eyes bulging, fit to pop.

'You don't tell me anything.' Mudge's saliva sprayed his face as he spoke. His breath smelled sour. 'You're in too deep to get out now. You know too much and you've done too much. If they find out your involvement they'll put you away for life. If we decide we don't need you any more then we'll kill you. If we kill you we'll have to kill a few other people as well, including your wife. I think you know we would not hesitate to do that if we had to. We have invested too many years and too many lives in this war to let you fuck it up. Do you understand?'

He punched Lex hard in the stomach and pushed tighter onto his throat. Lex let out as much of a gurgle as he could, afraid Mudge was going to kill him accidentally, not realising his strength. He was aware of his own weakness. A youth spent playing squash and school rugby did not build the sort of peasant strength he could feel throttling the life from him in Mudge's forearm.

'Don't ever bring the subject up again.'

Mudge released him and returned to the contents of the

briefcase as Lex struggled to get air into his lungs. After a few minutes he had regained his balance and moved a few feet back so he would have time to react if Mudge attacked again.

'With risks this big I have to get more out of it than a percentage,' he said, to save face as much as to make more money.

'Are you saying we've been ungenerous?' Mudge growled and Lex fought to overcome his fear and face the man down. It was vital he kept some dignity.

'I'm saying I need more to make the risks worthwhile.'

'Like what?'

'I want an introduction to Gaddafi. I want access to the oil markets.'

If he wanted to expand the company, the oil business was an obvious place to go, and Gaddafi was someone not many people could be seen to do business with. Everyone, including the Provisional IRA, denied they were dealing with the Libyan regime, but Lex knew that the Provo connection was his best way to reach them. If he could get to Gaddafi it would unlock incalculable profits and might make the risks of staying in business with Mudge and his masters worthwhile.

Mudge glanced across at him. 'You've got a fucking nerve, man, I'll give you that.'

The Range Rover left the road for the desert sands without so much as a bump. Through the tinted windows Lex watched the last of the palm trees and the simple roadside houses disappear from sight. They drove on for another hour and he wondered what would happen if the car broke down. Most probably the sun would bake them to a crisp long before anyone came to find them. His driver, however, seemed unperturbed by any such thoughts, keeping his eyes straight ahead and his hands on the wheel, saying nothing.

After an hour, a cluster of white tents amongst some palm trees broke the monotony of the sand dunes. The driver pulled up, climbed out and opened the door for Lex, as formally as if he was dropping him at a front door in Belgravia. Men in traditional desert robes, but with Rolexes on their wrists, led him to a large tent, which was to be his home for as long as he remained at the oasis. He had no idea how long that was likely to be. No person here was going to give him any clues as to how long he would have to wait for the President to arrive. There was nothing to do but relax and enjoy the hospitality. No one had actually promised that he would get to meet anyone. The instruction he had received in an anonymous phone call was to catch a certain Gulf Air flight to Tripoli and he would be met by friends. It was all the motivation he needed.

Over the following days he slept soundly in his tent, dined lavishly with his hosts, and talked with a variety of visitors, all of whom appeared out of the desert in Range Rovers and Mercedes and gave no clue as to what their roles in the country might be. They were all interested in doing business with someone who mined gold and diamonds, but it was hard to ascertain which of them had real power and which of them were there for political reasons, testing him before he was allowed access to their leader. Several of them seemed to understand the sort of deals he was looking to negotiate. As the days passed, he began to wonder if Gaddafi would ever actually show up, but even if he didn't, and if only ten per cent of the business he was being promised actually came to fruition, his desert sojourn would still have been time well invested. There was huge money in the air, he could almost smell it, and the aroma made the hairs stand up on the back of his neck.

The President arrived early one morning with no warning and

no fanfare. A cavalcade of black Mercedes and Landrovers swept into the encampment and there was a flurry of activity around the huge central tent area.

'The President will see you now,' one of his minders informed Lex as he was sipping his morning coffee.

Lex hid his surprise at the sudden announcement and followed the man out of the tent and across the sand to where Gaddafi was waiting, surrounded by advisers, seated on a chair that looked a lot like a carved throne. An identical chair stood empty beside him and Lex was ushered towards it while Gaddafi pretended to be too busy listening to his advisers to greet him. Other people fussed around, ensuring that Lex had coffee and a plate of delicacies within reach. After a while the other men were dismissed from the tent and Gaddafi turned a stern eye on his visitor. His face was impassive, impossible to read. Dark glasses covered his eyes and his mouth was set in a straight line, neither smiling nor frowning.

'How do you like Libya?' he asked with a polite bow of the head.

'You have a beautiful country, full of hospitable people.' Lex returned the bow and kept his own face expressionless, mirroring the President.

'Your South Africa is also a beautiful country,' he said.

'Indeed. I hope one day you will be able to visit as my guest,' Lex replied. 'So that I can return some of this hospitality. Or perhaps in London.'

'London?' Gaddafi allowed a slight smile to break through. 'I don't think I would be very welcome in London. The British Government does not like me.'

'Then they are making a mistake.'

Gaddafi nodded thoughtfully. 'The British have not treated the South Africans any better than they have treated us or the Irish.

They plundered what they wanted from all our lands and now they believe they have some right to tell us how to govern ourselves,' he said. 'Why do you want to live amongst them?'

'It is always helpful to know your enemies well,' Lex said, hoping his answer sounded suitably wise and mysterious.

'And to choose your friends carefully.' Gaddafi appeared happy with whatever he was hearing.

'Indeed, I make it my business to choose my friends very carefully indeed.' Lex allowed himself a smile, determined not to allow Gaddafi's presence to make him nervous.

'They tell me you would like to do business with Libya,' Gaddafi said, getting straight to the point. 'Do you not realise that I am an outcast in the international community?'

'As a South African I understand how that feels. It often doesn't take much for outcasts to be welcomed back into the fold.'

Gaddafi fell silent and thoughtful for a moment.

'I've brought this gift for you, Mr President,' Lex said, passing over the small parcel he had been carrying in his pocket ever since arriving. 'To demonstrate my admiration for you and your country. A gift of friendship.'

Gaddafi turned it over and over between his fingers for a few moments, as if savouring the delay and then opened the stiff leather box, revealing a large, perfectly cut diamond.

'With the compliments of the South African people,' Lex said with a small bow of the head.

Gaddafi nodded his acceptance of the gift and Lex felt he had passed some sort of test.

'I believe we have friends in common,' Gaddafi said after a few moments.

'They speak highly of you,' Lex lied, knowing they were talking about Mudge and his coterie, none of whom thought anything of Gaddafi at all beyond the fact that he was a good source of funds and arms.

'Many people speak highly of you too,' Gaddafi returned the compliment.

'It would be an honour for me to serve your government in any way I can,' Lex said.

'They tell me you are a clever and influential businessman.'

Lex said nothing, waiting for him to go on.

'There are a lot of opportunities in this country for someone with vision, and international connections.'

'I would never underestimate the potential of Libya or her leadership,' Lex replied. This meeting, he thought, was proceeding better than he had expected and was going to make him very rich indeed. With a friend like Gaddafi he would be untouchable.

The Nigerians had suggested a meeting at their suite in the Waldorf Hotel in Manhattan. Lex had been wary about the first contact. They'd approached him through the Nigerian embassy in London, inviting him to official functions and dinners without telling him why. He knew that African businessmen had mixed feelings about South Africa and about companies like Goldfields who exploited their labour force, but these men didn't seem to hold any animosity. None of them mentioned the fact that he was South African, treating him as if he was a native of London. They had won over his confidence enough for him to accept the invitation to meet in New York without having more than a vague idea what the agenda would be.

At the Waldorf they had come clean about their motives. They wanted to mine for diamonds in their own country and felt they needed the expertise of an established company to help them. They were a serious minded collection of bankers and entrepreneurs, all of whom spoke disparagingly of the politicians and corruption in their country. Lex left the meeting feeling optimistic and his driver dropped him back at Trump Tower, where Goldfields owned a company apartment, so he could pack for his flight back to London.

As he let himself into the apartment he sensed something was wrong, but his mind was busy with a dozen different thoughts. When he felt the cold steel barrel of the gun pressing into his back his mind was suddenly clear and he knew his senses were right. It had been the man's aftershave that had given away his presence. Nervously, Lex raised his hands as instructed, his heart thumping uncomfortably, believing himself about to be robbed, hoping they wouldn't kill or maim him in the process. The fear made every inch of his body prickle with sweat, and he had no intention of playing the hero when he would be able to recover any losses from his insurance company. The opulence of the apartment was bound to attract thieves, but all the valuables and effects were replaceable.

When the other man emerged from the sitting-room Lex realised he was not being robbed and his fear became deeper as his mind raced over the possibilities. Could this be Mudge's men come to end the arrangement? Or someone sent by Gaddafi? Both men were wearing sharp-cut pencil-grey suits, crisp white shirts, navy blue ties and tight haircuts that suggested they were highly disciplined operators, whatever their chosen field might be.

The man with the gun frisked him quickly and professionally. Apparently satisfied that Lex wasn't armed, he put his own gun away and produced identification instead.

'CIA?' Lex was startled as he read the proffered badges. 'My God, couldn't you just have made an appointment?'

'We need to have a word,' one of them said.

'Do you want a drink?' Lex asked, leading the way into the sitting-room, 'because I certainly need one.'

Both agents looked unsure how to respond. They were there on business, they did not expect to have to make small talk. How come this man wasn't showing them due respect?

'We would like to ask you a few questions about your friend Colonel Gaddafi,' the second man said, following Lex into the sitting-room. Lex sat down in one of the low leather chairs with a glass of Scotch, but didn't ask either of them to do the same, so they hovered uncomfortably in front of him, like naughty schoolchildren called up in front of the headmaster. He had regained the high ground.

'You flatter me,' Lex said, secretly impressed that they already knew about the connection and more uncomfortable about it than he intended to show them. The stakes in this game he was playing were rising and he felt the adrenaline pulsing through his body. 'He's not my friend.'

'Friendly enough to stay at his desert camp,' one of the agents snapped.

'It was just business,' Lex smiled, catching sight of himself in a tinted mirror across the room and pleased with what he saw. He looked like someone who won every high stakes poker game he played.

'There are international sanctions against Colonel Gaddafi's regime,' the other man reminded him, irritated by the way Lex's confidence seemed to be swelling by the moment. 'The man funds terrorists. But then you know that.'

Lex ignored the final comment as if it wasn't worthy of his time. 'I'm a South African, he and I have a lot in common when it comes to sanctions. You people turn us into outsiders, we only have one another to trade with.'

'Your company is not unduly hit by sanctions,' one of the agents said and for a second Lex was disquieted to find out he knew so much, as if they had been researching him. 'But it could be.'

'Is that a threat?' Lex felt a shiver of apprehension. A smear campaign against Goldfields could undo all the good work he'd done in public relations, building the image of an international company that was beyond local politics.

'The American Government doesn't threaten people,' the agent said, 'we leave that to the sort of people you like to deal with. We're merely warning that you're dealing with highly dangerous people . . .'

'Thank you for your concern.' Lex was willing to bet these men were jealous of him, of his wealth and success. He liked that idea.

'And suggesting that we might be able to help protect you, should things not work out as you hope.'

'Protect me?' Lex was puzzled as to where the conversation was going now. He liked to think of himself as being above needing protection from authorities like the CIA. He liked to think of himself as independent and self-sufficient. 'Why would I need you to protect me?'

'Well, you could help us, and in exchange for that we could allow you to continue with your business dealings.'

'Allow me?' Lex raised an eyebrow at the man's effrontery.

'Yes, Mr Goldman,' the agent's voice was as cold as steel, 'allow you.'

In that second Lex realised they knew all about his Irish connections, but were willing to overlook them if he gave them something in exchange. 'How would I be able to help you?' he asked, cautiously, aware that the stakes in the game he was playing might be about to rise.

'We need detailed inside information. We'd like to think we could rely on you to provide us with it, in return for our discretion.'

Lex nodded. 'I understand.'

He could see now that the agents both understood him far better than he had imagined. He had been assuming they saw an international businessman of stature in his million-dollar apartment. What they actually saw was an international gambler and pirate and a man who might conceivably be of more use to them in business than out of it. But if he had information that they needed and wanted, that put him in a strong position. If he was clever he could exploit this to his advantage; chances were he was going to be able to trade with the US Government as well as Gaddafi and the Provos. The rush of adrenaline he felt at the thought made him feel good. He could easily get addicted to this game or maybe he already was.

As they walked towards the Black Boys Inn together, Mudge pointed up towards the sign swinging above the door, named after the local Gaelic football team who played in black jerseys.

'Now, that's something you wouldn't see in South Africa, I guess,' he grinned.

Lex looked up and saw the name of the pub. 'Yes, it might mean something a bit different back there,' he agreed.

'Don't envy you with that problem,' Mudge muttered as they pushed through the doors.

'What problem?'

'The blacks. We've never really had that problem over here.'

'I'd noticed, I don't see too many foreigners here,' Lex said. 'Mind you I would have thought you'd have seen us as their problem rather than the other way round. It was their country first.'

Mudge ignored him, following his own train of thought. 'England's gone soft on them boys, letting them in in droves, and look at the problems they've got as a result. They say the Irish are stupid. We're not that stupid. We don't let the bastards settle in our patch. The only niggers we ever see over here are the fuckin' British soldiers.'

Lex was used to hearing racial prejudices like this back in South Africa, but it was a shock to hear them being voiced in Ireland, especially *Catholic* Ireland.

'A good friend of mine would like to meet you,' Mudge whispered once they'd been sitting for a while with their drinks. It was late evening and Lex was tired from weeks of travel and work. He'd hoped to just hand over a briefcase full of money as usual and go home to bed, but he could tell from Mudge's intent tone he was going to insist.

'Who would that be then?' Lex asked.

'He's a man who could help you with the business,' Mudge said, taking a long, loud sip at his Guinness.

'Does he have a name?'

'Not that you need to know at the moment.'

'Is he here?' Lex looked around the bar, but no one was taking any notice of them.

'No, but I will take you to him.'

'When?' Lex asked, trying to visualise his diary.

'Now.'

'Now?'

'If you've nothing better to do,' Mudge smirked. He liked taking Lex down a peg or two whenever he could. He'd heard the rumours about Sophie and liked the idea that Lex was being made to look a fool by his young wife and knew nothing about it.

'Okay,' Lex said, draining his drink.

As they got into Mudge's car Mudge handed him a scarf. 'Tie this around your eyes and make sure you can't see.'

A scene came back from deep in Lex's memory, bringing with it a surge of nausea. He remembered the night Zak had driven him to the party where he'd met Reshmine. For a moment he remembered all the joy he'd experienced as a result, and all the pain that had followed. It felt as if someone had punched him in the stomach.

'You all right?' Mudge enquired. 'I can't take you unless you wear that fuckin' scarf. You'll have to wear it right through the meeting, and all the way back. If you fuck about we'll kill you.'

'Okay.' Lex bit his tongue; there was no point antagonising Mudge unnecessarily. His tone was already aggressive, as if he was just looking for an excuse to attack as he had before. He tied the scarf around his eyes and sank down in the seat so he was less likely to be noticed by anyone in a passing car. He needn't have worried; the tracks that Mudge drove him down didn't see much traffic at that time of night. Mudge drove fast and didn't avoid the bumps, causing him to bounce around uncomfortably in his seat. After about an hour's driving they reached their destination. Mudge drew up the car and came round to help him out, handling him more violently than he needed to. Lex stumbled as he walked across rough ground and Mudge caught him and jerked him back onto his feet, pushing him through a door and into the warmth of a house. Lex didn't protest, not wanting to give Mudge the satisfaction of knowing he was hurting him.

'Put your hands out in front,' Mudge grunted, 'in case you decide to pull off the fuckin' blindfold.'

'I'm not going to do that,' Lex protested, even as he felt himself being forced down onto a hard chair and his hands tied tightly and painfully together. There was someone else in the room and he felt a hood being pulled over the top of the blindfold. 'For fuck's sake, Mudge,' he gasped. 'You trying to suffocate me?'

'Just shut the fuck up and listen to what you're told,' Mudge replied. There was the sound of people moving around. A door opened and closed and then a new voice spoke. It was deep and cracked, as if it belonged to an older man, someone who had smoked a great many cigarettes over the years.

'Lex, good to meet you at last.' Lex said nothing, letting the voice continue. 'I wanted to say thanks to you in person. You've been a great contributor to the cause.'

Still Lex said nothing, waiting to see what would come next, unsure if the voice was being sincere or setting him up for a fall.

'It's a long and hard war we're fighting here,' the voice croaked up again. 'We need people who are with us for the long haul, freedom fighting is a dirty business.'

Lex nodded, aware that he must look ridiculous in a hood, aware also that Mudge must have told this man about his attempt to back out a few months before. They knew they didn't have his complete loyalty, that he was only with the cause for the profits it could bring him. Was it possible they'd brought him there to execute him?

'Sure, the relationship is benefiting you as much as it is us,' the voice went on. 'You've been making a fine living off the back of us.' Did he detect a hint of a threat there? 'And so you should do. A man should be rewarded for his efforts, for the risks he takes.'

It went quiet and Lex waited, having no idea what to say next, bracing himself for a blow or the sound of a shot.

'We'd like to offer you the chance to make a great deal more money.' Another pause. 'I mean, truly, a great deal more money.'

A picture of the agents at Trump Tower flitted through his mind. Whatever they were about to ask him to do was bound to come to the attention of the CIA, but would they care? They seemed happy to let him do as he pleased as long as they believed he was reporting back to them anything that might be of interest. Despite the rivulets of sweat that were starting to run down his face inside the airless hood, he allowed himself a wry smile – the game just kept getting more exciting. Whatever he did, he came out with bigger and better rewards. It seemed that he just might be on a winner all round if he simply continued letting everyone think they were getting what they wanted.

'We need you to take charge of a major part of our business. It would mean you would have access to pretty much bottomless funds. Would that be interesting to you?'

Still Lex said nothing. It was too ridiculous to talk from inside a hood. He had a feeling they'd already decided what they wanted him to do, and they would not be changing their minds. All he had to do was wait to see what the offer was. The idea of having access to bottomless funds made his heartbeat quicken. He had been finding the restraints put on him by the Goldfields board of directors increasingly irksome. The money that Mudge and his connections had been putting his way had been useful, but it could hardly be described as 'bottomless'. He liked the idea of moving up the ladder. If they didn't meet his needs, maybe he could 'sell' them to the CIA. Either way he would come out the winner. The danger had passed, leaving only a feeling of elation.

Now that his father had gone, Lex did not like being answerable to anyone. There was no question he was the chief executive of Goldfields, but the company was far too big for one man to run. Before he died, Sol had ensured that the boardroom was filled with steady hands: loyal men who he'd known for years and who had a deep understanding of the mining industry. Not many of them were entrepreneurs and none of them were cosmopolitan in the way Lex was, but they knew their business. They also understood that if Lex's role was to take the company forward into the international arena, theirs was to ensure that he took no undue risks with the legacy that his father had created for him.

The moment he walked into the boardroom in Johannesburg, Lex immediately felt like a young boy again, and resented it. The table was surrounded by faces that had been familiar all his life, but he was surprised by how old they were all growing. He was going to have to find ways to get some new blood into the room, younger people who understood better what he wanted to do with the company; people who would not look at him as if he was a naughty schoolboy whenever he suggested changing anything.

'Good morning, gentlemen,' he said, taking his seat at the head of the boardroom table, keeping his tone breezy. There was a murmured response.

The meeting progressed along predictable, businesslike lines, everyone ignoring the feeling of disquiet that lay beneath the surface. Various directors reported what had been happening in their sectors and Lex listened and commented if required. On the whole he was happy to leave the day-to-day running of the company in such capable hands, especially when it was turning in such mighty profits, as long as they didn't interfere with his plans for the future or his personal freedom to manoeuvre.

'So,' he said after several hours of talk, anxious to leave the room and clear his mind before flying back to Europe, 'any other business?'

David, an elderly man who had been with Sol for many years,

made what sounded like a coughing noise and all heads turned towards him. In many ways he was the senior figure amongst them.

'David?' Lex raised his eyebrows expectantly. Perhaps the man was going to offer his resignation; that would leave a space he could fill with someone more on his wavelength.

'We hear rumours, Lex,' the old man said slowly, 'that cause us concern.'

Lex could see now that the others were nodding their agreement, as if they had all been planning whatever was coming next.

'Rumours?' Lex enquired, shuffling his papers together and putting them into his briefcase to show that he was preparing to leave.

'About the sort of people you have been doing business with.'

Lex was anxious not to give him time to be specific; once names like Gaddafi and the IRA were actually spoken out loud they would be on the record and impossible to ignore.

'I have to meet with many people that I might not choose to,' Lex said. 'It's the way business works. The company does not become involved in anything without the board knowing and approving.'

They all looked at him in silence for a moment and he realised they knew that was not true.

'In many ways you are the company, Lex,' David said eventually. 'The company may not be legally involved in whatever you are doing, although I think you have involved it, but it is still tainted. Business is booming, Lex, we do not need to take unnecessary risks.'

'You are all men who have lived through hard times,' Lex said, aware that such an acknowledgement pleased them. 'You know that downturns can return at any time. We must make hay while the sun shines, gentlemen, who knows when the storms will return?'

Now he was on his feet, smiling broadly, pretending he couldn't hear that several of them were now speaking at once.

'I'm sorry, gentlemen, but I have a plane to catch, and I promised I would say goodbye to my mother before leaving.'

None of them could argue with that. They had all known Eva a long time and knew she was sick; they couldn't keep her son from her bedside. Once he'd left the room, however, they all knew that they had achieved nothing in their attempt to rein in their headstrong chief executive. But then again, maybe he was right, maybe they should just enjoy the good times while the business was so profitable; certainly none of them felt inclined to make any sort of stand and risk having to resign from a company that was earning some of the biggest profits in the sector.

The old men in the boardroom might have known how sick Eva was, but it was a shock to Lex as he walked into his mother's bedroom and saw the tiny, frail figure propped up on the pillows. There seemed to be no flesh left on her and her hair had thinned to allow her pink scalp to shine through. A fluster of small dogs yapped at him, rolling over to be petted as he sat down on the edge of the bed.

He squeezed his mother's hand, shocked by how tiny it felt, although her grip was still strong as she clung on to his fingers.

'How are you?' he asked.

'They're all trying to kill me, you know,' she said, rolling her eyes towards the servants' quarters.

'No they aren't, Mother, they all love you, although God knows why, the way you talk to them.'

'You sound like your father.'

Lex smiled and sighed. 'I miss him,' he said, surprising himself.

'*You* miss him?' Eva raised her eyes. 'What do you think it's like for me, lying here day in and day out? At least you're doing something to honour his memory.'

'What's that then?' Lex was genuinely surprised. Eva had never said such a thing to him before.

'You're building on the legacy he left behind. I know what's going on. I still read the papers. I'm a shareholder in the company, remember, they have to keep me informed. I'm proud of you. He would be proud of you.'

For a second Lex felt a twinge of discomfort. Would Sol be proud of him if he knew the sort of people he was working with? Surely he would understand that he had to take risks if the company was to go on growing.

'You know what would have made your father truly proud?' Eva asked.

'What's that?'

'Grandchildren. After all he went through, he wouldn't want the family to just die out. You're the only one left, Lex, all the others have gone.'

'I know.' Lex squeezed her hand, wanting to stop the tears that were rising in her faded eyes.

'So many good people killed, for what?'

'That's all over now,' he tried to reassure her. 'You're not in Europe any more.'

'Sure it is. So how come that wife of yours isn't pregnant? Is there something wrong with her? Are you seeing doctors? I'm not going to be around much longer, I want to hold my first grandchild at least.'

'You're going to be around for a while yet,' Lex told her, not wanting to discuss his marriage to Sophie, not even sure what the true situation was himself. He should spend more time with his mother but she was too frail to move to England now. There were so many things he needed to attend to; there was just never enough time for everything.

'Don't go yet,' she pleaded, her fingers gripping his with little strength.

'I have to go. I have a plane to catch. I'll ring you soon,' he promised.

His mother stopped protesting, apparently resigned to being left alone with her dogs and her servants once more, or maybe she was sulking, receiving the kiss he planted on her forehead without attempting to return it.

He tried to sleep on the flight back, but his mind was restless and refused to switch off. By the time he walked into the house in Hampstead he was exhausted and ill-tempered. His secretary was waiting for him with a grave face and the tragic news that Eva had died a few hours after he had departed for London. He was now without both his parents. He suddenly felt very alone.

Eva's funeral was a huge affair. Every Litvak in Johannesburg seemed to be there as Lex looked around the synagogue, exchanging nods of recognition and respect. Many of the faces were familiar, but had grown old in his absence like those of the board, making him aware that a whole generation was dying out, all the people who might remember the ghettos of Europe and the murder of whole families. If these men could create big fortunes from such small beginnings, he thought, imagine what he would be able to create by the time it was his turn to start saying goodbye to his contemporaries. He felt a shiver of pleasure as he reflected how far he had come already. Everyone in that synagogue knew he was now one of the richest men in the country.

After the funeral he received guests back at his mother's mansion, looking every inch the dutiful and grieving son with his beautiful wife at his side. Guests queued up to pay their respects, but out of earshot they gossiped freely and speculated on just what the glamorous Goldmans got up to in their secretive private lives. Everyone had heard different rumours, each more tantalising than the last.

He noticed a lot of the women stealing glances at Sophie. Her beauty was enhanced by the black of her mourning outfit, as was the danger that lurked in her deep eyes and the sensual mouth, which seemed, he thought, to have grown a little cruel in the last few years. He wondered if motherhood would soften her, if it ever came. Losing Eva had focused his mind even more acutely than usual on their inability to produce an heir. He wanted a son to hand the growing empire on to. If that didn't happen what was the point of it all? Just to die one of the richest men in the world? They'd had so many false alarms, their spirits rising for a few days whenever Sophie's period was late, and then plunging once more. He was beginning to think there might be something wrong medically, but Sophie pooh-poohed the idea of talking to doctors. He wasn't sure that she really cared for the idea of motherhood. She liked sex and she liked danger, neither taste was conducive to successful mothering. Lex had assured her he would be quite happy to hand over the care of any children to professional nannies, but still nothing changed and they seemed to spend more and more time apart.

In many ways Sophie's disappearances suited him, leaving him free to travel and work wherever and whenever he wanted. The company and his private fortune had become his surrogate children, but they weren't enough to bring peace to his soul.

Sophie never seemed to resent him leaving her in London or

Ireland on her own. He assumed she was busy herself with Mudge and his fellow fighters. Sometimes he wished things were different, wished he hadn't allowed himself to become so caught up in their business, but he knew it was an addiction; where else would he be exposed to so much danger and excitement and money? He assumed it was the same for Sophie.

The fact that her husband never questioned her about her movements left Sophie free to please herself, but she too was unable to shake off a feeling of disappointment at the way her marriage was drifting. She had imagined Lex would turn out to be so much more of a hero. She had pictured them working together to fight for the freedom of Ireland and then moving on, side by side, to bring about the destruction of apartheid. But he only seemed interested in building his business and making money. Money bored Sophie, but then there had never been a time when it hadn't been there for her. She didn't spend as much time with Mudge and the others as Lex thought, distracted more often by the demands of the social world.

It had been a good hunting season in Ireland, particularly as there was a new huntsman in town, a young man from one of the rival brewing dynasties. He looked particularly good on a horse, and kept turning up at all the same parties she did, while Lex never seemed to be available for any social engagements. There had already been whispers about how close they were becoming on the various dance floors they shared, although no one cared to pass the rumours on to Lex.

An anonymous invitation to take a private jet to Havana arrived at the house in Hampstead by courier. There was no indication who might have sent it, but Lex had a good idea it was something to do with the new role the Provos had planned for him.

His curiosity was sharpened by the thought of visiting Cuba as well as the prospect of finding out how he might be able to gain access to the 'bottomless funds' that the voice in Ireland had talked about. He also assumed the CIA would be watching everyone who went in and out of Cuba, and a private jet landing in Havana would quickly grab attention.

He liked the idea that he might be considered important enough to be watched wherever he went; it fed his already inflated sense of his own importance and untouchability. He didn't, however, like the idea that the authorities could be building on his dossier every day without him even knowing what was going into it. He had a feeling he was moving to a position somewhere beyond the laws of any individual country. Such elevation made him feel slightly giddy with a mixture of vertigo and pride.

The crew on the jet knew no more than he did as to who they were working for or why. They had simply been instructed to fly an important passenger to the island and to look after him on the way. When they landed there was an old but shiny black Cadillac waiting on the tarmac to carry him up into the mountains, to a villa guarded by electronic gates and cameras.

'Mr Goldman,' a familiar voice croaked out to him from the pool area as he was shown through the house, 'thank you for accepting our invitation. My name is Joseph.'

Joseph Flint, the invisible, anonymous man who had interviewed him in Ireland, stood up from the sun lounger where he had been waiting, stubbed out his cigarette and extended his hand.

'You made it very intriguing,' Lex replied, not sure if it would be prudent to let the man know he recognised his voice.

'Take Mr Goldman to his room so he can change and relax for a while,' Flint instructed the houseboy who had brought in

Lex's bags, before turning back to Lex. 'Then we'll meet back here by the pool for a drink and a chat.'

Lex nodded his agreement and allowed himself to be led upstairs to a bedroom with windows looking out across the green of the mountains. Long net curtains moved in the gentle breeze and an awning across the veranda outside shielded the room from the ferocity of the afternoon sun.

An hour later, having cooled off in the pool, he was lying beside Flint on another lounger. Flint was talking, with the inevitable cigarette dangling from his lips as if permanently attached to the rough, chapped skin.

'You've done us proud, Lex,' he was saying, 'and we want you to know we appreciate it. Because of you we've been able to finance ourselves for several months, and achieve a lot. We're grateful and we want to show it.'

Lex said nothing, just sipped his drink and waited to hear what would come next.

'It takes a lot of money to run a war, I'm sure you can appreciate that, being a businessman yourself. There's a limit to how much we can raise from well-wishers back in the homeland and the States.'

Lex nodded curtly, well aware that most of the money he'd been laundering for them had come from the proceeds of crimes like armed robbery and protection rackets rather than charitable donations, but he thought it prudent to go along with the line Flint was selling.

'We have some contacts in South America, particularly Columbia, who are very keen to work with us. The scale of their operations is far larger than anything we have dealt with before, larger even that your own operations in South Africa.' He smiled grimly.

Lex nodded, but kept his eyes focused on the view down the valley beyond the pool. There was only one sort of business in South America that could rival the African diamond and gold mines for profitability – the narcotics industry.

'We'd like you to take over the logistics and the financial side of our South American interests,' Flint said. 'It'll be a major commitment for you, we appreciate that, but the rewards are greater than you could hope for in all your other business interests.'

Lex looked across at him and raised an eyebrow. This was news he did not think he would share with his new friends at the CIA.

'Logistics?' he said.

Flint lit a fresh cigarette from the stub between his lips before replying.

'The biggest problem is the movement of the goods,' he said. 'It's dangerous and difficult, so anyone who successfully undertakes it is able to add a large percentage to the price. The South Americans are very happy to be paid what they ask for, but the consumers in America and Europe are more than happy to pay a thousand per cent more for the product when it's delivered to them.'

'That is a good profit margin.'

'Of course it is. But it has to be earned. The logistics of moving the goods are complicated and dangerous. The financial rewards are big but the risks are high. If a shipment is seized then the original investment is lost. We need a man who has the stomach for some big risks.'

Lex was unable to stop himself from smiling. Just thinking about the excitement and danger of overseeing these clandestine operations and the possibility of making untold riches made his heart beat faster. There was no way he was going to miss out on this opportunity, whatever the risks.

'So,' Flint said. 'Are you in or out? If you take this on, there will be no going back. Not ever. You've got to stay the course but if you do, your cut of the wedge will be beyond even *your* wildest dreams.'

Lex wasn't sure if Flint had added that line deliberately, aware that he was hardly going to be able to resist the lure of getting his hands on so much easy cash.

'Oh, don't be in any doubt, Joseph, I'm in all right,' he said, hardly able to disguise his glee.

5

The explosion of gunfire took Lex by surprise. He hadn't even seen the guns before they started spraying bullets around the room. The noise was deafening. Blood and small cauliflower-like particles of the men's brains splattered the walls and furniture around him. He dived for cover as bullets ripped into the sofa and wall behind, showering him in splinters of wood and bits of plaster. In the few seconds' bedlam of screaming and shouting, he couldn't work out if they intended to kill him too, or whether he'd been hit already and hadn't yet felt the pain. Where had the guns come from? More blood splattered the fading white walls above his head as the ear-shattering noise finally subsided to a ringing silence.

A few minutes earlier the seven of them had been sitting around the small room drinking beers, laughing and talking. Most of the conversation had been in Spanish so he'd been on the outside, smiling and nodding now and then in response to some comment obviously directed at him.

Juan Baptista and Garcia Mendez, two Colombian cartel members, had met him at San Jacinto International airport near the city of Cali, off a connecting flight from Mexico. He'd been introduced to them by Joseph Flint, after an elaborate charade of codes and signals. Even after such a cautious introduction they seemed suspicious of the stranger who'd been foisted on them and unwilling to make him feel either safe or comfortable. Flint had told Lex they would be introducing him to the full logistics of the business.

To start his education they'd brought him straight to a small beach house in the coastal area of Choco Bay, about an hour's drive from Cali. They hadn't bothered to make any small talk on the way over, occasionally grunting something to one another, puffing on cigarettes and leaving him alone in the back seat with his thoughts. His instincts told him they were not men he wanted to fall out with. Not knowing what was in store was unsettling and exciting in the same measure. He felt he was on the verge of making some very big money indeed. He was unsure of his own safety and the speed of his heartbeat was exhilarating as he assessed what was going on around him.

There were four men waiting for them in the beach hut. They looked as if they'd be more at home in the mountains that Lex had seen towering above the coastline as they came in off the beach. They were swarthy, hirsute and pungent. They gave Lex a wary welcome and seemed anxious to ingratiate themselves with Juan and Garcia. By keeping quiet and listening, Lex managed to work out that these four men were part of a drug cell. A typical cell, he knew from his research, consisted of a stash house sitter, a cocaine handler, a money handler and a cell director who also acted as the bookkeeper for the coterie. Juan and Garcia were part of the shipping department attached to the same cell, but they obviously operated higher up the hierarchy than the men in the beach house, with their designer sunglasses and Gucci loafers worn on bare, tanned feet.

Tired from the long flight, Lex had been willing to let them take him wherever they wanted without question. He'd been told he could trust them with his life, but from their demeanour he wasn't so sure. The four men waiting had offered them beers the moment they were through the door, grinning broadly with gold-filled teeth, eager to please.

As they got the beers, Lex noticed the giant fridge contained no other groceries. It looked like the beach house was a rental rather than someone's home.

'We need to bring some more stuff in from the car,' Juan had said, nodding for Garcia to come with him and holding up his hand to tell Lex not to bother moving. 'You relax, get to know the guys.'

Left on their own, the other men seemed unsure what to make of him and tried to communicate in broken English and broad grins, laughing loudly and nervously. He smiled back, unsure what to expect and who to trust. When Juan and Garcia burst back into the house pumping bullets, their faces didn't give him any clues as to whether they intended to kill him as well. Lex had dived for cover, the other men's bodies falling in jerking, twisted contortions around him as they tried in vain to escape the hail of bullets.

When the guns fell silent Lex stayed very still, waiting to be told what would happen next, aware that if they wanted to kill him there was nothing he could do since he had no gun of his own and they were standing between him and the door. His heart was thumping in his ears and he wished he'd never taken up Flint's offer. All the excitement had now turned to cold fear in his veins.

Juan was wiping blood off his shoes and Garcia was stretching and yawning, his gun still in his hand. It seemed they had performed all the executions they wanted to for the moment. Lex pulled himself to his feet, trying to cover his shaking by dusting down his clothes. The other four men were most definitely dead, their faces unrecognisable from the close-range impact of the bullets.

'See what happens,' Garcia said to him, gesturing at the carnage surrounding him, 'if you try to steal from the cartel? It will never be tolerated. We have to have loyalty.'

Lex shrugged, giving the impression he witnessed such scenes every day of his life, but he was unable to find his voice to reply. He checked himself to see if he'd caught any of the blood on his pale linen suit, but he hadn't.

Juan and Garcia set about systematically searching the house, ripping up floorboards and punching holes in the walls, calling out to each other in Spanish as they found things. They didn't seem to be in any particular hurry, just businesslike and meticulous. After a few minutes they'd found two large cardboard boxes and had filled them with packets of cocaine, which they seemed to find with the efficiency of airport sniffer dogs. Juan pulled a suitcase out from under a bed, opened it, gave the contents a cursory glance and zipped it back up. They stacked everything by the door, ready to leave.

'Help us,' Garcia instructed Lex, gesturing at the pile.

Lex nodded his agreement, aware they were both still armed. Juan passed him the suitcase and he was startled by how heavy it was. The other two picked up a box each and led the way out to the stairs without even a backward glance at the bodies they'd left behind them. They moved efficiently but without any show of panic. There was no sign of anyone else in the surrounding houses coming to investigate the sounds of gunfire, but it must have been audible for some distance. He followed them to the Toyota Landcruiser they'd left parked across the street, the number plates obscured by mud.

A few village children gathered to watch as they stacked the boxes and the case into the back, but Juan and Garcia took no notice of them. When the bravest amongst the children came forward to ask for money Garcia handed them a few crumpled notes, which they snatched and ran off with. When the bodies were eventually discovered the children would know better than to give the police any descriptions of the men they'd seen leaving. Lex climbed into the back as Juan got behind the wheel with Garcia next to him. As they drove away Lex put on his dark glasses and stayed silent.

'Stupid bastards,' Garcia said after a few moments, 'they thought we wouldn't know they'd been stealing from us.'

'How long have you known?' Lex asked, pleased his voice had returned, even if it was a few octaves higher than he would have liked.

'Not long,' Garcia turned and grinned. 'It cannot be allowed to happen. This is a business where a man's word has to be trusted. We trusted them to handle a lot of money and a lot of product, but they proved untrustworthy. It's the same for everyone. You would have to be stupid to try to steal when there is so much money for everyone anyway.'

He turned back and switched on the radio, searching for a station playing American rock music. Lex felt a mixture of emotions. He was aware they'd staged this assassination while he was present to show him just how unwise it would be ever to try to double-cross them. At the same time he felt a sense of elation at the thought that it was so easy to kill four men and just walk away without making any attempt to clean up the scene of the crime.

He'd read up on Cali before the trip and knew that several thousand people a year were murdered in the area and hardly anyone was ever arrested. The authorities did little about it because they knew that virtually all the killings in town were gangland executions. The gangs did their own cleaning up and innocent citizens only occasionally became caught in the crossfire. Most of the police were in the pay of someone in the business, and those that weren't knew there was no point wasting time on investigations that would lead nowhere. It seemed to Lex to be further confirmation that people like him could do whatever they wanted if they had the right connections. It was just a question of having the nerve. The further they drove towards the lush green of the mountains, with music blaring from the radio, the more intense the feeling of elation. The adrenaline rush caused by his fear was now replaced by the glow of a greed that expected to be satisfied. He felt himself to be invincible, as long as he did nothing to make the guys of the cartel doubt his loyalty.

He slept well that night in a villa in the mountains. During the day he took to wearing his dark glasses all the time, partly because of the bright sunlight and partly because it helped him watch what went on around him without being observed himself. He kept his face expressionless and asked no questions, which seemed to have the desired effect on his two minders, who started treating him with the same wary respect he was showing them, as if they were all moving amongst unexploded bombs.

A housekeeper worked silently in the background, providing a breakfast worthy of a five star hotel, and by the time the first rainstorm of the day broke Lex took his seat in the back of the Landcruiser. Juan and Garcia continued with his familiarisation tour of the business they'd known and loved ever since they were kids on the streets. The sudden outburst of rain turned the jungle tracks to mud beneath their tyres as they bumped, swerved and slid their way up through the undergrowth that clung to the sides of the mountains. His guides seemed to know where they were going as he hung on to the strap, staring out through the rivulets of water on the window. Anything or anyone could have been hiding a few feet from those windows, totally invisible amongst the foliage.

The rain was still lashing down on the leaves when they turned into the clearing that was to be their first destination of the day. Only once the bonnet of the car had pushed its way through the foliage did the makeshift shelter appear from its hiding place.

'You want to see how we make the coke?' Juan asked proudly.

Lex nodded without saying a word. He'd been forced to remove his glasses by the gloom of the jungle and felt naked without them as he squinted around, aware now that Juan and Garcia carried guns and were happy to use them, unsure if he was being set up to witness another blood bath. Half a dozen peasants were sheltering from the rain under a noisy corrugated iron roof, which had been propped up on an assortment of pieces of wood, bound together with vines.

'Every three months,' Juan shouted over the noise as they ran towards the shelter, 'the cocoa plants give us another crop of leaves for free. The flowers and buds are picked off and then mashed into a thick pulp.' He nodded towards a couple of dirty looking oil drums at the far end of the shelter. 'They mix it up with some lime and salt, put it into the barrel with some gasoline, then add more chemicals, cook it into powder . . .'

Juan was obviously losing interest in the details of the process, if he knew them, which Lex doubted. Lex pretty much knew what happened next anyway, how it was packaged into bricks or 'kilos', boxed up and shipped out. One kilo brick, which had cost virtually nothing to manufacture, could sell for as much as fifteen thousand dollars on the streets in America. It was a mouth-watering profit margin by anyone's standards.

The gap between his snappily dressed, streetwise minders and the workers in the forest was as wide as the gulf between them and himself. He guessed these workers never took the risk of helping themselves to the finished product, although he noticed they were all rhythmically chewing on the raw leaves in order to help pass the time. Only one of them, an old man, exchanged looks and words with the visitors, the others kept their heads down and their eyes averted. Lex was shocked by the primitive surroundings. Whenever he'd heard about cocaine factories he'd always assumed they were buildings, hidden in the jungle like ammunition factories in times of war.

It was hard to imagine that these people, the poorest of the poor, were creating a product that the richest of the rich in other parts of the world would pay a fortune for. He was willing to bet they had no idea what happened to the cocaine that men like Juan and Garcia picked up from them in exchange for a few bags of rice, cartons of cigarettes and the occasional bottle of whisky. There might not be any apartheid in South America, he thought, but these people were just as unfairly enslaved as any of the black labourers working in his mines had ever been. He was pretty sure that if they ever showed any reluctance to continue working for the syndicate, they would be executed as mercilessly as the four men he'd met the day before.

As the days passed, Lex had to work hard to curb his impatience. He wanted to meet the people at the top of the cartel, but whenever he dropped any hints Juan and Garcia would look straight through him as if he hadn't spoken. He didn't want to insult them by insisting they took him to meet their bosses; he wasn't even sure that they had access themselves. He had a good inclination that everything he said and did was being reported back. He was continually being tested. When they were confident of him they would allow him more access, but how long would that take? It had been easier to get to Gaddafi than it was to get to these elusive drug barons. Juan and Garcia were obviously enjoying having an excuse to drive around, showing off their scattered empire.

'We're going back to the laboratory to collect,' Juan announced one afternoon, when the three of them had finished eating their lunch. 'We'll go now.'

Lex was getting used to these sudden announcements and followed the men out to the Landcruiser, only half concentrating on what was happening. Now that he knew a lab was no more than a few peasants working under a canopy in the jungle he was bored at the thought of having to drive all the way out there again just to collect a consignment. He didn't like to think of himself as a delivery boy, but he had no choice. He was still waiting to prove himself.

When they arrived at the lab the old man acknowledged all three of them with a nod and pointed to three boxes waiting in the shade. The others kept their eyes down as always. Juan asked for coffee and the old man shouted instructions at a woman who could have been his wife. After loading the boxes into the Landcruiser, the three visitors sat down on a home-made wooden bench to wait while the coffee was made, smoking as the workers shuffled self-consciously about their business around them.

The police must have been waiting and watching before the Landcruiser had arrived. Maybe they'd been trying to snare some visitors from higher up the organisation rather than just a few peasants, or maybe it was just plain bad timing that they happened to be there when the raid took place.

The first sign that something serious was up came from the old man, who suddenly looked up from the fire where he sat with the old woman. Like a wild animal sensing danger in the wind Juan saw the look on his face and was immediately alert, his gun appearing in his hand just seconds before the police broke out of the undergrowth all around them. They charged towards the lab firing their guns in the air. Juan shot the man at the front through the throat as Garcia pulled out his gun and ducked behind the bubbling vats for cover.

Realising they had more than a few unarmed peasants to contend with, the police brought their guns down and started firing at the workers as they ran for the jungle. Several were brought down, screaming in pain and fear. Two of the attacking policemen had axes, which they swung hard at the flimsy wooden supports, bringing one end of the roof crashing down. A sharp piece of bamboo slashed across the top of Lex's head, releasing a powerful flow of blood, which ran into his eyes. Staggering back to his feet he saw the frightened face of a young officer just two metres away with a gun pointing directly at him. The gun went off with what seemed like two explosions and Lex was knocked sideways at exactly the same moment as the young policeman.

As he pulled himself back onto his feet he realised he'd been hit in the shoulder, and that Juan had shot the policeman instantaneously. The boy was still alive and was pulling himself up to take another shot when Juan put a bullet through his ear. His terrified face disappeared in a spray of blood and Lex felt a surge of pain in his head as his nervous system registered what had happened.

Garcia was shouting at them to move quickly. The police who were still on their feet were concentrating on smashing the laboratory, while frantically looking for the boxes of cocaine they believed were still located there. The leader, seeing that the three visitors were escaping in the confusion and guessing they must already have the cocaine, shouted at his men to shoot at them. Half a dozen rifles swung round to take aim as Juan fired back at them, running as he went. Lex tried to run but stumbled, suddenly weak and overcome by the searing pain that went through his shoulder. Seeing he was down, Juan raced back to him and Lex was sure he was going to put a bullet through his head to ensure that he didn't survive to tell the police anything. If he could have found the strength he would have made a run for the jungle, but he didn't seem able to make his legs take the weight of his body.

Garcia, now under the cover of the foliage, let off a barrage of shots to cover his friend, bringing down two more of the policemen and forcing the rest to take cover.

Juan crouched low as he ran back, bending down over Lex as he struggled to sit up and defend himself. Sliding one arm under Lex's armpits he lifted him up, still firing at the remainder of the police with his free hand. Garcia had stopped shooting and Lex could hear the Landcruiser's engine gunning as Juan dragged him into the trees. The pain in his shoulder made him want to faint and the blood in his eyes almost blinded him, but he forced himself to keep going, to be as light a burden as possible. Garcia threw open the passenger door as they got close, and Juan pushed Lex onto the seat, clambering in on top of him as Garcia stood on the accelerator, forcing the giant car forward through the jungle.

Behind them the sounds of shots died away, but within a few minutes, as they looked back from the track, they could see a plume of smoke from the laboratory and knew it was being burnt to the ground.

'I owe you my life,' Lex said weakly. Now that they were speeding away from the scene the full impact of what had happened was dawning on him. He had just been as close to death as it was possible to get without toppling over the edge, and he felt simultaneously exhilarated to be alive and terrified of what he was getting himself into. Juan gave no indication of having heard him.

As the Landcruiser bumped and crashed through every pothole, sending spasms of pain through his head and shoulder with every new lurch, he was aware that they were carrying well over two million dollars worth of coke in the back. He forced himself to bite back the cries of pain that were struggling to escape from his lips.

Back at the villa Juan and the housekeeper cleaned up his wounds and bound them as best they could. There was an air of calm among them, as if they no longer needed to prove anything to one another. It was as if Lex's spilt blood had bonded them.

Juan and Garcia were not their usual relaxed selves. Juan spent most of the time on the phone, muttering urgently and occasionally letting out expletives.

'We've got to get this gear out of the country quickly,' Garcia told Lex when he asked what was happening. 'We're going to vary the normal route and get out before the police bust us again.'

'What's the normal route?' Lex asked.

'The cartel flies the stuff up to Mexico in a 727. Usually to a heavily modified airstrip near a town called Heroica Caborca in Sonora in the north. Then, depending on who we're supplying, it gets spirited over the border into the States.'

'So what are we doing instead?'

'Juan is organising a Cessna to be fuelled up and hidden in the jungle near the border with the US. We'll fly up to Sonora tomorrow where a couple of our local guys will meet us. We'll drive out to the plane and then leave in the night.'

The weather warnings for the following night were bad, predicting gale force winds and torrential rain. Juan and Garcia seemed unconcerned, and their apparent belief that they were above such considerations was catching. With his wounds patched up and his system full of painkillers, Lex once more felt ready to take on the world. If he could survive being shot and wounded by a bunch of armed police officers at such close quarters, he could survive anything. He wondered why so many schmucks felt the need to use cocaine to attain this sensation of omnipotence.

Another young Colombian man joined them on the flight up to Sonora.

'He's going to fly the Cessna over the border,' Garcia explained when Lex looked at him questioningly. The pilot wasn't much more than a kid, relaxed in a way that a regular drug habit can make you, and looked more suited to flying short hops between the Caribbean islands.

The flight up was bumpy, but Lex had been through worse. If this was as bad as it got, the journey wouldn't be anything more than uncomfortable. Once they had arrived, the four of them were met by a pair of jeeps. The drivers loaded the boxes without a word, and they headed out into the jungle.

As they made their way out to the plane waiting in the clearing, the rain returned, instantly drenching them, but there was still no sign of any of the predicted strong winds. The plane looked shockingly small, with just enough room in the cabin for the pilot and three passengers. In the beam of the jeeps' headlights he saw that it had only one propeller on the nose. The paintwork, white at the top and pale blue at the bottom, reminded him of model aeroplanes he used to see as a child in toyshops in Jo'burg. It was hard to imagine anything more lightweight for the job. The boxes and suitcase were wrapped tightly in plastic to protect them as they were loaded on board, filling every available bit of storage space.

After the shoot-out in the jungle he finally felt safe with Juan and Garcia. Whatever the future had in store, for the time being they were obviously keen to keep him alive. He was a sufficiently valuable asset, worth protecting.

Lex hadn't flown in anything with propellers since he was a boy in South Africa and never in weather conditions like this. The noise inside as the rain splattered against the aircraft's thin skin was deafening, and then the engine spluttered into life to compete. The pilot shouted something to indicate that he was about to take off, but Lex couldn't hear the words. He saw the jeeps backing away, the jungle instantly swallowing their lights. The plane took off into the blackness.

The moment it hit the cloud it started to rock and roll. The pilot let out a yip of excitement, and Lex wondered if he'd been snorting something before take off. Garcia and Juan were both grim faced from what he could see in the dimly lit gloom of the cabin. Suddenly the plane plummeted like a stone as it hit an air pocket. His own insides felt like they were about to desert him and he looked around to see if there was a sick bag. Juan and Garcia were already opening theirs and putting them over their faces. The pilot glanced back as he wrestled with the controls and laughed.

All Lex's delusions of invulnerability deserted him as the nausea racked his body. All he wanted was for the flight to be over and his feet to be on solid ground again, but they had only just started on the journey. As the plane bucked and reared on the thermals every pore of his body prickled with fear, adding to the feeling of nausea.

'There's no way we're going to make it too far in this weather,' the pilot shouted to them at the top of his voice. 'We'll have to put down just across the border somewhere.'

'Can you make it to the airfield outside El Paso?' Juan shouted back.

'I can try,' the pilot laughed, as if dying was nothing but one huge joke.

'Radio the boys on the ground and tell them to get someone to meet us there instead.'

Because of the storm warnings in the area there was hardly any air traffic coming in over Texan airspace. The Drug Enforcement Agency had almost decided to call off their surveillance on the small private airfield outside El Paso. They'd known for some time that this was one of the destinations the cartels were using to land narcotics into the States, but over the previous few nights there had been no action at all. They were used to hanging around and waiting, it was what they were trained for. With stormy weather setting in none of them thought that anyone would be stupid enough to try to fly a light aircraft in conditions like these, and all the operatives were keen to get back to their homes to check that everything was battened down against the incoming inclement weather.

At first, when reports of an approaching plane reached them, none of them believed it.

'Why the fuck would anyone want to be up in a light plane in conditions like this?' One of the agents voiced what they were all thinking, hardly able to make his words heard above the growing noise of the wind.

'Because these guys have burned their brains out so many fucking times they probably think they're getting a free ride on Space Mountain,' another replied.

'If they're willing to risk flying in conditions like this they must be carrying something big,' another suggested.

'Get into position,' their commander instructed. 'They won't be expecting us on a night like this any more than we were expecting them.'

The agents returned to their surveillance positions, and emergency lights had been turned on by the airfield's operators. All of them were drenched to the skin and were becoming wary of the branches and other debris, which were bouncing around them as the winds picked up force.

Lex didn't care any more if he lived or died, and wished he'd never even thought of going into the drug running business. His entire body was exhausted by the waves of nausea and vomiting, and the effort of bracing himself against the sudden lurches. Every nerve ached from the effort of controlling his fear and stopping himself from screaming. Juan and Garcia seemed to be coping like robots now they'd emptied their stomachs. The pilot, who'd managed to rub more cocaine onto his gums at the same time as hanging onto the controls as if riding a bucking bronco, had gone way past exhaustion into a world of his own, grinning through gritted teeth as the plane rolled from side to side, plummeting one moment and hauling itself back up the next.

'Wow, there's the runway ahead,' he howled over the double roar of the engine and the storm as he spotted the dotted lights of the airfield in the blackness below.

* * *

'Where the fuck are they going?'

The two men in the waiting truck could see the lights of the plane and it wasn't aiming at the airfield any more. They'd been parked a little way back for an hour after receiving a call telling them to get there as fast as they could to meet an incoming shipment, ready to drive in the moment the plane touched down if the coast was clear. The canopy that should have been covering the back of the truck had been ripped off and carried away by the gales, but both men knew they couldn't give up waiting. The roar of the wind made it impossible to hear anything outside the rocking cab. If the plane made it through and they weren't there to meet it the chances of them living to tell the tale were slight. They were well-trained soldiers and they knew the importance of obeying orders, no matter what the personal costs. The truck had been adapted to travel over terrain that non-military vehicles would fail on; the wheels were so high the occupants needed steps to get to the doors.

'Ask them what they're doing?' the driver yelled to his passenger who had the two-way radio.

'I can't hear a fucking thing,' he shouted back. 'We'll just have to track them and see where they end up.'

'Shit.' The driver threw the truck into gear and accelerated forward into the darkness as the lights of the plane moved further away from the runway.

The truck's headlights sliced through the blackness, illuminating the flying debris.

'We need to cut across the airfield,' the other man directed.

The driver swerved and headed for the airfield lights. As the giant wheels leapt over a ditch, the headlights picked up the frightened faces of two surveillance agents flushed from their hiding place.

'What the fuck?' the driver swore.

'Fucking agents,' his passenger shouted. 'It's a fucking set-up. Keep going!'

Lex could see the lights of the truck from the window of the plane. He could also see the airfield lights were now moving away from them as the plane coughed and sighed like it was on its deathbed. They'd become one more piece of flotsam in the wind. The pilot's eyes had taken on a glazed stare and his teeth were gritted so tightly now that there was no chance of him even being able to scream. He was attempting to wrestle the aircraft back onto a course for the airfield. Both Juan and Garcia were praying, their lips moving fast, their hands crossing and recrossing their chests as they tried to make amends with their creator.

Hitting a sudden patch of calm, the plane lifted beneath the pilot's hands and circled. The truck lights below stopped for a second to watch as the plane came down again towards the airfield, shaking and rattling like a child's toy. Just when it looked as if they were going to land safely a gust of wind came up under the wings and threw it off course once more, banging Lex's head painfully against the edge of the window. The plane lifted and dropped a few more times, and the headlights started moving once more, tracking it as it was carried towards some fields of weather-battered crops.

'Who the fuck was that?' the agents were all screaming into their radios at once as the truck crashed on past them.

'It must be their ground contact.'

'They know we're here.'

'Follow the truck and the plane!'

Breaking out of their positions, they all ran to their camouflaged vehicles, desperate not to lose sight of their prey. It looked like their patience was going to pay off and they were desperate not to let the chance of a bust slip through their fingers.

Lex realised they had no option but to crash. The pilot had virtually no control as the wind tossed the plane like a dead leaf. The airfield lights were moving further away and there seemed to be more than one set of headlights now, bobbing up and down. In front of them there was nothing but darkness, no way even of judging when the moment of impact would be. It seemed to take forever, every second stretching agonisingly on until he began to wonder if maybe it was already all over and he'd moved on into the limbo of the next life. Then they hit the ground in a roaring, tearing, spinning, screeching whirl of horror and pain, his head and joints banged against the fuselage and the corners of the seats. His shoulder wound opened up and the blood soaked through the dressings. The plane kept on and on spinning and rolling. It seemed as if they would never reach the end of the nightmare. When they finally came to a stop all of them were drenched in blood from a variety of cuts, but the pilot was the only one who wasn't moving.

Juan was the first to unbuckle himself and crawl from his seat. He pulled a gun from his waistband and put a bullet through the pilot's head without bothering to check if he was dead already. He'd served his purpose; he could be nothing but a liability from here on. Garcia was unbuckling himself and heading towards a gash in the fuselage big enough to allow them to get out. Lex followed, surprised to find he was able to move despite the pain. The fear of an ignominious capture drove him on.

Their priority now was to get as much of their shipment as possible out of the plane's carcass in the dark. Miraculously, most of the boxes and the suitcase had survived, but running in such strong winds over unfamiliar terrain in the dark was hard enough as it was, without being weighed down. Juan and Garcia, however, were not hesitating and he was pretty certain that if he showed the slightest reluctance to keep up he would meet the same fate as the pilot.

They stumbled toward the approaching lights of the truck as they bounced over the crops towards them, the DEA vehicles forming a ragged line behind. As soon as the beams hit them, the three men froze and waited. The truck halted beside them and two black clad figures dropped from the doors to the ground, herding Lex and his fellow travellers to the back. The case and boxes were snatched from them and thrown over the side onto the flatbed. Lex felt strong arms grab him round the thighs and lift him as if he was weightless, propelling him after the luggage. He let out a scream as he landed on his shoulder, the sound lost in the wind. He felt Juan and Garcia land beside him, and a few seconds later the headlights went out and the truck flew forward into the blackness.

The driver must have known the terrain well because he didn't take his foot off the gas, and the resulting ride had the three men rolling and crashing around on the flatbed. Robbed of their guiding light, the DEA vehicles fanned out, trying to locate their prey, their headlights providing just enough light for the truck driver to avoid the many trees that had fallen in the wind. Those he didn't manage to avoid he simply drove straight over.

One by one the pursuing vehicles hit obstacles they couldn't get round and Lex's team eventually pulled out onto a deserted highway on their own. The driver flicked the lights back on, confident the wind would be too strong for the DEA to be able to get a helicopter up to look for them. Lex became horribly aware of just how much pain he was in from the battering his body had received over the previous few hours.

They drove for about half an hour to the outskirts of a town. The wind had brought the power lines down and the streets were dark, only houses with their own generators giving off any sort of glow. In the headlights of the truck he could see they'd driven into an industrial building, where another man was waiting in a Toyota family car. The others were all talking in Spanish, but Lex could make out enough to know that the car was there to get them to Miami. He helped Juan and Garcia load the cocaine and money into the trunk of the Toyota. There was a makeshift bathroom at the back of the building where they patched up their cuts and cleaned off the worst of the blood. The man with the car had brought them some clean clothes, none of which fitted to the satisfaction of the Colombians, but had the desired effect of making them look like American workmen. An hour later they drew back out of the building in the Toyota, looking like three men returning home from a late shift. They needed to put as many miles as possible between themselves and El Paso by dawn, in case the police started erecting road-blocks.

Two hours later the wind dropped and they were able to travel at a steady speed, careful always to stay within the limits, not wanting to draw any unwanted attention to their anonymous looking car. Whenever they stopped, two of them would stay in the car while the third went to buy food or take a piss. They took it in turns to drive, while the others slept or munched on fast food snacks.

'Bastard bad luck,' Juan kept saying as he reflected on their arrival in the country. 'Bastard bad luck that they were waiting for us.'

'Actually good luck that we didn't land on the airfield,' Lex pointed out, 'or they'd have got us. Just as well the pilot was spaced out or we mightn't have been so lucky.'

'We're better off now he's out of the picture,' Juan said.

'Why do you say that?' Lex looked puzzled.

'His uncle works for the Medellin Cartel, our sworn enemies. He said he'd fallen out with that part of the family when he was a kid and we were never totally convinced we could trust him, but he would always take the plane up whenever we needed him to, so he was very useful to us. We suspected he might be linked to that double dealing we discovered but we couldn't be sure.'

'Fuck, I must make sure I never get a pilot's licence,' Lex thought to himself. His anxiety was growing at how untroubled these guys seemed about terminating colleagues.

Juan looked at him, chomping on a burger and licking his lips noisily. 'Goldman, you're a pretty cool dude for a gringo,' he said eventually.

Lex shrugged modestly.

'No,' Juan insisted. 'I mean it. I can tell you're a real rich guy who's never had to do a proper day's work, am I right?'

'I guess that's right,' Lex smiled. He was starting to like these two. He imagined this was how it felt to be in front-line action with fellow soldiers.

'But you do whatever needs doing without complaining or making out you're something special. You've kept your nerve through some nasty situations with us. That's cool.'

Garcia let out a snort of amusement. 'You must be some sort of king for Juan to like you,' he said, his eyes on the road as he drove. 'He pretty much hates everyone, especially gringos.'

'I'm honoured,' Lex said, his mouth full of French fries.

'That shoulder must hurt like fuck,' Juan went on, ignoring the interruption.

Lex raised his eyebrows but said nothing.

'See what I mean, Garcia, he's tough.'

Satisfied that he'd said all he needed to say, Juan returned his attention to his meal.

The hours of driving lulled Lex into a trance-like state as he struggled with the pain of his shoulder and his mind wandered to thoughts about the way his life was unfolding. To have come this close to arrest and death twice in a few days was sobering, but yet again he'd managed to walk away relatively unscathed. One thing for sure was he didn't intend to put himself in the front line any more. He felt he'd proved his loyalty and now it was time for them to start showing him the rewards.

Knowing what was in the trunk of the car added a frisson of excitement to the journey every time a police patrol car or bike cruised past them, but the thought of how much their precious cargo was worth made his heart beat just as fast as the fear of capture.

After two days of driving, they dropped him off at a beach-front hotel in Miami, where a suite had already been booked in his name, and the moment he lay down on the bed he fell into a deep sleep. Juan and Garcia departed without uttering another word but he wasn't bothered. He was happy to be on his own for a while to sort out his thoughts and plan his next move.

Twelve hours later he woke in exactly the same position, and found virtually every muscle in his body ached. As he struggled to move, he realised he must have cracked some ribs in the crash, and a glance in the mirror showed a variety of ripening bruises. Beneath the pain, however, there was a strange sense of elation at having survived once more. Not even a plane crash, combined with the might of the DEA had been able to stop him.

When he ventured out onto the roof terrace attached to his

suite, the weather had returned to a cliché of Florida sunshine, although the debris on the street and beach below still bore testament to how rough the storms had been right across the southern coasts. The sound of the suite telephone buzzing grabbed his attention. When he answered, an anonymous voice invited him to a meeting and informed him that a limousine would pick him up in an hour.

By the time the car delivered Lex to an imposing villa locked behind high walls and gates, he'd filled himself with painkillers, dressed in the clothes provided in the room and covered his bruising as well as he could, hiding his eyes behind dark glasses once more. He was pleased to be out of the working clothes he'd travelled in.

A security guard with an earpiece showed him into a lounge that looked out over a pool area where young children were playing, the noise of their splashing and joyful screaming silenced by the thickened glass of the windows. A group of men in shirtsleeves, looking as if they were fresh from a business meeting on a golf course, rose from various chairs and sofas to shake his hand. He did not return their friendly smiles or remove his glasses. He was not yet ready to lower any of his defences. He wanted to know who these guys were in the organisation before he showed any of his cards.

They soon made Lex feel at ease, if somewhat curious, by telling him how honoured and thrilled they were to meet him. It seemed they already knew a great deal more about him than he'd imagined; Flint must have briefed them. They made sure he had a drink and food and kept the small talk going for several minutes before it inevitably turned to business matters.

'You can imagine how excited we were to find that a man of

your calibre was willing to work within our network,' one of them said. He seemed to be the spokesman. Lex had been introduced to him as Sam. 'It's always great to work with guys from different areas of expertise.'

Lex remained silent. The excitement of the previous few days had left him feeling calm and confident. There was nothing these men could do to shake him. He just waited until they got round to whatever it was they wanted to say, feeling only slightly impatient. Eventually they got to the point.

'Our friends in Ireland,' Sam said casually, 'we'd be interested to hear what you think of them.'

'*Think* of them?'

'Do you feel you would be able to work more directly with us, rather than through them?' Another man, whose name he now couldn't remember, interrupted, 'Or is the cause something close to your heart?'

'The thing is,' Sam went on when it was obvious Lex wasn't going to give them an answer until he was sure he understood the question and why they were asking it, 'we're business people like yourself. We sometimes worry that they miss business opportunities because of political agendas that we might not feel the need to prioritise.'

Lex continued to listen.

'We'd just like to know if you would be interested in talking about doing things differently in the future.'

'We can always talk in the future,' he said, giving nothing away. He was starting to like these people, they were interested in the same things as him. He'd found the intensity of Mudge and his fellow republicans interesting in the beginning, now he just saw them as amateurs too detached from this exotic business world, and he wanted to move on.

'What happened in Texas,' Lex added quietly, 'can never be allowed to happen again. Juan and Garcia must handle all the physical stuff and everything must be planned meticulously. We all have too much to lose if it gets fucked up again. Is that understood?'

'I think we all understand what you're saying perfectly,' Sam grinned, and one of the other men refilled his glass. 'But I don't think Juan and Garcia would. They are useful men and we wouldn't want them to think they were dispensable in any way.'

Lex glanced up from his glass and saw them all looking at him. He nodded his understanding. Juan and Garcia must be allowed to go on believing that they were his equals.

That evening, when the limousine dropped him back outside the hotel, he decided not to go straight back in but strolled across the road to the beach to watch the sun setting. Workmen were continuing with their clearance work under mobile spotlights and the hum of generators mingled with traffic sounds. The air was eerily calm.

'Humbling isn't it, don't you think?' The voice from behind made him jump. He swung round to find himself just inches away from Mudge's face. He felt a spasm of guilt after what had been talked about at the meeting earlier.

Had it been a set-up? Had they been testing his loyalty to the cause? He tried to remember if he'd said anything that might have given away his wish to put the Provos behind him.

'The power of nature,' Mudge continued when Lex didn't speak, 'it reminds us just how insignificant we all are, wouldn't you say? A little puff of God's wind and all our feeble efforts can be blown away.'

'Have you been following me?' Lex asked.

'We need to chat somewhere private.' Mudge ignored the question.

'Do you want to come up to my room?' Lex nodded towards the sparkling façade of his hotel.

'Nah, not my style.' Mudge's lip curled to show his displeasure at the thought of such a place. 'I'm staying a couple of blocks back from the front. We'll go there.'

The owners of the motel he led Lex to hadn't bothered to put right any of the storm damage, and they had to pick their way through the fallen chairs, tossed tables and ripped umbrellas. Once they were in the room Mudge turned the television on to cover their voices from prying ears behind thin walls, and poured them each a whiskey.

'I was on my way back from Joseph in Cuba,' he explained, even though Lex hadn't asked. 'I believe you're carrying some of our wedge. I could take some of it back to Ireland with me.'

'I don't have it,' Lex said.

Mudge paused and stared at him hard. 'Don't fuck with me,' he said. 'Never fuck with me, Goldman.'

'I'm not fucking with you. You'll have to ask your friends over here what happened to the money and the gear. I don't have it. I would be quite interested to hear the answer myself.'

Mudge took a long, thoughtful drink before going on. 'Seems to me, Lex, you may be forgetting who your paymasters are, my friend.'

'The money is my patch, Mudge,' Lex said firmly. 'At no stage have I given you any reason to distrust me. I don't need to steal from you. Why would I bother?'

'People like you have been stealing from people like me since the beginning of time,' Mudge sneered. 'So don't pretend you own some special moral high ground.'

'Oh fuck off and give it a rest, Mudge.'

'You're a double-crossing little shit,' Mudge snarled, and Lex could see that his temper was brewing close to boiling point.

'Look, you can trust me,' he said, trying to calm the atmosphere. 'I've shown you that.'

'A man who can't control his wife,' Mudge suddenly shouted, banging his glass down angrily, making the whiskey slop over the sides, 'is not a man I would ever feel I could trust with any responsibility.'

'Don't push your luck, O'Connor,' Lex snapped, feeling a hot anger rising. He'd been deliberately forcing any thoughts of Sophie and their troubled marriage to the back of his mind, allowing the adrenaline of his jungle adventures to replace the empty feeling in his heart, and now Mudge had deliberately stirred them up.

'Don't fucking tell me what to do,' Mudge snarled. 'Remember who you fucking work for, you piece of colonial shit!'

'You think I work for you? Man, you are sadly deluded.'

For a second it looked as if Mudge was about to pounce and Lex braced himself for the impact. He was determined to stand his ground, knowing that if he allowed Mudge to intimidate him now, he might never regain the upper hand.

'I've been sent to tell you that things are going to be different from now on,' Mudge said, making a visible effort to restrain himself from punching the man who at that moment he hated.

'*Different*, how?'

'From now on you're answerable to me for every deal. You don't just hand me the odd case full of cash, you get approval from me on every deal before you make it.'

'You're a fucking idiot, Mudge, if you think that's ever going to happen.'

Lex's mind thought back to the cool calm meeting he'd just left and wished he could kill the Irishman there and then. His brain was racing. If he did kill Mudge, would the CIA be able to protect him with a new identity? He could give them plenty of useful information to make it worth their while.

For a moment it looked as if Mudge was going to choke on his own spleen as he struggled to maintain his self-control, more angered by the knowledge that Goldman was too valuable to the organisation to be dispensable, than he was at Lex's actual insult.

'Just remember,' he hissed, 'that I am your shadow, you arrogant bastard. If you even think of double-crossing us with your new friends in Colombia you won't know what hit you.'

'My new friends?' Lex laughed, aware that Mudge had been forced to back down, glad that he had temporarily won the upper hand. 'You guys introduced me to them, O'Connor.'

Mudge opened his mouth to say something else but Lex had already left the room, so he punched the bedside table instead, snapping it in two and making his knuckles bleed.

Lex was relieved to be back in New York, on familiar territory, especially within the safe environs of the Waldorf Astoria. He stepped out of the elevator onto the floor where his suite was, looking forward to a hot shower and a few hours of undisturbed sleep before his meetings the following day. The elevator doors closed behind him and he walked wearily towards the suite door, only vaguely aware of the two men walking towards him, apparently deep in conversation. As they approached they split apart to allow him to pass between them. At the same moment the nearest door in the corridor opened and everything became a blur. He was aware of a hand clamped painfully across his mouth and other hands lifting him by his upper arms, sending a sharp pain through his recently injured shoulder, propelling him through the door into a darkened room.

There was someone else in the room, but it wasn't until he'd been forced down into a chair and a light had been switched on that he was able to see it was an older man, with a heavy, scowling face and dark suit. The two men who'd snatched him from the corridor came into focus through his confusion. They looked familiar.

'What the fuck are you doing?' Lex shouted at them, genuinely affronted at being manhandled.

Neither of the CIA men replied, and he saw that the older man was extending a hand to be shaken.

'A pleasure to meet you at last, Mr Goldman,' he said, 'I'm Special Agent Trent Colby.'

'Why didn't you just invite me in?' Lex asked, deliberately not shaking his hand, but Colby didn't withdraw it.

'They like to make use of their field training from time to time,' he said. 'Indulge them a little, will you?'

Lex scowled, despite his anger and shook the man's hand. It was a powerful grip.

'What's been happening?' Colby smiled. 'You haven't been in touch for a while.'

'I haven't had any information for you.' Lex felt defensive. The last thing he wanted was for the CIA to discover his Colombian connections. He realised that if the DEA had caught him at El Paso these men would no longer be able to deal with him and he would have lost all his bargaining powers.

'A man called O'Connor was in Miami recently. He met up with you. Want to tell us about that?'

Lex remained silent, waiting to see if they would give away how much they already knew.

'I would be grateful if you could fill me in a little on the activities of O'Connor and some of his IRA friends.' Colby tried again. 'We've been getting a lot of heat from the Brits over tracing funds that are originating from the States to these guys; we need to get on the inside and find out what's going on.'

'He's an old family friend of my wife's,' Lex replied. 'What more can I tell you?'

His confidence was returning as he realised they knew nothing about his trip to Colombia or his bumpy arrival in El Paso. These men were no more than incidental government foot soldiers, what would they know? He could outwit them.

Trent Colby smiled, but didn't appear amused. 'The only point,' he said, 'in us keeping you out of jail is if you're able to tell us a few things we don't already know.'

'Send me to jail? For what?' Lex laughed in an attempt to appear unworried by the threat. 'I operate within the law.'

'We both know what you do, Mr Goldman.' Still his tone wasn't anything but benign. 'We could arrest you while our colleagues in the FBI look into your sudden investment in the Middle Eastern oil business. What would we find if we turned over a few of those little stones?'

Lex said nothing. His mind was racing. The confidence he'd felt a few seconds earlier had suddenly gone, leaving him feeling vulnerable. It looked like he might need to call on his new friends in Miami to provide him with some legitimate business alibis. But in exchange for that, would they want him to double-cross Mudge and the Provos? He felt a shiver of foreboding as he tried to work out all the possible permutations of his situation. If he made one wrong move now, the whole web could unravel.

Two hours later Lex was finally able to fall into his bed and try to sleep, despite the thoughts spinning round and round in his head as he attempted to figure out the best course of action. He'd given the CIA enough to keep them happy for the moment. He'd tested the idea that he might one day need to disappear with a new identity and they hadn't protested. He just wished he could be sure they didn't know any more about him than they were letting on. His confidence ebbed and flowed. At the moment he didn't think they were going to cause him any problems. If he could handle the minefield that the Provos and the Colombians presented, a few bureaucratic gofers shouldn't be allowed to give him any sleepless nights.

'I'm afraid I don't have time to fly back to Jo'burg at the moment, David.' Lex was busily signing letters that his secretary was putting in front of him at the same time as talking into the speakerphone on his desk.

'No need, Lex.' The older man's voice was authoritative, reminding him of his father, making him keen to end the conversation. 'How long are you going to be in London?'

'I have to be here for at least a week,' Lex replied.

'We'll meet you there then.'

The line went dead.

'Huh!' Lex punched the buttons on the phone, unable to believe they'd dared to hang up on him.

Forty-eight hours later David was back on the line. 'We're at Claridge's,' he growled. 'Can you meet us here this afternoon?'

'I'm really busy, David, I can't just drop things.'

'Then we'll come to you.'

'Wait!' Lex didn't want to be cut off again. 'I can make it at six.' He hung up quickly. If the whole board had flown to London to see him, it must be serious.

He deliberately didn't arrive until seven and they were waiting for him in one of the hotel's sumptuous meeting rooms. None of them smiled when he walked in except David, who shook him warmly by the hand.

'I haven't got long, gentlemen,' he warned as he took a seat at the end of the table. 'So, let's get straight to whatever it is that's worrying you.'

'You've brought us all halfway round the world at your convenience,' snapped the man on his left, who'd been in business with Sol Goldman from the beginning and was too old to be able to curb his impatience with his former partner's arrogant son. 'The least you can do is spare us some time.'

'I wish I could spare more.' Lex spread his hands helplessly, trying a little charm. 'It's you I'm working for.'

David smiled quietly, as if at some private joke, but none of the other faces cracked.

'Lex, we all have a lot of respect for you,' he said. 'But we all loved your father, and our first priority is to protect the legacy he left behind.'

'We are in agreement on that,' Lex grinned, but the frosty atmosphere remained.

'We think it's time you and the company went separate ways, Lex,' the man sitting next to him blurted. 'Our interests no longer coincide.'

'Don't be fucking stupid!' Lex laughed. 'It's my company.'

'No, Lex, it's a public company and you are becoming a liability,' the man opposite tried a more reasonable tone. 'We can't have the Americans threatening us.'

'What do you mean?'

'You can imagine what I mean. As long as they have you in their pocket they can exert pressure on us. We can't allow that.'

'I'm not in anyone's pocket.'

'You are in more people's pockets than the Artful Dodger,' the man next to him snapped. 'So don't give us any of that crap. Your father would no more have done business with terrorists and drug runners than he would have sold his children to the Nazis.'

'Give me a break!'

'That is our plan,' David said quietly. 'We wish to free you from your obligations to Goldfields, so you will be able to follow your other "business" interests. We're making you an offer for your shares.'

He tossed a sealed envelope across the table. Lex stared at it for a moment, breathing deeply, trying to work out a game plan. No one spoke. He picked it up and opened it.

'You stupid old men,' he snarled, 'that's less than half what my shares are worth, and you know it.'

'It's not negotiable,' the man opposite warned. 'It will be paid the moment you sign. How much money can one man need, Lex?'

'It has nothing to do with need, as you fucking well know. This is my business and it's not for sale, not at this price.'

'You deserve to hang, you little shit!' one of the others blurted and David put up his hand to quieten him.

'We've heard enough of it,' the man opposite snapped.

'Enough of what?'

'Your bullshit, Goldman. It's time to face some facts.'

'My entire life is spent facing facts!' Lex felt a surge of anger that these old has-beens dared to question him in this way. Hadn't he more than quadrupled the personal wealth of every man in this room with his recent deals? 'What exactly is it that's worrying you?'

'You're worrying us, Lex,' the man next to him snarled. 'You've become a liability to the company.'

'What are you talking about?' Lex tried to laugh but it was a hollow sound. 'I've increased the value of this company tenfold and the potential for growth now that I've opened up international markets is unlimited. If anything is a liability it's having a reactionary board who all learned this business in another age. It may be time to make some changes around this table.'

'Anyone can strike lucky if they take enough risks,' another voice spoke from the end of the table. 'The risks you're taking now are too big. If you end up in prison you could tarnish us and bring down the whole company.'

'What do you mean, "end up in prison"?' Lex was genuinely shocked. How could they imagine that a man as rich and as powerful as him could ever end up in prison?

'You've lost all sense of reality,' the man opposite replied. 'You deal with dictators, gangsters and terrorists. You launder dirty money through the company accounts. No one can get away with that sort of behaviour for long.'

'You don't know what you're talking about,' Lex sneered. 'Every businessman has to take risks.'

'You can take all the risks you like with your own reputation,' the man next to him snapped angrily, 'but not with ours, or with your father's legacy.'

'Maybe that is what you're all forgetting,' Lex hissed, like a snake about to strike. 'This company is my father's legacy, and I keep you all on this board out of respect for his memory. It may be time to rethink that policy.'

'Are you threatening us?' the man opposite voiced the outrage of the whole room.

'Merely putting my cards on the table. I'll run this company in any way I see fit. If any of you are unhappy with that your resignations will be accepted.'

The anger in the room now was almost tangible, a thick cloud of fury. Lex noticed David was the only one who didn't seem to be talking. He was smiling quietly to himself, as if at some private joke. At least he appreciated the foolishness of their stance, Lex thought.

'I'm afraid that's all the time I can spare.' Lex stood up as their angry voices rose around him. He gave a curt nod to the room and walked to the door. David stood up and followed.

'Lex,' David's calm voice caught him as he stalked down the corridor outside. 'If you could spare me one more moment.'

Lex paused and allowed the older man to catch up. He could still hear the outraged voices coming from the meeting room.

'Can we meet later?' David asked with a friendly smile. 'Just you and me.'

'I really can't spare any more time for this nonsense,' Lex said.

'I think I may have a solution, but I would like to discuss it with you in private. I plan to take supper at Rules, will you join me there later?'

Lex paused for a second. There was something in David's manner that suggested he would not take no for an answer.

'Oh, very well then.'

David was ensconced in a corner table in the famous old restaurant in Maiden Lane, behind the Strand. He was already eating when Lex arrived.

'Excuse me for not waiting,' he said as Lex sat down opposite him. 'I wasn't sure what time you would arrive.'

That's all right,' Lex said, 'I'm eating later.'

The waiter poured him a glass of wine and he toyed with a piece of bread as he waited to hear what the older man had to say.

'I really think you should reconsider that offer,' David said quietly. 'It's a good price.'

'Is that all you've got to say?' Lex asked, glancing at his watch. 'Because you're wasting your time and mine.'

'It can't carry on, like this, Lex. It would be better for all of us. Without a company tying you down you would be free to do whatever little surreptitious deals you want.'

'Are you accusing me of doing illegal deals?' Lex was outraged at the suggestion. How could he make these foolish old men realise that he had moved above the law, that he belonged in a different world to their humdrum, workaday existence. He was successful because he no longer lived by their petty rules.

'Are you denying it?' David sounded almost amused at the thought.

'Of course I'm denying it.'

Putting a large forkful of food into his mouth, David sat back, pulling a neatly folded sheet of paper from his pocket and passing it over without a word. He watched as Lex read it, chewing thoughtfully.

Lex felt a chill run through him as he read through a precise list of transactions he had executed in recent months through the company's bank accounts with a number of bogus commodity trading companies in Switzerland. He pretended to study each one in order to avoid looking up into David's eyes, giving himself some time to think.

'Who else knows about this?' he asked eventually.

'No one,' David said quietly. 'I did a little digging on my own. You covered your tracks well but I dare say if I kept digging I would find more.'

Lex said nothing. Trying to compose his thoughts.

'If even a whisper of what you've been up to gets into the media,' David continued, 'your shares will be worth a lot less than the price we're offering you today.' He pulled the envelope with the offer back out of his pocket and laid it on the table. 'You're a gambler, Lex; you should know when to cash in your chips, son.'

'Don't patronise me, you old fuck!' Lex's voice was louder than he intended, making heads turn in the hushed atmosphere of the restaurant. David continued eating.

Silence fell again as Lex struggled to work out what he should do. Even fifty per cent of the paper value of his shares in the company would give him a massive cash mountain. Did he need the aggravation of being answerable to a board of directors any longer? There was a lot to be said for taking the money and putting it to work. But he didn't like the idea that he'd been manipulated so easily by a parochial bunch of old fogies. How could he have allowed himself to get into such a vulnerable position? Too many things on his mind; juggling too many balls at once. This was tantamount to blackmail.

'I'll need your signature,' David said, sipping his wine.

Realising he no longer had any option, Lex took a pen out of his pocket and smoothed the papers out on the table in front of him. 'Five years, David,' he growled, 'and I'll be running a corporation so big I'll be able to buy you out from petty cash!'

David said nothing, simply watching as he signed.

Sophie was waiting for him at Le Gavroche in Mayfair, so he took a cab straight there. She made no fuss about him being late and he sat down without even pecking her on the cheek.

'I've already ordered,' she said, passing him the menu.

'I'll have the same as my wife,' he said and the waiter poured him a glass from the bottle of champagne Sophie had cooling beside her.

'Bad day?' she asked after a moment.

'Just did the biggest deal of my life,' he replied.

'Congratulations.'

'Nothing is ever quite what it seems though, is it?'

'Meaning?'

'I've been forced out of Goldfields,' he said, looking deep into her eyes.

'Ah,' she said. 'Sorry, I didn't realise.'

'But that isn't the only thing that isn't as it seems, is it?'

She said nothing, waiting for him to go on.

'Mudge tells me I've lost control of my wife.'

She laughed and he remembered how much he still desired her. The thought that he might be losing her brought a stabbing pain to his chest, reminding him how he felt when he lost Reshmine. He wasn't sure his heart would stand the strain of going through that again.

'Have I?' he asked.

'You can't control people,' she reminded him, 'not even you.'

'Is there someone else?'

'No one special.'

'Do you want a divorce?'

'Do you?'

He sighed. There were so many things he wanted he didn't know where to start.

'No,' he said, 'I don't want a divorce. But what are we going to do?'

'Why don't we go on as we are? We lead more or less separate lives anyway, who'll notice the difference? A divorce would just draw attention. There's no one else you want to marry, is there?'

'Good God no!'

'So, why not keep up the pretence until one of us wants something different?'

He nodded, relieved when the waiter began fussing with the cutlery, allowing him to take another swig of champagne and look away in case Sophie saw in his eyes how much he was hurting. In one evening he'd lost his company and his wife. Now all he was left with was a pile of money and a place in a network of international criminals. As the stark reality of his new situation set in, he knew his world had changed for ever.

6

The security staff at Trump Tower were faultlessly polite, but immovable. The first Lex suspected anything was wrong was when his key didn't open the lock of the apartment door. Small glitches in the smooth running of his life always infuriated him. He stormed down to the reception to demand another key, doing his best to control his temper when the two stony-faced security men appeared from nowhere and informed him that the locks had been changed and he was no longer allowed to have access to the apartment.

'What? On whose instructions?' he barked, forcing himself to keep his composure. These people, he reminded himself, were just doing what they were instructed to do. They also didn't look like the sort of men who would give in to intimidation. He'd hired people like them in the past to suppress troublemakers at the mines and he knew their tactics in situations like these. He was also well aware that he had to maintain a psychological advantage to stop things turning physical.

'The owners, Mr Goldman,' the more senior and slightly smaller of the two uniformed men replied.

'I am the owner,' Lex smiled with what he hoped was disarming charm.

'I'm sorry, sir,' the man said, 'the instructions came from the owning company.'

Lex sighed and took a deep breath. The man's patience and politeness almost made the insolence seem more offensive. He realised immediately that David must have moved quickly to exclude him from all of Goldfields' properties. The important thing was to maintain his dignity over the next few minutes. The security men were equally keen not to have to physically eject a man who might well turn out to be someone of influence with their bosses.

'Look, guys, I have personal possessions in the apartment that I would like to retrieve,' he said.

'All your personal possessions have been taken care of and are in storage, Mr Goldman,' the receptionist interrupted, pleased to be of service. 'If you would like to let us know where to forward them I will be happy to arrange it.'

'What? You've already cleared my belongings out of the apartment?' Lex was shocked to find he actually felt threatened by this invasion of his personal space. They were only clothes, after all, a few suits and shirts, a few pairs of shoes and some personal effects. Why should he care? But he did.

'The owners arranged it, sir,' the receptionist explained.

'Send it all to the Waldorf,' he snapped and stalked out of the building.

The staff at the Waldorf hid their panic immaculately as they went into overdrive to clear and prepare a luxury suite for a valued customer who had arrived unexpectedly and had announced that he wanted to make the hotel his base for the foreseeable future. They offered Lex a bottle of champagne in the bar while he waited, and he was glad to accept the offer. He needed some time to himself to think what his next moves should be.

Although he had been fully aware that David meant what he said about disassociating him from the company, the reality of finding himself locked out of an apartment that he had come to think of as his own was a shock. He suddenly felt vulnerable. Having the financial muscle of Goldfields on his side had given him the security to take risks. The company had been a huge part of his life, supporting his international business credibility, but now he was on his own and if he made any mistakes he would no longer be shielded from the negative consequences. He had to tread more cautiously if he was going to repair the huge loss to his wealth that David's clever tactics had engineered. The painful realisation of the *actual* worth of his holdings in Goldfields was a jolt to his system. Along with the cost of settling Sophie in order to maintain her high standard of living, he was burning cash at a massive rate on his own lifestyle. As he gathered his thoughts he could feel his resolve strengthen. He was going to recover from this set-back, now that the shackles of Goldfields were off, and be even more daring than he had in the past.

Lex knew he needed to liquidate as much cash as possible to replenish his funds for investment. While the maids scurried around upstairs preparing his suite he rang the estate agent in London who had acted on the sale of Hampstead Hall and instructed him to put it back on the market. Now his relationship with Sophie had waned, he had few reasons to be based in London and fewer still to have so much capital tied up in a big stately home there. There were much better ways to invest the money.

By the time the hotel reception staff came to tell him his rooms were ready he had polished off most of the champagne and was again lost in thought. The hotel manager came by to accompany

Lex and show him up to his suite. He was pleased to discover on entering the room that his clothes had already been sent over from Trump Tower, and the maid was busy unpacking them into the wardrobes.

Once the staff had all gone and he was alone again he sat by the window and stared out across the Manhattan skyline. His main worry now was that if David had been able to uncover his Swiss trading activity with bogus commodity firms so easily, others might be able to do the same. He didn't like the idea of anyone else being in a position to blackmail him, and he also knew that the detailed information he was passing to the CIA could become suspicious if someone started to burrow too deeply into his private life.

'Speed,' he said, surprised to find he had spoken out loud. 'That's the answer.'

He had to move fast to fix up a few lucrative deals with the Provos and the Colombians if he was to increase his fortune substantially and his security. Ultimately, Lex always felt his only real protection would come from his wealth and being able to buy himself out of trouble. Although he hated having to do business with men as crude as Mudge or as sinister as Flint, they were the only ones he knew who could orchestrate the really big money deals. Together with the Colombians they provided him with the global distribution network he needed in order to realise significant profits from drugs and arms. He felt confident he had shown Mudge who was boss, and now was the time to harvest some of the rewards for all his labours over the previous few years.

That night, feeling tired and alone, he made a call to an escort service for company. The girl they sent round was beautiful and charming and made perfect conversation in the restaurant as they dined, despite the fact that he was distracted by his own thoughts and was not good company. She graciously accepted the invitation back to his suite with the usual reluctance and they had business sex as if they were in a loving relationship, which was exactly what Lex wanted from such encounters. Once she had left though, the loneliness of his life returned.

Breaking out of a fitful sleep, he returned to staring out the window at the city below, fighting the urge to ring Sophie and tell her he loved her and that it was a mistake for them to be apart. He knew he would feel different once dawn broke and there were phone calls to make and deals to be struck. He just had to hang on until that moment of despair had passed.

His memory wandered back to his nights with Reshmine in South Africa and he felt a stab of pain in his chest. Even after so many years, the images of her in his head were as vivid as if he had seen her yesterday. Everything, he knew, would have been so different if he had had her by his side. He would have been a different person with different priorities, making different decisions. His opulent lifestyle and all its trappings would not have impressed her, he knew that. She wouldn't have approved of any involvement with Mudge or his cronies and certainly not the Colombian drug runners. The brutal end to their relationship had left a deep emotional void in him and there was nothing else he wanted to achieve with his life apart from accumulating wealth, his one and only skill. His course was now set and there was no turning back.

If he hadn't always been in such a hurry to cash in his profits early, Lex would have invested in the telecommunications business. Portable phones were still cumbersome, unreliable and expensive creatures in 1988, but the technology was a quantum leap ahead of the old landlines the world had been relying on for the previous century.

'They're the future,' he was fond of saying to anyone who showed an interest in his chunky portable phone. 'By the turn of the millennium everybody will be using them.'

Most people laughed at the idea that a portable phone would ever be something that anyone other than the business community would be able to afford.

'Would you buy one if it was affordable?' Lex would follow up. 'I mean, if it was retailing really cheap, no more than buying postage stamps or paying your normal phone bill? Wouldn't you want one then? Especially if all your business associates and friends had one?'

In the face of his evangelism, most people ended up agreeing that if the technology meant the phones worked well, they would find it hard to resist having one. Lex would shrug, certain that he was right. Once he had his fortune secured, he mused, he would launder it by investing in the telecommunications sector. But not yet, there were more pressing engagements before making any long-term investments in early stage telecoms start-ups.

Aware of the danger of putting all his eggs in one basket, Lex made sizeable initial investments in two unrelated projects. Acting decisively made him feel a familiar glow as the adrenaline pulsed through his veins. Juan and Garcia had told him they were planning a major drug run. They were going to use an innocuous looking fishing vessel, pack it with cocaine, and sail it in through the Gulf of Mexico to unload on the east coast of the States, if he wanted to buy a piece of the action.

'Too much fucking radar,' they had explained to him when he asked why they were using the sea route. 'It's becoming too hard to get planes over the border. It's okay, you can carry more cargo on a boat than a plane anyway. The risks are lower.'

Lex had made some initial calculations and felt sure the load they were talking about would have a street value of well over a hundred million US dollars. His slice of the action would be very lucrative in relation to any initial investment he cared to put in.

'We need friends to oversee the arrival,' Juan had said. 'Someone we can trust completely.'

For a second Lex considered approaching the IRA, but changed his mind before opening his mouth. Why give them a percentage if he could keep it for himself?

'I'll be your friend,' he said after a moment's pause. 'You know you can trust me.'

Juan understood without asking any further. He was happy to involve as few people in the operation as possible. Lex had proved himself to be entirely reliable on their previous adventures.

His second investment was in contract oil. The Libyan contingent came to the Waldorf for a private dinner in his suite. The escort agency provided them with the right sort of female company for the evening, but before dinner got under way the Libyans made Lex an offer to join them in a syndicate as a major investor in a large contract shipment of oil.

'Our President,' their spokesman told Lex, 'felt sure that this would be something that would interest you.'

'Ah, President Gaddafi.' Lex nodded approval. 'How is he indeed?' It seemed that his patience in the desert had paid off. He liked the way these people trusted him and wanted to do business with him. It made him feel invincible again, just what he needed after taking such a hard knock to his ego from David and the other relics. 'He is a wise man, your President. I would trust his judgement.'

The other men smiled their acceptance of his compliment, but no one in the room believed he was being sincere. Nor did they care. This was business.

Within a few months of being usurped from Goldfields and locked out of Trump Tower, Lex felt he was already back at the top of his game. Sizeable amounts of his fortune were now reinvested in projects that could provide a tremendous return within a relatively short time. He was so confident of making huge killings he'd also invested a large chunk of the funds he owed to the IRA. If one of the deals was delayed for any reason, the other would ensure that he was still in a position to pay them what they were owed, while he waited for things to come good. If they got wind of what he was doing he would have to give them a percentage of the profits, but he hoped to get away without that if things worked out right. All he had to do was keep stalling them on the money he owed them. A dangerous game to play . . .

'It's a fucking big ocean to try and find one little fucking boat, sir,' Johnstone complained when the intelligence report arrived at the Surveillance Support Centre at Corpus Christi, Texas. His commanding officer raised an eyebrow but said nothing about the language he'd just heard; pilots as good as Johnstone were hard to find and he knew he had to make allowances for a maverick like him, even in the Customs Service.

'You've done it before,' he said, 'I know you can do it again. They think this could be a really big one.'

'Coming from where?'

'Cargo originating from Colombia. They don't want this dope getting through to the streets.'

'We'll do our best, sir.'

Johnstone and his crew were up in the air within minutes of the briefing, but four hours later the P-3 Orion radar plane was just about to give up its search and return home to refuel when they spotted a small blip on their screens.

'Any idea who else that could be, apart from the target?' Johnstone asked his navigator.

'No other vessels reported in the area,' his navigator replied.

'Could be our guy then.'

'Could be.'

'Call in the coastguard, then we can get back to base for a meal and a few hours sleep.'

Carlos, the captain of the *Santa Anna* had been an honest fisherman for the first forty years of his working life. He had a reputation in the ports of Colombia for being willing to put up with any amount of rough seas and danger if it would get him to the shoals swimming in waters that rival captains were too cautious or too lazy to attempt.

'If I don't bring home any food I'm going to die of starvation anyway,' he would joke whenever anyone challenged the wisdom of some of his missions, 'so what's the difference?'

By the time Juan and Garcia came across Carlos, they'd already heard a lot about him. The Carlos stories told in the bars that fishermen frequented sounded more like legends about some mythical figure; many of them he had started himself when half-cut. The two men kept going to the bars until they eventually came across the man himself, holding court after drinking the best part of a bottle of brandy. They stayed all evening, pretending to drink at the same rate as everyone else, but saying little, drawing no attention to their presence. Eventually Carlos began to quieten down and become more melancholy. Garcia moved closer to listen to the older man talking.

'A fisherman's life is a dog's life,' he was moaning. 'Every day the same, risking your life just to bring home enough to feed your family.'

'They say you're one of the most successful fishermen on the coast,' Garcia said. 'You must have made enough money to retire by now.'

Carlos gave a mirthless laugh. 'Fishermen don't earn enough to retire; they just get too old to be able to pull in their own nets. I need to win the *Loteria del Tolima* if I want to retire.'

The word went back down the line from Garcia that they had probably found their man, someone with courage and seamanship, and a need for more money. For several months Juan and Garcia made sure to be in the same bars as Carlos whenever he was on dry land and gradually got to know him as a friend, building up trust until they could be sure of his discretion and his potential allegiances. By the time they came to load the eight tons of cocaine beneath the *Santa Anna's* normal cargo of fish and ice, Carlos seemed almost like an older brother to them.

The American intelligence services had spotted Carlos as a potential courier even before the cartel did. In fact, they were surprised he hadn't been approached before. Their operatives were in the same bars, observing and noting characters and awaiting their chance. When they saw Juan and Garcia moving in, they knew they could be on the trail of a big haul.

'That was a spotter plane,' one of the crew shouted to Carlos over the roar of the engines and splashing surf, but by the time the captain looked up into the skies the speck had vanished.

'You sure?' he yelled back.

'No,' the man looked doubtful, 'but I think so.'

'Maybe we need to change course a little, take in some more scenery,' Carlos grinned, staring out across the endless open seas that surrounded the boat. 'Then we can come back down the coast when we're closer in.'

'We don't have that much fuel,' the man warned.

'We have enough.' Carlos liked it when things got dangerous. It made him feel he was going to be earning his money fairly. They'd hired him because he was braver than other seafarers. He liked that.

Lex was already in radio contact with the *Santa Anna*, sitting with a driver who had been carefully selected from the cartel's network in an empty truck in the back area of a truck stop. They were ready to drive to meet the boat as soon as the landing place had been confirmed. By the time the coastguard's powerboat appeared on the horizon, a few miles from the *Santa Anna*, the truck driver was already getting nervous. This news added to the tension in the cab.

'Don't worry,' Carlos shouted to Lex over the roaring of the engines, 'we can outrun the bastards.'

'It's a fucking fishing boat,' the truck driver snarled, 'how the fuck does he think he can do that?'

'I doubt he does really,' Lex said, 'he just likes the idea of being a pirate. But they have guns, they can defend themselves.'

'Shit.' The driver lit a fresh cigarette to try to calm his shaking hands and Lex made a mental note not to use him again. People who became anxious were capable of losing their nerve just when they needed it most.

* * *

Part of Carlos's deal was that the *Santa Anna* would be fitted with new engines before the trip, paid for by the cartel. Now he was looking forward to trying them out. The engineers who fitted them had boasted that he would be able to outrun anyone he wanted, but he knew they were only talking about rival fishing boats, not coastguard pursuit vessels. As he pulled the engines to their maximum he could feel a surge of power beneath his feet and the *Santa Anna* lifted out of the water like a speed boat, crashing violently down over the waves, making Carlos laugh happily and the rest of the crew grit their teeth to stop themselves crying out in fear.

They kept a watch on their pursuer through binoculars, but it was impossible to judge if she was catching up or falling back. Carlos ordered one of his men to take over the helm while he signalled two others to come below with him. Once inside his cabin, doing his best to steady himself against the violent movements of the boat, he pulled up a section of the floorboards. Reaching in, he lifted up two machine-guns and half a dozen handguns. He kept one of the machine-guns for himself and tossed the rest to the two ashen-faced men. By the time they were back on deck it was obvious the coastguards were gaining on them.

'Turn around,' Carlos shouted at the helmsman as he loaded the gun. The other men followed his lead.

'What the fuck do you mean, turn around?' the frightened man screamed.

'Turn the fucker round and head straight for them!' Carlos pointed the loaded machine-gun at the man's head and grinned.

'What the fuck!' The man spun the wheel and a sheet of spray hit the windows, obliterating their vision for nearly half a minute as they plunged forward into the unknown.

As the water cleared they could see the coastguards approaching. With both of them travelling at full throttle the speed of the chase had accelerated and they were hurtling towards each other with little time for decisions.

'Hold your course,' Carlos shouted at his helmsman, bracing his body against the side of the cabin, preparing himself to fire and nodding to the others to do the same. 'Keep going straight for them. Make them swerve round us. Then hold your course so they have to turn round.' He turned to the others. 'Open fire as soon as we're alongside. We have to cripple them quickly.'

The others nodded, grim-faced and determined. They knew if they were caught they wouldn't be seeing their families for many years. They had no choice but to do as Carlos ordered.

'They're not changing direction,' the helmsman screamed as the two boats headed straight for one another.

'Hold your course,' Carlos commanded.

The helmsman's knuckles were white as the boat ploughed straight on ahead. When the bows of the two boats were just yards apart the coastguards made a slight adjustment to their course and there was a terrible scream of grating metal as the two hulls scraped alongside one another at full speed. The moment Carlos saw the startled faces of the coastguards alongside them he opened fire, screaming at the helmsman to keep his course. The coastguards just had time to let off a short burst of return fire before the boats were already too far apart for any hope of accuracy. They turned at full speed to keep up the pursuit, losing valuable seconds in the process.

Carlos didn't realise he'd been hit for several moments. He saw the blood first and then felt the pain in his shoulder and chest. As the boat crashed down onto the water he lost his grip and stumbled, banging his head on the deck as he fell. Two of the crew ran to help him up, both stumbling and skidding as the terrified helmsman kept on going, aware the coastguards had now turned and were closing the gap behind them.

'He's dead!' one of the men shouted.

Without their leader the crew of the *Santa Anna* had no will for anything but flight. They managed to retain their lead on their pursuer for nearly an hour, all of them shouting at one another at the same time as they tried to work out what to do, and then the fuel ran out, the engine coughed and died and the *Santa Anna* was left bobbing helplessly on the waves as the coastguards approached, shouting orders through a megaphone. The crew made their way to the rear of the boat, with their hands in the air, and one of them took the time to shout into the radio that they'd been caught, before throwing it overboard.

'The job's off,' Lex informed the truck driver, 'forget we ever met.'

He handed him an envelope of cash before getting out of the cab and walking briskly to his car on the other side of the truck stop. His brain was racing as he climbed behind the wheel. The truck was already drawing out onto the freeway. He sat for several minutes, breathing deeply, taking in the enormity of the disaster, before driving steadily back to the airport. It was important that he was away from the area as fast as possible.

None of the crew spoke as the coastguards came on board, simply obeying the orders to lie face down on the rolling deck, under the watchful eye of an armed guard, while the others searched the boat. Opening the holds they dug through the mounds of fish and ice until they came across the neat lines of cocaine stacked below. They didn't have to check any further, it was time to head towards the shore with their trophy.

Once safely back at his hotel, Lex allowed his anger to erupt in a primal roar of frustration. Pouring himself a drink, he flicked on the television news channel to see if the coastguards had started to boast about their haul. There was nothing. He swallowed the drink in one and poured himself another. If the radio transmission was true and the boat had been seized, then there was no chance he would be able to recover any of his investment. His money had vanished within minutes. If, on the other hand, it was some sort of double-cross by the crew or the cartel, there might still be a chance he could find out who was behind it and reverse the situation.

Two hours later a 'breaking news' strapline splashed across the screen concerning a major drug bust off the coast in the Gulf of Mexico. He now knew it was true. The newsreader reported that it was thought to be one of the largest hauls ever. Lex stared at the screen without moving a muscle. His anger had now turned to a white-hot fury burning inside him.

He was finding it hard to concentrate fully and several other news items slid past him before he realised he was watching a scene in the Panama Canal. There were a lot of people shouting angrily at one another and something about it seemed familiar. As he pulled his brain back into focus he realised it was the name of the oil tanker in the background that was familiar. He turned the volume up on the television to try to work out what the reporter was saying. There was an angry mob of dock workers shouting while a sweating politician in a white suit was explaining why the strike was unreasonable and why they all needed to get around a table and negotiate.

As the news moved on to another item he flicked frantically through the channels, trying to find the same story somewhere else, but there was nothing. Several phone calls later he had managed to discover that a wildcat strike by dock workers in the Canal had brought all shipping traffic to a halt.

'They're just workers for fuck's sake,' he bellowed down the phone at his Libyan contact. 'Why don't they kick their fucking backsides until they go back to work? If they shoot a couple of the ring leaders the rest will get the message!'

'You're not in South Africa now, my friend,' the Libyan at the other end chuckled, fuelling Lex's fury.

'At least in South Africa we know how to run our businesses,' he stormed. 'We don't let the fucking unions run them for us. What kind of men are these who allow the rabble to hold them to ransom?'

'You just need to be patient,' the Libyan cooed. 'The oil is not going to spoil, it is not fruit. It may take a few weeks to sort out, but your oil will still be there.'

'Weeks?' Lex screamed.

'Maybe months, or maybe days, who knows?'

'I can't afford to wait even days. I need to realise my money from this deal, and I need to realise it now.'

'I'm sure there are people who would be willing to buy the oil contract off you at a price,' the Libyan purred.

'Rip me off, you mean. I can't come out of this deal with less money than I invested.'

'Then you will have to wait, just like everyone else. Hold your nerve, Mr Goldman, hold your nerve.'

The line went dead and he knew there was no point pursuing the man any more, because what he said was true. Unless Lex was willing to take a heavy loss on the oil he had no choice but to wait. Fate had conspired to deal him a savage double blow. Would the IRA be willing to wait any longer for the money he owed them from deals he had done on their behalf? He doubted it.

A few days later Lex got his answer. He recognised Flint's voice the moment he picked up the phone. He didn't have to introduce himself. He gave Lex the name and address of a bar in the Irish sector of Manhattan and told him to go there. Before Lex had a chance to protest that he was busy Flint had hung up. He didn't like taking orders from anyone, but something told him that if he didn't make the meeting, Joseph Flint would come looking for him and he didn't want any unpleasantness at the Waldorf, where he was sure his every move was being reported back to the CIA. Dressing himself as inconspicuously as possible, he left the building by a side entrance that he'd discovered and walked for several blocks before hailing a cab.

The bar was busy and noisy enough for him to be confident no one could spy on him or overhear a conversation. He couldn't see Flint anywhere, but knew better than to stare too hard around the badly lit pub. There were bound to be a lot of people who wouldn't take kindly to being noticed in such a place.

He took a seat at the bar and ordered a beer. He was only halfway through it when Flint lowered himself onto the next stool and ordered a whiskey. Neither man bothered with any of the usual polite niceties.

'What the fuck is going on?' Flint asked quietly.

'Going on where?' Lex forced himself to remain calm.

'Don't fuck me about,' Flint warned. Anyone watching them

from across the room would have thought they were two strangers striking up a casual conversation. No sign of any emotion appeared on either of their faces. 'There have been deals done. Jobs have gone down with your name on them, and we ain't seeing any of the wedge.'

'You've been getting plenty of money from me.'

'Do you think that the fact you have honoured some of your debts makes it okay to steal our money on others?'

'If anybody is stealing your money, it's not me,' Lex replied.

'Wherever funds have gone missing, you seem to be somewhere close.'

'Some of the money is invested. It isn't always the right time to sell out early.'

'Fuck off!' Flint growled. 'Do you think you're selling me a fucking pension scheme? You owe us money. We want it. You were told Mudge was to oversee every deal you made, but you haven't made contact with him.'

'He knows where I am.'

'You would do well to remember that fact, Lex.' Flint almost smiled. 'We all know where to find you. But don't make us come visiting, you wouldn't like us when we're *really* angry.'

Lex turned towards him to warn him against making idle threats, but Flint was already halfway out of the bar and not looking back. The barman cleared the empty glass, another customer sat on the stool and it was like Flint had never been there. For a few moments Lex felt unnerved in a way Mudge had never been able to make him feel. Then he began to rationalise the situation. Why should he be frightened of these people? They needed him more than he needed them. They would just have to wait for their money like he was going to have to. Even as he gave himself this pep talk, he was aware of an uneasy stirring in his stomach. Flint was not a man to cross and Lex knew he would not hesitate to carry out a death threat if he felt he had no option. He was acutely aware that he needed to raise at least some of the money as fast as possible.

Not wanting it to be too well known that he was living at the Waldorf, Lex had arranged for a meeting with some investment bankers at the Pierre, in a suite overlooking the corner of Central Park. He had tempted them there with the promise of a gourmet lunch, and it was while they were enjoying the splendid food, having listened to his pitch for some short-term funding to help him while he waited for the strike to release his oil consignment, that he received a call from hotel reception to say an urgent package had been delivered for him.

'Send it up,' he instructed, puzzled as to how anyone apart from the invited guests in the room could have known he was there.

He answered the discreet knock on the suite door himself and took the small brown packet from the bellboy. He ripped it open as he walked back towards the assembled bankers, all of whom fell silent and turned to look at the sound of something metal hitting the marble floor. Every eye in the room focused on the silver bullet as it rolled slowly to a standstill. Lex bent down and scooped it up, while reading the enclosed note as if it was nothing remarkable, and the bankers went back to their conversations, aware that it was none of their business.

'The next bullet,' the note told him, 'you won't see coming. *Tíocfaidh ar Lá*.'

In that split second Lex knew it was from Flint and that he meant what he said. The Irishman had run out of patience and he was letting Lex know that wherever he went they would be able to find him. If these bankers did not sanction a loan for him, he was going to have to take immediate evasive action if he wanted to survive. By five o'clock that evening he knew his pitch had fallen on deaf ears. His Goldfields' connections were not there any more to support him. The bankers could sense he was desperate and they certainly didn't have to take on such risky business. With an air of resignation, Lex knew the game was up this time and Mudge's words uttered so long ago were coming back to haunt him – 'with us for life'. His was now in deadly danger.

Lex didn't hide the fact that he was going away to the Caribbean for a few days' break, but he didn't advertise it either. It was to be a diving holiday, so he would be on a boat, travelling from island to island on the whim of the captain, and it would be hard for anyone to track him down. It had been a long time since Lex had freed up even a few days to be away from the constant churn of telephones and meetings. The idea of a holiday had always seemed distant to him. He enjoyed his work too much to want to take breaks from it unless there was an ulterior motive.

People who had met Lex Goldman on the various islands the boat had docked at, later told reporters that he had been in good spirits, laughing and joking with all the restaurant waiters, bar and hospitality staff he had come into contact with. None of them knew who he was until the media descended on the island with photographs, looking to confirm his identity, and asking questions about how he had acted. When their memories were nudged, many of them remembered him as a man who didn't seem to have a care in the world.

The loud noise of the explosion could be heard all along the coast of Antigua. Some of the debris even landed on the beach, despite the boat being nearly five hundred metres off shore, such was the force of the blast. By the time the rescuers reached the site it was impossible to find any identifiable bodies amongst the shattered pieces floating in the water polluted by a multi-coloured slick of oil.

Within hours of the explosion, investigative reporters from the British 'red top' tabloids were frantically digging into their files to try to find someone who could give them a lead on the story. The more thoughtful, quality press were not far behind, sensing this was a story that would interest the business elite of the world as much as the man in the street.

Despite the fact that Sophie's telephone number was known to only an inner circle around London, several of the reporters managed to find their way through to her. It hadn't taken long for their editors to make a link between a fatal explosion and a possible Irish connection to the most famous of the boat's passengers.

The severity of the explosion off Antigua lifted Lex Goldman from being a story only of interest to the business page editors and planted him firmly on the front pages. Tales of his wealth and business genius became wildly exaggerated as each editor struggled to find a new and more outrageous headline with which to capture the attention of readers. No member of the board at Goldfields would comment, which merely fuelled the rumours of incredible wealth and possible corruption, and there were plenty of staff from further down the company chain who were willing to tell tales of Lex's ruthlessness when it came to his dealings with the workforce. Within a week of the story breaking several escort girls from around the world had come forward to sell stories of their nights of passion with one of the world's biggest spenders.

While the journalists tutted and smirked over his business methods and personal morality, they couldn't quite keep the admiration out of their tone. This was a man who had done exactly what he wanted in his life, regardless of the consequences to himself or others; it was a reputation to be simultaneously disapproved of and envied by more timid men. His name became synonymous in the public's mind with great international wealth, and because he hadn't survived to contradict any of the exaggerations, his reputation took on mythical proportions. Conspiracy theories took root and multiplied; some speculated that the explosion was the work of the IRA, others suspecting British Government or ANC involvement.

Sophie Goldman refused to comment and vanished from sight. The lawyers she instructed to take care of her affairs were able to inform her that Lex's death was not going to affect her income or her way of life. A trust had been set up in Switzerland entirely for her benefit and was overseen by independent trustees. As a result, it wouldn't become involved in any probate problems. Money, however, was not the biggest issue on Sophie's mind. What troubled her most was the thought that her childhood friend could have been responsible for the death of her estranged husband. These two men had had the greatest impact on her life to date, and they had only come into contact because of her. She was devastated and unable to take in the enormity of the news.

No one at Chase Pacific Bank in St Louis could find any fault with the new Head of Research of precious metals and commodities, although there were plenty on their way up the hierarchy who would have liked to.

'Where the fuck did he come from? How come we didn't even know they were looking for someone?'

George Lombardi had been the subject of a great deal of water-cooler speculation amongst existing staff.

One or two of them had been to his mansion on Signal Hill, over to the east side of the city, a spectacular house on top of the bluffs, reached through acres of winding boulevards and landscaped grounds, with commanding views of the St Louis skyline. There was no denying this man was a player, but how come no one had ever heard of him before? Despite their jealousy, his detractors couldn't help but be impressed by a man who appeared to have already made his fortune without having to serve the long apprenticeship they had all endured. They would have liked to be able to say he wasn't good at his job, that he didn't understand the precious metals or commodities markets, but they couldn't. It was obvious he was an asset to Chase Pacific, a highly reputable private investment bank, whose clients consisted of a select number of large US corporations and high net worth individuals whose headquarters were based in St Louis. What had particularly impressed other executives about Lombardi was his eagerness to network with other aspects of the business beyond his own remit. He had been particularly fascinated by the booming brokerage department, which was doing significant business with Wall Street.

Lombardi was keen to grow synergies within the bank and took up every invitation that came his way to meet 'market moving' players. The most impressive introduction was to Vince Walker, Head of Debt Finance at Drexler Burnstone, one of the fastest growing brokerages on the Street. Walker had become a star through his innovation and syndication of junk bonds, a combination of high-risk debt and equity, which carried high interest rates.

'Well, legally, they're debt,' Walker had explained to Lombardi with a disarming grin the first time they met. 'In the event of bankruptcy the bond holders essentially become equity investors. My niche is servicing mid-sized firms with limited access to bank and capital markets.'

Even before they met, Lombardi had heard from others that Walker was known as 'Mr Junk' on the Street and was becoming one of America's wealthiest financiers. His specialty was in trading 'fallen angels', bonds issued by firms who had seen better days before getting into trouble. His real skill was in getting these deals fully syndicated.

'That's why they offer such exceptionally good returns,' Walker explained. 'People who get beyond the stigma of junk can make very handsome profits. Drexler have been getting more and more of these deals away, selling to portfolio managers all over the Street. They just can't get enough of them, and it's gonna get bigger and bigger. Junk is the biggest growth area for raising capital.'

There were a number of older heads on Wall Street who didn't wholly approve of the burgeoning trend, although they couldn't deny the enormous profits it was creating for Drexler Burnstone, or the massive riches for Walker who was conducting this orchestra.

Walker was a man who hated the day-to-day scrutiny and bureaucracy of a bustling Wall Street business, and it had been only a matter of time before he moved his junk bond operations team over to the West Coast and had set up a sumptuous office in Beverly Hills. His bosses could hardly argue as this division was accounting for ninety-five per cent of all the firm's profits. Lombardi kept in almost daily contact with him, aware that the younger man was moving faster than anyone else in the business.

It was rumoured that Vince had probably generated more wealth than any other broker or investment banker on the Street over the previous five years.

'I wanna get out of that place,' Lombardi said, sitting in a downtown hotel room with the curtains drawn.

'What, Chase Pacific?' Casper Franks sounded surprised. 'Are you serious, Goldman?'

'Lombardi,' Lex corrected him.

'Have you any idea what we had to go through to get you into that place?' Franks ignored his interruption. 'Do you have any idea how much it costs to give someone like you a new life? We have used up a hell of a lot of our resources and string pulling to make this happen for you and we don't take kindly to being jerked around.'

'I'm not a company man, I guess,' Lex argued. He was aware just how much work must have gone into getting him a new identity backed up by a credible paper trail, complete with passport, driver's licence and bank accounts holding what was left of the Goldman fortune, but he didn't see why that didn't mean he could move forward as George Lombardi as long as he was discreet and moved in totally different circles. He didn't intend to stay in the one job for the rest of his life. 'They're all trying to play it safe in an unsafe world. Who are they kidding?'

'Shut the fuck up, Goldman,' Franks rasped. 'You came to us for protection and safety, so don't give me any shit about us putting you in a place that is too safe. How you want to take your career as George Lombardi from here is up to you, but don't fucking whine to me, because I'm not interested. To be honest, you are pretty expendable to us right now.'

There was something odd about Casper Franks that Lex had

never felt with any of the other CIA operatives he had come across. Franks was older than most, he was also leaner and meaner than any man he had ever met. His CIA role had him specialising in the witness protection programme and covert operations, which he never spoke about. However, he did seem very well briefed on the Colombian drug network, especially the Medellin Cartel. A couple of times Lex had tried to feed him false information and Franks had picked up on it instantly, immediately threatening to end their protection unless Lex stopped lying. Lex was beginning to wonder if he would have been safer taking his chances with men like Mudge and Flint; at least he knew where he stood with them. He had a horrible feeling that this agent knew more about his past than he had thought when he surrendered himself and asked for a new identity to escape from the IRA.

'You do whatever you think you should,' Franks snarled, 'but don't forget we own you and we can end the charade any time we want. Who the hell would know or care if George Lombardi disappeared off the face of the earth tomorrow?'

Vince had accepted Lex's invitation to stay over in Missouri eighteen months after their first meeting and was settled into the guest wing of the mansion.

'Nice place,' Vince said as they stood together on the terrace the first evening of his stay, looking out across the manicured estate. 'Must cost a fair bit to keep up.'

'It does,' Lex laughed at the young man's cheek. Vince reminded him of himself at that age, before he became so entangled in his own lies, ambitions and deceptions.

'Do they really pay you enough at Chase?'

'They pay me just enough.' Lex chose his words carefully.

'Enough doesn't sound like what you should be worth,' Vince said. 'How are you ever going to make big money if you're tied to a bunch of corporate wankers?'

Lex would have liked to have opened up and told Vince just how much money he had made and lost in his life, but he knew he could never do that. If even one person outside the CIA knew that George Lombardi was actually Lex Goldman, he would never be safe again. Innocent lives had been lost in the explosion in the Caribbean, and the CIA would never allow anyone to find out what they had done in exchange for the information he had given them. The darker side of CIA covert operations was not something the average US citizen would easily recognise or approve of having done in their name. If the CIA thought he had blown his cover they would terminate him rather than take the risk of him talking. That was if Flint and his men didn't get to him first.

'Why don't you do what I did?' Vince was still talking. 'Move away from all that red tape. You could do big trades for yourself. Set up an operation here, you have plenty of room. You'd never need to leave this pad to get round the clock access to all the major currency and commodity markets.'

All Lex's entrepreneurial instincts told him this was good advice. For the first few months at Chase Pacific he had enjoyed the challenge of connecting with the investment banking world, seeing it from the opposite side after so many years of being the client. He had also enjoyed the security of living under a new identity. But he had to admit that Vince's stunning success excited him and he liked the idea of emulating it, maybe even becoming involved with the younger man and his golden business circle. Great wealth could be accumulated in a short space of time with the right strategy on these fast moving, highly liquid markets.

Maybe he could make this the way to rebuild his lost fortunes and take responsibility for his own destiny again.

Lex installed a state-of-the-art dealing room in one of the grand rooms of the Missouri mansion and was trading within two weeks of making the decision. Screens lit up with various bank quotes as the split-second world of high stakes currency speculation took centre stage. First he built up long dollar positions against the yen and Swiss franc, holding his nerve when the positions looked like serious loss makers before eventually closing out for a big profit when his view was vindicated with a swift dollar rally.

Lex didn't bother to legally challenge the bank when they refused to settle his employment contract on the grounds of leaving with insufficient notice. He was consumed by the magic of the screens, and his knack for making the right call was raking in the profits, which more than recouped what it had cost him to get into this high stakes game for himself.

Days crashed into nights and back to days as the US markets closed to make way for early Asia prices and then on to European time, and back to New York opening. Having large margin accounts with all the main banks meant Lex could trade at any time, day or night. Over time, George Lombardi was becoming a major currency speculator in his own right, with the palatial mansion set-up allowing him to shun publicity and trade with anonymity. Every day he was on the phone to Vince in California, the two men breathless in recounting the deals of the previous day, telling each other of the bigger and bolder deals they were working on, constantly striving to make the next one better than the last.

At the same time as becoming firm friends, Vince was also

Lex's mentor in his new trading world. With his extensive banking connections he was able to provide Lex with invaluable market moving information. But on one particular trade Lex allowed his discipline to drop and let his sentiment take over. His very large 'short dollar' position had got out of hand with the dollar strengthening on the world's money markets. By doubling up his position he had made the situation far worse in the forlorn hope of breaking even. Now his exposure on these trading positions was growing more serious by the hour.

'Listen, man,' Lex confessed late one night when he and Vince were talking business gossip for the day. 'I've been running with some bad positions for the last few days. I got careless and lost my focus, I'm in for a very big hit.'

'Don't worry about it,' Vince dismissed his fears. 'You can make it back if you hold your nerve. Want to know what I do if some of my bonds look like they are going down the pan?'

'Sure.'

'I just reschedule the debt before any of them look like defaulting with higher yielding debt over a longer time period. . .just pushing the debt further into the future. I don't let them default, that's the secret! Whoever said necessity is the mother of invention, was spot on. Who can predict the future with any certainty? Nobody can!'

Lex hung up feeling elated. Vince was right, the money was pouring in at an unbelievable rate and this one bad position wasn't going to make him lose his nerve. He was becoming the master of his own universe again, and this time it was all legitimate. As George Lombardi he was going to experience again the feeling of power and the trappings of great wealth, and with his new identity secure he didn't have to keep looking over his shoulder, running and hiding.

Now with Vince Walker, the most powerful player on the Street by his side, what twists and turns could his life be about to take? Lex was soon to find out.

7

'Listen, pal, if I want any *fucking* advice, I'll ask my girlfriend, do you understand?'

Vince Walker had gone from normal conversation pitch to a screaming frenzy within two seconds. He was taking the urgent call on a speakerphone, so George Lombardi could hear clearly what was going on. Vince seemed suddenly unaware that George was in the room with him, completely wrapped up in his fury at what he was hearing. A minute earlier the two of them had been swapping jokes about mutual acquaintances on Wall Street and then the call had been put through. The caller had informed Vince that Drexler Burnstone had been left out of a major refinancing deal on a Leveraged Buy Out, and Vince did not take kindly to being dropped out of any big money-making opportunities.

George liked the fact that his friend trusted him enough to behave so openly in front of him. It was one of the reasons he came out to the mansion in Beverly Hills as often as he did, anxious to let Vince know how interested he was in being part of his world, wanting to win his confidence.

LBOs had become all the rage on Wall Street and every

investment banking firm wanted a piece of the action, having seen how much easy money Drexler Burnstone had been able to generate. As a result, the company's total dominance of the market had started to erode under the smooth, experienced and ruthless machines of the big name banks on the Street. Drexler was still the undoubted king of the junk bond business but it didn't have the market to itself any more, and that made Vince very angry. He wasn't happy being the biggest player in the business, he wanted to be the *only* player. He felt his personal fiefdom was being invaded by people who had previously looked down their noses at him, and it made him mad.

George had already got the message that he would only be invited to dine at Vince's banquet as long as he showed him total loyalty and never tried to eclipse him. Having seen the results that Vince was achieving, George was more than willing to give that loyalty, and was even happier to remain anonymously in the background. The last thing he wanted was the media trying to find out about his past. The moment they realised he didn't have one, they would never give up hunting.

No one from his previous identity meeting him now would have recognised him. In the months after Lex's 'death', while the CIA had kept him in hiding and tutored him in his new identity, he had lost nearly a quarter of his body weight. His face had grown gaunt, and in some ways more handsome. His hair had also started to grey, particularly the neatly trimmed beard and moustache that he now cultivated. He had known for some time that he was going to need to get glasses, so he made sure they were heavily rimmed and changed the shape of his face. He had gone from looking like a young man to becoming middle aged and distinguished in just a few months.

Given that he was now a mature man, he was surprised to

find how much he admired Vince. He had never before met someone in whom he was so willing to put all his faith. He had always prefered to be the one leading the field, but it seemed Vince was offering the impossible: a 'sure thing' bet.

George had watched enviously as Vince's golden circle of clients, all of them well-known takeover raiders and market participants, had made fortunes from the avalanche of innovative financial engineering and restructuring ideas that had been overrunning corporate America for most of the eighties. The media was giving Wall Street a lot of coverage and not just on the business pages. Not everyone was convinced that the trend was to the advantage of the targeted companies, and the editors were quick to dramatise events with screaming headlines like: 'The Greed of Wall Street', and 'America's Finest Drowning in Debt', but most people were just caught up in the casino-like atmosphere of telephone number profits and unquestioning optimism.

The sober, dissenting voices, however, had risen to such a pitch that Congress had found it necessary to respond to the increasing calls for regulation by selecting committees to closely monitor big deals as soon as they became public knowledge. Higher risk financings were throwing up some very exotic financial products, and teams of frighteningly young whiz-kid investment bankers and lawyers from the big Wall Street firms were treating America's blue chip companies as little more than personal playthings, crunching out opportunities to exploit break-up values and eye possible hostile takeover targets. As the months rolled by, George had allowed himself to become deeply involved, but with the financing structures growing more complex, along with the compulsory buy-backs of other syndicate members closing out stock positions, Vince was the only one who really knew what George's full exposure was at any given time.

Walker was the undisputed king of the jungle. His ability to syndicate massive junk bond placings meant his firm was the centre of the universe when a takeover bid or LBO target was being evaluated. Greenmailers and takeover artists were beating a path to his door in droves. The rocket fuel effect that his junk bond currency gave to corporate raiders was awesome, and Vince's slice of the action had staggered George. He was used to seeing big profits, but nothing like this. He could see that Vince knew exactly what he needed to do to keep the merry-go-round turning, allowing all the members of his circle to participate in other fundings, giving himself a huge and powerful network of inside information and ready buyers. Loyalty and these compulsory buybacks of other syndicate members closing out stock positions seemed to go hand in hand. It looked as if it was impossible for him to lose, and George loved that idea.

George had been used to living with wealth from as early as he could remember, but he was still impressed when he first arrived at Vince's palatial mansion in Beverly Hills. Vince had sent his personal Gulfstream jet to bring him over for a meeting, and a Rolls-Royce had been waiting on the tarmac when he disembarked. The mansion was an imitation of a Tuscan palace, and the glamour of the place stretched all the way to the towering gates. A long drive was lined with Renaissance statues imported from Italy. A butler was waiting at the bottom of the house steps to open the car door and escort him up through the front door into the first hall. Pools of light on the terracotta walls lit up a collection of Renoirs and Monets, many of which George recognised. The whole collection must have been put together over a number of years, and every one of the pictures would have cost Vince millions. The furniture looked mostly eighteenth-century French and had obviously been sourced at enormous expense, along with the Persian rugs scattered across the flagstones.

'You must have a whole team sourcing for you,' he said as Vince led him through room after room, airily waving at one masterpiece after another.

'About a hundred of them dotted around the globe,' Vince agreed. 'Sotheby's, Christie's, they all come running when someone like me emerges. They think . . .' he stopped for a moment and confided with a smirk, 'that they'll get their commission off me while I'm on the way up, and they'll get another bite of the cherry when I overreach myself and go belly up and have to sell the lot. Fortunes come and fortunes go, but these bastards score their percentage every time. But they've met their match in me. This collection will still be in one piece the day I finally kiss this life goodbye.'

'It's amazing what you have achieved here over the years,' George said as the tour of the mansion continued.

'This is only the beginning,' Vince grinned. 'I'm still young, if I can do this in a few years, imagine what I will be able to do in a few decades!'

'It's fantastic,' George purred, unable to hide his admiration. So few people had impressed him in recent years, but this guy was special.

'It will be,' Vince said. 'You should come along for the ride.'

'I'd like to.'

As the months passed, their relationship grew and Vince convinced George into taking on commitments for more and more junk bond placings. George was aware of the irony in allowing himself to be so heavily influenced by a younger man when he had spent so many years struggling to dominate everyone he came into contact with.

Not only did George see that Vince held the key to him rebuilding his fortune, he believed that by doing it Vince's way he could multiply it far further and far faster than he could ever have done in the past. Dealing in junk bonds was going to open up a treasure trove that could better any fortunes that had come before.

The other benefit of doing business with Vince was that it took his mind off the emptiness in his personal life. If ever an uncomfortable memory threatened to surface during the night, he could always go back to his dealing room and make calls to Vince. The global markets were open twenty-four hours a day and Vince only seemed to sleep for the odd hour here and there, keeping himself going on a diet of amphetamines and alcohol. Keeping up with Vince had added to the changes in George's appearance, making him seem thinner and more tightly wired. He found it was quite possible to forget how lonely he felt when he was in the middle of a deal and the figures were flying around, the phones ringing and the adrenaline flowing. Pushing the boundaries of what was possible and making big amounts in minutes was better than sex – or so he told himself.

Sometimes both of them would be exploding with so much adrenaline and energy that they would want to break out of their luxurious surroundings and spend some of the profits they could see racking up. Vince would usually be the one to suggest a celebration.

'I'm sending Air Force One to collect ya,' he would announce down the line in his New York drawl, 'we're going to party.'

The Gulfstream would arrive at an airport near to George's estate and would then head on to Vegas or Atlantic City, where Vince and other members of his golden circle would gather at the best hotels to gamble and drink and let off steam with the party girls provided by the management. Everyone in Vince's circle was male and fired with the same urge for world domination, and none of them had ever been so rich. They would boast and laugh and compare deals late into the night, no one ever actually mentioning the fact that the whole edifice might be balanced on mountains of paper and promises, like castles built on sand.

'We should do this more often,' Vince announced as they sat round a dinner table in the Venetian in Las Vegas. George had been introduced to the other men at the table. He knew they were all part of Vince's inner circle and were dealers responsible for some of the biggest corporate takeovers in America, but he knew nothing about any of their private lives. 'Why don't we take a weekend away?'

'Sure,' the others all nodded their agreement. No one wanted to disagree with Vince; there was too much to be gained by agreeing. 'Great idea, Vince.'

'We could go to the Caymans for the weekend,' he went on. 'That would be cool. I could see if Barry wants to come.'

'Barry LaVine?' one of the others asked.

George pricked up his ears. Everyone in the financial markets had heard about LaVine. He worked for Booker Lynch and was inextricably linked with Vince, they all knew that, although no one could be quite sure exactly what they were up to. LaVine was a figure of considerable mystery on Wall Street, revered, envied and feared in equal measure. George looked forward to meeting him.

LaVine and Walker were at the villa in the Caymans the night before the others were being flown down. However much Vince valued George and the other members of the golden circle, it was Barry LaVine who held the key to everything he needed. Between them they were amassing extraordinary riches.

'Who's this George Lombardi?' LaVine asked as the two of them sat on the deck gazing out to sea past the masts of the boats moored below. 'His name keeps coming up but I can't seem to find any trace of him.'

'He's very private,' Vince shrugged. 'Never really talks about his past. I never really ask him.'

'Sure,' LaVine could believe that, Vince was always too busy talking to ever want to give the floor over to anyone else. 'It might be an idea to know more about him.'

'All you need to know is that he's one of us. He wants to be part of the golden circle and he knows what it takes to stay there.'

'So you vouch for him?'

'Yeah,' Vince waved away the other man's doubts, 'he's sound. He wants to be part of the action.'

The next day Walker's Gulfstream brought the rest of the guests including Lombardi down to the islands and they were driven straight to the yacht that was going to take them out to sea for complete privacy. LaVine was just as loud and brash as George had expected. He knew that Barry LaVine lay at the centre of virtually every deal any of them had been involved with. For the first part of the day he hung back, watching and listening, trying to get the measure of the man and work out how he could best use him to further his own goals.

After lunch, as the heat of the sun increased, many of the other men began to doze on deck. George was sitting a little apart from the others and watched through his shades as LaVine made his way over, trying to give the impression he was just taking in the views of the islands as the yacht glided past them.

'Great boat,' George said, just to let LaVine know he was awake.

'You got one of your own?' LaVine asked.

'Not at the moment.'

'Lombardi, isn't it?' He extended a hand for shaking. George noticed how bony it was and how tense the grip. 'Vince's mentioned you.'

George nodded without saying anything, waiting to see what LaVine would say next. He said nothing, settling himself into a lounger alongside and lying back as if intending to rest. Eventually he broke the silence.

'I work with Vince a lot, he's a great guy.'

'Yeah.' George was still determined to give nothing away. Vince had already told him about his links with LaVine and how LaVine ran secret accounts for him and his close associates, some through a web of banks spread round the islands, in return for highly profitable junk bond and stock option bundling. They were all banks that were known for not asking awkward questions of their clients. George wanted to be part of the same package, but he didn't want to let LaVine know how much he wanted it, not yet.

By the time the yacht was drifting back towards the docks, with the sun setting behind it, George had managed to coax LaVine into inviting him to become part of his network. Their plan was for him to use George's bank accounts with a power of attorney for market sensitive trades. The agreement was sealed with another firm handshake on deck before they went ashore for a lavish dinner at the villa.

George was well aware that trading shares on inside information was technically against the law, although he had no idea of the extent of LaVine and Walker's activities, but so what? He couldn't remember the last person prosecuted for such a crime. Who cared if a few wealthy investors made money from bits of gossip passed around their own social circle? Like Vince and

LaVine, George saw the lawmakers as small-time pen-pushers. His group moved in a different orbit, beyond the realms of such petty considerations, and were creating a whole new universe of financial possibilities, which ordinary mortals like law enforcement officers couldn't hope to understand. He felt he was once again rising above the reach of rules that governed the lives of ordinary people.

'So,' Vince sat back on his dining-room throne in the Beverly Hills mansion, once he had finished screaming down the phone at the bearer of bad news, and sucked contentedly on a Havana cigar, 'where were you before Chase Pacific?'

For a second George was taken by surprise. Vince never usually showed any interest in anyone's past, only their potential for future wealth creation. He gathered his thoughts quickly, remembering the long hours of briefings he had endured with Casper Franks after the highly publicised demise of Lex Goldman.

'I worked privately,' he said, mirroring Vince's relaxed body language and puffing on his own cigar.

'How do you mean?'

'I mean I worked privately for clients I'm not allowed to talk about.'

Vince gave a lizard-like smile. 'Aw come on, buddy, you can tell me, just between friends.'

George wetted his lips from his brandy glass before replying. 'Would you want to be in business with someone who might one day betray your secrets to another "friend"?'

Vince's eyes narrowed even further than usual as he squinted at George through a cloud of smoke. 'You are so damned right,' he drawled eventually. 'Discretion. Shit, that's the only position to work from.'

George said nothing, taking another sip from his brandy glass.

'But your accent,' Vince continued after a few moments, 'doesn't sound American.'

'My family travelled a lot when I was young. Children adapt to fit in with their peers and surroundings.'

Vince nodded thoughtfully. 'You like your privacy, don't you, George? I noticed you don't like talking to the financial journalists.'

'I leave that sort of thing to you,' George laughed. 'You're the showman here – the star of the Street!'

Vince grinned with pleasure at the suggestion.

'I'd like to be involved in more of your syndications, Vince,' George went on after a while, not bothering to add that his reason for wanting to be more involved was to try to subsidise some of the terrible losses he'd been racking up in the currency markets.

Vince and LaVine had managed to cast such a glow of confidence over all who surrounded them that it was easy to assume it was safe to hold on tight to their coat-tails. The short dollar position that had first caused George to worry eventually had to be closed out, and the loss made him think that currency trading was no longer the business for him.

'Cutting profits early and running with losses is a common mistake people make with currency speculation,' Vince consoled him. 'No amount of reserves can neutralise that failing.'

'I don't want to take any more losses,' George said. 'I don't have time for it. I want out of that and into more of your high yielding stuff.'

'Wise move, old buddy,' Vince nodded sagely. 'Currency speculation can be very risky. Better to gamble on sure things. Stick with me and you'll stay hot on the money.'

George was sure he was right. Vince was generating such huge returns on his deals through his virtual monopoly on junk bond syndications. As George subscribed for more of these junk bond new issues it meant his cash reserves were being called on at a scary rate but, he told himself, as soon as the boom in takeovers began to ebb he would withdraw part of his fortune and diversify again. But for now he was going to put all his faith in Vince and his golden touch.

'No one makes a fortune without having faith in their instincts,' Vince would say at moments when George needed his nerves soothing. 'Your instincts are amongst the best, trust them, follow them, don't betray them.'

He had a way of making it sound like the only thing in the world to do.

There had been a number of meetings at the Securities Exchange Commission to discuss the explosion in junk bond debt and particularly the rising fortunes of Vince Walker and Barry LaVine.

'Maybe they are just a bunch of very skilled operators,' someone round the table suggested. 'They do their research well and they have their ear to the ground, so hey, they are able to predict what is happening.'

'With such deadly accuracy?' Phil Brown interrupted testily. 'No one is that skilled. Every time they position into stocks, sooner or later there is a corporate announcement that multiplies the value of their stake out of all recognition. Every time.'

He slammed his fist down on the table. He had been trying to draw his colleagues' attention to the notion that these stars of Wall Street were actually just trading on inside information, cashing in on their privileged access, which in his eyes made them no better than crooks. But everyone else seemed to be so in awe of the size of the fortunes Walker and LaVine and their cronies were building up that they were hesitant to step forward and challenge them.

'Men like this could tie us up in the courts for years,' his boss had told Phil the first time he went to him with his suspicions. 'For Christ's sake, you're calling the whole credibility of Wall Street into question. You will need to have a cast-iron case before you go after these guys. They have virtually unlimited funds.'

The very idea that anyone could be considered above the law because of the size of their wealth was enough to send Brown straight back to his research, certain that if he could just make enough connections he would be able to prove his case. Everyone at the SEC knew this had become his obsession, so when an anonymous call came through the switchboard, wanting to impart information about some insider dealing scam, it was routed straight to Phil's desk.

'Who's calling?' he enquired.

'You need to look closer at the trading going on over at Booker Lynch,' the voice said.

'I would be interested to hear about anything you might know.' Phil's heartbeat quickened. The voice sounded authoritative, not like a crank. This man might not want to give his name yet, but he wanted to give information.

He convinced the caller to meet up in an anonymous coffee shop in mid-Manhattan. When he got there the man's appearance was as impressive as his voice, five thousand dollar suit, thousand dollar shoes and a tie from Hermes. He was obviously someone of substance and, more importantly, someone who understood the workings of Wall Street. Only on their third meeting, however, did Phil manage to elicit the information that his informant was a star trader from one of the rival brokerage houses on the Street. By that time he had managed to win the man's trust and a promise that he would step forward and give evidence if Phil managed to get the case to court.

'These guys need to be stopped,' his informant said. 'Otherwise they could end up bringing the whole of Wall Street down. It could be worse than the great crash.'

'What you need to do,' LaVine lowered his voice and leant close to George's ear, ignoring the food on the plate the waiter had just placed in front of him, 'is open a string of stock and bank accounts, and then sign power of attorney over them to me. You will be cut in for a large slice of the action and no one gets hurt! I'll handle all the introductions you need. Then you leave the rest to me.'

LaVine knew from Vince that the one thing George Lombardi liked was his privacy. He didn't know what it was in this man's past that made him so keen to keep it shrouded in secrecy, but he didn't care. All that interested him was what use he could make of George's urge to remain in the shadows. He had worked hard to win the man's trust and respect, now he felt he was in a position to make his offer.

They were sitting at the best table in La Grande Terrasse flagship restaurant of the Palace Hotel in Gstaad, one of Switzerland's finest mountain resorts. Vince had organised the trip at the last minute as he always did in these cases, ringing his closest colleagues and telling them that his jet would be picking them up and whisking them off. Places like Monaco or Mustique, Saint Tropez or Venice were typical locations, or sometimes the crowd just went for a golfing weekend at Pine Hills in New England or Bear Creek in California. No one amongst the inner circle ever turned down any of the invitations because the information passing amongst the other guests was always worth too much to be missed.

The snow-covered mountains provided a picture postcard backdrop and both men were wearing dark glasses to protect against the dazzling white glare, which made it harder for George to read LaVine's expressions. The other members of the group had gone off skiing but he had been intrigued by LaVine's invitation to stay at the hotel for a private lunch. Vince had already tested him on the idea of allowing Barry LaVine to use his accounts, in exchange for a cut and a massive fee. Vince had guessed correctly that George was now so entwined with him financially that he would be willing to take this extra risk, especially if it helped to swell his own wealth.

LaVine fell silent, concentrating on his eating, leaving George to mull over his thoughts. As he sat back, he savoured the special atmosphere. Looking round the grand room, its buffet table laden with silver dishes of food from every corner of the earth, the sun glinting on his cut crystal champagne glass, George realised he was an addict. He was addicted to the lure of money and he was greedy for the luxury that came with it. He knew LaVine was one of *the* men of the moment, a big winner, as were all of Vince's friends, and he was back amongst them. He had struggled clear of the sleaze of drug running and arms deals, and he was now sitting in splendour at the top of a Swiss mountain resort with the whole world at his feet. It was an intoxicating feeling. LaVine didn't need to say another word, he knew he'd made his pitch perfectly and that George was going to play the game his way.

'It seems you're gaining support in high places.' Phil Brown's boss at the SEC had arrived in his office unexpectedly.

'Yeah?' Phil decided to play dumb.

'I'm getting pressure from Congress to take an active interest in all this junk bond financing. They seem to be worried about these debt instruments your friend Walker has spawned. They don't like the way they seem to be so central in all these takeovers. They're getting jumpy. These takeovers are getting too big for comfort, especially when they all seem to be financed with junk. They think they may need to bring in regulation. There's some real heat coming from Washington over this issue.'

'They should be jumpy,' Phil agreed. 'The whole thing is like a pack of cards just waiting to collapse. Every time a major corporate news headline breaks, if you look back over the preceding days you can see massive movement in their stock. Someone is dealing in information and dealing big.'

'Well, let's see if we can bring it under control without toppling the whole of Wall Street.'

'Can't promise that,' Phil muttered, but his boss chose to ignore him.

Now that he was beginning to understand how the myriad paper trails and stock deal funds sluicing around the banking system worked for people like Walker and LaVine, George was becoming painfully aware of just how primitive his own system had been when he had been involved with the IRA and the Calis in Colombia. The speed and sophistication of LaVine's transactions took his breath away as he watched them flash through his accounts, and he wanted to understand the complexity of it all as completely as LaVine. This was money laundering *par excellence*.

George wasn't the only one wanting to be part of the action. Virtually every investment banker on Wall Street could see that

LaVine and his cronies were onto something big. Two young traders at a firm of executing brokers called Lexington Securities who were handling some of their stock orders noticed a pattern of winning lucrative trades on orders originating from particular Bank of Nassau accounts. They began to piggyback on these transactions for their own personal accounts. The bubble was inflating every hour of every day.

The guys from Lexington were brash and hungry and did not share George Lombardi's need for anonymity. Celebrating another day of heavy trading and even more chunky profits, they took over Le Cirque restaurant on Madison Avenue, a favourite haunt of the Wall Street crowd, and ordered the best champagne in the house to be served at their table, regardless of cost. They soon attracted a group of other traders also out on the town. As the night wore on, their chatter, fuelled by the alcohol and sumptuous surroundings, quickly led to their boasting becoming louder and less discreet. The star trader who had been briefing Phil Brown was seated at a nearby table and was soon able to hear clearly what they were saying.

Listening to their boasting opened up wounds from his own past. He remembered when he was a young trader at Booker Lynch, having to listen to LaVine crowing when he was picked to head up the new mortgage department they had set up in the early eighties. It should have been his job, but when the burgeoning market proved to be one of the most profitable on Wall Street for banks and traders alike, it was LaVine who had become the golden boy, and he had missed his chance. He could still taste the bitterness that had been with him when he left Booker Lynch, even though he had gone on to greater things at another investment bank on the Street. Having to listen to how his old rival was now making the biggest killings in history, and from the mouths of such foolish kids, ruined his evening. When he got home that night, still burning with resentment, he dialled the private number that Phil had given him.

'Sorry to ring you so late . . .'

'I told you,' Phil said, suddenly awake, 'any time.'

The trader reported what he had overheard in the restaurant.

'You should do something to stop this guy,' he said. 'Show you have some teeth. He's laughing at you.'

The next day Phil took this latest report to his boss, along with the dossier he had been compiling for months. His boss nodded him to a seat and started reading there and then.

'Jesus fucking Christ,' he said before he had even got past the first page. 'No one has ever had the balls to manipulate the market like these guys have been doing.'

Phil said nothing, relieved that at last he was being taken seriously. His boss kept reading with one eye, while making calls at the same time, setting wheels in motion.

'There are endless examples of sudden stock price movements and with big volumes traded,' he told someone, 'before deals are announced, linked back to positions of specific related parties. In other cases, there has been concerted build up of stock positions to weaken target companies' managements, and we can see a lot of examples of stock option entitlements being linked to junk bond investments. It all leads back to Drexler Burnstone, and specifically to Walker. We've got him.'

Phil smiled to himself. The ball was rolling now. Nothing was going to stop it.

The first inkling George had that something was up was when he saw Vince being escorted from his mansion on television. The report was sketchy, the news anchor obviously unsure what it was exactly that Vince was being accused of, just aware that it was a big scandal story with huge financial implications. They were already labelling it 'the biggest corruption investigation in history'. George felt a cold chill running through him as his brain raced ahead, trying to retrace which trails might lead investigators to him from Vince and thinking how to close them. All his fears regarding the extent of his exposure rose up to haunt him, making him feel nauseous.

He felt totally vulnerable and isolated. All his cash was now caught up in the web that surrounded LaVine and Walker, even his Signal Hill mansion had been leveraged in the frenetic junk bond activity. He was desperate to think how he could access the bank accounts that he had given LaVine a proxy over before the authorities started freezing or seizing everything they found. If that happened it might be years before he was able to get them released, assuming all their fortunes didn't evaporate during the scandal.

A few hours later the news channels were reporting that Vince had been released on a ten million dollar bail. George immediately started dialling. It was another two hours before he finally got through to him. His voice sounded just the same. There was no sign of panic. He was laughing at it all.

'Keep cool, man,' he counselled. 'They're beginning to realise who they're dealing with. It may take a few weeks, but this will all go away, believe me.'

For about a day George did believe him, because it was always hard to doubt Vince when he was doing his sincere bit. He still tried to find ways to disentangle his bank accounts from LaVine's grip but it was impossible. The following day he received a call from another member of Walker's golden circle.

'Vince's offering up LaVine as the fall guy,' he said without even bothering to introduce himself. 'Anyone connected to LaVine is going to lose everything.'

'What do you mean?' George wanted to know more, but the line had gone dead. He flashed through the television channels until he found a news bulletin reporting on the arrest of LaVine from his residence. Now the reporters were getting a better understanding of how the world of junk bonds operated and how insiders had been able to make fortunes by buying and selling shares on privileged information tips.

George tried phoning anyone he knew who was connected to Vince and LaVine, but most of them were no longer answering their phones. These two golden boys had suddenly turned into pariahs. It was soon obvious Drexler Burnstone, with all its assets frozen and effectively unable to trade, was going to have to file for bankruptcy.

It was only a matter of time before the SEC discovered the web of bank and stock accounts in Nassau, and there was nothing George could do to get any money transferred out without LaVine's help. His only chance of staying out of jail himself was to deny all knowledge of the activity on the accounts, leaving LaVine to take the rap since he was the one with power of attorney over them. Initially the thought of losing his newly won fortune made him feel physically sick, but he quickly started to rationalise the move. It was better to be broke than to be in jail. He had been down before and managed to rebuild his fortune, he would just have to do it again. He was angry with himself as much as with Vince or LaVine. He should have guessed it was all too good to be true. If he had learned one lesson in his business life it was that you never put all your eggs in one basket, and that's exactly what he'd gone and done. He had been naïve and greedy and he had paid a heavy price. Looking back now he couldn't think how he could have been so trusting of Vince and LaVine when it was so obvious that they were both men who were out for themselves and nothing more, but then hindsight is always twenty-twenty, he knew that. He could have been angry with Vince and LaVine for leading him astray, but that would have been foolish. He was an experienced man who knew the way the world worked and he had allowed his greed to get the better of him yet again.

He was now left with a feeling of emptiness as the realisation sunk in that all the people he had been communicating with on an almost daily basis over the last three years were now gone. Even if they hadn't been arrested they were still not answering their phones. The golden circle had gone to ground. As his anger subsided, his survival instincts cut in. He put in a coded call to Special Agent Colby at CIA headquarters in Langley.

An anonymous voice called him back a few hours later and gave him a hotel location and room number to go to. When he got there he found Casper Franks waiting.

'I need you to intervene with the SEC for me,' George announced, seeing that Franks wasn't in the mood for pleasantries. 'I have some accounts in Nassau, which are caught up with the Barry LaVine investigation. You'll have to extricate the money for me.'

'And why should we do that for you?' Franks' voice was level but it was obvious he was having trouble controlling his anger.

'Because if I get involved I could blow my cover.'

'You arrogant shit!' Franks hissed. 'What makes you think we are going to lift one tiny finger to help you out of a mess you've got yourself into. Have you any idea how many man hours and how many taxpayers' dollars went into setting you up with this identity? And you endanger the whole thing for a few quick bucks.'

'More than a few, Franks, I think you'll find.'

Casper's fist crashed into his jaw, sending him spinning across the room. 'Shut up, you fuck!' he snarled.

The blow released all the anger that George had been keeping tightly contained while he struggled to retain control of his life. He leapt back at Franks and managed to land a punch on his shoulder. But Franks was fitter and better trained and brought his knee up into George's groin, sending him back down to the floor, punctuating his next sentence with a vicious kick between each word.

'Don't . . . ever . . . ask . . . us . . . for . . . another . . . fuckin' . . . thing. You . . . are . . . on . . . your . . . own . . . again . . . you . . . fuckin' . . . scumbag.'

He left the room without bothering to wait for an answer from George, who remained prone on the floor, groaning. Through a haze of pain George watched Franks' highly shined shoes as he let himself out and felt a surge of hate. He had felt something cold about this man from the first time he'd met him. He seemed like someone who had a lot to hide, a position George understood completely. He had assumed it must be because of his work. Making covert operations in the CIA a career, he thought, was bound to have made him a secretive and sinister character, but he had met enough people in that line of work to know that there was something else, something deeper that Franks was covering up. George's instincts told him everything about this CIA agent just didn't add up.

Wanting to get as far away from the media and the authorities as possible, George hired an anonymous looking car and headed south. Driving in a daze, sleeping whenever he became too tired to continue, not really knowing where he was going, he ended up on Sanibel Island, off the Florida Gulf coast. He arrived too late to book into a hotel and ended up walking the beach as the horizon began to lighten, trying to get his thoughts in order, his mind drunk with tiredness.

The sea was lapping gently against the pure white sands, the only sounds the cries of the herons and gulls as they stirred from their slumbers. Staring out across the water, feeling the sand between his toes and watching the sunrise, he felt an enormous lifting in his heart. Even though he'd lost everything, he was still standing on a beautiful beach at dawn, able to breathe the fresh air. He had come so close to imprisonment he had begun to fear the whole game was over for him.

Taking in a deep lungful of fresh salty air he allowed his mind to wander back over the previous three years, and everything that had happened in his life before that. He smiled at the thought of just how often he had managed to overcome adversities that would have destroyed most men. He remembered Vince making a gag about Wall Street having a graveyard at one end and a river at the other; at least his brush with the 'Money Street' hadn't buried him. With each disaster he had learnt something knew and come out stronger for the experience. From hanging with LaVine and Walker he understood better now how the really big money got laundered and had collected some top banking contacts with establishments who were more interested in how much money he could deposit rather than wanting to know where it came from.

As the sun started to rise above the horizon, he felt a new dawn rising. So far his life had been an amazing roller-coaster of highs and lows and it wasn't going to stop now. He had developed a new set of skills and had a valuable network of banking contacts to sell. There was only one destination he had in mind if he was to cash in big on its full money making potential . . . Colombia!

8

George had done his research, a lot of it, and he still wasn't sure how much of what he had found out about Pablo Ramos Rodriguez was true and how much was part of a carefully constructed myth. Many of the most colourful tales could have been invented deliberately by Rodriguez and his allies, or could have been spread by his enemies in order to try to do him harm. There had been too many years of lies and cover-ups to be able to untangle it completely, but he had discovered enough to know that anyone who came too close to 'Ramrod' Rodriguez was living dangerously, and many of them didn't live for long.

He had first heard the name a few years earlier, when he had spent time with Juan and Garcia in Colombia. The Cartel de Medellin were the Cali Cartel's biggest rival when it came to the domination of the Colombian drugs industry, and when talking about Rodriguez both Juan and Garcia wavered between hero worship and a cautious contempt. They saw him as the most powerful man in the country, but at the same time, in their more arrogant, drug-fuelled moments, they would boast that he and his entire cartel were now 'yesterday's men', that soon the Cali Cartel would be running him out of business.

'Ramrod has no idea how well connected we are,' Juan told him one evening when they had been killing time together in a hut in the jungle. 'He is an old-fashioned leader. He believes he is all-powerful and doesn't need to make alliances with anyone else in order to keep his position. We think differently. We understand that you need to work with the politicians, with the Americans, even the CIA, and you need to be diplomats as well as businessmen. He's just a gangster, who loves money and women too much.'

'And himself,' Garcia added, spitting on the floor to show what he thought of such vanity.

The fact that they thought him to be 'just a gangster' didn't stop them telling tales of Ramrod's infamous past like star-struck schoolboys, many of which had passed into folklore, illustrating his immense power, his ruthlessness and his extravagant tastes.

'The guy still makes over a million dollars a day,' Garcia shrugged when George pointed out their apparent admiration. 'He's not stupid!'

'How do you know so much about him?' George had asked.

'There's a guy called Lopez, very close to Ramrod,' Garcia explained. 'He is the uncle of one of the guys who pilots us.'

It had turned out they were talking about the pilot who had crash-landed them in El Paso, and who they had executed. George had made a mental note of the name 'Lopez' at the time, as he did with every scrap of information Juan and Garcia had let slip during their time together. You never knew when these tiny jigsaw pieces would fit together to make a picture.

Not wanting to rely on what seemed to be little more than gossip, George hired James Friar, a researcher who was an expert on the narcotics industry, to put together a report for him on Rodriguez and the Medellin Cartel. James brought the finished document to him personally. They met in a hotel in New York, and James had no idea who George was. The anonymous businessman had paid him a large enough fee for him to avoid the need to ask too many questions.

'Thank you,' George said when the report was handed to him. 'I look forward to reading it. Can you give me a verbal précis?'

'Sure.' James never needed to be asked twice to talk about his favourite subject. He had been studying the drug cartels in Colombia ever since he was at university; it was a subject that obsessed him. 'You want me to start at the beginning?'

George nodded and smiled encouragingly.

'Well, Rodriguez started at the bottom of the pile. His family were the poorest of the poor, dirt farmers without enough land to support them. He was always brighter than his siblings, and while they all scraped and scratched at the soil in the hope they could make a living, he went off to the city – Medellin – and started hustling. You've seen thousands of boys like him in every third world city; begging, stealing, selling their bodies, doing little drug deals, cleaning windscreens at traffic lights, you get the picture. His specialities were stealing cars and selling smuggled cigarettes. Even by the age of fourteen he was known to have killed people. While most of those street kids end up being killed themselves, he soon showed he was a survivor, tougher than all the others, more ruthless. There's a story that he stole tombstones from the local cemeteries, sandblasted them back to the stone and sold them on to smugglers from Panama.'

George laughed. He liked the sound of the young Rodriguez. It was the sort of thing he could have imagined himself doing if he had ever been that desperate for money. 'So how did he get into drugs?'

'They all get into drugs. Drugs are the currency on the streets, in the prisons, everywhere that a boy like that would be. Most of them just stick to using the stuff and selling it at street level, but Rodriguez had a career plan. The Cartel de Medellin was by far the biggest cartel in the country at the time, and they were always on the look out for young talent. A boy who was willing to kill and do whatever was needed was valuable to them, so they started to give him bigger jobs to do. Once he'd got a position in the organisation he started to play the politics, just as ruthlessly as he played the street scams. He hitched his wagon to the right people at the top of the organisation and he set about eliminating anyone who got in his way.

'He made himself an incredibly popular figure locally by putting money into the right pockets, building sports fields for local kids, helping the poor with food hand-outs, you know the kind of thing. The local church is in his debt and so the people worship at his shrine. At the same time he also gained a bit of a reputation as a ladies' man, always out in the clubs at night. His own drug use gave him the energy to party all hours. People began to believe he didn't need to sleep at all. He was and still is the ultimate party animal. By the time he was in his thirties he was the undisputed leader of the cartel and now he is the biggest landowner in the country, most of the land turned over to drug cultivation. No one in the area could or would stand up against him. Anyone who tried to was butchered. He is ruthless and probably the richest individual in the country.'

'But?' George prompted as James paused to sip his coffee.

'But he is essentially just a vicious peasant, and there are smarter, more educated operators in the field now like the Cali Cartel. These people are better connected internationally, better contacts politically and have better banking connections for money laundering. They behave more like a multinational corporation.

Ramrod is beginning to look old fashioned, like Al Capone beside Coca-Cola.'

George laughed. 'Sounds like Rodriguez needs a better team of advisers.'

'He probably does, but would he listen to them? And would anyone who knew anything about his past want to risk getting close? It's beginning to look as if the Cali Cartel intend to wipe him out.'

'How would they do that?'

'Many ways, but the one that would worry him the most would be if they were feeding information about his operations to the Colombian Government and the drug enforcement agencies.'

George fell silent. He could feel the adrenaline pulsing in his veins as he contemplated the risks he was planning to expose himself to.

'And where does he spend most of his time?'

'He moves about a lot, as you can imagine. But he bases his headquarters at Los Olivos, a heavily fortified ranch outside Medellin.'

As the plane from Miami came in to land at José Maria Córdova Airport, George was able to see the metropolis of Medellin sprawling out along the valley below. The plane dropped below the mountains and some of the shanty areas came into sharp perspective. What had looked like a long-lost Shangri-La from a distance started to look like something else, something far less idyllic. As the plane taxied to a halt there was still the promise of the lush greenery stretching up into the mountains from the other side of the perimeter fences, but the moment the door of the plane was thrown open the stifling heat fell over him like a blanket, sucking the air from his lungs. There was a light breeze as he stepped onto the steps, but it did nothing to cool the air, merely filling it with swirling eddies of dust that stuck to his teeth and his eyes, drawing the sweat from his skin.

He had booked himself into the Nutibar Hotel situated near the Plaza Bolivar, one of the city centre landmarks. The building was inconspicuous, exactly as he wanted to be himself as he got used to the lie of the land and found his way around. Knowing as much as he did about who ran the city, he could almost feel Rodriguez's presence in the heat. Once he had settled himself in he started to stroll around the streets, staying close to the walls to avoid the sun, his eyes covered by Ray Bans so that no one could see them flickering into every corner that he passed, scanning every face for clues. He was beginning to have doubts about the wisdom of his mission. What made him think he could track down a man in a place like this when all he knew about him was that his name was Lopez? How many men must there be by that name in a city of two million souls?

It wasn't hard to see how near the surface of the city's life the drug culture lay. In cafes and bars frequented by the wealthy, there were all the trappings of easy money easily spent. The designer clothes and expensive cars, all lovingly pressed and polished, seemed out of kilter with the grime and poverty all around. In the roughest areas young boys scratched livings in exactly the same way Ramrod had at their age, chirping and hissing their various offers at strangers. Even though he hugged the shadows and kept his eyes hidden, George still attracted a small crowd of followers, keen to sell him whatever he could be persuaded to buy. They ebbed and flowed in his wake, sometimes just one or two of them, sometimes half a dozen, all talking at once, all wheedling and charming him in their different ways. Sometimes they would squabble amongst themselves, snapping and snarling like hungry young dogs around a juicy bone. All the time he kept silent and kept walking, giving no clues as to what he was looking for, sweating uncomfortably.

Eventually, standing on the edge of a busy square, feeling safer, he paused and turned to the boys.

'Where is Lopez?' he asked in his best Spanish.

'I'm Lopez,' several of the boys said, grinning proudly.

George shrugged, as if he had given them a chance to earn a few pesos and they had wasted it. He turned and walked off. Some of the boys kept on his heels while others gave up and vanished into the side streets. He stopped for a rest and a beer in a roadside cafe, and the waiter shooed the rest of the urchins away.

Over the following week he repeated the exercise dozens of times. He would walk the streets, asking for Lopez. Some of the boys who had heard him asking the same question over and over decided he was mad and started to throw taunts at him as they ran alongside. Now and then he would hand out small amounts of money and the taunts would stop for a while.

'You want to meet Lopez?' a small voice asked one evening, just as he was going back into his hotel after another fruitless day of searching.

'You know him?' George asked, without much hope in his voice. As the days had passed he had realised just how slim a hope it was.

'He's my uncle,' the boy said and George smiled. God alone knew how many boys had uncles called Lopez.

'Does he know important people?' George asked.

The boy ignored the question. 'He is sometimes at the *Lambalas*.'

'What is the *Lambalas*?'

'A bar.'

'Where is it?'

'I can show you.'

George's heartbeat quickened as he strode out behind the small boy, only partly due to the pace he was forced to take, despite the heat. His little guide headed off down side streets so narrow and filthy George would not have thought to step into them on his own. He was aware that if a group of street boys sprang on him now he would have little hope of escaping. He guessed that if he just gave them all the money he was carrying they might spare his life. He had to trust someone, why not this kid? It was a risk, but nothing was ever gained without a risk.

'*Los Lambalas*,' the boy said eventually, nodding towards a narrow, unlit doorway, hung with beads. On either side there were heavily framed windows, the glass black with dirt and age.

'Thanks.' George gave him a five dollar bill and the boy smiled happily, revealing a row of rotted stumps where there should have been sparkling new teeth.

Determined not to show his fear, George pushed his way through the beads, waiting for a second for his eyes to accustom to the gloom. A few men sat at a table at the far end of the room and looked up at him through a fog of cigarette smoke without even trying to hide their aggression. The barman was leaning on the counter, as if he had been talking to them before the unwanted interruption. The feeling of being an outsider, stepping into a world where he knew none of the rules, reminded him of the first time he stepped into the pub in Kilburn and entered Sophie's other world.

Ignoring the open hostility, he bought a beer and sat down at the opposite end of the room, facing the wall. He wanted them to get used to his presence there before he started asking questions. When the beer was finished he ordered another and returned to his place. The men had restarted their conversation. Although his Spanish wasn't good enough to make out the words, their tone suggested they were talking about him.

By the time he was ready for a third beer there were about a dozen men sitting around talking and appearing to take no notice of him. The barman still didn't smile or speak, but he didn't look openly angry any more.

'Do you know Lopez?' George asked as he paid.

The man gave a shrug that conveyed nothing, scooped up the money and turned his attention back to other customers. George sat back down and stayed sitting, alone, for two further hours. When he finally stood up and left, none of the other customers even looked up. It was dark outside and he walked briskly back to the hotel. The following night he went back to the same bar and repeated the exercise, and the following four nights after that.

On the seventh night, having spent several hours drinking in solitary silence, he made his way back out into the darkness as usual. He had now perfected the fastest and most direct way back to the hotel, avoiding all the most dangerous looking dark corners. Even though nothing had happened to make him wary, he still felt a sense of relief whenever he emerged back into the main street. His guard would relax as soon as he saw the lights, which was why he didn't sense the men behind him until the blow felled him to the ground. Passers-by all turned their heads away as a car screeched to a halt and the unconscious body of the middle-aged foreigner was thrown onto the back seat. Doors slammed, the engine gunned loudly and the car was swallowed by the side streets. Life went on as normal, such events were commonplace in Medellin.

* * *

As George swam back to consciousness he was aware of an enormous heat. For a moment he was afraid he was drenched in blood, but gradually realised the wetness was his own sweat. On the inside he was parched, his mouth and throat dry and stinging, and the moment he tried to move, a flash of pain cracked across the inside of his skull, reminding him he'd been hit over the head. Pulling himself up gently he became aware of the smell of urine, acidic and stale.

It was probably only a few seconds, although it felt like much more, before his brain began to focus and take in his surroundings. Sunlight streamed in through the bars of a small window, dazzling him and making it hard to refocus into the darker corners of the hut he was imprisoned in. The heat came from the tin roof above his head, which was soaking up the sun's rays and slowly cooking him. He must have been unconscious all night. He could hear screams coming from somewhere outside.

Pulling himself to his feet he peered out through the bars. It looked like his hut was standing in the middle of some sort of military base. The soldiers mooching around outside, however, did not give the impression of being under any sort of discipline. The screaming intensified and his eyes were drawn to a group of soldiers who were standing around a prisoner, beating him with batons. His screams for mercy only seemed to incense them further, and even once he had fallen silent, they continued to kick his lifeless body around in the dust, laughing to one another like street kids with a football.

A mighty roar made George jump and for the first time his eyes focused on a high wire fence behind the men, where a huge male lion paced back and forth, and behind him several lionesses waited sleepily in the sun. When the soldiers had finished with their victim they threw his body into an outer pen, closed the door and then raised an inner door to the lions' enclosure. The lionesses immediately rose to their feet, obviously aware what this meant, and their leader pulled the man's body across to them as if it weighed nothing. The men stood watching and cheering for a while as the animals tore the body to pieces, and then lost interest and sloped off to smoke in the shade.

Thirst gripped George like a vice but he didn't dare call out. He didn't want to attract their attention. He had to wait until he understood better what was going on. For the first time in his life he felt truly afraid, aware that if these men chose to kill him there was nothing he could do to stop them. It seemed he had finally taken one risk too many.

The only way he could tell that the hours were passing was by the movement of the sun and the eventual relief of darkness. He drifted in and out of consciousness, occasionally awoken by shouting outside, or the roar of a lion. From time to time he would hear a volley of gunshots, which suggested people were being executed on the other side of the compound. Within hours of the sun going down he began to shiver with cold.

He was half awake and half asleep when the door flew open and the light of powerful torches blinded him. Rough hands dragged him out of the hut and threw him onto the ground. He couldn't even muster enough breath to plead with them before the blows started to fall. Through the pain he could make out a few of their words.

'Filthy American pig! Police shit!'

He tried to protest that he wasn't American, nor was he anything to do with any police force, but his cries just sounded like pleas for mercy. Having shown him what they thought of him, he was thrown back into the hut until morning, when the interrogations started in earnest.

The questions were all the same, interspersed with blows that would often knock him over, still tied to the chair, and he would lie helplessly on the floor, waiting for them to put the chair back on its feet and start the questions and blows again.

'Who are you?'

'George Lombardi.'

'What do you want?'

'I have useful information for Senor Rodriguez.'

'What information?'

'It is for the ears of Senor Rodriguez only.'

They were convinced he was a plant from the Drug Enforcement Agency, and the more he denied it, the more feeble his protests sounded. There was nothing else for him to do but endure the pain and keep repeating himself. Either they would kill him or they would eventually take him to their leader.

It was impossible for him to tell how many days and nights the interrogations went on for, because he was constantly passing in and out of consciousness, unable to tell how long he had been out for, but eventually they came for him, blindfolded him and hustled him into a car instead of beating him. He didn't ask any questions and they didn't offer any explanations. He would know soon enough where he was being taken.

When the blindfold came off he found himself lying on the floor in what looked like a palace. The polished marble they had thrown him onto sparkled with gold inlay, and tall windows looked out across terraces to gardens beyond. There were no raised voices now. His captors stood round him, whispering to one another in respectful voices. He heard a door opening and the feet around him shuffled back.

'They tell me you have useful information for me,' a new voice said as a foot prodded him in the ribs.

'Yes.' George knew this was Rodriguez from the respect the other men showed.

'Get him up onto a chair,' Rodriguez instructed, and he was lifted into an armchair. The cushions felt unbelievably soft after the hard floor of the hut.

'So?' Rodiguez stepped into his eye line for the first time. He was overweight but sleekly groomed, his clothes shining white, his hair black and oiled.

'It's confidential,' George muttered through broken lips.

Rodriguez's hand flashed out and George braced himself for another blow, but it didn't come. Instead the drug baron took a gun from one of the soldiers and pointed it directly between George's eyes. He signalled with his eyes for the men to leave and they obeyed instantly.

'You have withstood a lot to get this far,' he said once they were alone, 'so speak quickly.'

'I'm a banker,' George said. 'I know about moving money around the world. You need to change the way you move your money.'

'Why?' The gun was still unwavering between his eyes.

'Because the people you are using don't understand how it works. They are losing you millions unnecessarily. The amount of cash you are holding at any time should be doubling its worth virtually every year.'

'How do you know so much about my business?'

'It's my business too.'

'Why do you want to help me?'

'Because if you gave me just ten per cent of the money I made for you I would be as wealthy as any man could ever wish to be.'

At last Rodriguez lowered the gun and smiled, showing a dazzling set of teeth, all rebuilt by a dentist in Beverly Hills.

'You put yourself through all this just to get a job interview?'

'It would be a good job,' George said.

Rodriguez spun on his heel and shouted for the guards to come back in. He ordered them to take George upstairs for a bath and to bring him back to the dining-room for dinner in an hour. In the days that George had been kept a prisoner, they had checked up on his name and had found the paper trail that the CIA had so carefully laid for him when Lex seemed to have been killed. They had found nothing to indicate that he wasn't who he said he was, or that he didn't have the expertise he said he had.

Later, as he ate hungrily, he explained to his host exactly what he should be doing with his money laundering operations. Rodriguez was relaxing as the evening wore on and he was able to see that George knew exactly what he was talking about.

'I like you, George,' he said eventually as they left the table, both puffing on Havana cigars.

'I'm honoured that you say that,' George replied.

'I'll tell you why,' Rodriguez went on, his arm around his new friend's shoulders as he guided him through to another room. 'I have an army of people who do everything I tell them. Not one of them would have been able to go through what you have been through just to get to talk to me.'

'Sometimes you have to take the pain,' George said and Ramrod roared his approval.

Over the next couple of years George carefully and methodically constructed a new web of bank accounts across the Caribbean, creating a complicated financial maze to launder the cash proceeds of the cartel's huge narcotics business, drawing extensively on the contacts and expertise he had been exposed to with Walker and LaVine. Once he had decided to trust him, Rodriguez had opened up all his financial details, as well as the doors to his villa. He had known for some time that the Cali Cartel had a more sophisticated financial network than him, but he had had no idea what to do to remedy the situation. It was as if George had been sent to him by God. He wanted George with him every second that he was in the country. They ate together, went hunting together, and often ended the days in nightclubs together. As time passed George became firmly ensconced in the drug baron's world. It was as if Ramrod had discovered a long-lost brother.

When he was in the country George based himself in a permanent suite at the hotel in Medellin, although he spent most of his time at Ramrod's villa or down on the ranch with his new employer, admiring his lions and giraffes. Now and again he would find himself with a few hours to spare, and one evening he decided to fill some spare time with a visit to *Los Lambalas* bar where he had first made his enquiries. Most of the men he had seen sitting around the bar on those evenings were now known to him, including the elusive Lopez, who had been there all along, although he'd never had any intention of revealing himself to a nosy foreigner until he was certain he knew who he was. George needed to speak to a couple of couriers who were about to do a drop in the States and he was sure they would be in the bar, or would soon be found if he went there to ask for them.

It was already growing dark on the streets as he turned into the street that housed the bar's shady doorway. He had only taken a couple of steps from the corner when he saw the beaded curtains move and Lopez stepped out, deep in conversation with another man. George swerved back around the corner in one swift movement, and then peered back round. Neither man seemed to have noticed him. He had recognised the other man instantly, hardly able to believe his eyes. To his absolute horror and amazement it was . . . Casper Franks!

Shocked, he began to question the ramifications. Why would he be in *Lambalas*? Why would he be talking to Lopez? His heartbeat quickened and a dozen similar questions spun through his mind as he tried to see some logical reason why the man from the CIA should be in that small dingy bar in Medellin at the same time he was. Was he on official business? Was he there because he had heard about George's activities with Rodriguez? Were the CIA connected to the Cartel de Medellin? Why hadn't he seen any signs of that connection before? Did Rodriguez still not trust him with all the facts? None of it seemed to make sense.

He walked briskly back to the hotel and poured himself a drink to steady himself. He needed time to think through all the ramifications in order to figure out what to do next.

A few days later Ramrod invited him up to the villa for a party. George had been to enough of Ramrod's parties to know that it wouldn't be long before his host was high on a cocktail of booze and drugs, which was always the best time to get information out of him. Ramrod was already far into the party mood when George arrived and walked past the guards who were frisking everyone else for guns. The host and his private guards were the only ones allowed to be armed at the villa parties.

'George, my brother!' Ramrod embraced him and George knew from the strength of the hug that he was as high as a kite.

He returned the embrace and allowed himself to be guided back through the room and introduced to a pair of pouting women who he recognised as Brazilian models he had met with Ramrod in a club before. Ramrod swept all of them onto the dance floor, throwing his arms around and laughing wildly. It was easy to see why people who had never had to do business with him loved him so easily.

An hour or two later, having exhausted himself and needing a few moments of quiet with a cigar, Ramrod left the women, steering George out onto a terrace and indicating a couple of chairs for them. He was carrying a bottle of brandy and two glasses.

'You have been in town for a few days and haven't been to see me,' he said, wagging his finger in a clumsy impression of an angry schoolteacher. 'People will say you don't love me any more!' He roared with laughter at his own joke and slopped brandy into the glasses.

'I have been following a new line of enquiry,' George said, aware that he sounded prim beside his drunken friend. 'But I have met some possible stumbling blocks.'

'You talk like a damn lawyer,' Ramrod complained. 'What do you mean?'

'I seem to be tripping over CIA operatives wherever I turn,' George said, deciding to chance his arm with a bluff. 'It's hard to know who's a friend and who's an enemy.'

'I'm the only friend you can trust,' Ramrod said firmly, his face suddenly serious. 'Everyone else will lie to you.'

George stayed quiet and watched as Ramrod lit himself a large joint, putting his cigar to one side, and inhaled deeply.

'You must listen to me carefully,' he said eventually, his eyes glazing with pleasure at his own cleverness. 'The CIA is not a problem to us. Do you understand what I am saying?'

'Not entirely,' George admitted.

'Everyone has a price, my friend,' Ramrod boasted with a grin. 'The CIA, they know about our activities in the States, but they choose to leave us alone. Do you know why?'

George shook his head, taking the offered joint from Ramrod's fingers and putting it to his lips without allowing the smoke too far into his system; he needed to stay as alert as possible.

'Because we've helped them fight their dirty little wars in lots of ways. Like when we helped them finance the Contras in their war against the Sandinistas in Nicaragua.'

George handed back the joint and took a sip of brandy to give himself time to think. Could that explain why Casper Franks was in Medellin, talking to Lopez? It might. And if that was the case did it mean the CIA operative had known about Lex Goldman's involvement with the Calis all along? An involvement he had not thought it wise to mention to Ramrod. He gave an involuntary shiver at the thought of what would happen if Ramrod discovered that link.

'You cold?' Ramrod asked, suddenly the concerned host.

'No,' George assured him. 'I'm fine. Is the CIA working with the Cali Cartel in the same way?'

Ramrod's grin spread even wider.

'The Cali Cartel will soon be finished in New York and all the other big cities.'

'They are well established,' George ventured.

'You can't tell me anything about the fucking Calis,' Ramrod snapped, making George jump. 'I know every move they make. I know everything. I give the right information to the CIA and they will smash their whole operation in New York, leaving the market free for us. I want to see those guys killed. They have screwed us for so much money.'

George was struggling to get his head round this new information as the fumes from the brandy threatened to confuse him. He knew that Ramrod was talking about Juan and Garcia, even if he didn't use their names. He could imagine just how much damage their operation had done to the Medellin traffickers over the years. If Franks was involved in this planned sting he almost certainly knew all about Lex Goldman's involvement with the Calis, and might pass it on to the Medellins. It was imperative that Franks didn't get to hear of George Lombardi being in town.

'So, how many people in the organisation have contact with the CIA?' George asked.

Ramrod looked surprised. 'How many?' He laughed. 'Are you feeling jealous, George? Do you think there are other people in the organisation I trust more than you? No one else has contact. You are the only person in the organisation I have ever told. I am their only contact.'

George nodded his understanding, but his brain was racing. If that was true, then it meant Ramrod knew nothing about Lopez and Franks meeting. So was Lopez double-crossing Ramrod, or was Franks? Or was Franks operating at an unofficial level, nothing to do with his bosses? Was Lopez just doing a bit of freelance business on the side? So many unanswered questions . . .

George didn't like to use the phones in Colombia; he was pretty sure the Medellins, the Calis, the local police and the CIA between them had virtually every line tapped, so he waited until he was next in Miami before putting in a call to Colby on his secure line. After his last meeting with Franks he certainly didn't want to have anything more to do with him. Colby was irritated that George had made contact and his assistant came back on the line to tell him Colby was 'in a meeting'.

'Tell him this is a call he'll want to take,' George said enigmatically.

The assistant hesitated for a second, thought better of arguing, and went away again. He was back a minute or two later.

'Mr Colby says if you would like to leave a contact number . . .'

'Tell Mr Fucking Colby that if he wants to know how Rodriguez fits with the CIA he had better ring back straight away.' He gave the number and hung up.

The phone rang a few minutes later. 'What the fuck do you want, Lombardi?'

'A meeting.'

'You've wasted enough taxpayers' money and time already . . .'

'You'll want to hear what I have.'

'Casper Franks is on a covert in the Gulf, talk to him when he gets back.'

'I don't want to talk to Franks,' George replied. It seemed Colby knew nothing about Franks being in Medellin, so he must be there as a freelance, he thought. 'I want it put on record that I asked you for a meeting and you declined the offer.'

'Fuck off, Lomardi.'

George hung up. His mind was racing. If it was true that the CIA were working on busting the Cali operations in New York on Ramrod's information, Juan and Garcia would almost certainly be eliminated. He felt a nasty twinge of conscience. Juan had risked his own life to save his when the jungle laboratory had been destroyed in the police raid, and that wasn't something he could ever forget. He had often wondered why Juan had risked everything to save him when it would have been much easier to leave a wounded man behind in their escape. The bond created between them that day was still fresh in George's memory as he relived the horror of those fateful events.

On his next visit to Ramrod's villa, he flicked through all the Medellin and associated bank accounts to check for any clues. He scoured the lists of transfers that had been made over the previous few years. Once he knew what he was looking for the evidence seemed to scream from the pages – regular payments to someone called 'Conrad Franks', none of them big enough to attract attention, but when added together, a sizeable amount.

He had so much information spinning around in his head that it was hard to hold onto a clear picture. All he did know was that Juan and Garcia were soon going to be snared in a deadly trap and he needed to warn them somehow, without letting them know that Lex Goldman was still alive, and without letting Ramrod know that George Lombardi was double-crossing him.

9

The forecast heavy fog had arrived early and O'Hare International Airport, Chicago was quickly lost in its cloak. An eerie silence had settled around the planes, which now stood invisible on the tarmac. Air traffic was at a standstill and nothing was going to be coming in or getting out for hours. Detective Investigator Chip Murray took several deep breaths as he stared at the departures board with its rows of 'flight delayed' notices, willing himself to be patient. There was nothing else he could do but endure it like everyone else caught up at the airport. His colleagues would have to manage without him in New York for a little while longer.

To take his mind off the mountain of work he knew was waiting for him on his desk back at the precinct he headed for the bar, ordered a beer and sat down on a stool next to a scruffy looking hippy, whose rucksack took up most of the leg-room between the seats.

'Sorry, man.' the hippy looked up ruefully as Chip struggled to get his legs in, then a look of shock came over his unshaven, sun-burned face. 'Chip?'

'Do I know you?' Chip stared at him closely. Now he was looking past the distractions of his outer appearance there was something very familiar about the boyish face grinning back at him. 'Blaine? Blaine Harmon? Jesus Christ, what happened to you?'

Blaine looked crestfallen for a moment. 'Happened?'

Chip realised he'd been offensive. 'Sorry,' he said quickly, 'it's just that you looked a bit different last time I saw you.'

'Well you didn't,' Blaine laughed, genuinely happy to see his childhood friend after so long. 'You hardly look any different. How've you been, man?' He leant across from his stool and gave Chip a passionate hug. Chip noticed the odour of his unwashed clothes, while Blaine was aware of the smell of Chip's aftershave and his freshly washed shirt. He knew that he'd let himself go, that he was an anachronism in the go-getting, materialistic eighties, and was embarrassed to be reminded of the fact by the crispness of his friend's appearance.

'I've been good,' Chip responded. Now he was over the shock of meeting someone he had once known better than anyone else in the world, he felt his conscience pricking. He remembered how Blaine's mother had asked him to protect and watch over her only child just before she died. He'd promised her faithfully that he would do that, and he'd meant it. But things had become difficult when Blaine and his dad moved away from New York to Chicago to escape the unhappy memories. He'd intended to visit regularly, but his career had taken over and somehow the years had slipped past. In fact he never had time to visit his own family and they lived in the same city, so there was little hope of visiting Chicago. Initially they had exchanged a few letters, but the gaps between each one grew until eventually he assumed Blaine had moved anyway, which was a suitable excuse to stop bothering altogether. He hadn't even tried to get in touch when he knew he was going to be in town on police business. Now that he saw the dishevelled state of his friend he realised he had let him down badly. He should have stayed on his case, like he'd promised he would.

'How's your dad?' he asked.

'He's okay,' Blaine shrugged. 'He married again pretty soon after Mum died. I don't really get to see so much of him now. He's always busy, you know. So, what about you? I heard you joined the NYPD.'

'Always said I would, didn't I?'

'Yeah,' he laughed with genuine affection at the memory of all the times Chip had told him how he was going to be a big time crime-buster. Many times they had played cops and robbers and he had always had to be the one who was arrested and led away in cuffs. Later, when Chip realised that all good policemen needed a sidekick, he had promoted Blaine to the post, and they had stalked around their area in search of wrongdoers to capture and crimes to solve. There hadn't been as much crime about in those days, but sometimes a local store would be robbed and they would spend many happy hours getting the storekeepers and any other witnesses to retell their stories, in the hope of picking up a vital clue that the grown-up police had missed out on.

'You always knew where you were going. That's why Mum loved you so much. She was always saying, "why can't you be more like Chip? You need to find a direction in life, like Chip. Stick close to Chip, he'll look after you." Sometimes I wondered if she wouldn't have preferred to have you as a son.' There was no malice in his voice; he was too fond of Chip to resent him.

'Nah, she loved you more than anything. She just worried you were too laid back, that you would drift through your life and not make use of your brain.'

'I guess she was right,' Blaine gestured down at his ragged

appearance. 'Not much direction. Not much brain work. So, what do you do in the NYPD?'

'I'm in the narcotics division.' Chip noticed the flicker of disquiet that went through Blaine's eyes. He was used to seeing it whenever he told people of his own age or younger what he did for a living. Everyone had experimented with drugs at some stage and they all became guarded once they knew he was on the other side of the fence. No one wanted to get a criminal record. 'Oh, don't worry, Blaine, my job is to bust the suppliers, not the users.'

'Don't know what you mean, man,' Blaine grinned sheepishly and returned his attention to his beer, aware that Chip was staring at him, lost in his own thoughts.

'My God,' Chip said after a few moments. 'It has been too long. I've never made another friend like you, you know.'

'Me neither,' Blaine agreed. 'We go back a long way.'

'Do you remember that first day at school, how old were we? Four?'

'Yeah, I remember. You were ambitious even then, wanted to be milk monitor or whatever the best job was.'

'And you didn't give a damn. Even then. Your mother used to get so exasperated. "Talk to him, Chip, make him see he can't just drift through life," that's all I remember her saying.'

'Poor Mum, I guess she'd an idea that she wouldn't be around to see me grow up. She wanted to make sure I would be okay.'

'So, are you okay?' Chip could remember clearly how devastated his friend had been when his mother told him she'd been diagnosed with cancer and had little time left. It was as if the life had drained away from him at the same time. He had never been confident like Chip, but all the composure he did have disappeared. Where before he'd been a serene child, smiling sweetly out at the world, at the age of thirteen he became dark and introverted.

'Yeah, I guess. Done a bit of travelling, seen a bit of the world.'

'So what do you want to do now? What do you want to do with your life?'

'There you go again. Does everyone have to "do" something? Maybe I could just "be".'

'So, what do you want to be?'

Blaine laughed again, but it sounded strained. 'I don't know, man. It's okay for you, you've always known. Is it as good as you hoped?'

'Better. I really feel I'm helping make a difference. Drugs have destroyed so many of the people I knew, people we both knew as kids. The guys who run these narcotics around the city are ruthless. Those bastards put no value on life. Most of the homicides we get called out to are squabbles between dealers and couriers and punters. You should come back to Queens with me and see the state of some of them, their lives over already. If I can do something to stop even some of this poison getting into the community, then it will have been worthwhile. A lot of the work is monotonous, sure, but sometimes it's exciting, better than sex even!'

They both laughed together, remembering their early, unrequited crushes on girls in school. The hours they had wasted talking about love and sex, dreaming of the impossible or squabbling over Jenny or Marina or some other girl they both fancied. With their laughter it was as if the missing years had disappeared and they were still two kids, hanging around the Beechhurst neighbourhood after school, with Chip holding forth about how he was going to change the world and Blaine day-dreaming in his own world. Right from the beginning Chip had been the more forceful one, the one who would step in to deal with any bullies who spotted Blaine's vulnerability. It wasn't that Blaine was a weakling or a coward, far from it, he just never seemed to see the danger coming until it was on top of him.

'Have you ever thought of joining the police?' Chip asked once they'd been reminiscing for a while.

'Me, a cop?'

'Sure, why not? We could be partners again, like we always used to be.'

'Me as your sidekick, you mean?' Blaine grinned.

'We really need to work at that self-esteem of yours.'

As the weather outside grew worse, neither of them cared any more. The hours, which would otherwise have dragged past, were filled with reminiscences as they both revisited years and memories they hadn't thought about in ages. Blaine talked about his travels and how he felt about his father and stepmother, while Chip explained as much as he was allowed to about his rise up the NYPD. He talked about the crime wave that had hit the streets of New York, making life almost unbearable for city dwellers, and how he felt sure the drug culture was the root cause of most of the problems.

'I really feel I can be a force for good in the city, leave a legacy.'

'That's great, man, I'm really pleased for you. We need guys like you.'

By the time the fog finally lifted and planes started to take off, they had renewed their friendship as if the links had never been broken, and Chip had persuaded Blaine to change his ticket to California for a flight to New York. He intended to ensure that he fulfilled the promise he'd made to Blaine's mother all those years before. He might have been neglectful in his duty up until then, but now he felt he was going to make up for it.

Chip had been telling the truth when he said he hadn't made another friend like Blaine. He always got on with the other guys he was teamed up with in the force, but he never felt much like socialising with them once the long hours of work were over. Most of them seemed to treat their police work just as a bureaucratic job, none of them sharing his intense dedication for clearing narcotics from the streets and breaking the Cali Cartel's vice-like grip on cities along the east coast. Blaine still seemed as happy as always to let him go on talking, just as had when they were boys.

It was the first time Blaine had ventured back to New York since his father had moved them away, fifteen years before, and he was shocked to find that it no longer held bad memories. Even when Chip took him out to the Beechhurst area of Queens, where they had spent their childhood, he felt only warm memories. Watching his mother die a lingering death when he was so young had been hard, particularly when he saw the pain and anguish it put his father through. But the years in Chicago and travelling the world had healed most of the mental scars, and now, like Chip, he felt only regret that so many of the people they'd grown up with or knew were dead or in prison. Those who were left seemed worn down by worry, living on their nerves, their eyes constantly wary, never knowing where the next attack might come from. New York felt like a city under siege from enemies who were already inside the walls, sometimes invisible, sometimes all too visible on the street corners or lurking around the tenements. Desolation had gripped its soul.

But despite all that, Blaine felt a fondness for this area that he had never managed to feel in the new home his father had bought in the suburbs of Chicago. His father had found it difficult being alone, and had married again soon after settling in the area. Blaine's stepmother had done her best with the boy she'd inherited, but she had no children of her own and didn't understand the moody teenager lounging around in her new husband's house. Their relationship had never managed to develop, and his father's time became more and more filled with pleasing his pretty new wife.

'Together we could really make a difference here,' Chip said, knowing just how to press Blaine's buttons.

'How can we work together? You've been in the NYPD for years. You're a proven man. They aren't going to team me up with you the moment I join up.'

'Not right away, but if you show them what you can do, and I keep prompting to have you on the team, they won't be able to say no for ever.'

'You really think I could do it?'

'No doubt about it. If I'm going to have anyone in the world watching my back, I want that person to be you.'

'Supposing they don't accept me?'

'They'll accept you. You might need to get a haircut and a decent shave though!'

Chip's predictions turned out to be exactly right. The NYPD happily accepted Blaine's application, and four years later Chip was granted his wish for his friend to be seconded to his unit; to become his partner, just like they had acted out so many times as children.

'You'd better be right about this guy, Chip,' his boss warned him. 'I've put my neck on the line fast-tracking him like this on your say-so.'

'You won't regret it,' Chip promised him. 'I know this guy almost as well as I know myself. He'll be a major asset to the cause.'

There was never any doubt in Chip's mind about the importance of 'the cause'. When he first stumbled across evidence that some of the drug dealers he was tracking were paying off senior officers, he didn't believe it. In his innocence he was sure he must have been fed false information by someone with a vested interest in staining the reputation of the police force. So convinced was he that it must be a lie that he took the information to his boss.

'Shut the fuck up, Chip,' his boss snarled before he had even managed to get his whole story out. 'Spreading crap like that could get you drummed out of the force, or worse.'

'Worse?' Chip was genuinely puzzled by the response. 'What do you mean?'

'Junior cops meet with accidents all the time,' his boss sighed, as if talking to an imbecile. 'A stray bullet in a shoot-out, an unsolved revenge killing with no witnesses. Things like that happen all the time. Don't set yourself up for trouble. You're a good officer, I can't afford to lose any more good men.'

'Are you saying . . . ?' Chip tried to piece together what he was hearing.

'Get the fuck out of my office,' his boss shouted. 'And don't talk about this crap to anyone else, ever!'

Chip knew the man well enough to know when not to argue and backed out of the office. Over the next few days he did some serious thinking and the truth began to dawn on him. The more he fitted the pieces of the jigsaw together the more horrified he became, realising that a significant percentage of the NYPD, especially in the upper echelons, were in the pay of the Cali Cartel.

'You can't take on the whole of the New York police force *and* the drug cartels,' Blaine protested when Chip finally realised he had to share the knowledge with someone and went to the one person he trusted above all others. They were sitting together in the corner of a noisy bar after a particularly frustrating day on duty.

'So what's the alternative?' Chip demanded. 'To look the other way and pretend it isn't happening? What would be the point of even turning up to work each day if we're going to do that? If we're not intending to run the drug dealers off the streets then we might just as well be corrupt and get rich ourselves, like the rest of them. Do you want to do that?'

'We?' Blaine looked anxious. 'Since when did this become my campaign?'

'Since the moment I decided to tell you everything I know,' Chip grinned. 'If we are going to rid the streets of narcotics then we are gonna have to expose the corruption in the force at the same time.'

'Listen, I'm just a rookie. There's nothing I can do to help. If you decide to open this can of worms you are going to be facing the consequences yourself.'

'Ah, you'll be there for me. You're always there for me.'

'I'll be there for you as a friend, but that's all I'll be able to do.'

'That's a lot, Blaine. Under the circumstances it's a hell of a lot.'

'Buy me another fucking beer then,' Blaine replied. 'And tell me what you want me to do.'

'Do you think the boss is one of the ones on the take?' Blaine asked an hour later, when Chip finally stopped to draw breath.

'I don't think so. His name hasn't come up anywhere, but he isn't likely to want to stand up and speak out. He's getting on a bit, I know he's looking forward to his pension and enjoying his grandchildren on his knees.'

'Not planning to commit hara-kiri, like you then?'

'I think he would back me if he was sure I had the proof.'

'Hmmm . . . are you sure he wouldn't panic?'

'It's a risk, but unless I take a risk I can't move in any direction. It makes my job a million times harder when I can't tell who I can trust, who I can share information with safely. If you can't trust your own bosses, what are you supposed to do? These people disgust me; they undermine the whole basis of a decent society. They take on positions of responsibility and deliberately use them to enrich themselves. I want to see New York free of this poison. Don't you?'

'Sure.'

'So we have to start somewhere. We have to trust someone. The boss is a decent guy, he'll want to clean up the city for his grandchildren too.'

'But he may not want to end up as another homicide statistic in the process.'

Before returning to see his boss, Chip prepared a detailed dossier on all his findings, copies of which he lodged with a number of different firms of attorneys, giving instructions that the dossiers were to be released to influential congressmen and selected journalists in the event of his death. When he explained what he had done to his boss, and placed another copy of the dossier on the desk in front of him, the older policeman fell silent. He stared for a few moments at the document before leaning slowly forward and picking it up. He then thumbed through it, picking pages at random, still saying nothing. Chip waited in silence.

'And you intend to present this to the media?' he said eventually.

'Only in the event that the NYPD chiefs don't do anything about it. Or if I meet with any kind of unfortunate "accident".'

His boss nodded his understanding. He wasn't smiling, but he wasn't shouting expletives either, which seemed promising to Chip.

'I've always thought you were an exceptionally good policeman, Murray,' he said eventually, 'and this proves it.'

'Thank you, sir.'

'You know this will do the most incredible amount of damage to the reputation of our force.'

'I understand that, sir, but I don't think it's possible to keep it quiet. It's gone on too long and the repercussions go right to the top. The public have to know that the force is being cleaned of corruption if they're ever going to trust us again. They already know that this kind of shit goes on, they just don't know the details, and don't have the evidence.'

'Until you came along.'

'Yes, sir.'

'You're a brave man, Chip.' He sat back in his chair. 'Braver than I've been.'

'Sir.'

'I'll stand behind you on this.'

'Thank you, sir.'

'Don't thank me, Chip, you haven't left me any alternative. If I end up with a bullet in the back of my head you're going to have to be the one to face my wife and kids.'

'I hope it won't come to that, sir.'

'I hope so too. I really do.'

Within a few days Chip's boss had fulfilled his promise and Detective Chip Murray found himself reporting to a hastily convened pack of congressmen. It wasn't long before the dossier was leaked to the media, and the streets of New York descended into anarchy as every bent cop tried to cover his or her back and the Cartel struggled to regain the initiative. But Chip's research had been too thorough for anyone to be able to undermine it in any substantial way. Other straight policemen, emboldened by his lead, came forward to testify, and every day the newspapers were filled with new and more shocking revelations of the scale of the corruption that had been going on for years, touching all parts of the city. Chip had managed to turn his 'cause' into a public campaign, and most politicians in the city wanted to be part of the process. It didn't take long before any number of senior figures had stepped forward to take credit for being at the forefront of the campaign to rid the NYPD of corruption, and Chip was soon able to slip into the shadows, back to working at street level where he felt most comfortable. It would take time before the public trusted their police force again, but eventually they would learn to.

Chip had made a lot of powerful enemies in the force throughout this time, but one by one they were prosecuted and removed. Those who were left found that the mood within the NYPD had shifted and they had to change their ways if they wanted to fit in. Any whiff of corruption was no longer tolerated at any level. Eventually Chip found himself being accepted again and not treated with suspicion by colleagues, but for a long time after the dossier was made public Blaine was the only man he felt he could completely trust and depend on.

As the corrupted members of the force were named and shamed and then removed, it became easier to see the routes and network that the Cali Cartel was using to get its drugs into the city. Chip and Blaine stayed doggedly on its trail.

By the beginning of the nineties 'the cause' had narrowed itself down to being a private war between the NYPD and the Cali Cartel, which was still supplying virtually all the cocaine that was flooding onto the streets. As far as Chip and Blaine were concerned it was a war of attrition, an endless chipping away at the wall of fear and money that the cartel had managed to erect around itself. It was almost impossible to get meaningful information out of anyone, especially when everyone was well aware of how powerful and ruthless the Colombians were, and how well they rewarded loyalty, even amongst their most lowly foot soldiers.

The most time consuming part of the job was the surveillance work: long nights of sitting in the dark, usually in cramped conditions, watching the comings and goings of low-life couriers and dealers as they came and went from known addresses. Blaine was entirely happy to be back in the company of the person who had always watched out for him as a child, more caringly than his father had ever done. He knew Chip had steered him towards a career in the NYPD to fulfil the promise he had made to his mother at the end of her life, and he was grateful to him. He would never have imagined himself as a cop, but he actually enjoyed the work. A lot of it was tedious, but working with Chip took the edge off that, and every so often it was exciting, setting the adrenaline pumping as they rushed from their cover to make an arrest. Their suspects nearly always tried to make a run for it and had to be chased, just like in the movies, and sometimes they faced grave danger when a knife or a gun was pulled on them and the bullets started to fly. He felt good to be attached to a colleague of the highest integrity, who was acclaimed for having set the ball rolling on the biggest internal anti-corruption drive the NYPD had ever undertaken.

They had been watching one particular address for months. They knew it was a post box, through which any number of couriers came and went, and they hoped that eventually someone higher up the cartel's hierarchy would turn up. Day after day and night after night the two of them sat in a darkened room in a seemingly derelict building across the street, watching through a crack in the boards that covered all the windows. They took it in turns to watch and to sleep, talking in whispers during the hours when both of them were awake at the same time.

'Chip!' Blaine hissed one night, when his friend was asleep.

'What is it?' Chip was immediately awake.

'I think it's Juan and Garcia.'

'Shit!' Chip was up and with his eye to the crack, but he was too late to see more than a couple of shadowy figures disappearing into the house opposite. It felt like the names of Juan Baptista and Garcia Mendez were engraved on his heart. All his research and investigative work told him that if he could eradicate those two, the cartel's entire east coast operation would be mortally wounded. No doubt they had other people they could promote in their place, but it would take time, and in the intervening period of chaos the authorities would be able to do a lot more to stop the smooth running of supplies. Their ruthlessness and experience had made them legends and Chip had more or less given up hope of ever being able to apprehend them on the ground.

'Are you sure?'

'No, I'm not sure, but it looked a lot like them.'

Chip only hesitated for a split second before getting on the radio for reinforcements. Within twenty minutes the building opposite was surrounded by snipers. Chip and Blaine emerged from their hiding place as cars glided quietly to a halt at each end of the street. Armed figures ran to meet them, crouched low like attacking soldiers. Instructions were given in sign language and then they struck, smashing through the door with a battering ram and following in a sudden thunder of boots. The half-dozen men inside the house scattered and headed for windows and fire escapes. One of them, cornered and desperate, drew a gun from his belt and fired directly at Blaine, his hand shaking with fear. Chip lunged forward as his friend crumpled to the floor, grabbed the gun and sent the man back into the wall with a ferocious punch.

The rest of the gang had all escaped out of the building and they could hear shouts, gunshots and the sound of running feet in the streets. Chip knelt down beside Blaine and gently opened his blood-soaked shirt. The bullet, it seemed, had just grazed his flesh, making him bleed but not entering any vital organs. After a few minutes gathering his strength, Blaine pulled himself painfully to his feet, using his friend's shoulder as a crutch, and they limped outside to see what was going on.

It looked as if everyone who was in the house had been rounded up. There were a couple of bodies in the gutter. Chip checked their faces, but neither of them looked like Baptista or Mendez. He went through the ones who were left standing before they were taken to the waiting vans, turning their faces up towards the light. They were the same bunch of punks they had been watching for months. None of them would lead them any further up the organisation. Either Juan and Garcia had escaped, or they had never been there. Their cover was blown now and all the work of the previous months had yielded a few small-time couriers who would clutter up the courts and the prison system and cost the taxpayer yet more money.

'Fuck it!'

'I'm sorry, Chip,' Blaine muttered. 'I thought it was them.'

'Don't apologise. It could have been. It was my call and it was worth a try.'

Blaine stayed over in the hospital, getting his wound patched up, while Chip stood in front of his boss.

'That was a fucking cock-up.'

'Yes, sir.'

'What made you decide to blow your cover like that, for God's sake? After all the work you've put in getting into place.'

'I thought we had Baptista and Mendez in there. I was sure of it.'

'But you were wrong.'

'It seems so, sir. Unless they got out before we went in.'

'Does that seem likely?'

'They're clever enough for anything, snakes in the jungle, sir.'

'But we are left with no snakes in the bag, just a bunch of pawns, as usual.'

'Yes, sir.'

'They're laughing at us, Murray. These bastards are laughing at us. All we're doing is scratching the surface. They've hundreds of people at the level of the ones we rounded up here; thousands probably. They're worth nothing to us. You'd have done as well to arrest a dozen rowdy Irishmen for being drunk.'

'Yes, sir.'

'You've got to get beyond this, Chip. You've got to crack this otherwise they're going to review all the extra funding we have been getting. We need results and some good headlines. You've got to bust the major players and soon. Is Blaine going to be okay?'

'Looks like it, sir.'

'Then the two of you need to get the fuck back out there and catch some criminals who are worth fucking catching.'

Later that day Chip fetched Blaine from hospital. He looked pale but the doctors said they didn't need to see him again. The two friends made their way to a favourite Irish pub to drown their sorrows.

'What are we going to do now?' Blaine asked.

'We're going to start all over again if necessary,' Chip said, taking a long drink.

'These bastards can't be allowed to stay in business.'

Chip's frustration was growing at the ever-increasing stranglehold that the drug dealers had on supplies into New York. After the exposure of the corruption within the NYPD and the clear-out that followed, he had assumed that it would only be a matter of time before the forces of law and order won the day. He had been shocked to find that in many ways the war against the cartel had actually become harder since the corrupt elements of the police force had been removed. The officers who had been in their pay had also been the ones in the know about what was happening at street level. In many ways they had kept the supply of cocaine under control, not wanting to endanger their own necks by sticking them out too far. Now with them all exposed and prosecuted, or else driven further underground, the dealers had vanished into the shadows and found new markets for their products. There had never been such an easy supply of cocaine flooding onto the streets of New York, and the police were at a loss as to how to stem the tide.

'The government are shitting themselves,' Chip's boss told him. 'It's not just New York that's drowning in a sea of white powder; it's the same throughout all the big cities. It's rife. They want us to co-ordinate our efforts to cut these bastards' supply route off at the roots.'

In June 1994, the new multi-jurisdictional campaign was launched and code-named 'Operation Lifeline'. Detective Investigator Chip Murray became known as its most tireless advocate, helping to co-ordinate the various law enforcement agencies involved. It became a joke that no matter how small the detail, Chip would be on top of it, and usually Blaine would be there beside him as they spent virtually every working hour of the following two years travelling from meeting to meeting, stake-out to stake-out. The more they discovered about the cartel and its organisation, the more impressed they became with the level of sophistication of their operation. Despite the massive amounts of information they were accumulating, including contact names and witnessing deals being executed, they made no arrests, but kept on acquiring more details, building the picture, waiting until they were certain they had found what they were looking for. Sometimes it seemed like a waste of time.

'There's pressure building from every side,' Chip confessed to Blaine after another fruitless week. 'The media are pressuring the politicians, the politicians are pressuring us. We just need one major break to get us on the inside of the cartel so we can do some real damage to their infrastructure.'

'My Dad says the cocaine problem in Chicago is worse than anyone can ever remember.'

'It's the same everywhere. We're losing the bloody war, Blaine. We have to find a way to get inside their organisation.'

Most days they spent piecing together minute scraps of information, none of which seemed important in isolation, all of which they hoped one day would build into a picture clear enough for them to undermine and overcome their enemy. Blaine's greatest strength was his ability to get on with people at all levels. Anyone who saw Chip walk through a door could tell he was a man with a mission, but when Blaine sidled into a bar or a party no one gave him a second look. He could hang around the edges of social groups as they drank or got high, smiling amiably and attracting no attention. Chip had taught him how to listen and how to make sense of what he heard, and many of the leads they got came from Blaine's initial undercover groundwork.

'They've taken in a guy down on the west side,' Chip told him one day. 'They've busted his house and it looks like he's a major staging post. The place was stacked with coke waiting for distribution. Do you want to go see if he looks familiar?'

An hour later Blaine was observing the prisoner through a screen.

'Yeah,' he nodded. 'I do know him.'

'What do you know?' Chip already had his notebook in his hand.

'Hang on, I'm trying to remember. He was at a party. He'd just come in from Miami. I remember because he was complaining about missing the sunshine.'

'Whose party was it?'

Back at the office Blaine checked back over the notes he'd made after every activity over the last couple of years. It took forty-eight hours for them to piece together all the suspects the man might have had contact with in Miami.

'He must have been one of the distribution agents for big incoming supplies,' Chip said eventually, rubbing his eyes to try to fight tiredness off for a few more hours. 'He must have got a promotion.'

'This could be our way in,' Blaine said.

'Fancy a trip to Miami?'

The following day they were on the ground in Miami, talking to DEA officers, who recognised pictures of their man in custody. They were taken to meet local grasses who filled in gaps in their knowledge. Blaine could see that Chip was becoming excited, like a hunting dog that had finally picked up a scent after years of sniffing round and round in a field, confused and directionless.

'They don't make the fucking stuff here,' a world-weary DEA officer told them when Chip kept asking for more and more information. 'You need to go to Colombia or Nicaragua if you want to stop these fuckers.'

'It's kind of a big haystack to start looking for needles,' Chip admitted.

'We have some leads in Nicaragua that you might want to take a look at.'

'You have names?' Chip sounded shocked. 'Why haven't you shared them with us before?'

'Don't give me fucking grief,' the officer growled. 'Since when did you guys in the "Big Apple" share anything with anyone?' He managed to get more contempt into New York's nickname than Chip would have thought possible.

'It's always hard to know who should be allowed into the loop . . .' he said, his voice trailing off.

'Yeah, right.' The older man drawled, as if he'd heard every line in the world before and none of them impressed him any more. 'Well, if you want some leads, I'll give you some. I'm too damn tired to do anything about them myself. You guys can go get yourselves killed in my place.'

Later, when they were on their own, Chip checked that Blaine realised what they were getting themselves into.

'If we go down to Nicaragua we'll have to go quietly. If things go wrong there won't be anyone to come to the rescue. Are you sure you're still up for it?'

'Think I could let you go down there on your own? You wouldn't survive a minute.'

Chip laughed. 'Not sure this is the kind of thing your mother had in mind when she asked me to look after you.'

'She would have understood. This is a job worth doing.'

'We're gonna get these bastards, Blaine,' Chip assured him, 'whatever it takes.'

Chip was surprised to find that the local police in Nicaragua were keen to co-operate.

'No one ever asked us before,' the chief of police told him when he demanded to know why none of the information they held had ever been passed over to the United States authorities. 'The only people they send down here are ill-informed politicians or CIA men who think they can throw their weight around. If you really want to get close to any of the Colombian cartels we can help you do that. We have ways of finding out what they are planning.'

'They must have a lot of people down here on their payroll,' Chip suggested.

'Policeman, you mean?' The chief raised his eyebrows.

'We've seen a lot of it where we come from.'

'Just deal with me.' The chief smiled to show he hadn't taken offence. 'Then you can be sure there won't be any leaks.'

Something about the man told Chip he was a man of integrity and that he could be trusted. He listened carefully to everything the chief told him, not bothering to take notes for fear they might fall into the wrong hands.

'Our contacts tell us they have a big shipment of cocaine planned, destined for the east coast. They will try and bring it in through Miami.'

'Are you planning to bust it?'

'No,' he spread his hands in a gesture of helplessness, 'I don't have the manpower. And what good would it do me? I could never prosecute any of them here, the judges would be too intimidated. You guys have the resources to make something stick.'

'I appreciate the information.' Chip grinned. 'How are they intending to move it?'

'Well, in the past they've moved it secreted in drinking straws, usually hidden away in boxes of seafood. They will probably do the same with this shipment. We think they intend to move in two or three days.'

Three nights later Chip and Blaine were crouched in the darkness in some undergrowth outside a refrigeration plant on the outskirts of a town neither of them had ever heard of before. They had been there for nearly twelve hours, when the gates were rolled back and a lorry rumbled out of what looked like an aircraft hangar. Blaine had an infrared camera ready and zeroed in on its number plates. The sound of the camera firing off was muffled by the roar of the lorry as it set off on the first leg of its journey.

The ship that the lorry was preparing to rendezvous with had been under surveillance by another team who Chip had called in for back-up and had flown in from Miami. Every stage of the off-loading and reloading was photographed. They even managed to get some muffled but audible recordings of the voices of the men who had brought the lorry up country.

By the time the ship was sailing up the Caribbean, Chip and Blaine were already co-ordinating with the US coastguard as they drove to their own waiting plane. Stopping to pick up their support team along the way, they'd all get to Miami several days ahead of the refrigerated load.

'This shipment represents our best chance of bringing them down,' Chip told Blaine as they chatted together on board the plane, looking down at the blackness below, while the rest of the team started to doze in the cabin. 'By the time this dope reaches the streets of New York, we should be able to bust every single person who has handled it along the way from Nicaragua. It may not be the biggest haul in history but it's covered with all the right fingerprints. It goes right to the heart of the cartel. No mistakes, we've got to get them this time.'

10

It felt good to George to be back in New York, and to be able to walk the streets anonymously. The city still excited him as much as it had when he first arrived nearly twenty years before. His appearance had changed so radically since he was last living there he felt confident that no one would recognise him unless he made a point of introducing himself, but he still stayed away from his old haunts. He booked himself into a Marriott Hotel in Times Square, nothing too grand and nothing too seedy. He wanted a big place where no one would notice him as he moved around amongst the crowds of tourists and business travellers. He had decided the only way he would be able to get in touch with Juan and Garcia would be if he let it be known on the street that he was in the market to buy a large amount of coke. He knew exactly where to start his search.

'I can do that for you, man,' the dealer he contacted insisted. 'You don't need to talk to no boss man.'

'Fifty pounds is a lot of coke,' George insisted, understanding the business well enough to know the guy would not want him taking his business to a rival. 'I need certain assurances.'

'You can trust me, man,' he whined, 'I have a good reputation.'

'That's why I contacted you, but for this order I need to speak to someone else.'

'Okay, okay. Stay cool. I'll be in touch.'

There was no call back for five hours and George began to wonder if he'd hit a cul-de-sac. Had they checked him out and found out something that spooked them? He was fast asleep when the call finally came through.

'Got a mobile number for you, man,' the voice said. It sounded like he was high.

George fumbled for the light switch and a pen. He scribbled the number down and the line went dead. He waited a few minutes for his head to clear before dialling the number on his own mobile. It stopped ringing but there was no voice at the other end.

'Juan?'

The line went dead. He dialled again and an automated voice told him the phone had been switched off. He was surprised by the feeling of disappointment that came over him. He had found himself thinking more and more about Juan, remembering the way the Colombian had risked his own life to save his. No one else had ever done something like that for him before and he felt an urge to see the man again, to let him know how much that act of friendship had meant to him.

His phone rang and made him jump. 'Who's calling?' a voice with a heavy Colombian accent asked.

'My name's Lombardi.'

'Who you want to speak to?'

'Juan or Garcia.'

'What you want?'

'Fifty pounds of merchandise.'

The line cut again. He tried to recall the number but it had been withheld. He felt optimistic, at least he was in the system. Throughout the night calls came from what he assumed were a number of different mobiles, each call imparted another nugget of information until eventually he found he'd been given a time and a place for a meeting. Then the calls stopped. He had eighteen hours to prepare himself for the rendezvous.

Special Agent Franks, in the Directorate of Operations of the CIA had left a long-standing request to be informed of any surveillance on large-scale Colombian drug trafficking to the US east coast. When he got to hear about Operation Lifeline's target, and learned that the consignment Murray and Harmon were trailing had already been landed in Miami, he was puzzled as to why he hadn't been informed about it earlier. He put in a call to Chip's boss over at NYPD headquarters.

'We wanted as few people to know as possible,' Captain Amigo Serrano told him abruptly. He was used to other departments trying to muscle in on the prestigious jobs and he was annoyed that the Miami police had felt it necessary to bring in the DEA and CIA. He had managed to persuade them to leave Chip and Blaine alone until they'd finished the job, but it still resulted in calls like this one from time to time.

'There are other people involved in trying to wipe out these fucks you know,' Franks growled threateningly. 'The President has expressed a personal interest . . .'

'The President isn't the one out in the field with his ass on the line,' Serrano interrupted testily. 'My boys need protection. The fewer people who know what's going on, the more protected they'll be.'

'From now on you keep me in the loop. That way I won't have to interfere.'

Amigo grunted non-committally and hung up the phone.

Franks sat for a moment, smiling like a cat with a mouse squirming under its paw. This, he thought might be his chance to eliminate the Cali big boys once and for all. As soon as he got free of the office he found the time to put in a discreet call to Lopez on one of his secure lines.

'Ramrod *will* be very pleased,' he started . . .

Captain Serrano, still fuming from his earlier telephone conversation with Agent Franks, was in a determined mood as he finally tracked down his detective on the third attempt to his mobile number. 'The longer you delay, Chip, the more likely someone is going to leak,' he said. 'I've just had some specialist freak attached to the CIA breathing down my neck, wanting to know why he isn't part of the action. You can't keep stalling.'

'If we jump too soon, sir,' Chip protested, 'we run the risk of blowing the whole operation after all this work. If they get away this time we will never be able to lure them back into our web.'

'I know, I know. But if you hold on too long you could lose them just as easily. They've reached the safe house now, right?'

'Affirmative.'

'So what's stopping you going in? Do you want more back-up?'

'No more back-up, they'll spot us.'

'Just do it, Chip, for Christ's sake.'

'We're gonna get it right this time, sir.'

Chip hung up and swore.

'Is it because of me?' Blaine asked after a few moments thought.

'Is what because of you?'

'Are you being extra cautious because of what happened to me last time we went in too quickly?'

'No,' Chip snapped, then sighed. 'Maybe. It's something to take into consideration.'

'Would you be holding back if I was just another partner you'd been assigned?'

'You think I'm holding back because I'm frightened of letting your mother down?'

'I think it's possible.'

'Then you're a dick.'

Both men laughed, which relieved the tension, but both of them knew it was true. Chip was in danger of letting his personal feelings get in the way of his professional judgement.

Chip made a decision. 'Okay, let's get out to their lair.'

George's instructions had been sparse but specific. He was to drive out of New York in a rented car to a first location. Once he was safely there he would meet a car to follow and they would be able to see if he was being tailed before leading him to the safe house.

He got the hotel to rent him a mid-range Toyota, the sort of family car no one would give a second glance to, and set out to the arranged meeting point just as the light started to fade, merging with the streams of commuters leaving the city and heading for the suburbs. He drove for two hours.

He'd been instructed to park up at a gas station on a crossroads, which seemed like the middle of nowhere. He sat in the car for over an hour, watching as the occasional night-owl customer came and went from the small convenience store next door. A pick-up truck was filling up with fuel and the driver, casually dressed in jeans and work boots, went inside to pay. When he came back out he stared directly at George before climbing into his cab. He flashed his lights twice and drew slowly towards the road. George felt his heartbeat quicken as he started the engine and followed at a discreet distance. The traffic was thinning now that the rush hour was over and it was easy to draw out behind the truck and stay a respectable distance. They drove for close to an hour and George was concentrating so hard on keeping the tail lights in view he had no time to read the road signs or work out where he was going.

When he saw the truck's brake lights flick on for no apparent reason and the hazard lights flash twice, he realised they'd reached their destination. The truck sped away and he turned into a driveway so overgrown on either side he wouldn't have noticed it without the signal. He crept the car forward, peering from side to side, trying in vain to make out some sign of where he was heading. After about half a mile of bends and potholes, his headlights picked up a house. None of the windows showed any lights and he wondered if he'd made a mistake and turned into the wrong driveway. He stopped the car and cut the engine, leaving the lights on for a moment. A sharp tap of a gun barrel on his side window made him jump.

'Shit!' he swore. The man had come from nowhere.

'Step out of the car with your hands on your head,' a familiar voice commanded.

He did as he was told.

'Put your elbows on the roof of the car.'

He obeyed again. There were two of them now and one of them was searching him with gloved hands for weapons and wires, not missing any of the crevices of his body. Once the search was complete and Garcia stood back, a torch clicked on, shining directly into his face. It stayed there for a moment, no one speaking.

'Juan?' he ventured. 'Garcia?'

'Who's asking for them?' Garcia snapped.

'Don't you recognise me?'

The slap round the face took him by surprise and knocked him to the ground, but even so he knew better than to retaliate.

'Don't play fucking guessing games,' Garcia snarled, kicking him viciously in the ribs. 'Who the fuck are you?'

'Lex,' George gasped, trying to get the air back into his winded lungs. 'Lex Goldman.'

'Bullshit!' Garcia lashed out again with his boot. 'Lex Goldman is dead.'

'Wait,' Juan interrupted, bending down over George's prone body and shining another torch into his eyes. 'It *is* Lex.'

'Hi,' Lex said, inadequately. 'Good to see you guys too.'

'*Hijuepuerca!*' Juan exclaimed at him in amazement as he helped him to his feet. 'Where the fuck did you come back from?'

'How do we know it's him?' Garcia demanded to know, but his voice was already becoming less certain.

'Look into his eyes,' Juan said, giving Lex a brotherly hug. 'It is Lex, back from the fucking dead!'

'So where the fuck have you been?' Garcia wanted to know.

'At least let the guy get inside before you interrogate him,' Juan said, helping Lex to limp towards the house. Garcia growled like a suspicious guard dog as he followed them in.

Blaine touched Chip's arm to wake him, but the sound of the car crawling up the drive had already penetrated his shallow sleep. They had been lying for more than twelve hours in the shrubbery, just watching and waiting, taking it in turns to doze, not sure what they were waiting for. They knew very little for sure. They knew the property was some kind of safe house, although it had been impossible to find out anything about the owners, beyond the fact that they were domiciled abroad. They knew that the lorry they had been tracking all the way up from Miami was secreted in a barn behind the premises and, as there had been very little activity since it arrived, they assumed the cocaine was still on the premises. Even with the change of personnel at one point along the way, they were fairly sure that there had only been two men entering the house from the lorry until this third man arrived, but they hadn't yet been able to ascertain who they were. Chip didn't want to spring his trap only to discover he had caught two more underlings. He wanted Juan and Garcia and the moment he was sure it was them he would pounce.

Chip was instantly awake and taking in the movements close to the house. They watched the two shadowy figures appearing beside the car as it stopped and heard voices, straining to hear what was being said.

Most of the words were impossible to make out but then they heard the man from the car say, 'Juan? Garcia?'

At that moment Chip wished he had a few dozen back-up men surrounding the house. If the two of them stormed the place now there was a chance the men would get away. They would need help, but if their prey heard any unusual noises they would vanish into the night. He had to make a decision and he had to make it fast, an opportunity like this might never present itself again.

Once Juan was sure that it actually was Lex Goldman, he wasn't able to suppress his pleasure at seeing his old friend alive. He could tell Garcia wasn't so sure, but then he had always known that Lex and Garcia held a mutual suspicion for one another. Ignoring Garcia he threw his arm round Lex's shoulder and propelled him towards the house.

'Hey *pinga*,' Garcia barked, 'car keys!'

He held out his hand for Lex to toss him the keys.

'What about them?' Lex asked.

'I want to check the car.'

'It's rented,' Lex said.

'Give me the fucking keys!'

Lex shrugged and tossed them over. Garcia snatched them angrily out of the air with a gloved hand and went back to the car to start his search, while Juan and Lex went inside to talk. Lex was surprised at how easily they connected again, like soldiers who had fought together in some past war.

Garcia wasn't a man who liked surprises and as he searched the car he tried to work out what could have brought Lex back to them after so long . . . and from the *dead!* He partly wanted to check that the car wasn't bugged, but he also wanted some time to try and work out what the hell was going on . . .

When he saw the third man following the other two into the house Chip made a note of the car's licence plate and gestured to Blaine to move down the drive so he would be ready to cut them off if they tried to make a dash. He had made his decision; they were going to take a chance on rushing them. He couldn't let this opportunity pass.

Blaine disappeared soundlessly into the darkness and Chip moved out of the undergrowth and towards the house. If only he'd had enough men to surround the building, but he dared not radio for help, certain that the slightest whisper in the darkness would carry to the ears of the men inside the house. He knew which room they were in because he'd seen the blackout blinds drawn down during the day. No light could escape and no one could hope to spy in on them. Once he was close to the wall he edged his way round to the back of the house. His plan was to rush them from the back and bring down at least one of them. If the other two got away he would flush them out the front and send them down the drive towards Blaine. The moment he knew his cover was blown he would radio for help and all the surrounding roads would be blocked off within a few minutes. He wished the plan was more foolproof, but it was the best he could do and he didn't think he was ever going to get a better chance of taking Juan and Garcia out of the game.

'Did you find anything?' Juan asked Garcia as he came into the room.

'No,' Garcia shook his head. 'But I don't trust him.'

'You should listen to what he has to say,' Juan said. 'He's risked his life to come and warn us that Ramrod and his cronies are setting us up to be busted by the cops. He's on the inside with the CIA and he's planning to take over our patch with their blessing.'

'*No joda!*' Garcia spat onto the floor to show his contempt for such an idea. He held on to Lex's car keys to ensure he had no means of escape. 'So why did you fake your death and not contact us till now?'

'Our mutual Irish friends didn't like my banking arrangements too much and they threatened to kill me, so I needed to disappear quickly. It's a long story but I had other business interests to take care of, and I wanted to get close to Ramrod.'

'You got close to him?' Garcia was interested, despite himself. 'How did you do that?'

'Through Lopez.'

'You're lying.' He swung triumphantly round to Juan. 'He's lying. No one gets close to Lopez, you know that.'

'I think he's telling the truth. Test him.'

Garcia narrowed his eyes and thought for a second. 'Tell me something about Lopez then,' he challenged.

Lex held up the fingers of his right hand and then folded the little finger down so there were only three left standing. 'They say it was cut off on Ramrod's orders when they suspected Lopez was double-crossing the cartel.'

'Satisfied now?' Juan demanded of his friend. 'Come on, relax, have a drink.'

Garcia allowed Juan to pour him a glass from the whisky bottle they were already drinking from, but he didn't relax, pacing around the room, firing off questions, listening to the answers and then allowing a silence to fall as he pressed his ear to the blind on the window.

Lex's answers seemed to satisfy Juan and he became even more mellow as he refilled both their glasses. Garcia left the room and Juan knew he had gone to check the rest of the house.

'He never relaxes,' he told Lex. 'Always like an animal in the jungle, expecting danger. It is better than having a hundred guard dogs.'

Garcia could hear his friend laughing and knew he would be talking about him, but he didn't care. He knew that his alertness had saved their skins a hundred times. If they'd been relying on Juan for their safety they would have been dead or imprisoned years ago.

The crash outside banished all other thoughts from his mind and he was immediately running back to Juan.

'It's a trap,' he shouted. 'They're coming round the back.'

Juan knew Garcia well enough to know when he was serious and the two of them were running out through the front door before a dazed Lex was able to even gather his thoughts. Garcia still had the Toyota's keys in his hand.

* * *

Chip had stumbled into a barbecue, standing invisible in the shadow of the house. There must have been half a dozen metal cooking implements hanging from it, and in the silence of the night they hit the flagstones of the terrace like a detonating bomb. He knew he had to act fast. They wouldn't be coming out at the back of the house now. He snapped his radio into life.

'They've been spooked. Move up towards the house, shoot if necessary.'

Blaine responded in a crackle of static as Chip ran round to the front of the house, just in time to hear the car's engine exploding into life, the tyres spinning up a cloud of dust and gravel as it leapt forward towards the opening of the drive.

'The fuckers are heading your way,' he shouted into the radio. 'I'm following.'

As he ran he fired off some shots at the tyres of the car, but he had little chance of hitting them in the darkness.

Blaine heard the shots and the roar of the car engine as he pushed his way out of the undergrowth and onto the drive. He could see the headlights approaching through the trees. He knew they wouldn't see him until they came round the bend. Jumping to the side of the road, he positioned himself so he could shoot into the windscreen the moment the car appeared, before they had time to take evasive action. It was only a matter of seconds before the headlights were dazzling him, but it seemed like an age.

Chip didn't stop running, his lungs ready to burst with the effort, as he followed the car's tail-lights. He stopped firing for fear of hitting Blaine. The car was reaching the bend and he was sure Blaine would be waiting for them on the other side. He wanted to reach the corner at exactly the moment Blaine opened fire, so he could help to finish the job off. The car was going so fast as it went into the bend that the back wheels slid to one side, sending a spray of gravel up into the bushes, and the lights disappeared from his line of vision for a moment. He heard Blaine letting off a volley of shots and knew they had driven straight into the trap. He forced his legs to go even faster in his desperation to get there in time to stop them running off.

The car was swerving wildly by the time it came back into sight and he could see Blaine in the headlights, his arms still raised to aim the gun, his finger pumping the trigger. He didn't move as Chip shouted his warning, just kept on shooting, right up until the moment when the front of the Toyota hit him at full speed, sending his body up into the air and over the bushes.

The car kept going, accelerating away towards the road and Chip kept shouting into his radio for an ambulance as he ran towards the place where Blaine's body had been thrown, giving out the car's licence plate number, torn between his urge to ensure they didn't get out of the area and his need to get to Blaine as quickly as possible.

The moment the car reached the road, its lights vanished and a terrible blackness descended. As his eyes adjusted achingly slowly to the dark, he forced his way into the undergrowth, the branches slashing at his skin, thorns digging into him as he flailed around trying to find his friend.

'Blaine! Blaine! Where are you? Hold on, I'm coming for you.'

Lex heard the screams of the car engine and the shots from where he was inside the house and knew things had gone badly wrong. He froze in the kitchen for a moment, listening and waiting for whatever would come next, unable to decide which would be the best direction to run in, his heart pounding with nervous excitement. He had no idea where he would find another car on the premises; he was going to have to escape on foot. He expected to hear the sound of the police breaking in through every door and window, but all the noise seemed to be coming from the grounds at the front of the house.

As the sounds of the car engine faded, he made his way quickly to the back of the building, found a door and let himself out. He paused again for a second, like an animal sniffing the air for the scent of enemies. There seemed to be no one there. He set off into the darkness at a steady trot, aware that he'd been granted yet another lucky break. He was being offered one more chance to get away with it and he experienced a familiar glow of invincibility. He could feel the adrenaline pulsing through his body, giving an edge of fear to his relief at being able to walk away unscathed. He had come too close to the edge again, endangered everything by trying to outwit the whole world. The possible ramifications if he was traced back to this house didn't bear thinking about and it wouldn't just be the NYPD who would be after his blood. If word got back to Ramrod or to the CIA before he'd time to explain things, they would both be out to kill him. He could feel the heat coming from both ends of the burning match as he stumbled away into the night with no idea which direction he was headed in.

A cloud moved past the moon just as Chip came across the body of his friend. He knew from the first moment he touched him that Blaine was dead. There was a terrible heaviness about the twisted limbs and torso as he tried to lift him out of the undergrowth and onto the drive. He could hear the distant sound of sirens and a helicopter approaching. His priority was no longer catching Juan and Garcia, all his attention was focused on trying to straighten out Blaine's distorted body, to give him some dignity in death. All he could think was that his friend wouldn't be lying there dead if he hadn't talked him into joining the police and hadn't insisted on him working as his partner. He felt that his grief and guilt were going to overcome him like a tidal wave, sweeping away everything in their path. He'd been chosen by Blaine's mother in her dying days to be the one to protect him and guide him through life, but instead he'd led him directly to his death and his friend's blood was now literally on his hands.

Juan and Garcia had travelled about three miles from the house. The windscreen had been shattered by Blaine's bullets, but neither of them had been hit. The wind was making their eyes stream, and Garcia was finding it hard to see the road as it wound through the countryside. His foot was flat to the floor as they hurtled into each corner, desperate to put as many miles as possible between them and the house with its hidden lorry.

One of Chip's bullets must have grazed a tyre, because it blew with an explosion like another gunshot as Garcia took a tight bend and the car careened off the road, spinning for what seemed like an age before impacting against a tree, making every bone in their bodies jump.

There was a few seconds of stillness as the two men took stock of their injuries before the adrenaline overcame the pain and they forced their way out of the battered doors. Both of them were able to run and, without saying a word, they set off in different directions. They had fled scenes like this many times before and knew exactly what to do. Neither of them was bleeding enough to leave traces in the car and both were still wearing their gloves. The wreck they were leaving behind would have the fingerprints of any number of rental customers, including George Lombardi, but not theirs.

* * *

The house that had been so shrouded in darkness and quiet was now a riot of lights and raised voices as police cars, helicopters and an ambulance converged on the site. Spotlights illuminated the whole area as it was cordoned off and sealed. Special operatives from the DEA took control of the lorry in the barn, which still contained its load intact.

Once he had seen Blaine's body safely stowed in the ambulance, Chip's focus turned to the man who had killed his friend, the driver of the car. A battery of patrol cars was called to the area, the empty roads were blocked for miles around and they slowly closed the net in. The thought of these men getting away now, when Blaine had given his life to capture them, was unthinkable. The guilt that riddled him was boiling up into a terrible anger.

'We have the car,' a voice crackled down the radio. 'They've come off the road.'

'Have you got the driver?' he asked.

'No, he's not here. He can't have got far, the engine's still warm and he must have been injured.'

'Seal the area for a mile around the car and comb every inch. I'm on my way.'

Chip took the location of the crash and commandeered a driver. Maybe this one clue was going to be enough to unravel the whole Cali operation and find the man who'd killed his best friend.

A build-up of cloud obscured the moon and stars again as Lex stumbled and crashed through the unfamiliar terrain surrounding the house. He'd no idea where he was heading or how far he had come. He no longer even knew which direction he was walking in. All he knew was he needed to get as far away as possible from the house before dawn. To be constantly falling and pulling himself back onto his feet was draining his strength and he was finding it harder and harder to keep going. He was tempted to stop and rest, but he knew he couldn't afford to do that. If he was found asleep in a hedge he was bound to raise suspicions.

The dawn light eventually arrived and showed him he was travelling east, although he had no idea how far he'd gone. In fact he'd been going round in several circles before finally straightening out his course, and he was no more than three miles from the house. There still seemed to be no sign of any buildings, no crowds that he could lose himself in, no mall or garage where he could find a bathroom to clean himself up. He was so tired his concentration was waning, and suddenly, as he rounded a corner, he found himself confronted by the barrel of a policeman's gun. He instinctively turned to run and found three more guns trained on him from behind. There was no point in attempting to escape, or even to protest his innocence of any crime. He stood very still and silent as they cuffed him, read him his rights and led him to a waiting police car. Further up the road he could see the wreck of his rented Toyota. He wondered if Juan and Garcia had survived the crash and whether they'd been arrested, but he stayed silent. He didn't intend to say a word until he had a lawyer advising him.

Having pushed him into the back of the car, a policeman stood on each side to ensure he didn't try to get out, but none of them got in with him. It was as if they were waiting for something. He could hear police radios, but he couldn't make out what was being said. He waited in complete ignorance of what had *actually* taken place, only knowing that it didn't look good for him. Did they know who he was? Did they know Juan and Garcia were drug dealers from the Cali Cartel? He would do nothing but stay silent and wait to see what would transpire.

An angry white face appeared from nowhere at the window beside him, the palm of a hand slapping hard against the glass, making him jump.

'You son of a bitch,' Chip shouted, wrenching at the door handle, obviously intending to attack him.

Two uniformed officers respectfully but firmly grabbed the furious detective and moved him away from the car before he could say or do anything that might damage their case.

'I'm going to destroy you, you fucking cop-killer.'

Having no idea what had happened at the front of the house, Lex looked genuinely puzzled at such a violent reaction from a man he assumed was a professional policeman.

'The guy who was hit by the car was his buddy,' a uniformed officer explained once Chip was out of earshot.

'Hit by the car?' Lex asked.

'He was killed by the impact.'

Lex was about to protest that he had not been the one driving the car, hadn't even been in it, but thought better of it. It would be better to say nothing until he had a lawyer with him. He had no alibi and no ally. He was going to need a lot more than his own wits and a bit of luck to extricate himself from this predicament.

Chip was already regretting his outburst. He wanted to stay in control of his emotions. This man could be the one to lead them to the very heart of the Cali Cartel, he had to win him over, gain his confidence, deal with him as effectively as possible. The last thing he wanted was to force him onto the defensive. The first thing they needed to do was to take his fingerprints and compare them to the ones that the forensic team had taken in the car wreck.

* * *

Once he realised the pace of Chip Murray's operation, Casper Franks made sure that he heard about every development. The first major piece of news that came through to him was that an NYPD trap had been sprung, but had gone badly wrong. A detective on surveillance duty had been killed and two of the three suspects had escaped.

When he discovered that neither Baptista or Mendez had been captured, together with the murder of an NYPD detective, he felt a stirring of extreme disquiet and sickness in the pit of his stomach. Ramrod had been led to believe that the Cali Cartel had been about to be dealt a terrible blow, one that would damage their east coast operations for years, taking out two of their most senior operatives. As long as Juan and Garcia were still free nothing much would have changed. They might have lost a large consignment of coke, but the consequent increases in prices at street level would more than compensate for their financial loss.

A few days later his world was turned upside down when he heard that the man who had been captured, who had rented the Toyota, was a George Lombardi. His were the only fresh fingerprints on the wheel and door handle. Casper sat very still as the news sank in, his mind racing over the possible ramifications of this new development. George *fucking* Lombardi! Back again like a bad smell. Where did *he* fit into this jigsaw?

What was this going to mean to him and his relationship with Ramrod? Was Lopez double-crossing him? He knew of Lopez's distant family connection to Juan and Garcia, but how in God's name could George Lombardi have got mixed up in this drug bust? Now he could see that the potential repercussions of this explosive news could have devastating consequences for him personally.

IRONIC

He sat for so long, staring out the window of his apartment, puzzling over every possible angle, that he didn't even notice the light had faded back into night.

11

The shock for Lex was absolute. The moment he entered the 105th precinct station in New York he became less than nothing, and everything around him and within him seemed to have changed in a matter of moments. He could see the contempt in the stares of the officers as he passed them by. To them he was just another drug runner willing to kill in order to save his own worthless skin. They might pay a begrudging lip service to the idea that he was innocent until proven guilty, but their eyes told a different story as they stared at him hatefully. Their glances told him he was scum from the lowest of the low. He now realised he was trapped in a desperate situation that he might not escape from. To have been caught up in the murder of an NYPD detective and to be accused of that murder was grave enough, but not to have a credible alibi . . . his situation was just too awful to contemplate. It seemed like lady luck had finally stopped smiling on him.

Lex decided it would be better to remain silent throughout the interrogation while he tried to figure out what his best tactics for survival might be. There were too many conflicting thoughts buzzing through his head for him to form a clear strategy, so it was best not to incriminate himself while he waited to see what developed.

Detective Murray wanted to be present for every moment that the police teams were sifting through the contents of the house and the lorry, stripping both of them down until there was no chance of any hiding places remaining. He didn't trust himself yet to be in the same room as George Lombardi. He wanted to give himself time to calm down and to ensure that he knew exactly what evidence he was going to be able to put together before confronting him.

Searching the lorry didn't take long; within a couple of hours they'd found all the straws containing the cocaine, and had set to work removing every panel on the vehicle to make sure there was nothing else that their intelligence had failed to tip them off about.

'Chip,' a voice behind him made him jump as he watched the forensics team going over every inch of the truck, lost in thought. 'You should see this.'

He followed the fellow officer into the house. Other officers had tugged some panels off the old walls of the dining-room and pulled out a selection of anonymous-looking leather briefcases, which they now opened up on the floor, revealing bundles of used money.

'How much is there?' Chip asked.

'Gee, it's hard to say, but at a rough guess . . . about two million bucks.'

He let out a whistle of pleasure. 'Anything else?'

'A lot more coke,' the officer said, gesturing to a plastic sack filled with small packets.

'This should nail the bastard,' Chip said, his voice low and even, all the early hysteria drained out of it. He felt a cold sense of triumph spreading through him.

'Take it slowly, Chip,' another officer warned. 'Don't let your feelings take over the investigation. Don't risk blowing it by going off half-cocked.'

'I'm not going to risk anything. This man is a cop-killer and he's going down and I'm going to make sure every single nail is in place before I fix down the lid on his coffin.'

The other officer nodded his understanding, knowing Chip well enough to realise that he didn't need to question him any further. They all wanted the same thing.

Lex was taken to the visitor's room at the precinct where he was told an attorney had been appointed to represent him. He didn't like the idea of having someone else choose his attorney for him, but at that moment he couldn't see he had much choice. All he could do was hope.

The man who was waiting for him was overweight and sweating.

'Mr Lombardi?' He wiped the palm of his hand on the shiny seat of his trousers before holding it out. 'I'm Jack Crew. I'm your attorney, appointed by the legal panel.'

George nodded and wiped Jack's sweat off his own palm before sitting down. He could see the other man had noticed the gesture. The attorney loosened his tie awkwardly, showing a light fraying around his collar.

'It doesn't look good, my friend,' he said, gesturing down at the papers on the table in front of him. Lex said nothing, waiting for him to continue. 'They're going to indict you on a charge of capital murder. That carries the death penalty. That's what they're going to be looking to get.'

Jack looked up from the papers, obviously surprised by the lack of response from his new client. Lex said nothing, just staring at him and nodding very slightly.

'Is there anything you would like to tell me, Mr Lombardi?'

'Like what?'

'Like whether you are guilty.'

'No I am not guilty. I wasn't even in the car.'

'They've got your prints all over it.'

'I had been in the car earlier. I hired it. I stopped off at the house to ask for directions and the guys stole the car when they heard the police were coming. I panicked and ran.'

His story had begun to come together in his head while he had been sitting in the cell. It didn't sound too plausible, but it would be hard for them to disprove if they didn't have Juan Baptista or Garcia Mendez to contradict it.'

Jack Crew unwrapped a stick of gum without offering any to his client and chewed it methodically, staring hard at Lex.

'I don't know that I am going to be able to sell that, George, I really don't.'

'Then maybe you aren't the man for the job,' Lex said, holding his voice steady, managing to disguise the panic that was mounting inside him.

Jack made a facetious show of looking all around the room. 'Don't see anyone else queuing up to take over from me,' he sneered.

'Are you going to fight to get me justice here, Mr Crew, or not?'

'I'll do my best, George, I'll do my best.'

Lex wasn't sure that Crew's best was likely to be very good. He was feeling nauseous at the thought and for the first time in his life he was truly petrified. If his future lay in this man's hands there was absolutely no chance he would gain an acquittal.

* * *

'So you just happened to stop at this particular house for directions?' Chip Murray was staring hard into Lex's eyes, as if hoping to burn a hole through to the truth he was certain must be hiding inside Lex's head.

'That's correct.' Lex was feeling tired. He'd been in custody for two days and every waking hour someone had been questioning him. None of the interrogators had broken any of the rules but they'd stretched them as far as they could in the hope of piling on the pressure.

'Out of fifty million or more homes, you just happened to come across the one where two of the country's most wanted men happened to be holed up?'

Lex nodded.

'Even though that particular house was well hidden from the road and way up a long drive?'

Lex nodded again.

'So, by coincidence you turned into the drive in the hope of getting directions, and then found two old friends waiting to greet you.'

'I didn't know them.'

'You greeted them by name.'

'I didn't know what their names were.'

'We have you on tape, George, greeting them as Juan and Garcia.'

'They looked South American. Chances were they would be called Juan or Garcia. Maybe I should have tried Carlos? I didn't know what their fucking names were, they were just two guys with South American accents.'

'So if they'd been Chinese you'd have called out 'hi Chin, hi Chan'. Is that what you're telling me?'

'Okay, I plead guilty to some racial stereotyping. Is that any reason for me to be locked up?'

'This is a crock of shit, George,' Murray suggested through gritted teeth. 'You're taking the piss and I don't think that's appropriate with a policeman dead at your hands.'

'Listen, Detective Murray,' Lex sat forward, trying to overwhelm Chip with his sincerity, 'I'm sorry about your buddy, I really am. If I was you I would be looking for someone to pin it on too. But you've got the wrong guy. I wasn't in the car.'

Chip opened his mouth to let out a stream of invective, but caught himself just in time. 'Now you listen to me, George,' he said, with a forced calmness. 'You're up on a charge of killing a detective, and you have no defence worth a goddam. You could fight us all the way, waste a lot of taxpayers' money and piss everyone off, or you could just tell us the truth and earn our eternal gratitude. Do you understand what I mean?'

'I wasn't in the car,' Lex repeated, like a robot.

'Fuck!' Chip slammed his fist down on the desk, making everyone in the room jump. Exploding onto his feet, knocking his chair back against the wall, he stormed from the room, leaving his colleagues to conclude the interview and arrange for Lex to be escorted back to his cell. As he shuffled back down the bleak corridors, the gates clanging shut behind him, he could see no way to escape from the fate that now stared him in the face.

If Lex Goldman felt dispirited in the holding cell at 105th, the one they transferred him to in Shawangunk Correctional Facility destroyed the last vestiges of hope that he might be saved by one of his usual strokes of luck. It was one of America's tough maximum security prisons, located in Ulster County, about three hundred kilometres from Manhattan in upstate New York. None of his fellow prisoners were inside for any sort of white collar crime, this was the place where the authorities sent the scum of the criminal world, the murderers, the rapists, the pimps and the drug dealers, this was the place they believed George Lombardi, drug dealer and cop-killer, deserved to be incarcerated until the state got around to putting him on trial.

Nowhere in Shawangunk was Lex safe. He shared his cell with three other inmates, all of whom took sadistic pleasure in hurting him whenever they felt like it. His spirit broken, he became little more than their slave as he cleaned and ran errands for them while they relaxed on their bunks or entertained themselves by deliberately fouling the cell so he had to clean it again, laughing and swearing at his efforts. All the time his hands were busy working his mind was somewhere else, trying to work out how he could gain some advantage, some way of improving his position, of improving the odds against him.

The prison officers were no different to the cons, removing all his privileges without explanation, spitting in his food, pushing and kicking him whenever they were moving him from one place to another. Everyone in Shawangunk seemed to hold him in contempt and there seemed nothing he could do to break through the cycle of hatred, so he remained silent, his head bowed, biding his time.

Over at One, Police Plaza, the narcotics division had been focusing its attention on the investigation of one man – George Lombardi. The authorities knew that Detective Murray was obsessed and they were willing to let him work that obsession out if it resulted in a conviction. If they could pin the murder of Detective Harmon on Lombardi and then link it to the Cali or Medellin Cartels, they would stand a much better chance of getting the budgets they needed to go after the big fish in the cartels. As the months passed, Chip's initial rage calmed to a simmering white heat of determination. He didn't care how many hours he had to spend sifting through each tiny scrap of evidence and gleaning any information he could about George Lombardi. He wanted to know every move his suspect had made from the day he was born to the day he'd killed Blaine. His determination filled the whole station with its intensity, and his colleagues stood in awe of his colossal stoicism. There wasn't a man or woman in the building who wasn't aware of his need to convict the killer of his childhood friend, and they all wanted to do anything they could to assist him. Blaine had been a popular figure.

'There's a lot about this guy that just doesn't add up,' Chip said to the team still sitting with him late one evening.

'Like what?'

'Like the fact that he hardly seems to use his credit cards. Seems to prefer paying for everything in cash: hotels, airlines. Who pays cash for air tickets?'

'Someone with a lot of drug money to launder?' someone suggested.

'That's the other thing. He knew the guys from Cali, right?'

'He says not . . .'

'Yeah, yeah, just happened to turn up their drive in the middle of the night. He knew them, we can be sure of that. But we have no record of him ever flying to Cali, but Avianca has records of him flying several times to Medellin from Miami.'

'Maybe he works for Medellin and was just making contact with the Cali guys? Maybe they're thinking of working together.'

'Highly unlikely and it doesn't fit with our intelligence.' Chip shook his head, his eyes squinting at the effort of trying to see a pattern in all the evidence surrounding him on the desktops and pinboards. The thought of an alliance between the Cali and Medellin Cartels was too terrible to even contemplate. He couldn't believe that was possible. Was it?

'There are no mobile phone records, either,' he went on. 'How did he talk to people and not leave a trace?'

'It's not possible that it's a red herring, is it?' someone suggested. 'Could it be that he's telling the truth? That he really did just come upon the house by chance?'

'If that's true, how come he's got no regular address, no one coming forward to vouch for him? The guy hardly acts like a homeless bum, so where are his family? Where's his past. It's like he just materialises in and out of thin air.'

'What about the Chase Pacific Bank connection, has that led to anything?'

'Not really. He definitely worked there, moved in the highest circles. He'd some involvement with that guy LaVine who got jailed for that Wall Street insider trading scam five years ago, but somehow managed to keep his own nose clean. Everyone around him has been busted, but he seems to move on unscathed. I just don't get it. Maybe that was why he was driving so recklessly to get away from the bust, knowing he couldn't afford to get caught.'

'The bank must know where he came from, they must have a record of his past employers.'

'You'd think, but they don't seem to be able to turn up anything. The people I talked to there were as mystified as us. Someone put him into the bank with no history going on the record. He was such a good performer for them no one stopped to ask any questions. None of it makes any sense. And he just stonewalls every question.'

All Chip's colleagues could see how deeply he was hurting,

how much he wanted to nail the mysterious George Lombardi for Blaine's death. Everyone had heard how George's refusal to co-operate in the interrogation room had driven Detective Murray almost to the end of his tether. It had taken two officers to hold him back when his temper finally snapped after two hours of 'no comment' answers to every question he put.

All Chip could see was an image of Blaine's pale face as he lay dead on the cold ground that night. The sight haunted him throughout the days, and came back to him in his dreams when he finally managed to get to sleep. The only escape he could imagine would be to ensure that George Lombardi paid the full price for his crime.

'I can't get any further back than 1989,' Chip told his boss after another painstaking month of frustration. 'I need to ask for extra assistance.'

'From who?' Captain Serrano looked wary.

'The CIA, the FBI . . . Someone must know where this guy came from, unless he's some kind of fucking alien.'

Amigo grinned, relieved to see Chip could finally crack a joke. 'Do whatever you have to do,' he said. 'But don't expect them to fall over themselves to help.'

Chip Murray put the wheels into motion the moment he got back to his desk. He expected to have to keep chasing for at least several days before getting any response, so he was surprised when his call was returned within an hour by Directorate of Operations at CIA headquarters.

'We can make no material available to you in regard of George Lombardi. All such material is classified.'

'*Classified*?' Chip said out loud once the phone line had gone dead. 'What kind of a crock of shit answer is that?'

* * *

'George Lom-*fucking*-bardi!' Special Agent Trent Colby literally spat the words out the moment Special Agent Franks walked into his office at Langley, Virginia.

'What about him?'

'You're supposed to be in control of that son of a bitch.'

'He's under control.' Franks' temper was rising at being talked to like a school kid.

'He's killed a fucking cop and been swept up in a drug bust by the NYPD narcotics division.'

'Relax, the situation can be managed.'

Franks was bluffing. He had no idea how he was going to get the situation back under control once Colby had filled him in on it. His instincts were to have Lombardi eliminated, but that wasn't going to be so easy now he was held inside Shawangunk. It wouldn't be hard to arrange for an accident, but with the police so desperate to bring him to trial, an unexplained death would bring everyone out on the Lombardi trail.

'This guy was a loose cannon from the start,' Colby raged. 'That's why he was given to you. Now the police are poking their noses in and wherever they go the media are bound to follow. If they find out about our links to Rodriguez and the Contras the whole of the CIA will be severely damaged. This could be the biggest mess since . . .' He trailed off, unable to think of a mess big enough.

'Watergate?' Franks prompted helpfully.

Colby opened his mouth to respond but thought better of it. He rubbed his forehead hard and forced himself to calm down. 'I received a call from Lombardi some time ago mentioning the CIA connection to Rodriguez. I cut him off without listening to what he had to say. Now we need to know how he would have known about that.'

This was a disturbing snippet of news for Casper. His own position was now becoming increasingly vulnerable on two fronts, both of them potentially life-threatening.

'You didn't think to ask at the time?' Franks pressed his advantage without revealing his unease.

'Get your ass up to the prison,' Colby shouted, 'find out what's going on and what the fucker knows!'

The small bare room was filled with hatred. Neither Lex nor the CIA agent wanted to spend a moment longer with the other than they had to, but both knew their lives were now inextricably linked.

'What kind of a fucking shit hole have you dug yourself into?' Franks wanted to know, once he was confident the prison guards were out of earshot.

'One that should be familiar to you,' Lex snarled. 'It's down to you to get me out of here.'

'You're fuckin' kidding I hope. We bailed you out last time. This time you're on your own, pal.'

'Bad decision, Franks, very bad decision.'

'Don't talk down to me you piece of shit.'

'Listen, buddy, I know everything about the CIA involvement with Ramrod. I know all about the way you fund the Contras with narcotics money, and . . . I *know* all about you, you fucking double-crossing bastard. I could blow the whole thing open tomorrow.'

'Who the fuck would believe you, a cop-killer with no past? You are screwed, baby. We were your only hope and you've pissed us off. You've pissed everyone off, you greedy fucker.'

'If I go down for this killing, I'll be taking the lot of you with me.'

Casper Franks' fist bunched up to deliver a punch but he thought better of it just in time. 'What makes you think the CIA is involved in any of this?' he asked instead.

'I'm not telling you what I know or how I know until you tell me what the deal is to get me out of here.'

'We don't have to deal with you, Lombardi, you scumbag. You have nothing left to deal with. You're fucked and I've heard enough shit for one day.'

Franks stood up and banged on the door for the guard. There was a rattling of keys and the door opened. Lex rose to leave with his escort.

'Oh, by the way, *Conrad* suits you much better than Casper,' he said, before striding from the room.

Casper stood in the doorway with his mouth open but no words coming out. He felt a terrible numbness come over him as he realised that with those few words George Lombardi had shifted the balance of power and now his future was totally compromised.

'What do you want?' the CIA man shouted down the corridor after him.

'Get a message to Sophie Goldman, get her here.'

'How do I do that?'

'I don't care how you do it, but if you want silence, that's the price.'

Casper saw the prison guard's curious expression and knew it would be dangerous to say any more.

Back in his cell, Lex Goldman felt the first lifting of his spirits since the night of the arrest. His cellmates seemed to sense a change in his demeanour and stayed quiet, as if they knew he wasn't quite the victim he'd been an hour before. The expression on Franks' face had told Lex that he'd managed to score a direct hit, and had given himself the smallest of handholds on the slimy sides of the pit he'd found himself in. That was enough to revive his natural sense of optimism. He was back in charge, if only of a small part of his life, but it was enough for him to feel he might be able to get away with this yet. The rush of adrenaline had woken his brain from the torpor it had fallen into. He lifted his eyes off the floor for the first time since being incarcerated, and met the stares of his cellmates directly. They blinked and looked away first. The strategy he'd been searching for suddenly came clearly into his mind. This was a possible way out of his predicament, a chance to get back in control.

He tried to imagine how Sophie would take the news that her husband had not been killed all those years ago as she'd been led to believe. Maybe she wouldn't want to know anything about it. Maybe she wouldn't believe them when they told her. He couldn't blame her for a moment if she decided to ignore him. Allowing her to think that he'd been killed was a despicable thing to do, he realised that, and he deeply regretted it, but there had been nothing he could do about it at the time. He had tried to follow her career since then, but she'd kept such a low profile he had no idea whether she had met someone else. Now, having so many thoughts of Sophie, he found himself suddenly eager to see her again.

'Mrs Goldman?' one of the men on the doorstep enquired. Sophie could tell they were policemen just from looking at them. Since withdrawing to her elegant Georgian hideaway in Sussex, she didn't receive many visitors. That was the way she liked it. She had her writing and her dogs and horses to keep her distracted, she didn't need visitors, particularly strangers, particularly policemen. Her immediate thought was that the two detectives might be there perhaps to talk about her Irish connections. It wasn't an appealing thought. She always blamed herself for Lex's death, assuming that the bomb had been placed on the boat by Mudge or one of his sidekicks.

From the moment she had been informed of the mysterious explosion in the Caribbean she had severed all contact with her past life and had started writing detective novels under an assumed name. The books had become huge bestsellers, even without any promotion of the author, dominating the national bestseller lists. It wasn't that Lex hadn't left her amply provided for financially, particularly as she had inherited a large portion of the family estate on her father's death, it was more that she found writing a convenient way to drive out the demons of her past and the guilt she felt for Lex's death.

'Who's asking?' she enquired with a sweet, patrician smile.

The policemen showed her their identification papers. She read them slowly and deliberately, giving herself time to collect her thoughts and prepare herself for whatever questions would come next.

'You'd better come in,' she sighed, once she had satisfied herself they were who they claimed. She led them through to the drawing-room where a log fire was burning cheerfully. The dogs, which had set up an explosion of barking upon the men's arrival, settled back down on the warmth of the hearth. 'Would you like tea?'

The policemen accepted the offer and Sophie went to the kitchen to ask her housekeeper to bring it through, moving deliberately slowly to give herself more time to think.

'Are you all right, madam?' the housekeeper asked, shocked to see how pale her employer looked.

'I'm fine,' Sophie assured her with a brave smile.

When they were finally settled, and the policemen were confident that they were talking to the right person, they passed her a piece of paper with a number on it.

'We have been asked by the CIA in the United States to give you this number. It is a secure line. You need to ask for a Special Agent Casper Franks.'

She took the number from them and looked at it for a moment, as if just staring at the digits would explain the need for the call. 'What does Mr Franks want to talk to me about?'

'We wouldn't know, Mrs Goldman. We were just asked to pass the number on and stress to you the urgency.'

Sophie looked at her watch. 'Do you want me to call him now, while you're here?'

'Mr Franks should be at the end of the line by now,' the senior policeman nodded.

'All right.'

The men averted their eyes politely as she picked up the phone and dialled.

'This is Sophie Goldman. May I speak to Mr Casper Franks?'

'Agent Franks speaking.'

'I am unsure who you are Mr Franks.'

'I am from CIA Directorate of Operations, Mrs Goldman, and I would ask that you treat the information I am about to give you as highly confidential.'

'As you wish.' Sophie wondered if perhaps they had arrested one of Mudge's old cronies for something and wanted her to testify against them. She prepared herself.

'Your husband, Lex Goldman,' Franks said, pausing to allow her to take in the name.

'Yes?'

'He is alive and well and being held under the name George

Lombardi at the Shawangunk Correctional Facility, located in Ulster County, in upstate New York. He wishes you to visit him urgently.'

'Lex is . . . *alive?*' The shock of the announcement left her unable to breathe easily, and the two policemen sat forward in their comfortable armchairs, preparing themselves to help should she pass out.

'We can make arrangements for you to join the first flight to New York that the police can get you onto.'

'You have caught me rather unawares, Mr Franks,' she said, politely.

Her mind was racing over the possibilities, the adrenaline pumping in a way she hadn't experienced for many years, and had hoped never to experience again. If this was true, would it mean that her past was about to be dredged up for public consumption? The last thing she wanted was for the media to start digging into her youthful indiscretions.

'I would want my trip to be discreet,' she said cautiously after a few moments thought.'

'Mrs Goldman,' she thought she could detect a slight chuckle in the voice on the other end of the line, 'I can assure you that we are even more anxious than you to keep this matter discreet.'

'I see,' she said, feeling only slightly safer. 'I am trusting you at your word.'

'I have trusted you with my name and my title,' Casper purred, 'I wouldn't have done that if I thought there was any danger of media coverage.'

She paused again to gather her thoughts and then made her decision. 'All right. The police are with me now. I'll pass you over.'

Once the senior policeman had taken the phone from her and

started talking about flight times and arrangements, she tuned out, her thoughts a blur as she tried to piece together the startling news she'd just been given. How could it possibly be true? After all this time . . . Where had Lex been? Why hadn't he contacted her? She was surprised to feel her heart beating faster than usual; was that because she was nervous about the ramifications of this discovery, or was it just the thought of seeing Lex again after so long? Giving up hope of finding any answers, she waited for the detective to hang up and tell her what would happen next. Four hours later she was sitting in the first class cabin on a British Airways flight to JFK, still dazed and unable to comprehend what was happening to her. How was she going to feel about meeting the 'ghost' of a man she'd once loved and then grieved for?

As Sophie was shown into the honour room at Shawangunk she didn't immediately recognise the man sitting waiting for her. He was handsome but thin, gaunt-looking with horn-rimmed glasses and silver-white hair.

'No touching,' the guard snapped.

When she realised that this *was* Lex, she wasn't able to stop herself from letting out a sharp cry of surprise, and clamped her hand across her mouth.

'You've hardly changed at all,' Lex said, standing up, fighting back the urge to take her in his arms and cling to her. Sophie tried to find something polite to say in return, but could find nothing. 'I'm sorry, this must have been a terrible shock but I didn't have anyone else to turn to.'

'I'm so glad you are alive,' she said when her voice finally croaked back into life. 'I was so sure it was my fault.'

'Don't be silly. It would never have been your fault. I made all my own choices.'

'But I introduced you to Mudge and the others . . .'

'Ah, how is Mudge?' He smiled at the distant memory.

'Mudge is dead, killed in London a couple of years after you,' she corrected herself, 'at least two years after I thought you had . . .'

'Mudge . . . dead . . . what happened to him?'

'A bomb he was carrying in his car detonated prematurely. He was blown to pieces. It was all such a waste, all so stupid. We all wrecked our lives by letting ourselves be brainwashed and manipulated. We were just pawns chasing after the impossible dream. For what exactly . . . ? The two men closest to me . . . if only we . . . I'd . . . Oh, Lex . . . I am *so* overjoyed you are alive . . . but, how did you come to be George Lombardi?' Her voice had lowered to a whisper.

She sat down across the table from him and listened without speaking as he explained the bare bones of why he was imprisoned.

'They say I've murdered an NYPD detective. You have to trust me, Sophie,' he said, staring hard into her eyes. 'I didn't do it.'

'I believe you,' she said quietly. 'What can I do to help?'

'I don't have much time. I need the best defence legal team money can buy, and you have to get me out of here so I can prepare my case.'

'Christ, I don't know if I will be able to do that,' Sophie admitted.

'Sophie, you're my only chance.'

'I'll do everything I can.'

James L. Bates never had a business meeting without first finding out everything he could about the other party. By the time Sophie Goldman arrived in his plush lower Manhattan offices a few days later, his team had researched much about her family, her marriage and her dubious affiliations to Irish Republicanism in the early eighties. There was never any point in taking meetings with people who wouldn't be able to afford his fees, or whose profiles wouldn't help his reputation as the best, and most expensive, defence attorney, especially in murder trials. There was no doubt from the material his researchers had brought to his house the night before the meeting that Sophie Goldman was indeed a very wealthy woman, and any trial that involved her would be bound to bring a lot of media attention to all those involved. The initial telephone briefing had left him very intrigued, *especially* when he'd heard how her husband had been 'killed' and now had turned up with a new identity facing a murder charge!

He was even more impressed when he saw how attractive she was as she was ushered into the inner sanctum of the office, with its panoramic views across most of New York's fabled skyline. Good looks always played well in the media. Coffee was served discreetly and James Bates listened quietly as the elegant woman in front of him went into more detail.

'They tell me you have a fearsome reputation, Mr Bates,' she said once she had finished.

'Indeed I do, but I don't work alone, I head a large team. This brief could work out to be very expensive. Are you willing to foot the bills on your husband's behalf, and if there are bail requirements, to fund the amount? It could be, and I'm not promising mind, a seriously big number.'

'Yes, I am. Whatever it takes. To start with I want him out of that prison as quickly as possible.'

'There is almost no hope of that, Mrs Goldman. Bail in a capital murder case is virtually unheard of.'

'That's why I hired you, Mr Bates. My husband is completely

innocent. He was simply in the wrong place at the wrong time. You've got to try.'

'It couldn't have been more of a wrong place, could it?'

'There is a lot more to explain, but all you have to know at the moment is that he is an innocent man. He doesn't deserve to be executed for this poor detective's death.'

Bates sat thinking for a moment. He was impressed by Sophie's sincerity. He had met enough insincere people in his time to know the real thing when he saw it. He wanted to help her. He also sensed, even from the little that she had told him, that this had all the ingredients for a sensational trial. Indeed, it could become the media trial of the decade, keeping his name prominent on every news bulletin and newspaper headline in the States for several weeks at least, maybe even months.

'Let me see what I can do. I will need to pull a lot of strings. As soon as I have news I'll call you.'

The call eventually came a week later. 'Mrs Goldman,' he said, 'James Bates here. It was a real tough battle, but I brought an urgent preliminary hearing before a Justice Villars at the Manhattan Criminal Court and he's agreed to set bail at five million dollars. He's set the following bail conditions: your husband must stay within New York State, his passport will remain confiscated and he must report to a NYPD station every three days. Is that acceptable?'

'I will have the money wired to your account by close of business tomorrow, Mr Bates. And . . . thank you.'

'Don't thank me yet,' he said. 'We're only just at the start. Your husband is in big trouble and this judge has proved to be very difficult in past cases I've put before him. The odds are still massively stacked against us.'

* * *

A few days later, Lex and Sophie were strolling through Central Park, both of them feeling they needed fresh air, both of them feeling slightly shy, almost as if they were on a first date together. The moment he was free of the jail Lex had transformed back to his old self, standing tall, immaculately bathed and groomed, wearing newly purchased clothes. It was like the previous six months had been a very bad dream. He had bounced back again with all the energy of his youth. They made a handsome couple.

'I'm so glad you're alive,' Sophie said eventually, after they had been walking in silence for some time. 'When I first heard about the explosion and everyone said it was the work of the IRA, I felt like it was all my fault, I'd got you involved with them. If it wasn't for me . . .'

Lex interrupted, 'Look Sophie, I'm the one who's sorry, it was such a desperate thing I had to do, but I had to move fast. Flint threatened to kill me and he could have struck at any time. There was only one way I knew I could be completely safe. I had some involvement with the CIA over here and asked to be put into their protection programme. It was either that or be looking over my shoulder or fearing every knock on the door for the rest of my life. I wanted to find some way to tell you that I was okay, not to worry, but I couldn't take the risk of the message being intercepted. They would only agree to give me a new identity if I obeyed their every rule.'

They stopped at a stall to buy themselves coffee, sitting on a wall while they drank it and continued to chat.

'That must have been one heck of a journey, being wounded and chased through the jungles of Colombia, surviving a plane crash, then finding your oil tankers blockaded in the Panama Canal and having to fake your own death in the Caribbean,' said Sophie, barely pausing for breath.

'Well, every day was different, excitement and danger in equal measure, but what it really came down to was Flint and the IRA wanted their money and I couldn't deliver. I knew then I had to disappear or else they would kill me. So, at the end of 1988, with the considerable help of the CIA, a Mr George Lombardi surfaced in St Louis. Oh, Sophie darling, you really won't believe what happened to me next . . .'

12

'I'm sorry to have to tell you this, Ishani, but it really is time you moved on.'

The look in her uncle's eyes suggested that he wasn't really sorry at all. In fact he looked angry and offended, as if Ishani had somehow managed to insult him by having a child without first acquiring a husband. She wasn't exactly surprised by his words; she'd been expecting this reaction ever since she first had to admit to him that she was pregnant. She suspected he was under intense pressure from others to make this announcement. This wasn't the type of thing a good, deeply religious Asian family wanted to be associated with, especially within such a close-knit community of friends and neighbours. He wasn't even her uncle, strictly speaking, more of a cousin several times removed, but he'd been kind about taking her in nevertheless, until she 'let him down'.

'I have nowhere else to go, Uncle,' she said, hoping that he would be able to suggest somewhere for her to go as much as anything. She was still a stranger in New York.

'You must rent a room, Ishani, and be independent. It is the American way.'

She might still be a stranger in the city, but she'd been in New York long enough by then to know that she was not likely to get a good response from landlords when she turned up on their doorstep with her dark skin and a fatherless baby in her arms. She had already come to understand that although America called itself the 'Land of the Free', some were freer than others. It had been a disappointment to her. The newspapers talked a lot about the 'swinging sixties' and about 'free love' and 'racial equality', but on the streets nothing had really changed. The sort of people who would be willing to take her rent money without asking any probing questions owned the sort of properties that she didn't want to even attempt to bring up a child in.

'Do you know of anyone who will rent me a room?' she asked, hating to have to ask him for even this small favour. She could hear other members of the family in the next room, as they tried to eavesdrop on the conversation. They all wanted to be rid of her. The house was crowded enough before she arrived, and now they had the perfect excuse, making her expulsion from their home a matter of morality rather than a matter of meanness.

'I will ask around,' he promised. 'But you must be gone by the end of the week.'

'I understand,' she said, bowing her head politely. She owed him a debt of gratitude for taking her in at all in her time of need. Ishani knew that his life was not easy either and she didn't want to add to his troubles.

True to his word, her uncle made some enquiries, and at the end of the week she was able to move into a room of her own, which shared a bathroom with two other families and where the noise coming through the walls from the neighbours never seemed to cease day or night. Cockroaches hunted in packs around her kitchen floor and Kal, her newborn son, added to the cacophony with his continual screams, sensing his mother's unhappiness.

'Why do you wish to study law?' the stern-faced professor enquired. It was the fifth law school she had applied to since arriving in New York and the other four had all fallen ominously silent after her interview.

'I believe that there are not many women who are representative of me in the profession and I think that there's a need for people from all walks of life to be part of the legal system in order to ensure a fair society for all. A strong legal framework is the only way that a country can protect its more vulnerable citizens, and those who work within it need to understand the needs of those they are serving before they can hope to do it effectively.'

She could see that the woman on the interview panel was now staring at her intently, and the black man at the end of the row was smiling encouragingly. All the other faces, however, were stony, most of their eyes averted as they scribbled down notes.

'You're not going to offer me a place, are you?' she said, fighting to keep her anger under control.

'You have a small son, I believe, Miss Sharma,' another of the men enquired, choosing to ignore her question.

'Yes, I do.'

'Who will look after him while you study?' the woman asked, and Ishani could see that she had now lost her support as well.

'I have many relatives in New York who are happy to help out,' she lied. In truth she'd no idea how she would balance bringing up Kal and studying, she just knew that she intended to do it.

They were all writing now.

'Don't any of you realise,' she protested, unable to hold the anger in any longer, 'just how much prejudice there is in this country? The longer you go on trying to ignore the problem, the bigger the explosion will be when it finally comes.'

Now they were all looking at her, but only the black man was smiling, a little nervously.

'I'm sorry,' she said, 'but I feel very passionately about this. I came to America because I believed it was a land where everyone could be free and equal, but I find that it isn't so. I find suspicion and hatred everywhere. I cannot see why it isn't obvious to everyone in authority that something will have to change if you don't want to see bloodshed in the streets.'

'Thank you, Miss Sharma.' The panel spokesman silenced her outpouring. 'We will be in touch in due course.'

She knew from experience that that meant they would definitely not be in touch. Once she realised she was not going to get into law school, she concentrated on survival for herself and Kal. She took a series of menial jobs, just to put some food on the table. They were normally the sort of employers who would tell her they were willing to employ people like her, but not 'the blacks'. She would try to look grateful and not tell them what she thought of 'people like them', although sometimes she was unable to stop herself and ended up having to find another job the next day. She took Kal to work with her whenever possible, or spent her hard earned money on babysitters when she couldn't.

The unpleasantness of the ghetto she was forced to live in made her want to get out as often as possible, and in the evenings she would bundle Kal up against the cold and take him with her to any political meetings she could find.

Soon she came across the activities of the American Civil Rights Movement, and by spending many evenings in dingy local halls listening to a mixture of speakers, she learned more about its goals. The more she heard, the more convinced she became that the simmering melting-pot of racial tension was about to overflow and change everything. The media were also starting to take notice as celebrities like Marlon Brando and James Baldwin began to add their voices to the chorus, marching on Washington, demanding that blacks and Asians should be given equal rights throughout the country. Her own anger became edged with excitement at the thought that she might be able to play a part in the social changes that the Movement was striving for.

It was at a demonstration in Central Park that summer that she first heard Luther Woodson speak. The previous speaker hadn't been able to hold the attention of the crowd, and people around her had started to have their own conversations as he spoke, but as soon as Luther's rich, southern tones boomed through the tannoy system everyone started to pay attention. Ishani looked up at the stage, holding tight to Kal so he wouldn't escape while her attention was distracted, and was surprised by how young the speaker appeared. The authority in his voice had suggested he was a middle-aged man, but she doubted he was much older than her. He was also strikingly handsome, tall and athletic, more like a basketball player than a civil rights activist. Throughout his speech Ishani hardly noticed Kal's wriggles and protests as she held him firmly, and the moment Luther climbed down from the stage she pushed her way through the crowd to get to the front. She wasn't sure why, but it suddenly seemed vital that she spoke to him before he was swallowed up by the mass of people crowding round him. She felt fearful that she might never see him again.

'Hi,' she panted as she finally reached him.

'Hi,' he beamed at her with the broadest smile she'd ever seen and then lowered his eyes to Kal. 'And hi to you too, what's your name?'

'His name's Kal,' she said. 'That certainly was an inspiring speech,' she added, wishing she could think of something more intelligent to say.

'Thanks. It was a great audience.'

'There are so many things that have to be changed.'

'Well, I won't disagree,' he laughed. She could tell from the way he was looking at her that he was feeling the chemistry, just as she was, but he seemed to be handling it with a great deal more dignity.

'Listen,' he said, 'I have to go and meet with some people now. Is there any chance I could call you tomorrow and maybe we could get together for coffee or something? Be a chance to get to know you better. Bring Kal along too.'

'Sure.' She rummaged desperately through her coat pocket for a pen and piece of paper to jot down the number of the communal phone on the floor of her block. 'That would be really cool.'

She didn't hear the phone ring on the landing outside her room the next day, and one of the neighbours had to knock hard on her door to wake her up.

'Hey, honey, there's a call for you,' her neighbour shouted.

She staggered out to pick up the dangling receiver. 'Hello?'

'Hi, Ishani, you fancy some breakfast?'

'Sure.' At the sound of his voice she was suddenly awake, like an electric shock had passed through her entire body.

'I'll come by and pick you both up if you give me your address.'

She told him.

'See you in about half an hour then.'

If he was shocked by the squalor of her block he didn't allow it to show on his face when he arrived. It was as if he couldn't see anything except her and Kal, as if the sight of them so delighted him that nothing else mattered. Talking non-stop, they made their way to the nearest diner and he ordered them all breakfast. Ishani saw Kal's face as he stared in wonder at the tall handsome black man paying him so much attention, and realised she'd been staring at Luther in just the same awestruck way.

She'd never heard anyone talk so eloquently and with such passion about civil rights. He managed to put into words all the things she'd been thinking about for years. He seemed to mix eating, chatting away with her and occupying Kal with a calm assurance. Through his eyes she started to see life in America differently. It wasn't that he didn't see the same problems or tried to pretend that they didn't exist, quite the opposite. But despite the country's poisonous social atmosphere, he remained joyfully optimistic as the months passed.

'By the time Kal is a grown up things will be much different,' he assured her. 'There's a groundswell. Young people no longer think the same way as their parents. Things are going to change for the better, very soon. If you keep fighting you will get into law school one day and you will be a great lawyer.'

He made it all sound so convincing, especially when he would introduce her to some of the senior figures in the Movement, charismatic people who had great vision for the future. She and Kal travelled with Luther all over the country, listening to him speak at rallies and to others like him. The more time she spent with him, the more she realised she had fallen deeply and completely in love.

'Will you marry me?' Luther asked, just six months after their first meeting.

'You realise that if you take me on you have to take Kal on as well?' she said.

'Are you kidding me?' he laughed. 'He's a big part of the reason I want to marry you. So, will you marry me?'

'Oh, Luther, my darling, yes,' she said, 'of course I will.'

Kal, unaware of what was going on, laughed and clapped happily to see his two favourite people hugging and kissing each other.

Once they were married and had moved to a better apartment in New York, Ishani went back to her law books in preparation for another attempt at gaining admission to law school. Luther spent most of his time travelling, but for Kal's sake Ishani didn't feel she could travel with him all the time, however tempted she might be. There were a lot of lonely nights in the apartment once Kal had gone to sleep, and she would worry as she watched news bulletins reporting from the many violent flashpoints around the country. The deep southern states were getting most of the current coverage and that happened to be where Luther was doing most of his crusading.

'We have to talk,' Luther said to her one morning while they were lying in bed together on one of his rare visits home.

'We do?' She didn't like the seriousness of his tone.

'There is so much to be done down there now.'

'I know.' she stroked his brow, trying to smooth out the worried wrinkles. 'It's okay. I understand.'

'No,' he said, taking her in his arms, 'you don't. I'm going to be spending much more time down in Mississippi now. I'm going to have to base myself in Jackson.'

'Jackson? What do you mean "base yourself"?'

'We're going to have to move there, baby.'

'Move to Jackson?' His words were only just starting to sink into her brain. She hadn't visited that area but she'd heard enough about it to know that things would be a lot tougher for someone with coloured skin there than in New York. 'Is there really not a job you can do for the Movement up here?'

'I have to be there, baby. It's where our people desperately need us the most. These are the important years. If we can keep up the pressure now we can change things for the better for ever.'

'I know, Luther, I know all that. But taking Kal to Jackson? He's settled here. He has a home.'

'His home will be wherever we are,' Luther reasoned, 'with his family.'

Ishani felt the tears welling up as she looked into his kind, anxious face. 'You are such a good man, Luther Woodson,' she said as she stared straight into his eyes, and he knew she was going to agree to come with him.

Had Ishani realised just how bad things were going to be in Mississippi, she mightn't have allowed her love for Luther to cloud her judgement. She was already concerned about putting herself in harm's way but Kal and Luther's safety was worrying her a lot more. Kal, because he was just a small, defenceless child, and Luther because he was so stubborn, refusing to be intimidated by any of the bully-boy tactics of the segregationists. Even when thugs started fire-bombing the houses of some ACRM leaders, he still refused to stop speaking out and appearing in public, thereby making himself a continual target.

'I can't stop you from risking your own life,' she pleaded with him, over and over again, 'but what if they attack the house while Kal is asleep in his bed? What then?'

'We cannot allow them to win,' Luther would reply sadly. 'We have to be brave so that Kal and his children can live without fear and prejudice in their lives. If they think that they can silence us with threats of violence, what will ever stop them from continuing to grind us into the dirt?'

Despite all her fears, Ishani couldn't help but be grateful that her son had such a courageous and honest man as a role model. She knew Luther was right, but she was so happy now that they were both such a big part of his life that she couldn't bear the thought of it all being ended by a sniper's bullet or an arsonist's petrol can.

Luther wouldn't allow himself to be intimidated or to feel fear, otherwise he knew he couldn't credibly stand up on a stage again to show leadership to his people and shout down the hecklers and segregationists with their ignorance and racial hatred. He had to show them that they could not possibly win, no matter how many men and women they threatened or killed. Being brave had become something of a habit for him because he was deeply embroiled in this fierce struggle against racial prejudice.

Ishani was used to him coming home late at night from meetings. She would see the fire in his eyes as he came in, still fresh and exhilarated from the heated arguments. If he was speaking in Jackson, he would sometimes walk home in order to give himself time to calm down and gather his thoughts before reaching the house, always taking care to vary his route in case he was being followed. It was on one of those late night walks through the dimly lit and deserted streets that Luther's luck finally ran out. He heard the belches of a badly-tuned truck engine growling up behind him. He didn't bother to look round. If it was being driven by a black man then there might be some conversation and maybe a ride home, but if it was being driven by whites he didn't want to draw their attention to his lonely presence. He kept going at a steady pace.

The truck jerked to a halt a few yards ahead of him and he

paused to see if the driver was going to offer him a lift. By the time he realised that the three men jumping out of the cab were white and hostile, he'd left it too late to turn and run. There was the stench of beer on their breath as they closed in on him. He fought valiantly, but these were powerful men, obviously used to fighting. Within minutes of the truck stopping, he'd been over-powered and bundled into the back with two of the men holding him down, while the third revved up the truck. His desperate screams for help faded away in the darkness as the vehicle sped into the night.

It wasn't until the next morning that Ishani awoke and realised that Luther had not been home at all during the night. He'd never done that before without ringing to tell her, and she immediately feared the worse. Forcing herself to stay calm she got Kal up, dressed him and gave him breakfast before starting the rounds, knocking on the doors of all Luther's friends and colleagues. Most of them had been at the rally the previous night and told her that they'd seen him leave before midnight. She could see from the looks on their faces that they were thinking the worst, but she refused to believe it. Maybe he'd somehow injured himself and was just lying in a ditch somewhere, waiting to be found. Friends agreed to retrace all the various routes he might have taken home, but they found nothing.

By the following day she thought she was going to go mad with anxiety, imagining Luther held prisoner somewhere by the Klu Klux Klan or some of their bullies. She dared not imagine what they might be doing to him, and forced herself to attend to Kal as if nothing was wrong, although she felt her heart was going to break.

* * *

Two days after he disappeared, Luther's hooded body was found by the police in a small wooded area on the outskirts of town. From the marks and bruises on his skin it was obvious that he had been subjected to the most brutal of attacks. He had been executed with two bullets, fired at close range through the back of his head. As soon as he had been identified, a policeman was sent to inform Ishani about the grim discovery. He chewed gum methodically as he imparted the bare facts to her while she shook and shivered in front of him, unable to focus on his words, feeling like her whole world had collapsed. The shock of knowing that she would never see Luther alive again, never hear his voice, never feel his lips on hers, or his big hand encircling her shoulder as they walked together, was too much to take in. As if to protect her from the unbearable pain of the moment, her mind went back to her early life and all the horrors that had turned her into a woman who believed she was resilient and independent and able to cope with anything life chose to throw at her. At that moment she didn't believe she was going to be able to survive with the terrible grief that was welling up in her chest, as it threatened to choke her.

'What will happen now?' she asked in a tiny voice, her face cracked with agony.

'Happen, ma'am?' he asked, his eyes travelling up and down her body as he spoke, a smirk twitching at the corners of his mouth, 'why, we'll investigate the case thoroughly. This will be a full-scale murder investigation.'

He sat down at her kitchen table without asking permission and spent an hour taking her statement and making suggestive comments. When he'd finally got the message that she wasn't interested in playing his games, he snapped his notebook shut and left.

That night she had to break the news to Kal. He received it silently and dry-eyed. It felt as though she'd physically assaulted him as she tried to explain that Luther was gone, that he had been taken by bad men, and that now they must be brave together. She assured him they would be able to manage, however difficult. Later, as she lay in her own bed, she heard him sobbing quietly, as if he was trying to stifle the sounds so as not to wake her, and she could imagine just how hard it was for him to understand that anyone could hate the colour of another man's skin so violently that he would be willing to kill him. She remembered the first time she'd realised what the world was really like, and she had been older than Kal by then. She climbed out of bed and went through to his room. Without a word she curled up beside him and they both cried themselves into a fitful sleep.

As the weeks of silence from the authorities turned to months, she would go into the police station at regular intervals, but she could see the officers exchanging looks and knew they were laughing behind her back. Their apathy was staggering. Sometimes she would find a sympathetic policeman, who would assure her they were doing their best to identify the culprits, but the next time she went in that officer would no longer be there and she would be back to square one. It was almost like the murder had never happened. After a further two years of increasingly bitter frustration, she realised there was nothing more she could do and so, reluctantly, she packed up and they both returned to New York with heavy hearts. She was determined that Luther should not have died in vain and dedicated herself to working full time for the ACRM.

In 1988, watching Kal graduate from the famous New York Law School in Lower Manhattan, Ishani felt that maybe, just maybe, the sacrifices that she and Luther, and the many other martyrs and their widows had made, were worthwhile. No one seemed for even a moment to think that her son was out of place at such a ceremony just because his mother was of Indian descent. As she sat amongst the hundreds of other proud parents, applauding till her hands hurt, she was unable to stop the tears from streaming down her face. No one noticed; the entire hall was filled with pride and emotion.

When the ceremony was over and everyone was searching for their children, she spotted him across the crowd, so tall and handsome. As soon as she reached him she threw her arms around his chest and hugged, unable to get the words out.

'Luther would be so proud of you,' she eventually managed to say.

'If it wasn't for you and Luther I wouldn't be here,' he said, returning the hug, enveloping her tiny frame. 'All those stories you told me about him when I was a kid. His was the torch that led the way.'

She gazed up at him and laughed at his easy eloquence. 'You sound like you're making a speech already. I bet he's looking down from above and cheering right now. Oh, I'm so proud of you, Kal.' She squeezed him again, like she was never going to let him go.

'Now we can really make some money, buddy,' another new graduate roared as he passed them, slapping Kal on the back. 'Oops, sorry, almost forgot, you've got to save the world first!'

His friend gave a hoot of laughter and dived off in search of his own parents.

'The others all think I'm mad for not being so interested in making money,' he chuckled. 'They just don't get it.'

'They haven't suffered what we've been through,' Ishani said.

'You can't expect them to have the same priorities. Maybe in time they will come to understand just how many injustices there are in this world. They'll soon come across them.'

'Some of them, maybe, the rest will get nice cushy jobs working for Coca-Cola and on the Street. They all talk about the money they're going to make, the mansions they're going to buy, and the cars and the boats, I just don't see the appeal.'

'I know you don't.' She stretched up and pecked him on the cheek. 'That's one of the reasons I am so proud of you.'

Kal's integrity and honesty shone out so brightly that no one who came into contact with him could fail to be impressed. His work ethic and legal skills were soon taken for granted at the Justice Department, where he got his first job, and it was his dedication in helping those who were most needy that made him indispensable and assured his steady rise up the ladder. In such a competitive environment there were plenty of ambitious young lawyers who resented his success. They found his seriousness hard to take. There were also people who tried to tempt him from the straight and narrow with job offers laced with generous perks, but no one ever got close to succeeding. This was a man who knew the difference between doing things right and doing the right thing.

Once Kal was grown up and had been safely launched into the world, Ishani had a lot more time on her hands to follow her own interests. For many years she'd been following the plight of the Burmese people in the media. Having also read extensively on the subject, she felt a kindred spirit in them and believed that they were suffering from a growing brutal oppression, which seemed very similar to her own experiences in the sixties.

'I've been thinking about going out there, to see if I could help them,' she told Kal over dinner one evening.

'Oh, Mom, it's such a dangerous place at the moment,' he warned, 'highly unstable. Do you need to be putting so much risk in your life?'

His mother said nothing, just sipping her wine and looking at him over the rim of her glass.

'This isn't up for debate, is it?' he grinned. 'You've already made up your mind.'

'I would like to think that you approve, Kal.'

'Of course, Mom, I approve. I approve of anyone who wants to make things better for other people. But please be careful, I'm just a little frightened of losing my mother.'

'We have to be brave now if we want the children of the world to ever live without fear later.'

'One of Luther's sayings, by any chance?'

'Roughly paraphrased.'

'The man lives on then?'

'For ever.'

Kal raised his glass. 'Well, here's to your new Burmese adventure. Just make sure you don't get yourself killed.'

'You know I'll be careful,' she smiled, happy at receiving his guarded endorsement.

Ishani arrived in Rangoon in 1993, three years after the National League for Democracy won over eighty per cent of the national vote, but they'd still not been allowed to come into office. She, like many other concerned people around the world, had watched with horror as the military junta used every means it could to avoid handing over power, and started jailing the NLD leaders for criticising them. House arrests and intimidation had become the norm and the people of the country were left with no democratic voice. The thumping military iron fist was becoming more brutal with each passing week.

Ishani spent a couple of months getting to know the country and its people before stepping forward and joining the NLD. She knew that a foreigner with a track record for fighting other human rights battles was certain to attract the attention of the government the moment she declared her interests, and she wasn't disappointed. It was only a matter of days before she sensed she was under surveillance by the National Intelligence Bureau. They didn't even bother being discreet about it, obviously hoping to intimidate her as much as find out what she was doing and what company she was keeping.

The first time they took her in for questioning she made it clear that she'd no intention of changing her ways, and she could see they were frustrated at not being able to intimidate her in the way they could their own people, particularly those who belonged to ethnic minorities.

'Don't you realise,' she raged at her bemused interrogator – someone who was used to being the one asking the questions rather than answering them – 'that the whole world is observing what your government is doing in Burma? They are watching every rape, every execution, every case of child labour and forced labour. America had to give up slavery over a hundred years ago, don't you realise that you're bound to have to do the same?'

'None of your accusations are accurate,' the interrogator replied, with studied patience and politeness. He left the torturing of prisoners to other more lowly soldiers these days. 'You have been falsely informed by enemies of the government.'

'The whole world is against you,' she fumed, 'you will have to change your ways.'

But as the years passed, Ishani Woodson realised she was fighting a futile battle. Whereas she'd been able to keep her morale up during the sixties and seventies in America, where every step backwards in human and civil rights seemed to be matched by two steps forward, in Burma everything seemed to be going backwards all the time, and the people's plight was growing ever more desperate.

It was becoming increasingly difficult to communicate with the outside world, and sometimes weeks would pass with no news of how Kal was doing. She was depending on unreliable and clandestine Internet connections just to get her news out to him, and it was often months before she was able to get hold of any return messages.

By 1997 local tensions had risen dramatically. She'd now been in the country four years and had heard through reliable sources that the NIB's patience with her activities was growing thin. She had been a constant thorn in their sides. There were rumours everywhere that they were about to introduce Draconian new travel restrictions on foreigners, which would make it impossible to get back to America should she want to. Being in Burma of her own choice was one thing, being held prisoner there was quite another.

'You have done all you can for us,' an NLD leader told her at a secret meeting late one night. She'd eventually found her way to an obscure safe house on the northern outskirts of the city, and her clothes were still soaking wet after she'd been caught in a sudden downpour of heavy rain on her way there. 'You've worked tirelessly for our cause against impossible odds. You must not endanger your life any more for us. How would your son feel if he'd heard that you had disappeared or had been killed needlessly?'

When she thought about it like that she realised just how much she was missing Kal. She hadn't communicated with him in such a long time. She felt a strange yearning for him and a sudden excitement at the thought of going back to America. She suddenly felt she'd had enough of the overpowering heat and torrential rain, and the constant bad news as friends were removed or murdered around her. Maybe the NLD was right. Her work here *was* done. And so she decided, just as soon as she could safely arrange the logistics of her departure, she was returning home to New York to give her son the best present he could wish for.

13

Captain Amigo Serrano of the NYPD was a busy man with a hundred other cases cluttering his in-tray, but the murder of Blaine Harmon was always at the forefront of his mind. There was barely an hour of any day when he didn't feel a surge of anger at the thought that the man he was convinced had been driving the car at the moment of impact might get away with killing one of his detectives.

At the beginning of the investigation the captain had been worried that Chip Murray could lose his sense of proportion due to having lost his childhood friend, but as the months passed and they seemed to make no progress he became equally impatient himself.

'So who exactly is this Lombardi jerk?' he had asked Chip. 'I'm still not clear.'

'That's the point,' Chip said, fighting to disguise the exasperation he was feeling. 'We can't find out. He seems to have come from nowhere and the only people who seem to know anything about his past are the CIA.'

'And what do they say?'

'Nothing. They're just bullshitting, telling me their files are classified and I don't merit access.'

'That's bullshit.'

Chip spread his hands, feeling that he was finally getting his message across. 'That's what I've been saying, but they won't shift.'

'Tell them it's a fucking police killing we're investigating here, not to mention the fucking narcotics. Tell them they have no choice but to co-operate.'

'You think I haven't told them that? I've tried everything.'

'Give me the number.'

Chip passed over the number he had been so frequently dialling over the previous few weeks and watched as his boss put in the call.

'This is Captain Serrano of the NYPD narcotics division. Who am I speaking to?'

'Special Agent Colby,' the voice at the other end replied, sounding wary.

'We're investigating the murder of one of our boys, Colby, we need your co-operation. Any reason why you're holding back?'

'There's a problem with the classification status of the files on this one.'

'Is that right? I've had a journalist from the *New York Times* onto me about why we aren't getting any further on this case,' Serrano lied. 'Can I quote you on that "classification of status" bullshit, Special Agent Colby?'

'The media doesn't need to be involved in this case.' There was now more than a hint of panic in Colby's voice.

'Don't know what else I can tell them, seeing as I don't know what the fuck you guys are playing at.' Serrano winked at Chip, letting him know that he now had the upper hand in the conversation.

'You talk to the media, Captain, and you will be in contravention . . .'

'Don't try to threaten me, son,' Serrano snarled. 'I want some answers from you by the end of the day on this Lombardi character or I'm going to the top of your organisation and it's your neck that's going to be the one on the line. I'm getting the whiff of corruption in all of this and corruption will interest the media and your bosses, Colby. Are you willing to face this kind of scrutiny just to protect a cop-killer?'

'Let me get back to you.'

The captain sensed high-level corruption and it made him feel physically sick. In all his years of dealing with career criminals and street bums, he had come to hate the corrupt officials more than any other kind of crook. How could the system ever be improved if it was constantly being sabotaged by greedy, ambitious, cowardly insiders?

An hour later Colby rang Chip direct and invited him to a preliminary meeting at CIA headquarters at Langley.

'They're gonna open the files for us,' Chip told his boss after the meeting a few days later.

'Take a team with you; make sure everything that's said or done is recorded. These people will do everything they can to keep their reputations clean.'

'Thank you, sir.'

'Don't thank me; just bring back something that will make this case watertight. I want every corrupt son of a bitch in that organisation exposed!'

* * *

'Holy shit, no wonder they wanted to keep the lid on this one,' Serrano said as Chip finished telling him what he'd learned from the CIA files. 'Lombardi was this Lex Goldman guy? Can you believe it?' He shook his head in wonderment.

'It's incredible. Not only is the guy up to his neck in cocaine trafficking with the big Colombian cartels, he was also the main man in the money laundering operations of the IRA movement in Ireland and became a close friend and confidant of Gaddafi at a time when the guy was considered one of the biggest threats to world peace. This son of a bitch sure has some appetite for money. He doesn't know when to stop.'

'And the CIA took him into the witness protection programme?'

'Absolutely.'

'So where did he come from originally?'

'South Africa, where he was a big time gold miner. I mean real big time. This guy must be one of the richest men in the world, although I doubt anyone would be able to find a fraction of his money.'

'The CIA were protecting a man like this?'

'Apparently so.'

'He must have something big on them, or on someone who has influence on them.'

'It would seem likely.'

Serrano, a man who thought he had seen and heard everything in life, sat for a moment with his mouth hanging open. 'You think this could be the new Watergate, as in "cover up"?'

'I think we've a lot more digging to do and a lot more questions we want answers to,' Chip said, 'but yes, I think it could be as big as that.'

'Holy shit, and there was me hoping to slide peacefully into retirement.'

'I need to put together a crack team to help me with this. There is so much material to be chased up, particularly the Gaddafi link. These guys think they can get him off this rap just because he fed them information about some tin-pot dictator years ago. They believe that Blaine's life is worth nothing by comparison. I want to turn over every filthy rock and see what crawls out.'

'Keep a cool head on this, Chip,' Serrano warned. 'I don't want you to end up dead in an alley somewhere because you trod on the wrong toes. Make sure you make every move by the book.'

'Don't worry, sir, I don't intend to make any mistakes. I want to nail this bastard, no matter how many friends in high places he has.'

Kal Woodson's office at the Justice Department had suddenly filled up with files from the narcotics division.

'This is going to be a big one, Kal,' his boss had said when designating him to be lead prosecutor in the case against Lex Goldman. 'Don't make me regret my decision to trust you.'

'I won't, sir,' Kal replied, still unsure quite why so much was riding on this particular case.

'Brief yourself on as much background to the case as you can over the next week and then get back to me with your initial thoughts. There are a lot of high profile people who have a keen interest in knowing what's happening. This could make you a big name.'

'I've never been too interested in the size of my name, sir.'

'No,' the older man chuckled good-naturedly, 'I know you

haven't, that's what makes you the right man for this job. Keep me in the loop.'

All his other cases were passed over to other departmental attorneys to free up his time and he was left alone in his office with the piles of paperwork to start work on the arraignment. At first he couldn't make sense of what he was reading, even with his sharp, highly trained mind. When he did start to see the underlying story he couldn't believe that he was understanding it right and went back to the beginning to check that what he was reading was true. The sheer greed of the man he was reading about stunned him. How could anyone be prepared to take such enormous risks with his own life, not to mention the hundreds of thousands of lives affected by his actions, simply to enrich himself? Nothing in Kal's make-up allowed him to connect with such a person.

'So what do you think?' his boss asked him a week later.

'I think this man epitomises everything that is wrong with the way our country, and our world, works,' he replied. 'He sums up the depravity of this elite who think they can ride roughshod over all the rules, believing they're just for the "little people". This man is beneath contempt, he's evil and he needs to be shown to be so. We need to demonstrate to the people that the United States will not allow people like this to prosper.'

'Steady, Kal,' the older man cautioned, 'you have to keep a cool, professional head in dealing with this.'

Kal took a deep breath and stared hard at the older man. 'How can you stay so detached about things like this?' he asked.

'That's my job, and yours too.'

'But what is the point of doing this job if you don't feel passionate about it? How can you not feel that a man like this is beneath contempt? Imagine how many people have suffered and died because of his activities; the slavery of his workers, the narcotics he's peddled, the cash he's laundered for terrorists, the deals he's done with mass murderers. How can you not be angry?'

'If you get angry, Kal, you're likely to act hastily, and if you act hastily, you will make mistakes. Imagine you're a surgeon, taking a bullet out of the brain of a small child. You may want to weep for that child, and for its mother, and you may want to vent your fury on the man who shot him and the man who sold that man the gun, and everyone else in the chain of evil, but if your tears blur your eyesight, how much harder will it be for you to take that bullet out effectively? If your hand is shaking with anger, can you operate effectively?'

Kal nodded his understanding and took a few moments to compose himself. 'All my life,' he said eventually, 'I have been surrounded by people who believed in doing the right thing for their fellow men. It's hard when you see one man who has done so much to undo the good work of thousands of decent people. There are so many ways in which we can improve life for everyone on this planet, and so many ways that we can destroy all hope of improvement. I hear what you're saying and you can rest assured that I will not do anything that will in any way endanger my chances of getting this man convicted of murdering this detective.'

'Attaboy,' the older man sounded relieved. 'That's why I designated you for this case.'

The further into the background research he delved, the more determined Woodson became that this man should not escape the punishment he was due. It seemed to him that the killing of one policeman was almost the least of his crimes against his fellow men, but if that was the one that would bring him to justice, that was the one Kal would concentrate on.

'They've announced who's going to be hearing the case,' one of his assistants told him excitedly one day.

'Who?'

'Only the "*Double V*" himself! Supreme Court Justice Vernon Villars.'

'Yes,' Kal punched the air in jubilation, startling his fellow workers.

'That's good?' one of them asked.

'That, my friend, is very good. The lead defence attorney in this case is the celebrated James L. Bates. Justice Villars and Bates have had, let's say, a lot of "form" in previous trials. Believe me, they don't like each other and they've had plenty of fireworks between them in recent high profile jousts. It can only help us.'

'This is going to make you real famous, Kal,' his colleague laughed.

Kal paused, obviously puzzled by the relevance of the remark. For the first time since he became absorbed in prosecuting the case against Lex Goldman he realised his friend was right. This trial was going to be front-page news for months, and his name would be an integral part of the story. Personal ambition had never played a part in his make-up, he seemed to progress fine on ability alone, but he suddenly saw that if he could win this case the resulting publicity and kudos would give him the authority to take on many more. If he could become known as the man who led the successful prosecution of Lex Goldman, his reputation would soar.

James Bates' patience was stretching to the edges of his endurance. It wasn't that he regretted agreeing to take on the Goldman case, he could see that it was going to be the biggest media trial for many a year and he wanted to be part of it, it was more that Lex wasn't co-operating and actually seemed to be questioning his competence to handle the case. James wasn't used to being questioned.

To his eyes Lex didn't seem to be grasping just how thin the ice was beneath his feet. James liked to see at least some sign of nerves in his clients, to indicate that they understood just how important it was that they followed his every instruction. Lex seemed to have other ideas.

'I don't think we need to go into any of that,' Lex smiled with a hint of menace and no sign of humour when James asked him if he could clarify his relationship with Gaddafi. 'The only thing I am on trial for here is the running over of this policeman and his unfortunate demise. You just have to prove that I wasn't in that car.'

James glanced at Sophie but her composed expression was giving nothing away. 'That is likely to prove a little difficult, given that the car is covered with your fingerprints, you have absolutely no witnesses or alibis to back up your story and you were the first person, apart from the cops, to show up at the scene of the crash. What we're going to have to do is prove that there is sufficient doubt that it would have been you. The more mysterious and sinister your past looks, the less likely that we'll be able to convince a grand jury, or a judge, that you are likely to be telling the truth.'

'Doesn't sound to me like you know what you're doing.' For the first time James thought he detected a crack in Lex's voice. Maybe the message was finally getting through just how much trouble he was in.

'Listen, you stupid fuck,' James pushed his advantage, 'they're going to be out to rip you apart. Even if I get to prove you weren't driving the fucking car they're going to use this trial to lift every other rock that you've hidden under over the years.'

'Do you doubt my word, James?' Lex was on his feet and shouting, his raised hand trembling.

'At this moment,' James paused to try to retain his own cool, 'I have doubts about whether I can convince anyone else that you are a truthful person.'

'But do you doubt my innocence of this killing yourself?' Lex shouted.

Watching her husband, Sophie was reminded of why she had first been attracted to him, all the bolshie arrogance had returned, but she could also see that he was shaken, that James was getting to him. It looked as if the reality was finally dawning on him that he was on the verge of facing the death penalty. For the first time ever he was wondering if he was going to get away with this as he had got away with everything else over the years.

'No, Lex,' James said eventually, deliberately trying to calm the atmosphere. 'I don't doubt that you are telling the truth.'

'So, James, you simply have to demonstrate to the world whatever it is that has convinced you of my innocence.'

'Well I'll tell you one thing, Lex,' James's temper bubbled back up at the man's arrogance, 'you'd better have Sophie by your side at every possible moment, because she's a heck of a lot more convincing as an upright citizen than you will ever be.'

'We've got the wrong man for the job,' Lex snapped at Sophie, moving to the door as if to leave. 'We need someone who's on our side.'

'Sit down, Lex,' Sophie commanded with an authority that

surprised all of them. 'This is no time to play games. James is not only the right man, he is the *only* man likely to take you on at this stage. Have you any idea how hard it was to convince him to defend you? Have you any idea how hard it was to get you bail? He's the only man who could have got that for you. He's the only man who can save you now. You need to stop and listen.'

Lex could find no answers to her cool female pragmatism. He was moved to think she cared enough about him to make the effort to save him after what he'd done to her. He sat back down.

'Okay, James. Prove how good you are.'

'We need to talk about the possibility of a plea bargain,' James said quietly.

'Don't waste your breath,' Lex snapped again, his self-control now paper thin. 'There's no way I'm ever going to plea bargain over something I didn't do. I'm innocent of the crime I'm accused of. That's the end of the story.'

'Standing trial is going to zero in every spotlight in the world onto your past. Do you really think it can withstand the scrutiny?'

'I've never done anything I'm ashamed of.'

'What, nothing?' Sophie was startled for a moment out of her serenity.

'Absolutely nothing. I've always done what needed to be done. I've always been willing to get my hands dirty in order to get the job done. I've always been willing to take the risks that others weren't willing to take . . .'

'You can get off your high horse now,' James interrupted him. 'Everything about your past is going to produce sensational headlines, none of them good. The potential damage that the revelations in this trial could do to the CIA's covert operations is incredible:

their narcotics funding, everything they want to keep secret. Everyone is going to want you silenced and discredited. You have no friends left outside this office.'

'I ain't no pussy. I'm used to fighting my corner,' Lex retorted, but it was obvious James had him rattled.

A knock on the door interrupted them and James barked for the junior member of the legal team to come in.

'The discovery documents have just arrived, Mr Bates,' the young man announced.

'Have you looked at them?' James asked.

'Only quickly, we're going into the details now.'

'What have they got?'

'They're throwing everything at us. All the headline stuff they have is seriously incriminating. It's pretty grim.'

For the first time since she'd met him, Sophie could see that her husband was truly scared.

Late that night Bates and his increasingly tired team of juniors were still in the office, drinking shots of black coffee to keep themselves alert as they pored over the papers.

'This Kal Woodson is likely to be putting his all into this,' a young woman James had particularly high hopes for piped up.

'It could make him a star,' James agreed.

'Not only that, his whole background has been leading him to this sort of show trial. Lex Goldman is exactly the sort of man he would want to bring down.'

'Tell me more,' James said, topping up his coffee as he listened.

'All his life he's dedicated himself to social injustice. His mother worked for the American Civil Rights Movement before heading out to Burma to fight for democracy there. His father was Luther Woodson, a black activist and hero, brutally killed in 1963 in a racist execution in Jackson. This guy has been brought up on principles.'

'Why has no one picked up on this before?' James had sat forward, looking like he scented blood. 'What else do we know about him?'

'He's very young and very low key. He really doesn't seem to be in it for the glory. He's the ultimate bleeding heart. He would see Lex Goldman as symbolic of all that's wrong in the world.'

'That's how we'll get to him.' James slammed the palm of his hand on the desktop, making them all jump.

By the following morning James Bates was briefing a private detective who he knew he could rely on for discretion.

'This is Kal Woodson's background,' he said, sliding a sheet of information across the desk. 'I want the media to be aware of his agenda. I want them to be aware that my client is being set up by the bleeding hearts of the left.'

'Your guy is likely to get the death penalty if they find him guilty,' the detective pointed out. 'That's gonna get you plenty of publicity. Why do you want to stir up more?'

'I need it to be the right kind of publicity. I need to be able to walk into that courtroom with the world already aware that the Justice Department is going to try to make my client look bad for its own private agenda. These leaks can't be traced back to me, you understand?'

'Of course I understand. I never remember even meeting you,' the detective laughed as he left the office with James's sheet of information. He knew from past dealings with the man that James Bates was someone who always wanted to win, no matter what it took. He'd always been a master at manipulating and spinning the media and had designed almost every move he'd ever made to make himself the centre of attention. Whatever happened, there was no doubt that all eyes were going to be on that courtroom by the time the trial started, and all the main protagonists were likely to become media stars, whether they did anything to help the coverage or not.

Lex and Sophie discovered that their story was about to explode across the media a few hours before the general public when the phones started to ring and a crowd of reporters and photographers began to congregate around the doorway of their apartment block. James's leaks had opened the floodgates early.

Chip Murray heard a couple of hours later when the NYPD received an urgent request from Bates's office to move Lex to a hiding place outside the city while keeping the terms of his bail valid. The newspapers were just hitting the streets and the news anchors were reporting the breaking story of a witch hunt the left wing establishment were being accused of mounting against one of the world's richest men.

'That bastard shouldn't have bail in the first place,' Murray fumed when he heard.

'The papers are saying he's being framed by the left wing, made a scapegoat for the whole capitalist system,' Captain Serrano told him when he went in to protest. 'If we don't protect the son of a bitch someone may take him out before we can even get him into the courtroom. This is getting out of control. I'd like to know who leaked this stuff to the papers. The judge will go fucking nuts.'

'Probably Goldman himself. He seems to think he can do whatever he wants,' Chip said.

'We're gonna have to do it, Chip. We're gonna have to put him in a safe place.'

By lunchtime that day the Goldmans had been lifted from the roof of their block in a helicopter and whisked to a secured out of town hotel, while the news channels were filled with images of Justice Villars holding an impromptu press conference on his own front doorstep in a breaking news story.

'I will not tolerate any more leaks to the media from either side in this case,' he bellowed at the crowd of reporters. 'I will not have this trial jeopardised by gamesmanship. You people will abide by the letter of the law in this coverage or I will be coming after every one of you. Tell your proprietors that.'

James switched off the television in his office with the remote and sat back in his leather chair with a sigh of satisfaction. That, he told himself, had evened the odds up a bit.

The media did not need any more leaks, it now had all the material it needed to whip its entire world audience up into a frenzy of expectation. By the following Wednesday, when the case was due to come before a grand jury, the whole of central Manhattan seemed to have been turned into a real life theatre for the biggest show trial the city had seen in years.

That morning the limousine had arrived early at the hotel to pick up the Goldmans, flanked by police cars.

'Where's Bates?' Lex had asked as they made their way out of the building and down the steps. 'He should be here.'

'It's okay, Lex.' Sophie put a calming hand on his sleeve. 'James and his team will be there. Don't lose your nerve now.'

Holding onto her hand tightly he stared into her eyes. 'It's going to be all right, isn't it, Sophie? I'm not going to the chair, am I?'

'No,' she smiled kindly, touched by his sudden vulnerability and the fear she could see in his eyes. 'You'll come out of this smelling of roses, like always.'

He was grateful for her comforting presence, but he wasn't

fooled by her words. He knew just how bad things looked as the cavalcade drew away from the hotel, speeding towards Manhattan. As they came over the bridge two other cars joined the convoy, carrying James and his team. It was like a small army on the move towards the battlefield.

Despite the judge's warnings that he was on the verge of having his courtroom cleared of all onlookers, the cameras managed to hold their places inside, relaying the proceedings to the networks outside.

Even when the scene was relayed to the comfort of people's homes, it was possible to sense how electric the atmosphere in the courtroom was. The judge made his opening remarks, establishing his authority over the proceedings and making it clear he did not intend to be bullied by the lawyers, the media or the Establishment.

Kal Woodson called a couple of minor witnesses to testify about Lex Goldman's past, wanting to establish as quickly as possible the sort of man who was on trial. The media drank in the sordid details of money laundering for terrorists and drug dealing connections. Kal made no accusations, just asked quiet, damning questions while James interjected and protested at virtually every single one.

'Mr Bates,' Justice Villars fumed after an hour of building tensions. 'We are going to get nowhere with this trial if you continue in this obstructive vein.'

'I insist that my client be allowed the fair trial that he is entitled to,' James replied pompously. 'I will do all I can to obstruct what is little more than a witch hunt.'

'I take grave offence at the implication that I would allow a witch hunt in my court,' Villars boomed. 'If, however, you do not allow the prosecution to do its job I will be forced to have you removed from this courtroom.'

'Depriving my client of an adequate defence would merely confirm the view of the world that this trial is a mockery, staged simply to humiliate my client and all he stands for.'

'I do not give a fig for the world's view, or your view, Mr Bates, but I insist on being allowed to hear the prosecution's case. Be silent or be gone from my court.'

'I hope that the jury will take note of the tone in which this trial is being conducted,' James said ruefully, before finally sitting down.

Kal Woodson had expected Bates to try to impede his progress at every turn and ensured he remained meticulously polite, waiting patiently as the judge and defence attorney interrupted and contradicted one another repeatedly. Each time he would resume his line of questioning where he had been forced to leave off. By the end of the first day he'd managed to build a broad picture of Lex Goldman as little more than a modern day gangster, a man who'd built a huge personal fortune by dubious means and was responsible for any number of deaths as a result.

James Bates continued to insist that the judge was showing undue bias towards his client, and the judge continued to roar his denials. The world stayed glued to their screens, addicted to the cut and thrust exchanges between the protagonists, while the newspapers devoted pages of editorial to every one of the major players in preparation for the following morning's editions. They had all become household names.

Back at the hotel that night, now under a heavy police guard, Lex was uneasy. The press coverage resulting from the leaks and speculation had given him the impression he was going to be given an easier ride. He'd been shocked by the vehemence of the judge's attacks on James L. Bates.

'Is it sensible for us to have an attorney who the judge obviously despises?' he asked the room in general as they sat around in front of the television, flicking through the news channels and ignoring the food the staff had laid out. Every report seemed to confirm that Woodson had made a strong start for the prosecution and the world was shocked anew by some of the facts they'd heard relayed from the court about his past.

Sophie was as calm as she had been all day, although she now looked tired. 'Things always look bad for the accused when the prosecution starts to set out its case. James is doing the best job possible to force an element of doubt into everything the grand jury and the public are hearing. Would you want an attorney who just sat back and let them say whatever they wanted without protest?'

'The judge is prejudicing the case, James is right,' Lex grumbled. 'But the more he riles him the more prejudiced he's going to become.'

'It's not comfortable having your fate in someone else's hands, is it Lex?' Sophie said, with only a hint of a smile.

'No,' he replied, glancing away from the television and noticing how beautiful she looked. 'It is not.'

The crowds were just as deep on the second day of the trial. Before leaving the hotel, Lex's eye was caught by a legal affairs commentator on the television discussing Justice Villar's rise up the legal ladder.

'He was appointed by Governor Pataki,' the reporter was saying, 'who is a former colleague of his in a New York law firm. He was assigned to state Supreme Court, bypassing the lower Criminal Court. This is a man who has benefited greatly from Establishment contacts.'

'Is the thinking in local legal circles that he is up to the job?' the news anchor asked the commentator.

'There are mixed feelings on that. Many of the legal fraternity have been surprised by the speed and scope of his rise, and speculation centres on him being somewhat inexperienced in dealing with a trial of this magnitude.'

'What about Kal Woodson, who is leading the prosecution case? He too is relatively inexperienced in prosecuting such a high profile trial, is he not?'

'That is quite true and it is still early days, but on yesterday's performance it looks like he is well within his abilities. He presented his case calmly, wasn't thrown by the antics of his opponents in the same way the judge was. At the moment it looks like his reputation is going to be greatly enriched by this trial, whatever the final outcome might be.'

Encouraged by his progress the day before, Kal pressed steadily on with his questioning throughout the second day. By mid-afternoon he had established the link between Goldman and the Cali and Medellin drug cartels. Just before the end of the day, as the newspaper columnists were preparing their pieces for the following day's papers, he suggested the connection between the cartels and the CIA.

'Mr Woodson,' Justice Villars lowered his glasses threateningly, 'if you are intending to suggest an involvement on the part of the CIA in this alleged conspiracy, you will need to present this court with some very specific evidence.'

'I hope to be calling Special Agent Franks of the CIA Directorate of Operations to the witness stand at a later stage,' Woodson replied, 'which will establish the connection quite clearly.'

'I object.' James Bates was on his feet again and this time the judge did not silence him. 'My learned friend is implying that my client has some influence over the CIA. The defence would be pleased to hear anything that Special Agent Franks might have to say.'

CNN had set up a live feed from the Manhattan courtroom, which was being beamed all over the Americas and beyond and was now being viewed intently in sweaty silence in the lounge of Los Olivos ranch on the outskirts of Medellin. The men in the room could feel Ramrod's rage swelling beneath the self-control required to keep listening to the words, but all of them jumped when the gun went off and the screen exploded into tiny shards.

'Double-crossing son of a bitch!' Ramrod roared, continuing to fire bullets into the television, even though the first had killed the voice outright. 'Get him silenced now!' Two men scurried from the room to convey the orders down the line. 'And get another fucking television in here!' Others hurried to replace the destroyed source of his anger.

Casper Franks had been lying on his bed most of the day with the television flickering on the other side of the room, deep in thought. The remains of a bottle of scotch stood on the table beside him, and by the time he heard his name mentioned in the court, his spirits had already sunk almost as low as they could go. He knew they had just signed his death warrant. It would only be a matter of hours before Ramrod's people found him, and he knew the CIA wouldn't have any intention of protecting a man who had betrayed them.

Fumbling for the remote control, he flicked the sleep button and sat up, throwing his legs over the side of the bed, composing himself before getting to his feet. Walking slowly and steadily across the room he pulled open a drawer filled with neatly paired socks and withdrew a Glock .40 calibre pistol. With the utmost care he slid the barrel in between his teeth and pulled the trigger. The gunshot could be heard on the floors below and above the apartment and a call went in to the police.

On the third day of the trial, Kal Woodson called Detective Murray to the stand, knowing that he was going to be a star witness. Amidst all the talk of powerful drug cartels and government organisations like the CIA, Chip provided the grand jury and the world with a more accessible figure. Here was an honourable young man doing a difficult job to the best of his ability. He was also a man who had lost a friend. Under Kal's careful questioning his answers showed that he felt a burden of personal guilt for leading Blaine to his death. Chip kept a close control over his emotions, and his testimony was all the more compelling for that. Once or twice the cameras caught him glancing at Goldman, an urbane, cool, unemotional figure, and millions of viewers around the world could imagine the thoughts going through the young policeman's mind.

By the time the trial adjourned for the weekend, Lex Goldman's future had never looked so bleak.

Ishani Woodson's journey back to America was long and exhausting. She travelled first to the Thai border, only able to move during the hours of darkness for fear of being picked up by soldiers or the NIB. Now that she had decided to return home she didn't want to find herself locked in a prison cell, or be left bleeding to death in a ditch. From there she took a train to Bangkok and boarded a flight to JFK, via Hong Kong, which left her feeling tired and disoriented as she stumbled out of the airport to find a cab.

She had decided to go to a small hotel she knew in Queen's while she sorted out a new apartment for herself. More than anything, she was looking forward to seeing her son after being so long apart. It felt strange to be back in New York, having been distanced and isolated from the western world for so long.

The midday traffic was heavy and they became stuck at some lights as she stared out of the window at the passing street scenes. A newspaper vendor was shouting out his wares and, as he moved back from serving a customer, she spotted a *Daily News* board with the headline 'LEX GOLDMAN TRIAL LATEST'. Something lurched in her stomach before her brain even managed to bring a picture of Lex Goldman into her mind. The name was so familiar to her, but had been covered in so many layers of deliberate denial it took a moment before the full memory came back to her. How could Lex Goldman be on trial? He'd been killed years before, hadn't he?

'Just a minute,' she shouted at the driver as she opened the door and ran to the vendor.

She grabbed a paper and started reading it even before fumbling to find the right change. The taxi driver, seeing a gap in the traffic began hitting his horn. Wanting all the distractions to stop, she pushed a five-dollar bill into the vendor's hand and ran back to the cab, still reading as she fell into her seat and slammed the door behind her.

'You okay, lady?' the driver asked as he accelerated away, 'looks like you've seen a ghost.'

She didn't reply, not even hearing his voice. Now she read the name Kal Woodson in the same story and her mind refused to make sense of what she was reading. Why would Kal's name be in the same article as Lex's? What could have happened to bring them together?

Realising he wasn't going to get a reply, the driver went back to threading his way through the traffic jams as his passenger struggled to make sense of the story she was reading. Memories from deep inside her were bubbling to the surface, memories of a time when her name had been Reshmine and she had lived in South Africa. She remembered the night when she and Lex had watched the young black man being kicked to death by the police as they huddled together in Beauty's house. For the first time in years she remembered the feeling of being so intensely in love that nothing else in the world seemed to matter. Then there was the evening when Sol Goldman came to her parents' house with all his threats and bluster. At first she'd been full of bravado, wanting to stand up to him, refusing to even think of giving up Lex.

'If your daughter goes anywhere near my son I'm going to the authorities,' Sol had raged while she sat respectfully behind her father, her head bowed, her hands shaking with a mixture of fear and anger. 'You know what that will mean to her and to the rest of your family.'

He didn't have to spell out the violence that would be likely to follow any such revelation. A sin like the one she and Lex had committed could result in the deaths of her whole family at the hands of angry mobs. It wouldn't affect Lex so much because he was Jewish and had money. He could leave the country quickly if necessary, and no one would dare to threaten the Goldman family. She knew she'd put her own family in grave danger with her actions. How could she speak up and refuse to obey these elders if her actions could lead to the deaths of her own parents and siblings? She might be able to put her own life at risk for the sake of love, but she couldn't do it to them. She knew at that moment she was going to have to pay the price for her crime of passion.

There was nothing she could do but stay quiet and agree to whatever was arranged for her. In those few minutes she'd realised she would never see Lex again, not even able to say goodbye and explain why she was going. She realised too that she would never again experience such intense feelings, and that she would never lose the ache of emptiness and sadness that was left behind. She loathed Sol Goldman and everything he stood for, but could think of no way to fight back. The irony was that she could see he truly believed he was doing what was best for Lex, when she knew that he was actually destroying a part of his son's soul, as well as hers.

It wasn't until she arrived in New York, alone and frightened, finding herself lodged with relatives she'd never met before, and who obviously didn't want her there, that she had discovered she was pregnant with Lex's child. Part of her had been thrilled to think that a bit of Lex would always be with her, but the practical side of her knew that life was going to become even harder once the baby arrived. What if it looked like Lex? What if every time she looked at her child she was reminded of everything she'd lost? It seemed ironic to her that through his ignorant actions, Sol Goodman had cut himself off from his own grandson. He would never even know that Kal existed.

For a while she dreamed that Lex would come to New York looking for her, defying his father, walking out on all the Goldman influence and wealth, but he never came and she realised he'd been crushed by the power of hatred and prejudice as easily as she had.

Deciding to become known by her second name, in order to hide herself even more effectively from anyone trying to dig up her past, she became Ishani. Sol Goldman and the apartheid system had even managed to steal her identity. She also made the decision never to tell Kal who his real father was, wanting to ensure that that part of her life remained a closed chapter for ever, locked away inside her memory.

As far as Kal was concerned Luther was 'Daddy' and he was happy to respect his mother's wish not to talk about anything that might have happened in her life before Luther came along.

Years later she read in the newspapers about Lex Goldman's death in an explosion on board a yacht in the Caribbean and had experienced a terrible grief, one that she had been unable to share with anyone, not even her son, but at least once she knew he was dead she'd been able to come to terms a little with her separation from him. However much she'd loved Luther, it had been Lex who was always her first real love.

She was still in a daze when she was finally alone in the hotel room, re-reading the newspaper articles and scanning the news channels for any information on what was happening in the Manhattan Criminal Courtroom where her son was in the process of prosecuting *his own father*. Aware that she was the only person in the world who realised the truth, she was torn between her wish to keep the secret forever, and her instincts, which had always taught her never to lie. How could she face explaining to her son who his real father was when the eyes of the whole world were watching them locked in a court battle with such huge personal stakes.

She had always taught him the importance of honesty and integrity, but in keeping this one fact from him she'd created a situation that was now out of control.

Exhausted from her journey, she cried herself to sleep a few hours later with the light from the television still flickering around the room. She had intended to call Kal with the news of her arrival in New York the first moment she could, but the phone remained untouched. The next day was going to bring the most difficult decision of her life.

14

Despite the fact that his picture was all over the front pages, Kal Woodson didn't have time to study the newspaper coverage of the trial in any detail until Saturday morning. As usual for a weekend, he'd picked up all the papers while out for a jog and brought them back to his apartment on the upper east side of Manhattan. He scanned through them while he ate his breakfast, sitting in the bright rays of the early morning sun as it slanted in through the high windows.

Kal knew better than to feel smug at the way the story was being reported by the majority of journalists, but he had to admit to himself that the first week of the trial had all gone his way. The pile of prosecution documents and briefings, which stood ready for reading later in the morning, was evidence that he was still not going to take any risks of Lex Goldman getting an acquittal, however well he might be doing at that stage. He knew that James Bates' defence was bound to be robust, even if the defendant's cause looked hopeless at that particular moment. He'd seen enough trials change direction midway to know that complacency would be his biggest enemy until the verdict was finally in.

He sighed when the door buzzer sounded. He'd been hoping

for at least a few hours of peace and quiet after the previous frantic few days. Taking a sip of coffee, he walked to the intercom at a leisurely pace. Pressing the button, he was shocked to see his mother's face on the screen.

'Mom?'

He pressed the button to let her in and ran down the stairs to meet her, almost knocking her off balance as he threw his arms around her, like an excited small boy. All the way back up to the apartment he didn't draw breath; it had been so long since they'd spoken and he wanted to tell her everything that had happened to him since they last communicated, particularly the Goldman trial.

'I read a little about it in the papers,' she said, smiling bravely as he tried to convey just how much had happened in the previous few weeks.

'It's the most fantastic opportunity to show the world exactly how they're being manipulated by the elite that run big business and corrupt governments,' he babbled, too excited to pick up on the strained way in which his mother was smiling at him as he bounced around her. 'This Goldman guy is the worst kind of capitalist, the sort of man who brings the whole system into disrepute. His greed knows no bounds and in his insatiable pursuit of money he doesn't care who he hurts. If we can expose him and send him down we stand a chance of changing the whole perception of the way people are exploited for profit all over the world.'

'Is he really that bad?' Ishani asked, the muscles at the edges of her smile quivering very slightly as she allowed her son to settle her on one end of his sofa by moving aside piles of files and papers.

'Bad? You have no idea, Mom. When I started researching the case I assumed that I would find the man had at least some redeeming features as I dug further into his past, but it just got worse with every revelation. He has indirectly caused the deaths of hundreds, by exploiting the labourers in his goldmines in South Africa, by dealing in drugs and arms, by supplying known terrorist organisations. He's on trial for killing a detective just to save his own skin, but in fact that is the least of his crimes. This man is Satan, Mom, truly without a conscience, only interested in adding to his own wealth and power at the expense of everyone else. It also seems that he's been protected by the CIA. Either he has been working for them or he has something big on them, because they've been going to a lot of trouble and expense to cover his tracks over the years. This whole trial has such a stench of corruption, who knows where it might lead?'

He stopped for a second to catch his breath, realising that he was becoming overexcited and that he hadn't even taken the time to ask her about herself. To his horror he saw her coal black eyes welling up with tears.

'Mom? I'm sorry, I haven't even asked how you are. Are you okay?' He sat down beside her and took her trembling hands in his. She made no attempt to wipe away the tears as they ran down her cheeks.

'What's the matter?' he asked, agitated by her inability to speak, fearful that she might be bringing some terrible news about herself. 'Please, tell me what's wrong.'

'Oh, Kal,' she sobbed, clinging tightly to his strong fingers, feeling like her heart was breaking in two, 'I don't know where to begin. I don't know how to tell you . . .'

'Tell me what?' He hadn't seen his mother so distraught since the day they heard about Luther's execution.

'It's Lex Goldman.'

'What about him?'

'He's your father, Kal.'

'*My father?*' Kal couldn't make sense of her words. How could it be possible? How could there be any connection between his saintly mother and this man who seemed to epitomise everything that was bad in the world? He couldn't fit it together, it sounded like complete madness. 'What? Are you serious? How can that be?'

'We met in South Africa many years ago,' she said, and he had to strain to catch her words through the sobs. 'We were both very young, and life was very different back then. You cannot imagine how brutal the apartheid system was for people like us. Anyone who stepped across the divide, as Lex and I did, were risking their lives. He was so exciting, a real firebrand, so sure of himself, with so much potential to do good in the world, I couldn't help myself from falling in love with him. It was a stupid and dangerous thing to do, but that only added to the appeal.'

'Huh, so he left us,' Kal was still trying to suppress his disbelief, 'never even bothered to contact us.'

She shook her head. 'He thinks I'm dead, and he never even knew you'd been conceived.'

'What do you mean?'

'Somehow his father found out about us. Sol Goldman was a rich, influential man and he valued his family's good standing in the Jewish community more than he ever valued his son's happiness. He'd built a big gold-mining business, and his reputation meant everything to him. He paid a visit to us one night and made it very clear that he would have our whole family exposed to the authorities rather than allow me and Lex to stay together. I knew exactly what he meant by that threat. We would have had no choice but to leave South Africa anyway if we'd wanted to be together, and I guess he didn't want to lose his son and heir.

He had plans for Lex's future and they didn't include having a local coloured girl as a wife. I was told to leave the country and not to contact Lex again if I wanted to save my family. Lex was told that I'd been attacked and killed by racist thugs. My parents went along with it. They didn't believe they had any choice. They thought they were protecting me as well as themselves.'

'But what about me, what about his unborn child?'

'I didn't realise I was pregnant until I was already on the boat to New York. If I'd contacted Lex to tell him he was going to be a father I'm sure he would have followed me, and Sol Goldman would have seen to it that my family met with an "accident".'

'How could you have been attracted to such a man, someone with a father as brutal as that?'

'He wasn't like the man you have on trial,' Ishani spoke thoughtfully. 'He was such a good man, despite the way he'd been brought up. He was already struggling to reconcile his father's exploitation of the black miners with his own palatial upbringing when I knew him. If we had been together we could have achieved such wonderful things. After he lost me he must have changed dramatically. He must have hardened his heart and, if he did, no one could have blamed him for that. He went to work for his father and he must have thrown himself into building the empire, just as he had been trained to do from birth. I don't recognise the monster that Lex Goldman became as the same dashing young man I fell in love with.'

'But what about Luther?'

'Luther was a truly good man, and a good father to you. I loved him as much as you did, but it was never the same as the love I had for Lex all those years ago. I have never forgotten how I felt during those few months that we were together. I can still remember what it felt like to have him touch me or smile at me, to know how much he loved me and would do anything for me.'

'His father must have been a truly evil man.'

'He did what he believed to be right. It was ironic that a man who had managed to escape the dark shadow of Nazi oppression at the start of the war, and lost nearly all his family in the process, was so blind to the evils of the apartheid system that he was supporting. He thought he knew what was best for his son and for his reputation, but he turned a blind eye to what was truly going on because it suited him and he felt he needed to be wealthy to be safe, in order for his family to be protected. But the truth is, Kal, if you see something evil going on around you and you do nothing to try and stop it, you are just as guilty as the people perpetuating it.'

Kal sat back on the sofa, letting go of his mother's hand, and stared at her, trying to pull his thoughts into order. Part of his mind was trying to come to terms with the personal shock of discovering who his real father was for the first time, the other part was looking at the professional ramifications of what would now happen in the Manhattan Criminal Court. Now that he knew the truth, he saw Lex Goldman in a different light; when he imagined his face, he realised there'd always been things about it that were strangely familiar, expressions that he now realised reminded him of himself.

The two of them sat together on the sofa, both silent, both shaking and trying to take in the enormity of what was happening to their lives. Ishani stared at the floor, lost for words, waiting for Kal to give her a lead and tell her what he was feeling. But Kal wasn't sure what he was feeling. Seeing his mother in such distress broke his heart, but at the same time he felt angry with her, too angry to put his arm around her and comfort her. How could she have kept such an enormous secret for so long? How could she not have told him?

'Were you ever planning to tell me?' he asked. 'If this trial hadn't happened would I ever have known who my father was?'

'I don't know,' she said, her voice small and trembling. 'It was too painful to even think about, let alone talk about it.'

'Did Luther ever know?'

'No,' she shook her head. 'You are the first person I have told.'

'But he was your husband, how could you have lived such a lie all these years?'

She just stared at him, unable to find any explanations or any excuses, praying that he would find it in his heart to understand and forgive her.

His thoughts had been so filled with the trial and how to bring Lex Goldman to his knees, now suddenly that was all driven from his mind. It was like watching some terrible freeway pile-up in slow motion as his brain began to take in the enormity of this collision between his professional and personal lives. The eyes of the entire world were on him at a moment when he discovered the biggest secret of his life, discovered that he was genetically linked to a man he despised. His mother, the person he loved and trusted above all others, was telling him that he was wrong in his assessment of Lex Goldman: that Lex was a "good man".

Eventually he felt calm enough to speak, although his voice had none of its usual strength. 'So,' he said, 'what was he like?'

Taking a deep breath, Ishani started to talk about a time in her life that she'd never talked about to anyone since the day she set sail from South Africa. All the feelings of her youth came flooding back to her: not just her love for Lex, but her family memories and the horrors of living under apartheid. In some ways it felt good to finally share these distant memories with someone she loved, like a great weight had been lifted from her. She remembered the optimism she and others like her had felt at the time, believing they could change things and make a difference, overthrow apartheid and create a fair society for all. In a way they had, because apartheid had crumbled and Nelson Mandela had been freed, but so many new injustices had emerged around the world to take the place of the vanquished ones.

The two of them talked for hours as Kal struggled to understand the world that he had been conceived in, and Ishani fought to overcome her own demons and unlock doors in her memory, which she'd never expected to have to open again. Once the initial shock of the discovery began to wear off, he felt a growing anger burning inside him. How could his mother have kept something this important from him? He'd heard what she was saying about her childhood and about the political climate in South Africa and about how young she was and how in love, but still he couldn't stop himself from feeling resentment and a deep sense of loss: loss of the father he never knew, loss of trust in Ishani, and loss of certainty about how he felt about Lex Goldman and how he wanted to convict him at any cost. It had been many years since he'd believed that everything in life was either black or white, but still he'd wanted to cling to a few certainties.

'You must go now, Mom,' he said eventually, standing up to show he meant what he said.

'Will you be okay?' she asked, anxiously.

'I'm not sure,' he replied. 'I need time to think.'

She stood up on tiptoe and pecked him on the cheek, hurt that he didn't respond, but realising she was going to have to wait for him to come back to her, back from his state of shock.

As soon as the door snapped shut behind her he sank back onto the sofa, trying to get control of his thoughts and feelings, trying to work out what he was going to have to do now that everything had changed. Before his mother's arrival, his path forward had been so cut and dried and obvious. All he had to do was concentrate on winning the trial and obtaining the maximum sentence possible for a man who he had seen as the epitome of evil. Now he was going to have to decide how to deal with a man who he knew to be his father, and the great love of his mother's life. With the full glare of the world's media on his every move, the pressure would be more intense than anything he'd ever encountered before. After a few minutes of staring into space, he started to cry, great heaving sobs that seemed to come from the deepest parts of his body and his soul. His brain was in too much turmoil to be able to make sense of anything, all he knew was he felt totally alone, his life shattered into tiny little pieces, and in possession of a secret that he couldn't share with anyone unless he was willing to face the consequences.

When Kal woke on Sunday morning his head was already heavy with pain, even before he remembered why. The events of the previous night came back to him in a torrent, making him feel nauseous and anxious. He couldn't lie in bed for a moment longer, but there was nowhere else in the apartment that he could settle. Pulling on a coat, he went outside, not knowing why or where he was going, just walking, briskly, trying to clear his head. After a few blocks he reached the newspaper vendor who greeted him cheerfully. He didn't even hear the greeting as he handed over the right coins without speaking. He carried the papers back to the apartment, hoping they would provide him an escape from his own thoughts.

He tried to stick to his normal Sunday routine, throwing the papers down on the table and brewing himself a pot of coffee, hoping to find some physical comfort from the caffeine. He browsed the headlines, unable to read anything at length, when his eye was caught by the reported suicide of Agent Casper Franks, whose name had been mentioned in the Lex Goldman trial. He picked it up and read further. The body hadn't been officially identified but 'reliable sources' had assured the journalist that it was CIA Agent Franks. For a few moments he found himself distracted by this new twist to the story as he tried to work out what it meant to his case. He had been hoping that Agent Franks would become a crucial witness in establishing the reasons why the CIA provided Lex Goldman with a new identity. He wanted to make sure that Bates and his defence team would not be able to imply that there was some CIA plot to frame Lex for the murder of the detective. The timing and circumstances of Casper Franks' death meant there were now a lot more questions than there were answers.

Once the coffee was brewed he gave up on the papers and went back to reviewing the prosecution documents, his mind constantly wandering as he stared at the pages of dense print. Each time he read the name 'Lex Goldman' in the documents, he heard his mother's voice echo in his head with the words 'he was such a good man' over and over again. As he grappled with the alternatives, he knew he'd have to pull himself together by the following morning for what was fast becoming the most important day of his life.

Monday morning brought day four of the trial, and the prosecution called Lex Goldman to the stand. The atmosphere in the courtroom crackled with electricity as Kal Woodson stood up to face the man who everyone knew he believed to be evil incarnate.

'Mr Goldman,' Kal started, 'we have heard a great many stories about you.'

'That is exactly what they are.' Lex smiled smoothly, but beneath the veneer he was nervous. There was something about this young man that made him uncomfortable. He'd never met someone before who he was so certain wanted to end his life. He'd faced down danger many times, but they had been immediate, recognisable dangers, and he'd been able to make plans on how to sidestep them, but this young lawyer was more complicated than that. In other circumstances, Lex thought he would have liked Woodson, might even have employed him if the younger man would be willing to work for someone such as he. His own feelings puzzled him.

Slowly and calmly, Kal repeated the most damning evidence that had already been put forward, linking different events in Lex Goldman's life to show just how they all fitted into a jigsaw of greed and depravity. Some of the accusations Lex batted away easily, others made him appear uncomfortable. Step by step, Kal was winning the jurors over, convincing them that everything he was suggesting was the truth, that he was a man of integrity and Goldman was just as he described him. It was becoming a clear-cut battle of opposites, good versus evil.

'At the time of your arrest,' Kal said, 'no narcotics or "buy money" was found on you. That's correct isn't it?'

The judge looked up from his notes with a puzzled expression.

'Huh,' Lex huffed, looking equally puzzled as to why Woodson was asking him a question like that. Was he trying to lead him into a new trap? Surely the prosecution team would have known that he had exercised his right to remain silent during the arrest and interrogation process when they'd read the briefing notes from the Justice Department.

'Did you tell the arresting officer, the district attorney, or anyone else at the DA's office, what happened when you were arrested?' Woodson's unexpected questions had taken on a force that had everyone in the courtroom hanging on his every word. 'Did you assert to anyone that you did not commit the crime?'

'Objection,' Bates shouted across the courtroom, springing to his feet. He didn't understand what sort of game Woodson was now playing.

'Objection sustained,' Justice Villars ruled. After admonishing the lead prosecution attorney, the judge turned to face the jurors to explain his ruling. 'Members of the jury, please disregard that last question from Mr Woodson, who seems to be following an impermissible line of enquiry. These questions are bordering on prosecutorial misconduct.'

'I don't understand,' Kal said, looking crestfallen. 'What is the relevance of the objection? I ask you again, Mr Goldman, did the arresting officer . . .'

The silence in the courtroom was swallowed by murmurs of speculation and the repeated cracking of the judge's gavel as he tried to restore order.

'Counsellor,' the judge barked, 'please approach the bench.'

Kal Woodson approached the bench with a look of bruised innocence on his face. 'Mr Woodson, you're badgering the accused,' Justice Villars said. 'It's best you remember you are prosecuting this case on behalf of our government and our citizens. This is a very serious trial and not some sort of cabaret act. There are a lot of people observing this trial, Counsellor, and it wouldn't look good on your CV if you were seen to deliberately throw the fight. You're skating on extremely thin ice. Don't push me again. There are important issues at stake and I don't want to have to reprimand you again in this case for professional misconduct.'

'I wish to motion a mistrial, Justice,' Bates interjected, desperately trying to work out what Kal was up to.

Villars stared hard at Bates for a moment, not bothering to hide his dislike of the man, and then reverted his gaze to Woodson. 'I will reserve my judgement on that, Mr Bates. You, Mr Woodson have had your final warning. Do not continue questioning the accused along those lines.'

Woodson nodded his understanding of the warning, but said nothing. Returning to the floor, he stared at Goldman for a few moments, as if gathering his thoughts. He then launched back into his attack and the buzz of puzzlement built up in the courtroom. Four times he used the word 'uncontroverted' in further questions to Goldman, and each time Bates objected, with the judge sustaining each objection in turn.

'Mr Woodson!' Justice Villars finally exploded, 'approach the bench *now*.'

As Kal made his way back to the bench, Bates was on his feet again, petitioning the court for a mistrial on the basis that the judicial process has broken down through prosecutorial misconduct, hardly able to believe that Kal Woodson's behaviour was so deliberately aggravating the judge. The young lead attorney's egregious questions were in stark contrast to his cool, assured performance of the previous week. Pandemonium filled the courtroom as everyone speculated on what was happening and why. Had Lex Goldman somehow managed to buy Kal Woodson, the one man who seemed beyond reproach?

Justice Villars finally lost his patience as he struggled to bring order to the courtroom and slammed his gavel down, declaring a mistrial, an outcome no one could have predicted. Media pundits all over the networks remarked that such a decision was typical of Vernon Villars' style, and speculation immediately arose as to whether he'd ever been competent enough to handle such a high profile trial. Calmly avoiding the bedlam, the lead defence attorney spotted his killer moment.

'May I just confirm for the record, Justice,' James Bates was now on his feet taking over the floor with a patrician stance, 'that under the double jeopardy clause in the state constitution, Lex Goldman cannot be retried for the same offence after the declaration of a mistrial on the basis of your ruling and that he is a free man.'

Cameras all round the courtroom zoomed in on the judge's open mouth as he realised what he'd just done. Legal experts on the news channels explained to the public that because Justice Villars had ruled that the lead prosecution attorney had engaged in prejudicial misconduct, deliberately intending to provoke a mistrial motion, Woodson had in effect eviscerated Lex Goldman's right to complete the trial before the empanelled jury, and because of that, the double jeopardy clause might well bar a retrial. The *'Double V'* had made Lex Goldman immune from further prosecution for the crime of killing the detective by declaring a mistrial on the basis of prosecutorial misconduct. Much as that grated him, Villars was going to have to concede the point to James L. Bates. He could see that he'd been outwitted, but he couldn't see how, or by whom. Lex glanced across at Sophie, who smiled back encouragingly. He grinned and nodded his acknowledgement that Bates was right to quote the double jeopardy clause and that yet again he'd beaten the odds, wriggled free at the last minute against all the predictions of doom. Sophie and Bates both knew that it had nothing to do with Lex's skills, that it had been the sudden implosion from the lead prosecution attorney and the incompetence of the judge that had freed him, not his own legal wit.

'I grant the dismissal,' Villars snapped, pulling himself to his feet and stamping angrily from the court as a roar of questions and shouts rose around him. As the courtroom crowd spilled out onto the steps, the media rushed in to find those they knew were friendly sources of quotes, jostling with microphones and cameras as everyone tried to make sense of what had happened, speculating how Lex Goldman, the magician, had managed to so easily leap clear of the executioner's reach.

Back inside the courtroom, Kal Woodson sank back into his chair, his forehead resting on his hands as if he was too exhausted even to bear the weight of his own head. All around him his colleagues sat staring, unable to comprehend what had happened to the man who had been leading the prosecution with such authority.

Sitting quietly at the back of the room, Ishani Woodson felt a powerful glow of pride through the sadness that filled her heart. There were tears welling up in her eyes and she felt a deep sense of admiration for her son, his knowledge of the law and his skill in having manipulated such a clever legal conclusion to their terrible dilemma. She'd always known that Kal was a good, honourable man and he'd given her many opportunities to feel proud of him, but none as great as this adept display of selflessness and love. He had sacrificed himself, his career and his principles for her and for his father.

From another position in the courtroom, Detective Chip Murray sat impassively in his seat, unable to grasp the enormity of what had just happened. His eyes fixed firmly on Kal Woodson and his thoughts filled with the image of his fallen friend, broken on the ground the night he died. What had transpired at this trial sure didn't feel like justice to him. He felt an overwhelming sense of guilt at his own inadequacy. He was supposed to look after

Blaine; he'd promised he would. Not only had he led him to his death, he'd failed to get his killer convicted. There wasn't a shadow of doubt in his mind that Lex Goldman was guilty as charged. Knowing as much as he did about the history of corruption behind the scenes in the NYPD, and how it stretched out into every level of government, he was convinced that someone had managed to 'get to' Kal Woodson. If a man like Woodson could be got at, who was there left to stand up to elite men like Goldman and Bates and their like? All his hopes of seeing justice done for Blaine had been dashed. The only chance he had of seeing his friend's death avenged now was if he took it into his own hands.

Eventually he pulled himself to his feet and walked quickly from the emptying courtroom to the bathroom. He needed to be away from the crowd, to compose his thoughts. He couldn't believe that it could end like this. How could his friend's murder be brushed aside on a legal technicality? How could this man have escaped justice yet again? He'd put so many painstaking hours into ensuring the case was watertight and Kal Woodson had simply thrown it all away in some inexplicable moment of madness.

When Lex and Sophie appeared outside, arm in arm on the steps of the Manhattan Criminal Court, a small army of policemen and officials had to run to cut off the rush of the crowd as the media surged forward, threatening to overwhelm them and trample them into the ground. James Bates was quick to grab centre stage at the impromptu press conference that was starting to take shape. Basking in the glory of the moment, he stood in front of a battalion of jostling press reporters and camera crews among a forest of microphone stands, with the Goldmans at his side. It was impossible to make out individual questions from the mêlée of shouting and fighting at first, but Bates's experience in such situations soon allowed a short, meaningful exchange of questions and answers to take place. He made it clear that Lex Goldman would not be making any comment whatsoever and that he would only take a few questions.

'Mr Bates, are you surprised with the outcome?' inquired an aggressive reporter from CNN.

'No,' James lied blandly, 'my client was innocent of these charges.'

'Was a mistrial correct, in your opinion?' a BBC correspondent asked, leaning forward with his microphone.

'That's what the judge ruled,' James smiled to counteract any hint of irony in his voice, 'and he is a very well respected judge, as you all well know.'

'A lot of people will be unhappy with this verdict, what do you say to them?' a woman shouted from the side.

'Have a nice day.'

The reporters closest laughed with him, none of them able to hide their respect for the attorney who had apparently just pulled off the seemingly impossible.

'Lex,' a woman from a South American television news station tried her luck, 'what will you do now?'

'Okay, that's it, ladies and gentlemen.' James quickly ushered his client down the steps with Sophie in tow. 'We gotta go.'

Well-wishers stretched out their hands to shake Lex's and he responded with a gracious smile, like a politician winning over a crowd, ignoring the boos and catcalls from those who believed he was guilty and as evil as he'd been painted over the previous few days in court. The trio managed to inch their way down the steps towards their waiting limousine, the men in uniform forcing open a path for them through the throng.

'Lex . . . Lex Goldman,' a woman's voice suddenly cut through the babble, making him turn towards the speaker. He thought he saw Kal Woodson out of the corner of his eye, behind the woman who'd just spoken. She was very striking to look at, but there was something vaguely familiar about her that seemed to sink a hook into his memory. She smiled. 'It's been a long time . . . I'm not sure Sol would want us meeting like this . . .'

The words cut through his consciousness like a hot knife through butter.

'Reshmine?'

Suddenly he remembered everything. Everything that had happened in his youth and everything he'd been told had happened to the woman he'd loved more than any other.

15

'Reshmine?' Lex froze as the crowd pressed in, threatening to crush them underfoot. 'Is it really you?'

'Hey, we have to go, Lex,' James shouted over the noise. 'They can't control the crowds, there's going to be an accident.'

'Lex,' Sophie spoke gently, taking his arm, unsure what was happening, unsure who the woman was who had her eyes locked onto her husband's. 'We have to get in the car.'

'I can't talk now,' Lex shouted out to Reshmine as he felt the weight of the crowd forcing him away from her. 'I'll be at my attorney's office in about an hour. Ring me there. Please . . . ring!'

He tried to catch another look at her before she disappeared into the sea of faces, but he was being dragged away, and bodyguards were forcing him through the open door to the back of the limousine and the crowd had closed around her. For a terrible second he wondered if he'd imagined her there, if the stress of the trial had started to play tricks with his brain. Sophie was already seated inside the car, looking frightened.

'Who was that?' she asked as the doors clicked shut after them, cutting off the noise outside, and the driver gently pressed the car forward through the packed bodies.

'My God.' Lex was in shock, unable to comprehend what he'd just seen. 'That was Reshmine. *She's not dead.*'

Sophie looked quickly out the car window, not wanting Lex to see the consternation on her face at the sound of a name she hadn't heard him mention since the early years of their marriage.

'Reshmine?' James asked innocently.

'Oh, it's a long story, James, I'll tell you about it some other time,' Lex said, not wanting to talk about anything so intimate with his attorney. He wanted to regain control of his thoughts and emotions, find out the truth about his own past. If that was Reshmine, why was she not dead? What had happened to her all those years ago? 'Let me savour my vindication,' he said. 'It's been a bad six months, I need a few moments to adjust to being a free man again.'

An awkward silence enveloped the car as it left the crowds and purred towards James's downtown office, and Lex struggled to make sense of everything that had happened in the last few hours.

'Lex, you'll never know how lucky you are,' James interrupted the silence as the limousine approached the entrance to his offices. 'I've never witnessed anything like what happened this morning in thirty years of criminal trials. That guy, Woodson, just imploded. I don't understand it.'

'Maybe you're underselling me,' Lex smiled, 'and yourself. I always told you I was innocent. I've been in tight corners before and survived. Maybe this guy just got a conscience check.'

'I don't think so, Lex, not his style. Something happened, I just don't know what.'

'Perhaps, Lex, you should be grateful that you've your freedom back,' Sophie snapped. 'Maybe you should learn a little humility from this whole affair and stop living so close to the edge all the time.'

'Bullshit,' Lex snapped back, irritated at her carping. 'I never doubted for a moment I would be freed.'

Sophie opened her mouth to remind him how low he was feeling when she came to his rescue in Shawangunk, but thought better of it. 'Hmmm,' she murmured under her breath.

The champagne corks were flying as they hurried into the offices past the crowd of media that had made it there ahead of them, heads down, refusing to comment to any of the shouted questions from the hacks. James and Lex, like two returning battle heroes, were bursting with excitement at their unexpectedly fast and favourable outcome. In the general roar of congratulations and celebrations, no one noticed how sombre Sophie had become.

Eventually Lex noticed that his wife had separated from the crowd, lost in her own thoughts, and went over to her. 'You okay, Sophie?'

'That Reshmine, she was from South Africa, wasn't she? She's the one you used to talk about all the time.'

'Yes.'

'You told me she was dead.' Sophie was struggling to come to terms with the feelings of jealousy that were rising up inside her.

'I believed she was. That was what I was told.'

'What could have happened?'

'I have no idea. It was like seeing a ghost. I could hardly ask her any questions in that crush, with all those vultures waiting to pounce. To be honest, I think I went into shock a little bit. I haven't seen her for over thirty-five years. I hope she calls because I have no idea how to contact her if she disappears again.'

Someone interrupted them and he turned away to talk, missing the sad look that flitted across his wife's face.

A couple of hours after they'd left the Manhattan Criminal

Court steps, while the party was still in full swing, the receptionist came up to Lex and informed him a lady by the name of Reshmine Sharma was on the line. 'She's very insistent that she must talk to you. She's holding on the line. Will you take the call?'

'Yes, of course.' Lex was unable to hide his eagerness and Sophie felt a stab of pain as she saw the look of excitement on his face. 'Is there a private office I can use?'

'Use my office,' James chipped in. 'You won't be disturbed there.'

'Reshmine?' he said as the receptionist put him through, his head spinning as he tried to work out what he was feeling. 'Is it really you? They told me you'd been murdered. Where have you been? What happened?'

'Oh, Lex,' she said, her voice cracking with the emotion of speaking to him after so long. 'There's so much you need to know, so much I need to tell you. Can we meet?'

'Of course. I've been imprisoned in some hotel I've never heard off for the last few weeks. I'll get a private suite organised at the Waldorf; they'll be discreet. Meet me in the front reception area about four.'

'Come alone, Lex, I have very important things to tell you.'

After hanging up, Lex took several deep breaths before going back to the party, which was just starting to wind down. He didn't notice the worried look that Sophie shot him, too wrapped up in his own thoughts and memories.

'James, can you arrange a car to take Sophie back to the hotel? I have some private business in town to take care of.'

'Sure,' James grinned conspiratorially but Lex ignored him.

'Lex,' Sophie took his arm, 'can I talk to you privately for a moment?'

James moved away to give them space. He could see how agitated Sophie was, even if her husband couldn't.

'I can't tell you how I feel at the moment, Sophie, honestly I can't,' Lex admitted. 'I need to meet her alone. I'll see you back at the hotel later. My whole world is spinning, with so many things to take in at once, please understand.'

'Okay.' Sophie forced a smile, realising that there was nothing she could do to stop him going to see Reshmine, wanting to hide her jealousy, afraid that she'd been misreading the signs she thought she saw of their own relationship restarting. 'I understand.'

Sophie's serene world had also been turned upside down over the previous six months. The sense of guilt she'd felt at the thought she'd caused Lex's death by introducing him to the IRA had made her want to help him, but now she was beginning to feel an anger at the high-handed way in which he was treating her. Several times during the previous few months she'd thought the old sparks of passion were being rekindled between them, but now that Reshmine had returned from the 'dead' she began to wonder if she'd ever really had his whole heart, even in the early days of their marriage. His lost love from his youth had always been there, she had known that from the start, but only as a memory, as a ghost. Now this woman had become a reality and it looked like her husband might simply wander out of her life again, after waking her from what felt like a long sleep, and go back to his first great love. The next few hours were going to be an agony as she waited to see what fate had in store.

She remembered how she felt when she first heard that Lex had been killed in the Caribbean, the sudden sense of loss and desolation. Even though they had lived apart for a few years by then, just knowing that he was in the world somewhere, that if she really needed to see him again she would be able to make contact, had given her strength. To hear that he had gone for ever had been a devastating blow. The intense media interest had then bewildered her, with tabloid reporters stalking her for months in the hope of finding some connection or story to spin out the Lex Goldman saga for a few more editions. In her grief she had withdrawn even further from the world, finding solace in her writing and resisting all her publisher's attempts to lure her back into the spotlight. The previous weeks had reminded her of just how it felt to be swept along in Lex Goldman's wake, feeling the adrenaline rushing again after so long, and she'd surprised herself to find she didn't like the idea of losing him again.

'Don't tell me that was justice!'

Captain Serrano could see from the redness of Chip's eyes as he burst into his office that he'd been crying. He guessed that it was partly from a delayed grief at the loss of his friend, now that the pressure of the trial had vanished, and partly from his fury at the outcome. He felt the same way himself.

'I know, Chip, I know.'

The captain was well aware of just how many thousands of hours of painstaking work Chip had poured into the investigation in his determination to prosecute Lex Goldman and let justice take its proper course. He also knew that he was still racked with guilt at having been the one who convinced Blaine Harmon to join the NYPD in the first place. Serrano had worked closely with both of them through the two years of 'Operation Lifeline', and he knew just how close they were and how much pride the duo felt in serving their community with integrity and courage. They had bravely taken the fight to the cartel to try and reclaim the streets from its vice-like grip. Serrano still felt the loss of Blaine personally, so he could imagine just how bad it must be for Chip, who'd known him all his life.

'That Goldman bastard paid someone,' Chip insisted. 'Somehow he found a way to beat the system. How else can you explain what happened?'

'Calm down, Chip, calm down. I heard what happened. I haven't got an explanation any more than you have. I've never seen anything like that happen before.'

Chip struggled to control himself. He didn't like Serrano or the others seeing him like this. It felt like Goldman had beaten him. 'That so-called judge completely fucked up. Full of his ego and self-importance. What a bungler to let that killer back out on the streets.'

'I know, I know,' Serrano continued to try to calm him, 'but getting mad is not going to help anyone. I need you to stay cool so we can try to see what we can do.'

'You might be able to do that,' Murray said, and Serrano saw a glint of menace in the young detective's eyes, 'but I can't.'

No one in the foyer of the Waldorf recognised Lex Goldman as he hurried in, wearing a trilby hat, horn-rimmed glasses and an oversized coat borrowed from James. He was breathless, partly from the rush to get there and partly from excitement and anticipation. He had not felt anything so intense since he first left South Africa.

Reshmine was already waiting for him, pacing nervously up and down, and they were drawn together into an embrace as if by magnets. For two full minutes neither of them said a word, just clinging to each other, both overcome by a surge of emotion unlike anything either of them had ever experienced before, never wanting to let go.

'What is it that you wanted to tell me?' Lex whispered as soon as he was able to speak.

'Sh,' she put her fingers to her lips, 'not here. We have to be somewhere private.'

Lex tore himself free of her arms, impatient to get away from the busy lobby, but reluctant to let her go for even a minute. Holding her hand tightly he led her to the reception. 'Let me arrange some privacy,' he said.

Despite her immaculate training, the receptionist was unable to hide her surprise at finding the face that had been plastered over the front of every paper and blown-up behind every television newscaster for the previous week a few feet away from her across the desk, asking about a suite reservation booked in the name of Bates Attorneys.

'Please send coffee and sandwiches,' he said, 'and then we want complete privacy; absolutely no calls.'

They both walked briskly from the lobby, up a flight of stairs to the first-floor luxury suite, still in a trance-like state, neither of them able to look at the other for fear of the emotion that might spill out. Once they had settled themselves and the staff had left them alone, Lex asked her to start her story from the beginning. For two hours Reshmine talked, carefully explaining everything that had happened to her since their lives had been so forcibly separated. She told him about how Sol Goldman and his minders had visited her family and issued his veiled threats, how she had fled to America and found that she was pregnant. There was so much to tell him and he insisted she didn't leave out anything. She explained about her uncle and the early months of hardship and struggle with her baby, Kal, in New York, and her sense of isolation among the sea of strangers there. She talked about meeting and marrying Luther Woodson, aware that the thought of her being with another man caused Lex terrible pain, even after so many years.

Occasionally he interrupted with questions, nearly always wanting more details about his son, and all the years that he had to catch up on. As she talked, Lex could visualise the thousands of moments he had missed, and he started to weep, unable to control himself.

When he thought of how much damage his father had done to him with that one wicked act he realised that Sol had been controlling and manipulating him all his life, even from beyond the grave. Everything that had happened to him as an adult, every decision he'd made, stemmed from that fateful moment he was told that Reshmine had been murdered because of her relationship with him. The realisation that he was going to have to live without Reshmine had sent him down a bitter and twisted road, where the accumulation of money had been his only comfort, and greed his only friend. With no fear of danger, he'd grown to believe that he was invincible with every new gamble he landed, and he kept pushing the stakes higher.

The memory of Reshmine had always cast a shadow over him emotionally and he had been unable to move on until he met Sophie. How ironic that Sol had done what he'd done because he thought he was protecting his son's safety and happiness.

'What about your wife?' Reshmine asked eventually, as she watched Lex sobbing into his hands, unsure how to comfort him. 'Do you love her?'

'I suppose I did,' he said, pulling himself together enough to answer. 'She was a very exciting woman when she was young, still is I guess. But it never felt the same as it did with you. Nothing in my life has ever come close to the intensity of those feelings I had when I was with you.'

'She has stood by you through your troubles,' Reshmine reminded him.

'Yes,' he nodded. 'It's complicated. We did some bad things together I guess. She was young and exciting and I was seduced by the dark side of her life, led into a world of people who wouldn't think twice about killing you if you were no longer of value to them. I think she has a conscience over involving me in all of that. She wants to make amends with the world.'

'It seems you and I have travelled similar paths in many ways,' Reshmine said.

'How so? You're practically an angel, and I'm certainly not that.'

'I'm no angel, Lex, look how I lied to our son. We both faked our own deaths in different ways.'

'Yes,' he smiled at the thought, 'and both had to change our names to disguise our pasts.'

'They were horribly bad times in South Africa back then, they made many people do bad things.'

They both fell silent and thoughtful for a moment. Reshmine waited for Lex to say what was on his mind, and eventually he found the right words.

'Would Kal agree to come here and meet me properly? I know him only as a prosecutor trying to convict me for murder,' he asked. 'I would really like the chance to tell him how I feel, and show him how proud I am of him.'

'No, Lex.' Reshmine shook her head. 'It would be too risky after what happened this morning. If the media ever got wind of any secret meeting between you they would immediately assume that you'd bribed him.'

'Why would they think that?'

'Do you not understand what he has done for you?' Reshmine could see from the puzzled look on Lex's face that he still assumed he had won his freedom on his own merits. 'He threw the trial for you, because I told him who you really were, what you were really like. He made up his own mind how to deal with that. It must have been the most traumatic situation anyone could find themselves in . . . and to do it under the full glare of the world's media. He has ruined his career for us, sacrificed himself to save your life.'

'He did that on purpose?'

'Of course he did. Did you think he was so stupid as to make a mistake like that in the middle of the biggest trial of his life? When I got back from Burma and saw the headlines I knew I was going to have to tell him the truth about you. I went to see him and made my confession. I don't know what shocked him the most, finding out that you were his father or that I had lied to him. Our relationship had always been one of complete trust, and I had betrayed him by keeping the biggest secret possible. By the time we'd finished talking I was so afraid I had damaged our close relationship beyond repair. He basically told me to leave.'

'Did you go?' Lex asked.

'Of course, what else could I do, although it broke my heart to think of the dilemma that I was leaving him to deal with. I had no idea what he would do, but he dealt with it. He took this tragic dilemma, both personal and professional, and he found the right solution. He decided to spark Justice Villars' temper and give James Bates the opportunity he needed to destroy the prosecution case in one blow.'

Lex sat back in his chair as if he had been punched in the face as the truth dawned on him and he realised just how clever his son was, and how much he'd sacrificed for them both. Sol, he thought, even from the grave had managed to damage his grandson's life, without even knowing that he had one.

'It would be better if he comes to your secret location,' Reshmine said, 'after midnight perhaps.'

'Of course,' Lex nodded, 'whatever you think, but the wait is going to feel like an eternity. Can you come with him? I think that would make it easier.'

'I would like that. Will Sophie mind?'

'Sophie?' Lex was taken by surprise by the question. It hadn't occurred to him that Sophie would care at all; if anything he'd assumed she would be interested to meet Reshmine after hearing so much about her in the past. 'Why would she mind?'

'She must still be in love with you to have done so much to help. Can't you see that?'

On the way back to the hotel Lex's mind was a turmoil of conflicting thoughts and emotions. For the first time in many years he was being forced to remember the most painful period of his life. It still hurt when he thought about the way Zak, who he'd trusted with his life, had betrayed him to his father, even though he knew Zak had thought he was acting in his best interests. Sol too must have believed he was doing the right thing when he banished Reshmine from the country and constructed the lie about her being murdered. But if either of them had acted differently his whole life would surely have been better. Certainly, he would have been happier if he had known that Reshmine was alive, had known they had a son together and had been able to be with them. He wondered what path Zak's life had taken over the years.

By the time he was back at the hotel with Sophie, Lex could hardly contain his impatience to meet his son and see Reshmine again. He had thought of hundreds more questions he wanted to ask her. He found himself resenting every moment that he wasn't with her now that he knew she was alive. Her words of warning about how Sophie might feel had vanished from his mind.

He had no room to think of anyone except himself, Reshmine and Kal.

'In some ways it was like we had never been apart,' he enthused to the stony-faced Sophie, 'like those thirty-five years never happened. She's had the most terrible life since my father interfered. I have to make it up to her, and to Kal.'

'What makes you think they're going to want you in their lives?' Sophie interrupted, just wishing Reshmine and Kal would vanish off the face of the earth, but knowing they never would, feeling trapped and desperate. 'You may find it hard to believe, but some people don't want to be part of the Lex Goldman circus.'

'Don't be ridiculous,' Lex snarled, furious at having his dream questioned. 'He's my son. Think what I can do for him, how I can help him to build himself up a law practice. I could make him the most famous lawyer in New York.'

'From what I've seen he doesn't want that, he actually just wants to do some good in the world, like most people. Not everyone is like you, Lex, they don't all share your lust for world domination in everything they do.'

'Don't try to bring me down, Soph,' he shouted. 'It won't work. This is the most important thing that's ever happened to me. I have a son. You'll never understand how that feels.'

'You are an arrogant son of a bitch!' she spat.

'What?'

'Take a long hard look at yourself in the mirror, Lex, do you really like what you see? You use people like they're expendable. You'll use Kal just like you've used me!'

'How have I used you?' he demanded, his temperature rising.

'You don't even realise you're doing it, do you? You come to me for help after leaving me believing you were dead, you allow me to think that you might actually still care for me a little, and then the moment something better comes along – or something you imagine is better – I am no longer that important to you.'

'I'll repay every dollar you've spent on my defence, you know I will.'

'That's just it, it's not about the money!' she screamed. 'Not everyone is as obsessed with money as you are. I helped you because I really care about you. You were once my whole life, until more important distractions took you away. Now you have your ready-made family, something I can never give you, so that's the end of it.'

'You think this hasn't been tough for me? I've lost everything.'

'You'll rebuild your fortune, just like you always do. It's what you're good at . . . once money is involved. You lust after it and it's blinded you. And now you have your precious Reshmine and your son as well. You've ended up with everything, Lex, as always.'

'Maybe that's the thing about money,' he protested, 'it makes you do things you don't want to do.'

'But why, Lex? The only race in this life you're competing in is with yourself. Can't you see the things that are *really* important in life have nothing to do with money? I'm truly sorry for you, because I know now you'll never change. And I'm sorry for Kal to think what sort of father he has.'

Shocked by the vitriol in her voice, his tone turned quiet and cold. 'Maybe you're the one who doesn't understand what today has meant to me. My whole life has been turned upside down. Nothing can ever be the same again. Maybe we have grown too far apart . . . maybe it's best if we return to our separate ways.'

Realising that there was no way she would be able to persuade him to see sense, Sophie turned silently away and started packing. Lex sat with his head in his hands, tears oozing through his fingers. She didn't even look up to say goodbye as she left the room, carrying one overnight case. At reception she instructed the concierge staff to forward the rest of her luggage to her address in England and ordered a cab to take her to another hotel nearer to JFK Airport. The next day would see her board a flight to London, leaving Lex Goldman for ever.

It was just after midnight when the first spots of rain started to fall across the streets of New York. Reggie Coombs, a daring kid from the Bronx, realising he was being followed by the NYPD patrol car, stamped heavily on the gas pedal of the stolen Chevrolet and sped away down a near deserted street.

'Holy shit, look at him go!' exclaimed the officer in the passenger seat of the patrol car. 'Don't lose him.'

As the police driver pressed his foot to the floor to give chase, his partner hit the siren and radioed in to their base station.

'He's seen us and he's making a run for it, over.'

'Stay on his tail, we want this guy,' the disembodied voice replied.

'Will do.'

Reggie had started his life on the wrong side of the tracks and had never been able to cross over. There had been a couple of teachers who had spotted some potential in the boy at different stages, but the bad influences that surrounded him at home and on the street had soon stamped out any early signs of promise, removing any chance he might have had of making good. He was exactly the type of lad that Kal Woodson would have fought for if the two had ever met, someone who needed a break. The cops on his tail that night certainly weren't feeling in a forgiving mood.

For five kilometres Reggie barely touched his brakes, shooting every set of red lights, swerving in and out of the traffic, the patrol car staying tight behind.

'Looks like a kid,' the patrolman radioed in. 'He's driving like a crazed lunatic, someone is going to get killed here if we aren't careful. He needs to be stopped.'

'Don't let him get away.'

'We'll need a chopper to tail him if we're going to catch him, or we'll be the ones ending up killing someone.'

'It's on its way.'

'It's starting to lash down pretty hard now, these streets are getting too slippery. We should slow down, maybe take the pressure off him a bit.'

'Negative. Stay with him. The chopper is on its way.'

'Fucking hell,' the policeman muttered, hanging on tightly as his colleague accelerated the car across a junction, forcing a lorry to jam on its brakes, its horn blaring.

By the time the stolen Chevvy roared onto Brooklyn Bridge, Reggie could feel he was losing control. The car was careering back and forth across three lanes, in and out of the light night-time traffic as other drivers swerved away or punched their horns angrily. A truck, unable to move quickly enough, forced Reggie to wrench the steering wheel and he felt the tyres lose traction for a split second, sending up sheets of spray from the road surface as the car spun out of control.

The driver of the red Pontiac, making his way towards Manhattan, saw the Chevvy heading towards him and tried to accelerate out of harm's way. His passenger screamed as the two cars exploded directly into one another, the impact bouncing them apart, sending shards of debris flying in all directions as they both rolled over and over.

'Holy shit,' whispered the patrolman as they watched the

balletic movements of the doomed vehicles until they finally erupted in twin fireballs, lighting up the night sky and illuminating the police helicopter as it swooped in to take a look.

'None of them are going to survive that,' the police driver said, as he pulled the patrol car to a halt and they radioed for urgent assistance.

As he waited in the hotel room for Reshmine and Kal, Sophie's comments swirling in his mind, Lex remembered the terrible days in South Africa when he waited for Reshmine and she never came. He had the same feeling now. The minutes ticked into hours and slowly his devastation increased.

'Maybe,' he thought, 'my son doesn't want to meet me.'

Eventually, as dawn was breaking, he gave up hope and slumped onto the sofa, falling into a fitful, exhausted sleep.

At around eleven the door buzzer raised him to the surface and he stumbled to the door, finding the chambermaids standing outside. Without a word he waved them away and pushed the door shut. Wanting to pull himself out of his stupor, he called room service and asked for a pot of coffee, switched on the television and walked through to the bathroom for a shower. Room service arrived as he emerged in his bathrobe, drying his hair. The television channel came out of a commercial break as he poured himself a cup of coffee and tried to gather his thoughts. A breaking news story dominated the screen: KAL WOODSON KILLED OVERNIGHT IN CAR CRASH, and Lex's coffee cup fell from his hands, the hot liquid splashing the carpet.

As his legs buckled under him and he sank to the ground, stifling his sobs so that he was able to hear what the news anchor was telling him about the passenger in the car, Reshmine Woodson,

Kal's mother, who'd also been fatally wounded in the horrific crash.

Lex's brain ceased to function, slipping into a daze in its attempt to deal with the shock of losing them both again after only just finding them. Just as he had found the two things he wanted in life – Reshmine and their son – both had been snatched away from him. It was like someone had cut his heart out with a knife. Now fate had determined that he would never get to meet Kal *as his son,* his only memory of him as a prosecutor out to see him executed. He would never be able to tell him how proud he was to discover he was the father of such a fine young man. He would never be able to tell him just how ferociously he'd loved Reshmine. The thought of losing Reshmine again was unbearable, having felt her in his arms again after thirty-five years. The sobs that racked his body were unstoppable.

Chip Murray was coming out of his office when he first heard talk amongst his colleagues about the fatal car crash the night before.

'What crash?' he asked one of them as he passed by.

'Haven't you heard? Kal Woodson was killed last night. A kid lost control of a stolen car and went right into him.'

The idea of someone as young as Kal being killed shocked him for a moment, bringing back the feelings of the night when Blaine died. Then a brief smile tweaked the corners of his mouth. 'Poetic justice,' he thought, 'for Woodson's corruption that ended the trial. Or maybe destiny was playing its final card.'

For a second he wondered if Blaine's spirit had reached out to protect him, to stop him pursuing a vendetta against Kal Woodson that could have ended up destroying them both. Maybe

Blaine was looking after him in the same way he'd tried to look after Blaine for so many years.

Four days after the crash, Lex felt strong enough to be able to check out of his hotel room. Throughout those long days and restless nights he had searched deep into his soul. He'd come to realise that Sophie had been right in everything she had said to him, but he'd always been too blinded by his own greed to see it. In many ways finding out what Sol had done, and the repercussions his actions had brought about, felt like an exorcism of the demons that had been tormenting him all these years. The two hours he'd spent listening to Reshmine had filled him with glowing pride for what his son had achieved and what he had been willing to sacrifice for his parents. The devastation of having it all snatched away so suddenly and so finally had left him feeling sad, empty and lonely. Now he had lost both the women he'd loved and the son he'd never got to know.

A terrible realisation was dawning on him that two of the greatest gifts possible in life had passed right through his hands. By Kal and Reshmine being taken so tragically, he had lost real love for ever, and by losing Sophie he had lost the most loyal person he'd ever known. No amount of money would ever buy or replace either for him again.

Despite all the turmoil of his newly awoken emotions, however, the old survival instincts were still at work, ticking away at the back of his mind. He knew there were bound to be more vengeful ramifications from the publicity surrounding his release after the trial, and there was a very real danger that Ramrod and his cronies or the CIA would come looking for him. Fate had once more conspired to set his life on a completely different course.

He knew what he had to do next. He reached for a telephone in the lobby and dialled SAA flight reservations.

'Can you book me on the next flight to Jo'burg please, first class?'

'Certainly, will that be a return ticket, sir?' the reservation clerk enquired.

'No,' he said, smiling to himself, 'just one way, I've been away too long, it's time I went home.'